ALLIES OF MAJESTY
CHRONICLES

VOLUME 1

ALLIES OF MAJESTY
CHRONICLES

VOLUME I

· Hope Ann · Joshua C. Chadd · Althea Damgaard · Anthony Diastello · M.B. Everett · Erin R. Howard · Megan Huffman · Caedon Hull · Ellie Lerum · Bryan Timothy Mitchell · Gao Yu Qing · Nathaniel Sorensen · Merve Thomas ·

PureFun Media

PureFun Media
9477 Snyder Church Rd. NW
Baltimore, OH 43105

Book Cover by Simon Wong
Edited by Dawn L. Carter
Illustrations by Moreamh

ISBN 979-8-9992476-2-9 (Paperback)
ISBN 979-8-9992476-0-5 (Hardcover)
ISBN 979-8-9992476-1-2 (Ebook)

Printed in the United States of America
First Edition July 2025

To all our unseen, unknown, unthanked allies.

CONTENTS

FOREWORD

ANTHONY DIASTELLO

For me, *Allies of Majesty: Chronicles-Vol. 1* is a dream come true. It is the first published work in the *Allies of Majesty* world, a world 25 years in the making as of this writing.

My vision for *Allies of Majesty* is simple, yet expansive. My desire is to bring people together to have fun and explore the richness of Scripture. I hope people from all Christian backgrounds, those curious about spiritual themes, and even those who may be at odds with biblical principles, will all find a home here together. This project is not here to highlight one modern theology above another. Instead, it is meant to explore ideas from the times and cultures of the ancient biblical writers, brought to life through the landscape of storytelling and fantasy. The world of *Allies of Majesty* is fictional, but its foundation is built upon ideas and concepts drawn from Scripture and the ancient times in which it was written. Some aspects, like the divisions of angels, are very unlikely to be real fact. Within the context of this world, they serve the story well while at the same time reflecting imagery and concepts found in biblical text. As you explore with us, I encourage you to think of this realm as you might a parable. These are imagined stories, crafted to entertain, all the while pointing toward deeper truths.

Many of us have been taught to read the Bible like a reference book of answers or a law book of rules. If we approach the Bible like well-crafted literature, we will begin to see how interconnected it is. Though it follows a single people for most of its pages, it is a story of all people. All of God's children. You. Me. Those who came before us, those around us, and those yet to come. We are all in its pages. Not by name, but by calling. Our God is calling to us and the only question is, "Will we answer?" Will we answer His call to participate in this story and write the next pages? Not pages written on paper, but the pages He writes on our hearts.

Join me and 12 contributing authors for a journey of wonder that leads not to an unreachable pot of gold at the end of the rainbow, but to something real.

PROLOGUE

MERVE THOMAS & ANTHONY DIASTELLO

The soup steamed as Thomas ladled it into the last bowl. It had been a long day, and Thomas, tall as he was, stood slightly hunched, his lower back screaming. As usual, Ebby grasped the last bowl of the day. The lukewarm broth, mostly water, sloshed against the side, carrying hard root vegetables and gristly scraps of meat, presumably turkey, the bowl only filled halfway. It wasn't award-winning, but at least it was food. What more could Thomas do? He already volunteered at the shelter once a month, more than most people.

"Thank you," Ebby said. His salted beard crawled up his cheeks nearly to his eyes as he smiled. He always thanked Thomas for the soup, one of the few who did. One of the few who said anything.

Around the room there was little chatter. About a hundred people, mostly men, sat huddled against a hard life, their hands wrapped around tepid soup. The shelter provided a little food and a couple hours of warmth against the cold outside. They wore layers of mostly tattered coats and jackets, raggedy scarves, and holey gloves.

Ebby's thumb poked from his own pair. "How's Tom doing today?"

Thomas looked up, surprised. "Fine, I guess."

"Will you sit with me?"

"I really should get home."

"Please?"

Thomas shrugged and followed Ebby to an empty seat.

I

Ebby placed the soup on the table and sat. Before he ate, Ebby bowed his head. "Pray with me?"

Over ten years, since he was a junior in high school, Thomas had been handing out food at the soup kitchen, only to see the problem grow. More and more people filled the shelter, more and more wasted lives. Somewhere behind him, a man coughed, wet and phlegmy. "I'm not feeling too much like praying, Ebby."

"That," Ebby said, "is the best time *to* pray." But he didn't force the issue. He simply bowed and prayed silently.

Out of habit, Thomas bowed his head too. He had grown up in a church, and was currently attending seminary, though he was contemplating dropping out. He felt he didn't have it in him to lead a church. In fact, over the last five years or so, he had sort of forgotten how to pray. When he looked around at the people here, their destitution, he had trouble believing in an all-loving God. Frankly, he wondered where any of Ebby's faith came from.

"What did you pray for?" Thomas didn't know why he asked, it just sort of came out.

"Thanks, mostly."

Thomas scoffed. "Doesn't seem like you have much to be thankful for—" He shook his head. "I'm sorry, Ebby. I didn't mean…"

"I know what you meant." He slurped a bit of soup. "But I'm thankful for the protection God gives me every day. I'm thankful for the food, even when it's humble. And I'm thankful for the breath of life, just to experience it. So I prayed my thanks." His eyes met Thomas's. "I prayed for you, too." He returned to his soup, carefully eating it like it was gourmet, carefully constructing bites of broth, vegetables, and meat all in one spoonful.

Thomas flinched. A homeless man, praying for him. And why not? For years now, he'd devoted himself to God, but still lived in a cramped apartment. He worked most days and took online classes at night, dragging out his education for more years than it should. Lately, though, he'd been taking on extra projects at work, and it had paid off; he was offered a promotion. The money would allow him to finally buy a house and a car—he took the bus most days. The promotion would mean leaving seminary and the soup kitchen, but with a house and a car, maybe he wouldn't need pity from this man who would likely sleep tonight on a damp mattress under an overpass.

So why hadn't he accepted the promotion yet?

"I prayed," Ebby said, "you'd have eyes to see and ears to hear." His spoon scraped against the bottom of the bowl, chasing a lone chunk of potato. "And those might give you a mouth to speak." He stared hard at Thomas. "How's seminary going?"

"Fine," he lied. "I mean, okay." He didn't want to tell Ebby about the promotion. "I ace all my tests."

Ebby smiled. "But have none of the answers."

Before Thomas could react, Ebby stood and brushed his wrinkled coat straight. "Thank you again for the food." He carried his bowl to the dish receptacle and placed it inside. As he left, he stopped for a moment by the door and plucked an old hat from his pocket, pulling it down over his ears, and giving Thomas a little wink before leaving into the cold night.

Thomas stared after him for a moment before rising, ready to leave himself. As he collected his coat from the rack, he had to yank it a couple times to get it free. The hanger clanged to the floor. *Great, just great,* Thomas thought, bending to pick it up. His house was about a mile away, but he decided to forgo the bus... He headed out the door, head down, marching as much as walking. As he neared the alley shortcut he usually took, he turned, but decided to take the long way instead. The things Ebby said intruded his mind, like a burglar in the night, and he needed time to think.

I prayed for you, too...

Thomas shook away the pestering thoughts and continued staring at his feet as he walked. To his luck, he found a five-dollar bill on the ground and stooped to pick it up. Wind whipped through his hair as he did. He jammed it into his pocket, planning to give it to Ebby next time he saw him.

Once home, Thomas collapsed in his chair, exhausted. Many times he had considered leaving seminary, and now he could get a sizable raise and increase in responsibilities. It would mean no more volunteering at the shelter, too. Which was fine. He wouldn't have time to waste bailing water from a sinking ship. It's not like he was really doing any good, anyway. Again, the words Ebby had spoken echoed in his head. Again, he tried to shoo them away.

Eyes to see...

To see what? He already saw the suffering God allowed, even from many claiming to believe in Him. Sometimes, especially from the believers. Whatever God was doing up there, it didn't seem to be trickling down here.

Ears to hear...

Thomas shook his head and raked a hand through his hair. He needed some food and sleep. Tomorrow was the deadline to accept the promotion, and he couldn't let the words of some homeless guy preoccupy him.

Seriously, though. Why don't I see God doing more? There's a hundred miracles in the Bible. A few multiplied fish and loaves would have been handy today. What are You even doing up there?

Thomas stumbled to the kitchen and opened the fridge. Half a turkey sandwich stared him in the face. He'd been too busy at work to get to the store, and, having served turkey soup all day, the smell carried away his appetite. He slammed the fridge. *I should've gone to the store, not the shelter. I might as well go straight to bed.* No dinner. No shower. Maybe he'd brush his teeth.

Brother Thomas.

Thomas opened his eyes, but he couldn't see, the room dark around him.

Brother Thomas.

Thomas looked around but saw no one. The sound seemed to come from his head. He slapped his temple a couple times and lay back down. *Too much stress.*

"I believe you had some questions."

He sat up. "Who's there?"

The darkness before him shifted and distorted, coagulating into a shape—no, not a shape, a figure—standing before him. But this was no human figure. It was tall with four voluminous wings, two stretching to the ceiling of his bedroom. A soft glow came from the—man?—allowing Thomas's eyes to adjust. The being—definitely not a man—had three faces, and the one staring down at him was that of an eagle. On either side was the face of an ox and the face of a lion.

Great. I'm going crazy. Thomas shut his eyes tight until points of light flashed behind his lids. When he opened them again, the being still stood before him.

"Who?" Thomas coughed the sleep from his lungs. "Who… what are you?"

"Call me Hirael. You asked what the Most High does, and I am tasked with showing you. Now stand and come with me."

"Okay." Thomas laughed, climbing out of bed. "I get it. Ebby got all in my head and now I'm dreaming."

"This is no dream, Brother Thomas."

He looked down at himself. "And I suppose I fell asleep fully clothed? I guess at least I'm not in my underwear and late for work, like my standard dreams."

"You zonked out quite readily," the being replied. "You must have worked hard yesterday. I didn't have to wait long."

"Wait long?"

"I was here before you arrived. I greeted the other elohim who saw you safely home—thank your mother for that—and then came up here to wait for you to fall asleep."

"A little creepy, man." Thomas decided to play along. "Aren't you supposed to tell me, 'Be not afraid?'"

"Sometimes, yes. Sometimes…" Hirael seemed to grow, looming over Thomas, the feathers on his head puffing, his wings spreading, filling the space, his eagle eyes sparkling in the dark. "You are supposed to be afraid."

Covering his face, Thomas fell to his knees, his hands raised to protect himself, his whole body shaking. "Okay, enough! What do you want?"

Hirael stood straighter, now only slightly taller than Thomas. He reached out a hand and helped Thomas to his feet. Was that the slightest hint of a smile at the base of Hirael's beak? Can birds smile? This all seemed too random for a dream.

"I am an elohim, though I am concealing my glory, for this night I need your trust more than fear. You should appreciate that. Where we are going, you will see other elohim, some will not conceal their glory. But be not afraid"—definitely a smile—"it won't affect you in the heavens like it does here."

The heavens? Questions inundated Thomas's mind.

Hirael must have perceived this. "I can see you are confused. I will allow for three questions. I assure you, you'll prefer where we are going to talking in this… less than tidy bedroom."

"Hey!" Thomas scooped up a T-shirt crumbled on his floor and tossed it toward his hamper. It missed. "I'm busy at work."

The—elohim? That's what he called himself—waited, his head slightly cocked.

Thomas took a deep breath. "Okay, uh, what is the meaning of life?"

Shaking his head, Hirael lifted a hand. "Humans," he said. "Please, Brother Thomas, keep it relevant to this situation. I am sent here to guide, not reveal the mysteries of the universe, as if I even could."

"Fine." Frowning, Thomas considered all the things spinning through his mind. Finally, he stuck on one. "You called yourself 'elohim.' Isn't that God's name?"

"Elohim is a descriptive word sometimes used as a name, like the word *Father*. Your language differentiates with capital and lowercase letters; however, the old Hebrew and Greek you translate from do not. Those languages require context to decide whether 'elohim' is being used as a simple descriptor or as a name for the Most High. If it helps, you can think of elohim as meaning 'spiritual being'."

Thomas paced a bit, then snapped his fingers. "Okay, here's my next question. You keep calling God 'the Most High.' It's in the Bible, sure, but why use it so heavily?"

Hirael nodded. "It wouldn't mean the same for us to call Him Elohim because we are also elohim. But no other elohim is the Most High above all elohim. We also call Him 'Elyon,' which is just 'Most High' using an older tongue. You see, from our perspective, his relative position is the most relevant descriptor to acknowledge. Though, we will also use other descriptors as names such as Creator, Lord of lords, and others."

This was heavy. Thomas paced, snagging the shirt from the floor and finally getting it into the hamper. He'd get the socks later. "I have so many questions... This feels like all the hypothetical conversations you have about what three wishes you would make to a genie."

"I have never had such a conversation," Hirael replied.

"Right." Thomas was all in now, crazy dream or not. In his time in seminary, he had had about an hour on angels and demons, and it barely covered this sort of thing. After a brief pause, he was ready with his last question. "Are you missing a face?"

Hirael balked. "I'm sorry. What?"

"You have three faces. If I remember correctly, in Ezekiel, the cherubim had four faces." He counted out on his fingers. "Eagle, ox, lion... you're missing the man face."

Hirael grinned, his eyes softer. "Oh, I understand. Thank you. No, I am not missing a face. I am also not a cherub. The ones written about in Ezekiel were *serving* as cherubim.

"In our world, we care far more about a being's function than its form. Purpose distinguishes and defines. If an elohim stands guard over sacred space, they are performing the function of a cherub and can be called such. We are allowed to dedicate ourselves to the pursuit of a specific function above others. This is what we call a discipline. Each discipline is only available to certain orders of elohim... But now I see that I am creating more questions. Let me put it into layman's terms."

"That'd be helpful, thanks."

"These faces you see represent my orders, the purposes given me by the Most High. Unlike humans, who apply much effort to modify their appearance, I can change my appearance at will. Even the weapons I wield are my own creation."

As Hirael spoke the words, a bow manifested in his hands, and, as he drew the string, a flaming arrow materialized. He released the arrow. Thomas ducked as the bolt flew across the room, but before it struck anything, it dissolved into a streak of harmless light. The bow in his hands vanished as Hirael walked toward Thomas, shrinking down in size. As he came near, his wings disintegrated into sparkling wisps in the air, and he appeared, well, rather quite human. Though the weight of Hirael's presence belied his meager looks.

"That's how I thought an angel would appear," Thomas said. "Not that I expected any of this."

"Understandable. When elohim come as messengers, we usually appear human-like so as not to distract from the message. And I could conceal my glory fully, so that you would not feel I am an elohim at all. The author of the letter to the Hebrews mentions how some humans have received angels as guests without knowing."

"Right. 'Entertaining angels'. So, who actually wrote Hebrews anyway?"

"Ahh, that would be a fourth question, and not a relevant one." Hirael shifted back to his previous form. "Besides, I'm giving enough information from your third question to account for seven."

Thomas shrugged. "Can't blame a man for trying."

"Right. Anyway, back to appearance. When we appear in your world, we generally look more human. When your eyes are opened to see into our world, however, you see us as we appear natively, which is intentional and laden with meaningful imagery."

Thomas raised a finger, another question popping into his head, but Hirael shook his head and continued.

"We are not burdened with biology. For example," he glanced down at his human-like legs that ended in hooves. "I do not actually have hooves." His wings reappeared, spreading wide. "We don't have wings. I don't have three faces."

"Then why?"

"Your patience needs work. May I continue?"

Thomas closed his mouth tightly and nodded, not meeting the elohim's eyes.

After a beat, Hirael continued. "I wear these wings as a declaration of my general standing among the elohim and the holy watchers— those tasked to serve on the earth to guide and protect humans."

"Guardian angels," Thomas said, careful not to inflect.

"Clever use of language so as to not ask another question. But no, not exactly. Guardians are another discipline. But watchers may guard sometimes. Or sometimes guide. Our duties vary across assignments.

"There are four general standings of lesser elohim with archangel at the top. These four wings declare me to be an elohim of the second heaven, a middle standing, not the weakest, but not nearly the most powerful. Newly commissioned watchers of the first heaven are called 'fledglings' for their first several ranks. Your militaries and other organized squads use terms like 'green' or 'rookie'. But even archangels are considered lesser elohim. As I said, no elohim is like the Most High above all."

"That's..." Thomas chewed on his lower lip. "That's a lot of information." In truth, his head was spinning. "But you're avoiding the question. Why are you missing a face?"

"It is a lot, and I realize it can be overwhelming, even when I'm just giving you the basics. There is much depth I could get into, but I'll explain the faces. Each face represents a different order, or primary purpose, assigned to each elohim by the Most High upon their creation. He gives us the purpose, and we wear the face as a sign of our acceptance and cooperation with that purpose. There are four primary orders, and most elohim are given one or two of these purposes. As you see, I have three. Some are given all four, like the ones you referenced from Ezekiel.

"This eagle face," Hirael pointed to his current face, "represents the messenger order. Messengers are what humans commonly call 'angels'. We gather and deliver news and information." The eagle eyes went solid white, and Hirael's neck twisted. As the ox face came forward, color appeared in its eyes.

Thomas shivered.

The ox face peered at him, head slightly cocked, eyes holding a compassion Thomas had not seen with the eagle. "The ox face represents the ministering spirit order, who are tireless burden bearers, interceding and sacrificing for others."

The eyes went white. The neck twisted and the lion face stared blankly for a fraction of a second before its eyes too filled with color and life and ferocity.

Thomas recoiled.

"The lion face represents the warrior order, representing leadership

9

and strength. You don't want to witness what I do when I wear this face. Just be thankful that I do it."

Hirael centered back to the eagle. The whole switching faces things made Thomas's skin crawl. It was also pretty cool, though, if he was honest.

"The order I do not possess is the one that would be the most familiar to you."

"Yeah, man face." Thomas grimaced, hoping that wasn't rude.

Hirael assured him with a friendly nod. "Yes, the face of a man. That represents the minstrel order who embody passion and praise. Where the eagle points to divinity as it soars in the heavens, the man relates to humanity whose dwelling is the earth. Humanity is simultaneously higher than the natural creation and lower than the elohim. I hope you can see the beauty of the layers of meaning in the imagery. Even *we* realize a fresh nuance on occasion."

Thomas just stared. He could suddenly feel the messiness in the room around him.

Hirael placed a hand on Thomas's shoulder. "Come, we have delayed enough. I shared this information to help you focus during our journey." He motioned as if showing Thomas a wide landscape. "You are about to encounter many stories. I don't want you to miss their meaning due to distraction from foreign terms and concepts. There will still be many things you are not familiar with. Some of those will become clearer in time, and I will also share more as we go. But you know what you need to."

Thomas nodded, still a bit confused. Hirael gently nudged him forward and Thomas marched to his window. He looked at the public courtyard below and the bright lights of the city shining off the clouds. Then he looked down at his apartment complex.

Down?

Squirming, Thomas rubbernecked up at Hirael, who didn't seem to be carrying him. But he certainly wasn't flying on his own accord. He had no idea how he was moving, he just knew he was.

"Be not afraid." Hirael chuckled.

And Thomas wasn't. He marveled at the sights around him from this high up. The neighborhood in which he lived cut up into little squares, the moonlight bouncing off the windows of tall buildings he now floated above. He glanced back to Hirael, and his eyes went wide. "You're bigger now."

No way could this Hirael fit into the tiny apartment they had just left.

"To your eyes, yes," Hirael said. "We are not of this material world. Size is relative for us. We inherently adjust, rescaling to the situation. Free of spatial constraints, this is what you might call my natural size. However, several of us could fight a full battle inside one of your compact cars. True example, by the way."

Faster than felt natural—if flying *could* feel natural—they ascended above the clouds, and Thomas saw a ripple in the air ahead. Then a window of water appeared in the middle of the sky.

Thomas held his breath as Hirael led them into it...

So this is heaven... Thomas thought. When they came through the window in the sky, Thomas had found himself stepping out of what he was told was one of the west gates. A tall and mighty ox-headed elohim stood head and shoulders above Hirael. The cherub had six wings and guarded the gate. Thomas realized he was staring when the elohim gave him a warm, but stern, nod of welcome.

Everything he had seen so far was glorious beyond imagination. Reading accounts in the Bible honestly didn't compare to the experience of it. Thomas now understood Hirael's hurry to leave his room earlier. Everything seemed to be made of light—or rather gems that refracted light. Large crowds gathered. Hirael was right, there were many elohim, some smaller than Hirael, several as tall as a house, and among them walked righteous spirits. A low murmur of voices filled the air as they mingled. At first, Thomas expected to be distracted by— what did Hirael call it?—the 'glory' of the elohim, but instead he felt almost perfect peace.

Thomas lifted a finger. "Uh, more questions."

"Come." Hirael beckoned him forward. "There will be time. I want to show you the arenas before we enter them."

Hirael led Thomas up into the air as he had when leaving Thomas's house. Below them, Thomas could see a myriad of large bowls, each with a stage at the bottom. These arenas were dark, but dotted with the glow of thousands of elohim, almost like looking down at a night sky. The sight disoriented Thomas.

"These arenas are where we listen to the minstrels' stories." Hirael spread his hands, gesturing toward the arenas. "You will be a rare and privileged guest for several such stories this day." Hirael descended with Thomas toward one of the arenas along the outer rim.

Thomas took the chance to sneak in a couple 'relevant to the situation' questions.

"Is that what happens in *all* these arenas? Stories?"

"They are tales of all history upon the earth. That's a lot to recount. Think of it like your movie theaters, but far more of them, and all the movies ever made are repeated now and again. Elohim are not omniscient. This is how we educate one another as to the happenings upon the earth. We find much enjoyment from these tales. It brings new meaning to 'entertaining angels', as you said before. I believe your language afforded me what you call a pun."

Thomas chuckled. Since they entered the arena from above, they were able to land directly in two open seats. "Well, this is convenient. I wish I could do it all the time." He wondered why most of the elohim were shuffling amongst each other on foot, like they couldn't simply do the same.

"I was sad to miss the chance to greet many of my friends along the way," Hirael said.

Interesting. Thomas found the possibility of crowds being a *pleasant* thing, almost more astonishing than everything else he had witnessed so far. He realized how profoundly isolated his own culture was.

The shape of the arena made for easy vision of the stage, seemingly from any seat.

Two elohim walked past, one with three sets of wings and one with only two, both full of glory, though the one with more wings shone brighter, if that was the right terminology.

"Never realized there were so many different sizes of angels—er, elohim."

"Yes and no," Hirael said. "You observe the different standings I had touched on in our first conversation. Holy watchers are honored for our loyal service, promoted in rank, and eventually elevated in standing, which brings increased glory and a more commanding presence. As I pointed out then, this is also represented by the number of wings. It's all purposeful. It all communicates something." On cue, Hirael unfurled his four wings.

"To help you remember, think of each set of wings as a 'heaven'. Some ancient humans spoke of three heavens—first, second, and third—progressing from the sky to the throne of the Most High. We use those same terms to describe where our primary duties lie, progressing from individual to national significance. By 'nation,' I speak of spiritual, not earthly, authority. But let's—how you might say—put a pin in that for later. For now, just understand: holds, footholds, strongholds—these all refer to locations of spiritual authority upon the earth."

Before Thomas could process enough to form a question, Hirael moved on. "I have one more thing to quickly share with you before the stories begin. I spoke to you before of orders: warriors, messengers, ministering spirits, minstrels. They each have different ways of interacting with others. Warriors are often more tactile, and they fight using practiced maneuvers. Messengers, on the other hand, are often more perceptive and attentive to others and their surroundings. Ministering spirits, being especially compassionate, employ their strength of will to perform unique effects which range widely, but all stem from mastery of their resolve. Minstrels, as we are about to witness, express themselves artistically through music, verse, and song, which can influence others in powerful ways and can even produce magnificent manifestations of their meaning."

Hirael paused and winked before continuing and Thomas nodded, acknowledging the poetic use of alliteration to exemplify the minstrel, the one order Hirael lacked.

"If you hear a role that isn't one of those orders, like guardian, king priest, shepherd, it is likely the name of a discipline—a dedicated function, which elohim of an appropriate order can choose. There are many holy and unholy disciplines, and it would be too much to detail them all."

"What about—?

"Shh." Hirael gently shushed Thomas. "It's about to start."

A 'man face' elohim stepped out onto the stage humbly, but confidently, and the crowd hushed. After a dramatic pause, he began to speak in musical tones that projected effortlessly throughout the arena.

ONE STEP AT A TIME

NATHANIEL SORENSEN

I have generally considered it prudent to avoid being pinned by giant scorpions. My more robust partners normally handle those closer encounters. Unfortunately, this day's companion was occupied a short distance away with nuisances of his own. He had been mostly successful in drawing a couple of unclean spirits and three other spiritual beasts away from the Israelite woman now kneeling behind me, but this one proved too focused on inflicting anguish and despair. So there I found myself, staring the exception to my rule in his beady eyes.

The scorpion was easily twice my size. His carapace was singed, where my song of fire and holy fear had struck at its focus, but I had been little more than a nuisance standing between him and his obsession. Dodging jabs from his tail, I crescendoed into my chorus, causing a ball of cleansing fire to explode between us. The scorpion screeched with the impact and stepped back. I shook my head as the flames' sting refined my focus to prepare for the scorpion's next move.

I thought perhaps I'd gained an advantage until he lunged at me again and caught me in his pincers. Unable to move, I braced for the finish. His tail gathered for a last strike when suddenly the beast's head was replaced by the gleaming double-blade of a war axe. Just as quickly, a putrid plume of black smoke obscured my view and the scorpion's grip on me slackened.

The smoke thinned as Brute kicked the defeated beast aside, then leaned on the axe that had so efficiently severed the scorpion from his purpose. His lion's smile is never wholly without ferocity, but I detected a hint of smugness as he waited for me to gather myself.

I allowed myself a brief sigh before smiling back. "As momentous as that was, Brute, a moment earlier would not have been out of order."

"Just testing your resolve in the face of opposition, brother. You so rarely give me company here in the thick of things."

"Ha ha. Confess—that was your second swing. You missed with your first attempt."

Brute grumbled something I couldn't make out before nodding toward the woman behind me. "We should probably continue."

I turned to look at the woman kneeling on the ground. Her face was smudged and her dark hair tangled, but her weeping had abated. She sat unmoving in the dust, contemplating a short, bronze sword loosely held the wrong way in both hands. Its handle rested on her knees, the point laying against her chest. Her gaze was somehow distant, yet still unwaveringly fixed on the pommel.

"Right," I agreed. "Not out of danger yet."

Brute moved to her other side, laid his unseen hand on one of her shoulders and spoke words of comfort to her spirit, while I encouraged her heart to trust there would be purpose and goodness lying ahead in her life. I perceived interweaving layers of fear, loss, confusion, and exhaustion swirling around her. These weren't residue of the spiritual attack. Her human heart and mind were attempting to pick through the aftermath of chaos and trauma. And grief. Mostly grief.

If there are simple solutions to these moments, I have yet to discover them. The Most High has certainly not given to us elohim the ability to erase pain. To fortify, guide, encourage, comfort—all of these we do eagerly. And we do them well. But true peace for this woman would require more than we have to offer. For that, she would need to seek the Most High directly.

In this, I could sympathize. Brute and I both know what it is to lose loved ones, albeit to rebellion, rather than death, in our case. The pain of grief is not foreign to us.

Thus it was with tenderness and respect that I eased into a new song and manifested it not to be heard in her ears, but to be felt in her heart. It was something of a lullaby of waiting on the Lord. I attempted to soothe tensions and encourage stepping back from hasty reactions. Brute picked up on my lyric and complemented it with words of his own.

As I sang, I took another look around to confirm we were clear of further interference. It was a remote area, and having dealt with whatever unholy influence had followed her here, we appeared to be alone. Without interruptions, Brute and I soon succeeded in steering her out of the most dangerous areas of despair. Indeed, before I made it into a third verse, her eyes regained focus on what was in front of her.

I would have preferred she cast the sword away. Instead, she turned it around and held the hilt up before her face. Her previously vacant expression turned into clenched teeth and sharpened eyes. Her breath quickened as she studied the pommel. Standing, she turned and walked in the direction of her village, not hurried, but definitely leaning into her stride.

I concluded my song and stored it away for later. Please hear no arrogance when I say it was a good melody. Hardly the best in creation, but worth refining for another appropriate moment.

We watched her pick her way through the rocky hillside, satisfied in successfully navigating another touchy situation. Well, *I* was satisfied. Brute sounded contemplative as he turned to me. "I believe we are to continue with her."

"She did not bring herself harm in her grief, Brute. The mission seems a success."

"And yet..."

"You do realize I'm not the only one here looking wispy."

He glanced down at the white, smoky tendrils drifting up from his arms and torso, marking wounds received in our recent encounter. Looking back at me, he cocked his head to the side to show how little he was impressed.

The Most High *does* occasionally gives us additional instructions in the field. They rarely come with the same detail given in our formal briefings, however, and I'm one who is quite fond of clarity. Especially when working with humans.

Brute's second set of wings twitched, and I glanced down at my own. They were new to us, signifying our elevation to second heaven status. We had been told they would be accompanied by additional responsibility. Still, I didn't want to read too much into that and seem overeager when we reported back to our superiors.

I had worked with Brute often enough, though, to know he is not one to press an issue unless he's convinced, so I nodded. "Very well. Let's follow and see what comes next."

We *had* just encouraged this woman to have enough trust to go on another day. I supposed I could eat from the same scroll and do likewise.

Brute manifested a reddish-gold horse underneath him, his choice of blessing upon promotion to second heaven. Since he could easily outpace the woman without the steed's extra speed, I assumed he wanted the extra magnitude to discourage interference along our way.

Our briefing had told us the woman was away from her village earlier that day when a Canaanite group passed through. Whether or not they came to make trouble, trouble resulted, and several villagers were killed. In foresight of her finding her family among them, we were sent to ensure she did not come to harm in her grief.

By the time we'd arrived, she had already made the discovery. The freshness of her shock and disorientation drew a handful of spiritual beasts and unclean spirits who had been nearby reveling in the trauma of the conflict. Under their torment, she had wandered out to where Brute and I finally caught up and ended their influence, if not her grief.

Entering her village, it became apparent that the strongest evil had either left with the Canaanites or been in the group we had just defeated. Unclean spirits and weaker beasts in groups of two or three were still at work along the streets. They turned to study us as we passed through rows of tents and simple buildings, but our greater glory encouraged them to shrink back to easier spoils. Arriving at her dwelling, she went inside, changed into fresh traveling clothes, and began packing a small bundle.

Then came the hardest moment of our day.

Before leaving, she stopped in her main living area and knelt before a set of small, crudely carved idols. She confessed her weakness before these gods and invoked their aid in the task now before her.

Brute growled with disgust. "I can't watch this, Veta. The *Most*

High just intervened to spare her! How can she turn and offer allegiance to the *enemy?*"

"You know she does not see as we see. I do share your frustration, though."

"Is this not self-harm?" Brute asked. "Is it not our mission to put an end to this?"

"I see your point, but this action is not newly due to grief. This altar has been here for some time, and like many such altars in Israel lately, it is well-used. I don't think this is why we're still with her."

Brute sighed as he turned toward the door. "I'll take another look around outside."

It required most of my resolve not to join him, but it seemed one of us should keep eyes on her until we knew why this mission continued. My discomfort elevated as an unclean spirit entered from the other side of the dwelling. It eyed me with a triumphant gleam as it sidled up next to her.

"Careful, Minstrel," it taunted me. "She gives me right."

"You needn't speak rules to me, restless one. Know your leash is short."

Having confirmed I wasn't an immediate threat, it turned to whisper in her ear. I leaned in to listen, knowing some of these overeager spirits can be careless with their thoughts. Given the tone of her prayers, I expected to hear some incitement to vengeance and perhaps violence. There was that, but I also picked up on a layer of betrayal and renewed notes of despair. I assumed the despair was to keep her judgment clouded and her decisions careless. This theme of betrayal was harder to explain. The unclean spirit must have been playing on some knowledge of this family that I did not yet share.

Humans talk of life being a mystery. Though we elohim do certainly see more than they, I often find myself feeling a kinship in this respect.

The woman finally concluded her misdirected prayers and grabbed her bag. I noted a stony glint in her eyes as she tucked the sword inside. I didn't feel at liberty to address her carrying the weapon, but Brute and I *would* be within the mission to intervene if she tried to use it. I went through the door ahead of her.

"We're moving, Brute. And we have an undesirable companion."

23

Brute's eyes blazed when the unclean spirit came through the door behind our charge, and the spirit flinched to find an imposing warrior suddenly looming over him. Brute was quick to read the situation, though, and merely released a controlled snort as the woman readied a horse and headed north.

Our unlikely party traveled for several hours in silence. I must confess to questioning again whether we were simply chasing after wind, but I wouldn't do Brute the dishonor of giving voice to these reprised doubts.

I did not question his ability to receive direction. It was more that I usually fill the quieter moments on missions considering strategies and contingencies. Not knowing the Most High's specific intent, or even our destination, left me unclear on which details to focus. I eventually gave it up to work on that new melody, a timely reminder to rest my own spirit in waiting on the Lord.

Just after sunset, I finally had a place to turn my attention. We approached a well-established encampment spreading out from the cover of a lone, great tree dominating an open plain. The dwelling was less a village and more on the scale of a wealthy family with its entourage of servants, apprentices, and guards.

The woman left her horse hidden in a ravine, then carefully crept close enough to watch. Brute dismissed his horse as well. Stealth seemed prudent for the time being. As we watched, I would have expected the clatter, calls, and laughter of the humans' evening meal. The stillness that greeted us hung heavily in the air.

Periodically, a guard wandered into view, but nothing more. The woman took her time—whether from caution or uncertainty, I do not know. After nearly an hour, she got up and made for an area showing the least activity.

As we got closer, Brute and I noted the dark shapes of spiritual evil concentrated around a small group of humans quietly gathered at the encampment's main fire pit. Most were lower in power and making no attempt at vigilance.

"Do you perceive anything pertinent?" I asked Brute.

"They have the look of enjoying time away from a commander," Brute responded after a pause.

"So they do," I agreed. "That would explain the general inactivity. Some of the human household must be away and the leader of the unholy with them."

The unclean spirit turned with a sour look and addressed us for the first time since the woman's house. "If the tyrant were here, you'd have been sent crawling in shame before laying eyes on the camp."

"If this tyrant were here," I replied, "the Most High could have sent a larger force. Keep your poisonous thoughts to yourself."

The spirit received the rebuke with something like a human sneeze, but said nothing more.

The woman seemed to have an idea of what she was searching for as she slipped through the shadows. She looked rather comfortable avoiding detection, but the rest of us were more conspicuous. An unholy messenger approached to challenge us. Bold, given his single set of wings, but a familiar setting and a crowd of allies within earshot does lend one confidence. I could at least appreciate that he approached with words and not arrows.

"What have you to do here? You have no right to interrupt our operations. Best leave now and save us any trouble."

I attempted to keep things calm. "We're not here for you or yours," I responded firmly, but without threat. "We're with her." I gestured to our charge creeping behind a tent.

The messenger eyed the woman and the unclean spirit with her. "By the looks of things," he scoffed, "she *is* one of ours. Do you expect me to believe your mission involves the intentions I perceive in her?"

I maintained a calm tone. "The Most High has His ways and isn't to be questioned by the likes of you or us. Just be at ease to know we haven't come for you."

The messenger seemed conflicted, but nodded. "Very well. But I'll have to escort you. I would surely lose power if my captain returns to find I've allowed an interruption to his plans."

"Do as you must," I said, stepping past with Brute to keep up with the woman. Truth be told, having this messenger with us would probably lessen chances of unwanted conflict. I didn't really mind letting him come along, provided I didn't have to continue conversing.

Without further incident, we came upon one of the larger tents. It sat on the far side of the tree from the main fire and was a little apart from any tents around it. The woman listened for a moment, then slipped in through the entry curtain.

As often as I've repeated the exercise, I can't say I relish the tension of passing through physical boundaries into unseen spaces. I've grown quite used to scaling down in order to operate comfortably within human-scale rooms. It's quite another thing to make that adjustment while needing to scan for, and potentially react to, hostile inhabitants.

As we emerged into the tent, we found another woman reclined at her evening meal in the center of a large room. Her two attending servants looked startled at the interruption, but offered no immediate objection. Behind her stood an unholy ministering spirit with two sets of wings, accompanied by a minstrel of slightly less power. If their actual leader were away, this ministering spirit must have been a chief lieutenant left to mind the details at home.

The minstrel was quietly humming a tune to numb the senses on an easy evening. It had no effect on Brute or myself, but it wouldn't have been meant for us. I made a note not to underestimate this minstrel's capabilities should things turn hostile.

Their lazy postures indicated a night off, confirming Brute's earlier assessment. The only other spiritual presence was a low-ranking messenger to our left, looking more like a page than a guard. The ministering spirit probably didn't want others around, crowding out his daydreams of command and its glories. He wouldn't be thanking us for the intrusion.

While our escort moved closer to explain our presence, I noticed the woman at dinner looking over our charge's appearance with curiosity. "Welcome, traveler," she said with ease. "Find rest and refuge here in my tents."

Where our charge had previously moved with purpose, she now struggled to make eye contact and shifted her weight from one foot to the other. Some response or introduction was obviously expected, but none was offered. The silence seemed not to faze the impromptu host.

"Be at ease. My name is Yael, wife of Heber. Please, come share my table."

Our charge remained frozen, but Yael continued to show impressive self-composure. She simply lifted an eyebrow and settled in to wait for her guest to make the next move.

In the pause, the ministering spirit addressed us. "You must be quite the pair to follow her alone into our encampment. Please, give me your names so I can make record of this esteemed visit."

Tense silence seemed to be the theme of the day, so neither Brute nor I chose to rise to his mocking. The ministering spirit continued, "What are your plans here? Do know that I will have no tolerance for disturbances this night." He delivered the last words in a tone he probably thought was incredibly menacing. I kept my attention on the humans.

After a further silence even I must describe as awkward, Yael finally spoke to her servants, "You may leave, but don't go far."

After they left, Yael asked, "Now, what is your name?"

Our charge responded softly. "Ahava," finding her words at last.

"And what can I do for you, Ahava?"

"I thought when a Kenite family came, we would have friends among us."

"And... you feel that not to be the case?" Yael asked.

Ahava's grip tightened on her pack until the blood disappeared from her knuckles. "You are a betrayer of my people, and of the God of Moses and of your father, Jethro."

Yael sat back, her polished demeanor giving way to a slight grimace. She responded in a tone suggesting boredom and a touch of condescension, but no offense. "We may not be of Israel, but we do know of your covenant. Given its terms, you can hardly blame your current situation on my clan. I'll own that our peoples have long been close, but your covenant with Yahweh is your own."

"You claim not to be involved?!" Ahava's voice rose with increasing tension. "You are crafting weapons for our enemy! Your handiwork sheds our blood!"

She reached into her bag and pulled out the sword. As she did, the unclean spirit found the moment it seemed to have been waiting for and urged, "Do it. Do it now. Kill her! She deserves it! Take your justice!"

Ahava gripped the hilt and began to step forward.

Brute and I made eye contact and quietly agreed, "*No.*"

Brute formed a spear and flung it at the unclean spirit. It was a clean miss. An arrow had beaten him to the target, knocking the unclean spirit aside. We looked to the arrow's source and saw our escort watching us as he cautiously lowered his bow. To our left, the other messenger had a ready arrow trained on Brute.

The ministering spirit manifested a sturdy, yet ornately carved staff as he looked from our escort to Brute and back. "Explain yourself," he said, gesturing solemnly toward our escort with his staff, as though it should remind everyone of his authority.

"I… I knew its thoughts, my lord," the messenger said, eager to placate. "I heard it muttering its intent as we approached and suspected it would not restrain itself in deference to *your* wishes."

The ministering spirit looked thoughtfully toward Brute, who now held out open hands in a show of peace. It didn't look well-practiced.

"As we told the messenger," Brute said, "we're not here for you. The spirit crossed a line it seems we both wanted untouched."

The ministering spirit looked less than convinced but merely grumbled, "Your *assistance* is not welcome. There has already been more commotion than I desired tonight. Be certain I will not—"

He was cut off by the clatter of metal on wood. We all looked down to see the sword come to rest, thrown onto the table in front of Yael.

"Do you deny the mark of Heber upon this blade?" Ahava asked. Others may have noticed only accusation, but I heard notes of urgency and frailty in the timbre of her voice. "Has the craftsmanship of your house *not* been offered in service to Hazor?"

One of Yael's servants stepped back inside to check on the noise. Noting that Ahava moved no closer while waiting for a response, Yael waved the servant away.

"What does it matter?" she asked. "Jabin of Hazor conquered your people long before my husband and I came to Kedesh. We aren't tipping the scales in the slightest. You cannot seriously expect my husband and I to exchange opportunity for mediocrity purely for the sake of solidarity."

Hearing this exchange, I finally caught a glimmer of greater purpose in our continued assignment. I thought it was time to offer some distraction while the women talked.

Given this lieutenant's reticence to respond violently to the unclean spirit, and his seeming need for maintaining the status quo, I guessed at his chosen discipline. "Strange to find a pacifier overseeing a weapons-crafting operation."

My guess bore fruit and, as hoped, he needed little encouragement to boast.

"Lord Mishtarah has won great esteem in this dominion by bringing these metal smiths to aid King Jabin of Canaan. His skills, while admittedly great, are also limited to fear and domination. When it comes to the finer art of *maintenance*, he is as inept as…"

He glanced at the messengers, realizing there were others around capable of reporting his open derision to this master of fear and domination. Quickly masking his insecurity, he glared at each messenger as he finished. "…as any great leader in need of my particular skills."

I struggled to suppress a smile, and heard Ahava having a perceptive moment of her own. "The Kenites are not with you in this, are they, Yael?"

Yael's previous composure finally cracked as she blinked twice.

Ahava pressed further. "They actually resisted this choice, didn't they? You and your husband had to break from your own clan and come up here alone because they wouldn't back this self-seeking adventure of greed!"

Yael was now a touch less welcoming. "And just what has *my* clan's relationship to do with you and yours?"

Ahava's voice dropped to a whisper, but lost any traces that could be mistaken for frailty. "My family is *exactly* why I am here."

The pacifier stepped forward, waving his staff. "You need to *leave. Now.*" His voice trembled. He must have sensed the situation moving beyond his control and decided he'd had enough.

Brute lowered his hands and resumed a more ready stance. "We have our assignment. We're not leaving without her."

"Your assignment means nothing to me, Warrior," the pacifier snarled. "If your charge continues this conversation, unpleasant things will have to happen. *Be on your way.*"

Pacifiers are known to be adept in persuasion, and this one represented his discipline well. I must confess I froze for a moment. I had no inclination to *agree* with him, but in that moment, any well-reasoned response seemed beyond words.

Brute turned an inquisitive glance my way. Was the pacifier somehow playing on our mission orders? I shook my head slightly. More surprising things have happened in our experience, but the pacifier was probably just taking shots in the dark, hoping his ability to influence would see his suggestions to their marks.

Brute turned back toward the pacifier with a growl. "We will *not* be put off our assignment with words, Pacifier."

"So be it," the pacifier replied, stepping back. The light in the room somehow dimmed and warped around him, forming what looked to our eyes as a hole in space. He was there, but he was not. My eyes kept trying to slide off his position. As I struggled to adapt, the distortion drifted to our right and masked our view of the minstrel as well.

Brute kept his attention focused on the pacifier, though I knew he would be struggling with the same disorientation. He manifested his horse, simultaneously drawing his arm back as if to throw. As his hand reached his ear, another spear manifested, and he immediately threw it into the shifting darkness. Before it disappeared into the shadow, Brute charged forward with his great, two-headed axe hoisted above his head.

The messengers put arrows through the space Brute had just vacated. Their second shots were better aimed. Brute hardly seemed to notice, but I moved to deal with the messengers and save him the distraction.

As I turned toward the nearest, I noted that the minstrel's song had gotten louder, deepening from suggesting lethargy into a dissonant demand for slumber. It was a clumsy and ill-timed attempt. This minstrel had obviously lost touch with the nature of true rest. His lyric had more elements of paralysis than actual sleep. I have learned the dangers of underestimating an enemy, but perhaps I had over-compensated here.

Though his song wasn't a true threat, I did begin to sing my own. Rather than counteracting boldly and adding to the dissonance, I simply doubled the cadence of the song to introduce a sense of building speed without yet rushing the actual tempo. I knew this pattern would be familiar to Brute and the rhythm would give us both an extra step.

I then rhymed the minstrel's lyric with lines prompting fear of the Lord God Most High. No one would flee the room, but I watched the escort messenger recoil as I spread both sets of my wings and advanced toward him.

He awkwardly turned his bow to shield himself as I lifted my hand above my head and added fire to my song. A sword appeared, flames streaming from the edges. I brought it down hard and his bow could not slow it from biting deep into his shoulder. The flames blended with black smoke erupting from his wound, determination fading from his countenance. I struck again and his resolve left him. His bow dropped as he fell to his knees in submission.

I looked across the room to see the other messenger loose an arrow at Brute. Another arrow replaced it as he turned toward me. My display must have attracted his attention, which suited me fine. I deflected his arrow and started across the room.

As I passed behind Brute, the pacifier's voice reverberated throughout the room. "You have overreached yourself, Warrior. See how your flailing only wounds yourself! Cut your losses and leave while you can."

It had to be wearing on Brute's heart to stand against this nebulous void that seemingly swallowed his attacks. But his only response was to swing again. The axe head disappeared into the shadow and Brute's arms shuddered. He roared, but I could tell it to be a cry of pain rather than satisfaction.

From somewhere behind the pacifier, I heard a change in the minstrel's song. He dropped his lyric altogether, shifting into an awful wail to undercut the intensity of my song. Much as it may have been a true offense to the ears, it was unsuccessful in dampening my passion. Even his attempt to push against my beat and slow the song's tempo was little more than background noise for me. I was driving this song now. Easily maintaining my rhythm, I felt it speed me across the room.

This messenger gave no more resistance than the last. I am not counted among the mightiest of the Host, but a flaming sword's ability to discourage an enemy is not lightly dismissed. With my first strike, the messenger's eyes flashed around, desperate for escape. A second blow was again sufficient to bring defeat.

Glancing at the women, I expected no change and found none. Our shift into battle speed would have given Ahava only enough time to finish her next sentence.

I left them to continue and turned to see Brute visibly struggling. Pacifiers prefer to influence combatants more than attacking directly, but this one seemed skilled at turning his attackers' strikes against them. Brute's swings were still powerful, but growing wilder. I saw an abnormal tightness settling into his shoulders. The minstrel still had yet to be a direct threat, so I stepped toward the shifting cloud of darkness to help Brute gain an advantage.

Getting closer, I noticed Brute using my song to maintain a rhythm in his attacks despite his pain. As I built toward a new stanza, he gathered himself, bringing his axe high over his head. He pulled the axe down with a grunt, and this time the cry that filled the room was not his. For the briefest instant, the pacifier's silhouette coalesced, his form arched in agony. The glimpse passed quickly, but now a fierce grin stretched over Brute's mouth. Maybe a snarl. Probably both.

I used Brute's strike to time my crescendo into the chorus of a new song. Shifting into the major key, I burst from "Fear of the Lord" into a celebration of our Lord and King's true supremacy over all creation. Reaching Brute's side, my sword's sweeping arcs of light challenged the void's darkness. It was still near impossible to see what we were accomplishing, but we finally gained some encouragement with new billows of black smoke rising above the dark distortion.

It took just seconds (indeed, I could only be sure of landing one strike myself) before the darkness faded and our vision stabilized. The jet plume turned to whispers, then faded away. A pathetic groan escaped the oxen lips of the incapacitated *former* chief lieutenant.

Brute dismissed his horse, and the scale of the room readjusted as he settled back at my level, panting slightly. As I ended my song, he smirked and mimicked my tone from that morning. "You know, Veta, a moment earlier would not have been out of—"

"Yes, yes. I get it," I said, shaking my head.

I then realized it was quieter than it should have been. At some point, the minstrel had given up trying. I looked over to see him huddled in the corner, now thoroughly overwhelmed.

"I submit," he whispered in shame and self-loathing. "I submit."

"Probably shouldn't risk him bringing those reinforcements from out in the camp," Brute suggested.

I agreed. "Best we escort him from the area and send him on his way."

Brute walked over and crouched down to lock eyes with the minstrel. "You *will* be silent. Any interruptions or attempts to leave and you'll receive *no quarter* from me."

The minstrel nodded.

As we rejoined the women, Ahava was still pushing whispered words through clenched teeth, "... to find *this* sword bearing *your* mark standing upright in my husband's body. My *husband*. Laying next to my..." the effort to avoid collapse prevented her from continuing. A tremor appeared in her shoulders and her gaze dropped to the floor.

Brute went to Ahava, speaking courage and stability into her soul. Yael had gone quiet and was hard to read. After a brief moment, Brute's impartation enabled Ahava to continue.

"I know the sword was not in *your* hand." She lifted her eyes to search the ceiling. "I came here because... when I heard you'd come, I had hoped your presence in Kedesh meant support. Perhaps it was a sign that our time of oppression may be ending. You may speak true, and Jabin would be just as strong without you and your husband, but finding that my hope in you was unfounded seemed another black stroke laid on a picture of the night."

Yael looked down to study the contents of the table. When she spoke, it was with less confidence. "I... I am not without..." She searched unsuccessfully for an appropriate word. "Please do not think me unmoved. Perhaps we have been distancing ourselves from your suffering to avoid facing the part we have played in it."

Ahava leaned in, this time to make a plea. "I do not ask you to fight for us, Yael. It would just mean so much if we knew we still had friends around us. Go home. Reconcile with your clan. Stop profiting off our oppression."

Even before Ahava finished, I knew an imposing request when I heard one. I attempted to help by singing Yael a song of conviction. I didn't give it the intensity and force that might be received as a rebuke. Instead, I kept to an easy tempo with a melody meant more to woo a heart than to attack defenses.

Yael did not immediately respond. I could see two thoughts warring inside her. Or perhaps a thought in her mind warring with an infant passion stirring in her heart.

"I have no small influence with my husband," she said slowly, "but I am confident he will not leave this alliance—no matter what I say or do. There is too much potential profit and influence for us to leave.

"However, it is right to remind me of the friendship of our peoples. I may not be able to dissuade Heber, but I don't have to partner in this enterprise. And I can do more still. I don't yet know how or when, but I am strong and resourceful and will find a way to do more."

She rose to her feet, her tone warming from its previous formality. "Come. I earnestly hope you will never face a worse day than this. Let me prepare a place for you to rest tonight. You are welcome to stay as long as seems good to you. When you are ready to return to your people, I will send my best with you to see you arrive safely."

I brought my song to a gentle end. It's often hard to tell how much we, the holy watchers, truly influence these developments. Sometimes it's unclear whether we make a difference at all. We simply do what we can and trust for the best. Faith is hardly an exercise exclusive to the realm of humans, after all.

Brute turned to me and gave a satisfied nod.

I grinned back. "Are we allowed to go now?" I asked.

"I think she's in good hands from here," Brute said. "If we stick around any longer, we may attract undue attention to her."

I looked over at the minstrel. "Let's finish cleaning up here, then, and go make our report."

BIBLIO RUN

ALTHEA DAMGAARD

Thunder rumbled while torrential rain slanted across the land. Lightning flashes revealed gnarled trees. A monk struggled through the trees, trying to keep his prized possession dry.

Ibzan hovered just above the orchard. Keeping watch over the monk had drawn him lower than he usually preferred, as the land flattened on its way to the ocean.

The weather didn't hinder him like it did the monk, who worked to stay aligned with apple trees revealed in each flash. For the moment, the monk headed the right direction and was on pace to make his coastal destination on time.

As a watchman does, Ibzan scanned the surroundings for any spiritual activity. Perceiving nothing, he let himself drift in the sky.

The monk stopped and spun about. Ibzan swooped closer. How had he missed the enemy warrior now standing along the monk's path? Had he possibly approached from underground? Ibzan frowned in recognition. This warrior, Mahlon, was a strongman and could easily overpower him in close quarters. A prior altercation had taught him not to underestimate him. He would have to do his best to use his swiftness and ability to fight from afar if it came to that.

Mahlon raised his arms up and out as the monk unknowingly approached him. Ibzan's eyes narrowed. What was Mahlon doing?

As lightning flashed, Mahlon cast the shadow of a looming tree with reaching branches. The monk darted to his right. When the monk turned back to his left, Mahlon had moved to block him with a new tree apparition.

Mahlon's presence suggested the monk and his package had far more value than Ibzan had been aware of. He had been explicitly told to ensure the monk reached Hibernia. That included a trek to the coast of Frankia and then a ship ride that would round Britannia, a long and plodding journey for even the healthiest man. This weather, and now this warrior, were the only deterrents the monk had encountered once he had escaped the barbarians burning every written word they could find in the monastery's library. Ibzan had stopped the raiders from following the monk with tricks much like what the warrior used now.

Ibzan approached, making no attempt at stealth but keeping a healthy distance. He had witnessed the brutality of this warrior in the past. The memory and the intimidation that rolled forth depleted his desire to get any closer.

Mahlon looked up from toying with the monk. Seeing the watchman, his maw spread in a wide grin. "Why, Ibzan, what a surprise!"

Ibzan drew on his assurance of his place here, per his orders. "This is my charge. Leave him be."

"Ah, I suspected someone would be watching. You're aware, I assume, that you don't worry me much."

The monk corrected his path toward the coast, darting through the trees. Mahlon played off his distraction as he moved to get in front of the monk once more. "He can die just as easily at sea."

Ibzan followed, but kept his distance. "I doubt you have the right to sink an entire ship. Besides, think of the protection the other passengers may have. Would you dare to try it alone?"

Mahlon jumped and planted himself in the monk's path in time with a flash of lightning, his appearance momentarily shifting to a gnarled tree that came close to grabbing the monk.

This time, the monk stumbled and dropped his package. Scuttling across the ground, he snatched it close once more. He then settled in under an apple tree with his back against the trunk.

Mahlon taunted the messenger. "All I have to do is convince him to stay there until dawn."

Ibzan dared to move closer to the monk, attempting to affirm him with a sensation of purpose. He spoke to the monk's spirit. "The coast is so close. You can get there in time."

The monk's breathing steadied, but he did not move.

"Blast you, Ibzan. You know you can't win against me. Remember our last fight?"

"I remember it well. However, I have the true authority here, not you. Now move along or this could resort to something you *haven't* experienced before."

Ibzan prayed he sounded sure of himself.

Mahlon roared and flew toward Ibzan.

Ibzan created a bow with an arrow nocked. His swiftness allowed him to fly left, watching the much slower warrior as he passed. Ibzan taunted him with a pause and a slight wave of the readied bow to entice Mahlon into aiming everything at him and to forget the monk—daringly stupid with how close this allowed his enemy to get to him.

Mahlon succumbed to the desire, requiring Ibzan to evade another attempted grapple. The warrior's hand brushed along Ibzan's hooved foot, but did not gain a grip.

Several more zigs and zags and near misses worried Ibzan. If he did not end this soon, Mahlon would surely grab him. That would end it all for Ibzan and he would return defeated.

He put on a burst of speed, then pulled up short to concentrate on a shot aimed at Mahlon's right shoulder. The arrow flew true, knocking the warrior into a spin. Dark essence flowed steadily from the wound.

Ibzan formed a new arrow and aimed again. "Be gone or this one will do far more."

"You dare let me go?" Mahlon panted. "I'll be back with friends."

"Not in time."

Ibzan zipped away, keeping one eye trained on Mahlon, who stopped with a hand over his wound and a look of disbelief on his scowling muzzle. The watchman searched the orchard below for the monk. Furtive movement caught his attentive eye. Diving closer, he confirmed the monk had put all his resolve into running again and mostly in the right direction. The man would not keep the pace for much longer, however.

Ibzan spun about, working to perceive everything he could. Mahlon had left, rather than trying another attack. No other elohim were in the area. He could barely hear humans huddled in a house at the orchard's edge, soothing young children scared by the thunder.

He sighed with relief. To what extent should he help the monk reach his coastal destination, now that the enemy had displayed an interest in him? He pondered his options while closing in on the monk once more. Manifesting more into the man's world could leave him vulnerable to other elohim, an option he preferred to leave as a last resort.

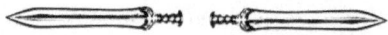

The monk reached a barn and leaned against the leeward side, gaining some protection from the storm. His chest heaved from the exertion of running through the orchard.

"Lord, help me reach the ship in time. This trying journey proves I carry something that should not be lost. However, I'm not sure I'd want to leave home again... ever. So much further to go."

He sank to the ground.

Ibzan flew closer. Was the monk that tired? If he fell asleep, he would not make it the last few miles. On a normal day, the monk could reach the mooring in an hour. Ibzan hung there, pondering the best path forward.

The monk pulled his package closer. His head lowered to rest against it.

Ibzan had to stir the man into moving. His destination lay so close. He spoke once more to the monk's spirit. "You're almost there. Keep going." He frowned when the monk did not move.

"I know I have to get up, but I can't," the monk heaved in a sigh, almost as if answering Ibzan.

Ibzan landed and assumed the appearance of a farmer as he entered the material realm. He rarely revealed himself directly to humans, but this man required a companion.

The monk's head snapped up. "Who's there?"

"Ah, there you are." Ibzan worked to pronounce the words correctly in Latin. He hoped it would intrigue the monk enough to distract him from any fatigue or fear felt after the run through the orchard. "It won't do you any good to stay out here in this." He stepped closer.

A flash of lightning revealed sunken eyes and a slackened jaw. Indeed, the monk had reached his limit this evening.

The monk pushed himself up the wall. A weak but welcoming smile spread across his lips. "I would love it more if I could make it to a friend on the coast." His brows creased. "You speak Latin well."

Ibzan shrugged. "The coast is not far. Do you intend to be there in the middle of the night?" He looked up, blinking rain out of his eyes.

"I would prefer such." The monk stopped leaning on the barn. "The storm gave me a fright in the orchard."

Ibzan nodded with a chuckle. "Gnarled apple trees can have that effect in a storm." He turned to face toward the shore. "Now that I am soaked, and you are so close, mind if I walk with you?"

The monk shifted his package to cover it better with his drenched cloak. His eyes narrowed when he looked at Ibzan once more. The scrutiny lasted a mere second before the smile returned. He stepped back into the rain, but staggered after only three steps.

Ibzan grasped the monk's arm just above the elbow to steady him. He aimed to ease the man's weariness.

The monk squared his shoulders. "That would be wonderful. I'm headed for a fishing village with a sizable mooring." He looked about. "I hope I did not get off course, foolishly plunging through the night in this." He raised a hand as if to catch the rain.

Lightning and then a more distant rumble of thunder answered.

"Ah, the storm is moving away. Even better."

Ibzan kept his hand on the man's arm as they walked. He plunged into chatter about the monks he knew as a kid to distract this one from how fast they truly moved. Thankfully, the dark, stormy night hid much of the landscape. His ward would make it to the mooring on time, rejuvenated by having company the last few miles to the sea.

Several minutes passed, but finally a lantern fighting to stay lit came into view. Its light revealed a building with a boardwalk.

The monk lurched to a stop. "Oh, we are here already? Amazing how a little company and chatter can make the road much shorter.

Blessings to you, my friend." He pulled out of the hold Ibzan had on his arm. "I presume you live back by the orchard. I'll not bother you further. My friend is close by and expecting me."

"I'm glad to have lightened a stretch of your journey. May God bless you and your friend."

"And may he bless you for your timely arrival. Did you have a premonition to come find me?"

Ibzan did his best not to react. Had the man seen through him the whole time? He needed a quick retort to get out of this and resume watching in a more traditional manner.

Laughing, Ibzan replied, "I saw you in a flash of lightning. It's not a good night for a run to the privy."

The monk laughed and slapped him on the arm with good humor. "Then I shall thank God for the man's need to relieve himself at the right time." He took a step away.

The rain ended.

Ibzan headed back the way they had come. He confirmed the monk had looked toward his destination and walked into the dark shadows of a building before dematerializing his fleshly form.

"Thank you." The monk's voice flowed after him. Seeing no one, he answered himself, "Well, God, I guess he had to get back home before someone missed him."

No longer manifested in the material, Ibzan flew into the sky, where he could watch the monk make it to his friend. He smiled at their jovial greetings, despite the hour.

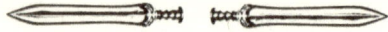

The rowboat scraped its bow into the rocky beach, having left the larger sailing vessel used to sail from Frankia to southern Hibernia in deeper waters.

Ibzan opted to perch on a cliff's edge and watch.

The monk leapt out eagerly with his parcel and threw himself on the ground, kissing it. A hearty laugh paused him, and he looked up with a grin.

"Welcome home, Rodhlann. I see you're overjoyed. Travels not so good?"

Ibzan used his fine sight to examine the welcomer, an aged monk with ink-stained fingers.

The monk, Rodhlann, climbed to his feet with his prized possession tucked in the crook of an arm. "We scattered when barbarians rampaged the village. I have the most treasured pieces of the library in my satchel." He patted the leather case. "I pray they survived the trek. God helped me, I am sure."

"Let's get you settled, and you can share the story after dinner."

An oarsman pushed the rowboat back into the water, leaving the two monks alone on the beach.

Rodhlann waved to the men in the rowboat. He then climbed the narrow cliff path behind the elder monk.

Ibzan flexed his wings. Something clouded the monastery. He didn't know exactly what, but it put an unholy pall on the place. Taking the two monks in again, he saw nothing untoward about them. What should he do? His mission had been to see the monk got home, which he had.

He did not feel right about leaving yet. It wouldn't take much to convince his superiors that he had checked it out to ensure a safe return of his charge. He needed to be sure if it was his feelings or a nudge from the Holy Spirit.

It only took a moment to fly to the structure. After a quick scan from above, he landed in the courtyard for a closer look. The chapel, with its wooden double doors, faced the main gate into the compound. A small shed and a workshop nestled against the outer wall. He had glimpsed more buildings on the landward side.

"What is your business here?" An unholy minstrel Ibzan had spotted earlier as he circled overhead, crossed his arms. "This is my domain now." The minstrel wore a crown with one large horn on display, proclaiming he was of the first domain. Not an impossible challenge, should a fight be necessary.

Ibzan opened his mouth to retort, but a loud whoosh came from behind the housing wing, followed by a plume of smoke. He cocked his head.

The minstrel looked quite pleased by this incident.

Several monks stepped out of the workshop and ran for the back. Shouts of them organizing a bucket brigade came in snatches.

"Are you sent to dissuade me from continuing here?"

Ibzan sighed. He had no authority here currently, unless it affected his charge. The feeling to remain grew stronger.

"If it does not hinder my charge, I will leave you be for the moment. However, I will report all I see here."

The minstrel harrumphed and waved a dismissive hand. "Expected. You are a fledgling messenger who poses no threat. Watch all you want."

Ibzan nodded. He tuned into his surroundings. Certainly, an ally would have sanction over this monastery. He turned slowly. His first glance into the open chapel demanded a closer look, but the feeling subsided when he kept his gaze on it. He kept turning, so the minstrel didn't take notice of his interest.

Once he completed his perusal, he strode toward the commotion.

"Wait. You said you would only watch?"

"Correct. I can see better without a building in the way." Ibzan chuckled while he kept walking. He stopped short when he reached the other side of the building.

Monks formed a bucket brigade into the fiery kitchen. Their combined efforts had a mixed effect of dampening the fire, but it had also spread. Someone had let hot oil get out of control.

Ibzan cocked his head. Someone had bolstered the monks with resolve.

"I told you not to interfere." The minstrel stomped up and jabbed a finger into Ibzan's chest.

"I don't have the power to influence all these monks at once. Not to mention the fact that you would see me doing it."

The minstrel looked about, a little confused. "Okay, it isn't you, I suppose, but your timing is uncanny."

"I just followed my charge. I will act if anything moves to harm his mission."

They stood in silence for several minutes.

The monks finished the firefighting but remained vigilant with more water at hand. Stone walls had kept the fire contained, though it had ripped through the thatched kitchen roof.

Ibzan stepped inside. Much of the kitchen had survived, at least in form. All of it had char marks. Much of the thatching over the cooking pit had come down to mix with the water in an ashy slop. The chimney had a great crack zigzagging up from its base, fracturing outward where mortar gave way. It would take the monks some time to repair everything.

That was the point if it hadn't burned the whole place down. This enemy minstrel hindered the work of the monks by misdirecting them. They had overlooked chimney maintenance because of it. What had their focus so much beyond the busy scriptorium?

Ibzan stepped outside, watching the monks tending to burns, to avoid being seen looking toward the chapel. Something was definitely working in the spiritual realm against the minstrel, and Ibzan couldn't shake the notion that the answer lay inside.

Rodhlann, his charge, arrived with the elderly scribe huffing to keep up. His satchel of scrolls remained clutched close to his body.

"Your charge may have arrived, but what he carries will not be saved."

Ibzan stepped closer to the minstrel. "You may delay things for a time, but I would be careful."

The minstrel huffed. "Their resolve will falter. Their protector fled after receiving a serious beating." His chest puffed out. "I could sing you into submission and then dance atop you like a stage."

Ibzan canted his head, looked down and then back up. "Perhaps, but you have no reason to invite me to dance."

A sigh escaped the minstrel. "True."

"You work to keep the monks from scribing. Perhaps you hoped for the fire to reach the scriptorium, even if it is on the other end of this building. This monastery has gathered many scrolls of history, stories, and the Bible. Many of them will make their way back into circulation at the right time."

"How do you know they will?" The minstrel narrowed his eyes.

"A feeling I have." He stepped back, putting some space between them again. "I'm sorry that I never introduced myself. I'm Ibzan, messenger of the Most High."

"And I'm sure you will tell all, so a new caretaker is sent unless I keep you here."

"Well, if I am to stay awhile, might I at least know with whom?" He played along with the other's posturing. He knew he could leave whenever he wanted.

The minstrel pointed at him. "You are aiming to have me let my guard down with you. However, so you know who bests you later, I am Ruahk, Dancer of Mayhem."

How fitting. He referred to himself as a dancer, but corrupt dancers were known as beguilers. He couldn't possibly have beguiled himself into believing he was not the one in rebellion?

Ibzan took in the monks once more. Order came quickly. Most of the monks returned to their duties. The few that had run from the workshop began discussing repairs. Two helped the worst burned victim toward the infirmary.

The elderly scribe said, "Looks like dinner may be a simple fare of bread, cheese and salted meats."

Rodhlann nodded. "Still better than eating on the road."

"Let's get your package sorted and then you can settle back in." The scribe looked about. "Or help where you see fit if you are up to it."

"I may help first. It feels good to have returned to solid ground and I could use some hard work."

Ibzan followed them to the scriptorium.

Ruahk remained behind to sing discord amongst the monks, who determined the best way to set up a makeshift kitchen. Good. Ibzan preferred Ruahk did not see what Rodhlann had brought back to the safety of this monastery.

The scribe cleared a table by a window. The scent of smoke wafted in on the breeze through the open shutters. A thoughtful architect had made sure the only windows in the scriptorium faced south for the best lighting when the weather permitted.

"This is the prized possession of all the writings we hastily worked to save." Rodhlann opened the scroll with gentle movements. "It's one of the more complete copies of John in the original language of

Koine Greek. This here is a partial translation into Latin." He waved at another scroll, still bound by its oilskin wrappings.

"Very good. There are few copies of this, but now that it is here, we can assure that more exist for when these troubled times are over."

Ibzan leaned close over the two men to take in the precise lettering of the scroll. Whoever made this copy had proved meticulous. Even the rainstorm had not marred its beauty.

His mission had succeeded. Or had it? A compelling desire to remain overwhelmed him.

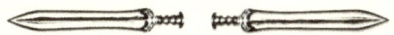

Night had fallen. The monks sat around a firepit, allowing them to produce a hot meal with items unaffected by the kitchen fire.

Ruahk stalked around, muttering to himself, the monks' continued resolve possibly bothering him. Ibzan had perceived its strengthening. He walked around the chapel as if admiring the architecture and the rare stained-glass windows. He had examined the entire complex to keep Ruahk in the dark about what he looked for. Despite sensing something off with the chapel again, he still could not pinpoint the source of the monks' bolstered resolve.

Ruahk stopped pacing to glare at him. "Your ward made it home. I'd assume your mission is over."

Ibzan shrugged. He worked hard not to show his delight when Ruahk spewed some choice words. His presence kept the minstrel on his toes and unaware of whatever was going on with the chapel. Best to keep him distracted.

"You are intentionally messing with me now. Leave."

Ibzan shook his head and pointed at his charge.

Ruahk scowled and puffed up, as if contemplating an attack.

Ibzan cocked his head as if to say, "Try it." He had a chance of besting the minstrel, who was alone here.

The minstrel slumped with a sigh, seeming to reconsider, and resumed his pacing.

Ibzan adjusted his wings and leaned against the stone wall protecting the monastery. He let his eyes slide almost closed and bowed his head. What compulsion was keeping him here? Rolling his orders over in his mind once more did not produce any answers. Rodhlann sat with his fellow monks, safe and sound. The prized scrolls containing the Gospel of John had found a secure place in the scriptorium's vault.

Something stirred in the chapel.

Ibzan's head snapped up at the same time Ruahk stopped pacing, both of them realizing at the same moment the ministering spirit who had stepped forth from the chapel and was standing before them. He had apparently created a haven for himself using his abilities. Thinking back, Ibzan remembered seeing a ministering spirit in the chapel, but it did not occur to him at the time as the source he sought.

Wisps of light still streamed from the ministering spirit's wounds. He planted his staff and did his best to stand with shoulders squared. Much of his support came from the staff by the way he leaned toward it.

"You will leave my dominion. The Most High set me here."

The ministering spirit's words rang with an assurance Ibzan wouldn't argue with. His eyes narrowed when the minstrel didn't flinch.

Ruahk hissed.

Ibzan pulled away from the wall, but did not manifest a bow.

"You are wrong, Tobiah. This is my dominion now." Ruahk sang the words while incorporating fearsome motions in a dance that somehow made the threat more believable.

Ibzan shook himself to remove the desire to flee.

Tobiah seemed unconvinced. "You failed to defeat me before. You only wounded me."

"I'll destroy you this time." Ruahk leapt forward.

Tobiah swung his staff up.

Ruahk pulled off a dexterous twist in the air to evade him.

Ibzan flexed his hands. He would wait for Tobiah, as the watcher over the monastery, to ask for help, unless his defeat appeared imminent. His orders still sat with his charge. As convenient as it proved before, it felt rather inconvenient now.

Ruahk continued to dance away. "I'll prove you wrong," he declared, weaving a raucous song of fury around the monks.

As Ibzan watched, a disagreement grew to a heated debate.

Several monks stood and gestured with emphatic arm movements, unknowingly mimicking the unseen motions of their invisible agitator.

Tobiah's staff thudded against the ground when he brought the end down. "The Most High's wings protect and comfort all those that take shelter there. Let it be so here." A soothing spiritual mist floated from the ministering spirit toward the arguing monks, but it burned away upon encountering the minstrel's fiery fury.

Ibzan leaned forward slightly with anticipation.

"Messenger of the Most High, I request assistance in securing this monastery against an enemy I cannot best alone."

On cue, Ibzan created a bow with an arrow nocked. He puffed himself up as he drew the bowstring back. Even the feathers of his head raised.

"I would stand down if I were you. I now have permission to wrest this monastery from your influence, Ruahk."

Ruahk screamed and whirled closer—the intensity of his furious song pushing the debate into a full argument—drawing other monks in.

Ibzan's arrow flew true, but one of Ruahk's feet slammed into his chest. He stumbled through the wall, sharp pain radiating from the contact point. He had misjudged Ruahk's speed because of the erratic dancing.

Stepping back through the wall, Ibzan watched as Ruahk pounced toward Tobiah with the arrow stuck through his side. Dark essence escaped the wound. As if untouched, he rained blows upon the ministering spirit, who only fended off half of them.

It took Ibzan three tries to pull his bowstring fully. He desired to bellow with pain while holding the shot to perfect his aim.

The arrow sliced through the air for Ruahk's head, but the pair twisted in their grappling. It scraped along the side of Ruahk's face and harmlessly phased through Tobiah's left horn.

Ibzan planted his stance, and with slow determination pulled the string back. He pushed through the distractions around him and the pain in his chest. This shot would end the fight.

He let the arrow loose.

Tobiah head-butted Ruahk and staggered back, free of the grapple.

The arrow slammed into Ruahk's right eye and had the force to come out the back of his head.

Ibzan grimaced as the minstrel slumped to the ground. He lowered his bow, watching the arrow slowly dissipating.

Ibzan's first killing blow had not sat well with him. Neither had any since, including this one. It did not matter that it had taken out an enemy in time. It did not matter that the recipient was immortal and would recover. Ruahk would be out of the game now for some time, as if dead.

He snapped out of his thoughts as Tobiah crumpled to the ground. With sure movements, he strode to Ruahk, confirmed his defeat, and then knelt beside his ally.

"Thank you." Tobiah's voice rasped with the effort required to speak.

"I am glad the timing of my duties allowed me to be here." Ibzan offered a hand to Tobiah.

Tobiah clasped it, and with the staff in his other hand, he found his footing. Healing warmth radiated from the ministering spirit that cleared Ibzan's wounds and eased the pain in his chest.

"I'll request you stay awhile and help me clean up here. It will give you time to recuperate and think about all this. It's never easy silencing a foe, regardless of the necessity. We serve the Mighty One who prefers life."

Ibzan relaxed. He had followed protocol and done what he had to. Now the monastery could settle down and scribe the scrolls that would one day spread throughout the world to reacquaint it with the truths of the Most High.

Summer sun flowed into the scriptorium. The elder scribe bent over his work, each stroke placed just so to create a replica of the text he copied. His gnarled fingers held the stylus with ease.

Ibzan hummed to the old scribe while leaning over him, watching every letter form. Soothing a human in this way was not his forte, but he had enough skill to allow the scribe to do more writing than he could have without the help.

The memory of how he took Ruahk out of the fight still haunted him. He found outright violence of that level revolting. He preferred shots that ended things with less impact, like the shot to the shoulder he had used on Mahlon. However, he knew he would do it again if he had to.

His choice of actions had brought attention to himself. He would be promoted in rank when he completed this mission. Many thought he would not bear the tedium of watching a scribe copy text, rather than scouting or protecting a monk on a long journey. To him, they held the same issues. If the enemy planned to return, they had waited too long. Both he and Tobiah had fully healed and had helped strengthen the dominion of the monastery.

He looked out the window.

The monks prepared their evening meal in the open firepit because of a fine day. Their industrious work under the watchful eyes of Tobiah had renovated their kitchen. The monks even joked about their spring foolery, while setting a better system of accountability. More villagers had filled the chapel pews than ever for the community service, which added to the coffers and physical labor beyond what the monks could do on their own.

Ibzan put his eyes back on the scribe.

The tremors had taken over his hand again. After a moment, he carefully lay the stylus down. He used his other hand to cap the inkwell.

"I made it to the end of another section. Time to enjoy a walk in the sun."

Rodhlann rose from where he sat verifying copied text. "Let me accompany you."

"Please. I can't move like I used to."

Ibzan nodded with approval upon scanning the drying ink of the latest words added. Not even a stray drop of ink. Yes, these copies would be the best and help the world in the future.

THE PERFECT STONE

NATHANIEL SORENSEN

There are few things in the Father's creation more beautiful than a child's smile. This child's name was Haven. She was two years old, and her face was alight because she had just found the most perfect stone in the whole world. It was perfect because she had found it and deemed it so. It was perfectly smooth; except for a dimple on one side, making it easier to grip with her finger. It was perfectly round; except for the way it tapered on one end, making it easier to suck on. It was perfectly brownish red; except for a swirly, cream-colored line, making it mesmerizing to stare at. In that moment, I was inclined to agree with her assessment.

I was part of a team of seven sent almost five years before to watch over Haven's parents when they planted a church in Missoula, Montana. After establishing our hold, three of us have been more permanently stationed here, facilitating support from others as needed. We were quite excited to receive such a prime assignment in expanding the Most High's kingdom.

What I hadn't expected was just how *amazing* it would be to care for a growing family. My team leader is most often the one with Dad or Mom when in their pastoral roles. My other holdmate and I rotate duties depending on the needs of the day. As a messenger, I am often sent to run errands or do recon around the city, but my favorite days are the ones when I get to play with the kids.

Children have an appreciation for the Most High's creation that I haven't seen as much in adults since Eden. Don't get me wrong—I love accompanying Dad on his Monday hikes in the mountains, too. He obviously appreciates and admires his Father's handiwork, but it lacks some of that extra bit of raw, delighted *fascination*. It tends to require more majestic discoveries to awaken the adult sense of wonder.

For Haven, though, an afternoon at the city park can be a trove of discoveries. One never knows what can be found, for example, in the soil just off the playground. That day we came across a perfect stone, and she could not have been more dazzled by a thousand shooting stars on a moonless night.

Haven looked over toward Mom and her smile brightened even further. The only thing better than a perfect find is sharing the joy with someone else. She got to her feet and took off across the playground. Walking was going pretty well, but running could still resemble more of a controlled fall. Her little legs barely kept ahead of gravity as she held the stone out and called for Mom to acknowledge their great blessing.

The catastrophe wasn't difficult to see coming. For me, at least. A few older boys had been testing their limits on the merry-go-round and, naturally, the next step would be to run off their dizziness. Thankfully, they had enough awareness to avoid running straight into Haven, but one of them cut too close in front of her and she ran into him. *Hard.* The boy was twice her size and already didn't know which way was up, so he seemed unfazed. Haven, however, was too focused on her mission to react. She caromed off the boy's hip and went down in a spray of wood chips.

I glanced up and saw Mom had already noticed Haven trying to get her attention. She was on her feet before Haven hit the ground. I knelt to look for potential injuries and knew it would be another second before Haven could process the collision. She quickly rolled over and sat up with a wobble. I could see she was free of noteworthy injuries, but then *she* noticed a couple splinters sticking out of her palms.

Uh oh. 3... 2... 1...

When Haven processes trauma, my brothers in Idaho hear about it. She doesn't yet know how to connect words with these experiences, so her only recourse is to sort it out with *volume*.

"You'll be alright, Haven," I soothed. "This pain isn't forever. Mom's coming for you."

Before you comment, I fully realize children of this age don't grasp concepts like 'forever'. I've learned with kids it's better to communicate more with sensations and impressions. The words were more for my benefit than hers. Regardless, Haven didn't seem interested in words *or* impressions.

Mom arrived during Haven's first long pause to take a breath. She picked Haven up and was promptly shown dainty hands now requiring triage.

"It's ok, baby," Mom said. "It's ok, Haven. I can make it better."

A mother's voice can be more potent than many medicines. Haven's crying did not stop, but the reassurances quickly lowered her intensity. Mom started back toward the picnic blanket where they'd set up a home away from home, and I knew she would have tweezers in her bag. Mothers often try never to leave home without being better equipped than I often am when sent on critical missions.

With Haven in good hands, I turned to make sure the boy truly was ok. He had looked to be eight or nine years old, and I was sure he routinely endured far greater interruptions. Still, it never hurts to check. What I saw made me pause.

The boy was holding Haven's stone. She must have dropped it when they collided. What really caught my attention, though, was the way he looked up toward Haven as Mom carried her back to their blanket. It was obvious he knew it was Haven's stone. Yet, his expression was nothing like the awed fascination Haven had shown. Calculations were running behind his eyes.

I went over to suggest he do the right thing. "Why don't you go give that back to her? I know you didn't *mean* to make her fall, but she could obviously use the encouragement. You could be a hero today."

Behind me, Haven's crying subsided into a soft sniffle. I turned and saw her looking back over Mom's shoulder. She recognized her stone in the boy's hand. I looked back and saw one side of his mouth pulled back into a half-grimace. His inner debate was apparently intensifying.

"Go ahead and bring it to her," I encouraged again. "You don't really have need of it yourself."

He tossed it in the air, caught it, then closed his fingers around it. Turning his back on Haven, the boy walked back toward his friends.

The renewed cry I heard behind me echoed the one in my own heart. I looked again to see Haven pointing toward the boy, her sobs now carrying a distinctly different tone. Mom looked back to see what had Haven's attention.

"I know, sweetie. He didn't mean to knock you down. It was just an accident."

Haven kept pointing, but her crying masked her attempt to communicate the real problem. As Mom carried her further away, Haven's arm drooped, and her eyes dimmed with the realization of loss.

I've seen that look many times. Just the week before, I was in the city with Haven's parents. They brought food to some people without homes. Most of the people expressed honest gratitude, but it takes more than a meal to heal the kinds of losses they had suffered. The kinds of losses they felt powerless to overcome.

It *is* just a feeling, however. A month before that, on a similar excursion, Haven's dad introduced a man to the Son. I watched hope come alive in the man's eyes as the Breath of the Most High entered him, transferring his citizenship to Elyon's kingdom. What a joy to observe the powers of this world prove unable to prevent his exodus! The man told Haven's dad that he somehow already felt new confidence that there could be more to his story.

But how to restore hope to Haven? In my time watching humans, I've observed far greater traumas and sufferings than a stolen rock. This particular injustice hardly seemed worth comparing. But Haven knew nothing of those deeper tragedies. It can sometimes be difficult to remember how much less pain is required to fill a world as small as hers. Yet, even having seen *all* of creation's struggles, does not the Most High sit alongside Haven in her hurts the same as He does the people her parents faithfully serve?

Haven's measurement of today's splinters will surely fade when she someday sprains an ankle or breaks her arm. The sting of this loss will be tempered when her brother someday lets her take the punishment for something he has done. Or when a boyfriend breaks up with her, seemingly without cause. Or when a co-worker gets her fired for nothing more than pettiness. I don't wish any of these things for her, but I've watched this world go around its star enough times to know such moments—or worse—will be lying in wait.

I must confess to a momentary feeling of powerlessness. I knew loss and suffering would mark her life, and I knew I couldn't stop all, or even most, of it. I quickly encouraged myself, however, with the knowledge she would be raised to seek and receive the presence of the Most High. The Good Shepherd would be with her in ways I never could. *He* would right some of the injustices quickly. And for the other times, He has shown an incredible aptitude for taking even what is directly meant for evil and turning it somehow to a good end for His people. Redemption is what He does, and He does it better than anyone.

It was time to stop stewing in the moment and start doing my job. I followed Mom and Haven back to the picnic blanket where Baby had slept through the brief commotion. Having remembered the Spirit of Elyon is always looking to turn injustice to some profitable end, I considered how to cooperate.

I looked over at Baby sleeping peacefully. Yesterday afternoon, Baby had not been so peaceful. He was nine months old already and crawling rather well. This meant he was learning how to get into Haven's stuff and Haven's space. Over the last few weeks, this had prompted some lessons from Mom and Dad on the concept of sharing, and how it is the kind thing to do for other people.

That might work. As Mom searched her bag for the smaller kit with the tweezers, I stooped down. Haven looked toward the playground's array of walkways and platforms. Just now, the boys were huddled underneath the higher platform—the one with the big pirate ship steering wheel.

No matter the boy's motivations or choices, I had to aim now for what was healthiest for Haven's soul. "This is a good time for sharing,

Haven. Maybe he needs a turn with the stone so he can have a happy moment too. Let it go for now."

I'd been striking out so far that afternoon, but I think a suggestion finally found its mark. Looking as though it tried every last bit of patience she had, she turned away from the playground and held her hand out for Mom to play doctor.

Mom picked the splinters out and determined no Band-Aids were necessary. Haven's hands must have felt tender, though, because she received her juice box with great care.

Discerning a good time for a break, Mom announced it was snack time. Haven grinned around her juice box straw. Easily gripping the juice box in one hand now, she held the other out with anticipation. Apparently, her tender hands were recovering nicely. I've observed this phenomenon before. Snack time seems to have restorative properties beyond what I've come to expect within the human dimension.

Several months before, I had taken a bit of a beating while defending our hold during a prayer meeting. Roga, my holdmate, offered me some manna to restore my wounds and its effects were immediate. I've never witnessed Goldfish, Cheerios, and cut-up bits of banana actually heal any physical wounds, of course. Still, snack time has an uncanny ability to divert Haven's attention suddenly and thoroughly away from many pains and discouragements.

This time was no different. As soon as the Goldfish finished turning into crumbs on the blanket, Haven played with some toys from home and the splinters were remembered no more. She seemed quite content to stay with Mom and Baby for the moment, away from the chaos of the wider world.

We had a few minutes of quiet. With snack time finished and both children close at hand, Mom pulled out her book of the week. I read along with her for a few minutes. I used to dismiss human fiction as frivolous. To be honest, I mostly still do. But after listening to hers and Dad's sermons these last years, I've begun to appreciate how humans can gain insights on life from the imaginations of other humans. How often those insights are actually helpful rather than misleading, I can't say for sure. But I've seen enough to know the profitable is possible. This book was one of a series I was a bit surprised to find myself enjoying. The protagonist was rather inane, but she had a bodyguard I found almost believable.

I glanced up to see Haven was ready to head back into the arena. I'd have to find a way to catch up on the book later. She made for the wooden towers and walkways, and I noted few other children in the area. The group of boys moving on might have been Haven's signal to feel like it was once again safe to explore.

The rope ladder and the rock-climbing ramp were still too advanced for her. I followed her past these to the stairs at the far end. She still half-crawled up the steps more than walked. I noticed she seemed to ignore her wounded hands, so I thought I should probably put it out of my mind as well.

We spent a few minutes walking the ramps back and forth between the three main platforms. The railings were tight enough that falling off was no concern. We just had fun for a while, being up on top of the world. Occasionally, I'd direct her attention to a pinecone I thought she'd enjoy or a moving part on one of the platforms. The pirate ship steering wheel was one of her favorites—that and spinning the Xs and Os on the big tic-tac-toe wall.

During one turn at the steering wheel, Haven looked out across the playground and got still. She didn't seem troubled, just focused. *What are you seeing, Haven?* I followed her gaze but couldn't tell what had attracted her attention. It might have been the spinning merry-go-round. The sun was also glinting brightly off the large slide. A couple of kids were on the swings, and they were moving pretty fast. She settled down in a squat and remained transfixed for a moment.

Nothing changed that I could see, but she abruptly stood up and walked deliberately toward the steps. Reaching them, I was glad to see she wasn't in such a rush as to be unsafe. She stopped and carefully let herself down, one at a time.

At the bottom, she turned and walked back around the wooden structure until she could again see what had captured her imagination. She paused behind one of the larger support posts, leaning against it as she watched. Then she craned her head to one side to look over at the blanket with Mom and Baby.

Oh. So that's it, then. Humans never need to be more sure of where their parents are than when they are hurt or contemplating breaking a rule. Of the three possible options, the swings were too high for her to get into by herself and the merry-go-round was still a bit too scary. The big slide was the only one that had been attractive enough and dangerous enough for Mom to put it off limits.

Mom looked up and waved. Haven just gave a half-smile but managed not to look *too* guilty. She quietly waited until she was sure Mom was reading again before looking back at the slide. "Let's go back up to the steering wheel, Haven," I redirected. "You can see really well from up there."

Haven looked up at the top of the slide and I realized my mistake. She could see just as well from up there, too. "Haven," I tried again. "Let's play tic-tac-toe. Mom would like that much better."

Haven looked back again toward Mom, but her expression showed she was hearing all the wrong points of my suggestions. She maintained that wide-eyed look of wheels turning and plots plotting. Daring deeds were still being contemplated.

A decision was made, and she moved toward the slide. *Some days, things just don't go your way.* The slide itself obscured Mom's view of the approach to the ladder. Haven arrived without detection, gripped the rails, and stretched one foot up to the first step.

"Haven," I pleaded, "let's see if Mom will push you on the swings. That would be *so* fun."

It was too late. All her focus was dedicated to the challenge of the first step. I could have attempted to lift her off and set her down safely on my own. I've seen too much of the stubbornness of humans, though, to think that would be the end of it. Odds were high Haven would have just tried again.

In a flash, I flew across the playground and was back at Mom's blanket. Moments like these are why I've become convinced that we messengers are the best at childcare. Sometimes you have to be *fast*.

I bent down to Mom's level and urged, "Look up." Immediately, she looked up and scanned the playground.

It still surprises me how quickly mothers respond to prompts from our dimension. It's unique—and it isn't just a parenting thing. Fathers don't react that much quicker, as a rule, than non-fathers.

Mom quickly tensed when her first quick scan didn't locate Haven. She was already getting to her feet as I added, "Slide."

Her eyes jumped to the slide, and she peered to see who was behind the ladder. She jogged in that direction, but I noticed the tension in her shoulders ease as she recognized Haven. I stayed back with Baby, now contentedly playing with his stuffed dinosaur, while Mom went to save Haven from herself.

The slide steps were not Haven-sized, so she had only managed the first step and was working on the second by the time Mom arrived to interrupt the climbing expedition. I watched them walk back, Mom not scolding so much as re-instructing. Haven was crying again.

I was getting pretty good at knowing the different cries. There's a cry that goes with getting disciplined. This one was subtly different. It was the cry that said, "I was prevented from doing something that I really, *really* wanted to do." Her version was much cuter than the adult version.

As they arrived back at the blanket, Mom said, "Let me get Jacob and we'll go play on the swings. Is that ok?"

Haven paused her crying to think about it. I could tell she wasn't really thinking about whether the swings would be fun so much as whether she could admit it was worth changing attitudes. Thankfully, the swings won, and she nodded while wiping away the last of her tears.

Mom strapped on the baby carrier and got Baby settled into place, facing forward. Holding her hand out for Haven's, she said, "All set. Ready?"

Haven responded by leaning forward with every bit of weight and strength she had.

The swings are always an interesting experience. At first, Haven yearns to fly. She hasn't figured out how to manipulate momentum for herself, so she calls for Mom or Dad to go higher and higher and faster. Then there comes that one point. That point has gradually crept higher, but so far it has always come: the moment when the height and speed suddenly exceed the reasonable limits of human endurance.

She used to panic right away, and Mom or Dad would reign her in pretty quickly. Lately, though, she's been learning. Dad probably started it. He'd keep going a push or two past the point at which he could tell she was done. A few park trips later, I noticed Mom doing the same. The last few times, I noticed Haven pushing through on her own. It was probably harder for Mom and Dad to see while Haven was in motion, but I have the benefit of a better vantage point.

Mom helped her get her legs through the holes in the swing seat, then started her moving gently. I looked forward to this. True to form, Haven quickly called for more. For a few minutes, she was truly and thoroughly thrilled. Delighted squeals. Face straining forward into the wind. I can fly, but it's different. She really makes g-forces and wind resistance look *fun*.

Then that point came. I got ready. Haven's eyes widened a little further. Her teeth clenched tight. Her fingers gripped the swing's chains as though they were the threads of life. In her mind, I suppose they were. She didn't scream, though. Despite being completely out of control, she told herself to endure.

This was where I stepped in to help. I didn't directly try to ease away the panic. Instead, I got close and encouraged her to trust.

"This is ok, Haven. Mom's got you. She can catch you. Mom can see if you actually need to slow down. She'll make sure you come down safely even if you can't see what's going on."

Then she broke.

"NOMAMA, NOMAMA, NOMAMA!"

She made it nine seconds. Nine whole, glorious seconds!! Two seconds better than her previous best. I'm so inspired by that kid. I suspect there are adults who have gone their entire lives without mastering what she was learning to do that day.

Mom waited until Haven started backward, then gently slowed her down. "You got *so* high that time, Haven!"

Haven gasped heavily as she agreed. "*SO* high! Hiya tees, hiya cowds. Hiya sun!"

"Even higher than the sun? Are you sure?"

Haven nodded emphatically. Mom lifted her out of the swing seat. "Well. Let's get packed up and then we can go tell Daddy about it."

When they reached the blanket, Mom started getting Baby settled into the back section of the double stroller. Haven was put to work putting toys back in the bag. As Mom turned to gather the blanket, I saw the chance I'd been waiting for.

I zipped back over to the wooden towers and looked around where the group of boys had been gathered under the main platform. I'd suspected games and friends would distract the boy from the stone sooner rather than later. Sure enough, it didn't take long to locate the stone carelessly tossed aside in the wood chips. I picked it up and turned back toward the stroller. Haven was helping Mom fold the blanket, so it was the easiest thing to drop the stone in the front stroller section without them noticing.

They packed the blanket and Mom lifted Haven to set her in her seat. As hoped, I saw Haven squirm awkwardly and reach behind her. Her eyes went big, and her mouth formed a perfect O when she looked down to see that her perfect stone was the hard thing in her hands. The shriek that followed carried just the same thrill as on the swing.

She thrust it into the air for Mom to see. Only, she was waving it around so much Mom couldn't make out what was going on. "What is it, honey? I can't see."

Mom picked her back up to settle her down. Haven eased her wiggling enough to thrust the stone inches away from Mom's face. "Oh wow, Haven! That really is beautiful. Good find!"

Haven released a stream of excited thoughts. "Kanna-bwinto-hum-dadda-wokshun?"

Ok. Something about home and Dad, I think. Was that 'conviction' at the end? No. She wouldn't be trying that word yet.

Mom jumped right in. "Oh yes! This will be perfect for Daddy's rock collection. He'll be so excited!"

Of course! Oh, the confounding wonders of that woman's perception! Among the host, it is taken for granted that we messengers have (by far) the best perceptive abilities. Yet, somehow, I still struggle to keep up with Mom when it comes to deciphering these cryptic communications. The week before, I rather easily got one that had Mom puzzled. But this week, Mom was already 17% more accurate than me. This made it closer to 19%. Not that we were competing.

Haven swelled with pride to have Mom affirm her good taste. She threw her arms around Mom's neck for a big, eyes-closed hug. It was the kind of hug that could warm the rings of Saturn. Or so I guessed. I would *love* to know what one of those hugs actually feels like.

Then Haven looked up and locked eyes with *me*. I wasn't manifesting myself to be seen, but she was definitely looking at me. I moved a little to the left and her gaze followed me. She lifted one arm off Mom's neck and hesitantly gave that bye-bye wave children give, whether coming or going.

I smiled and waved back. She ducked her head shyly, but kept her eyes up and studied me with relaxed curiosity. Held in Mom's arms, she had a quiet confidence that suggested I was an entirely acceptable part of her world.

Mom shifted her weight to lift Haven back into the stroller. On the way down, Haven held out her stone to show me and smiled the contented smile of a perfect day. Now that I think about it, I bet *that* is what one of those hugs feels like.

Thomas sat staring. It was hard to hold a thought in his head. What he just saw, heard, it seemed so… unreal.

"You're telling me all that happened?"

"Yes. Sharing these stories does more than inform. It also encourages us by hearing of the loyal service of others during their missions." Hirael stood and walked from the arena.

Thomas jumped from his seat and quickly followed. "But then why? I mean, who? I guess, God chooses you, but why these missions? Why help a little girl find a stone, but not Ebby find a place to live?"

Without turning toward him, Hirael kept marching. They were in a street of sorts, colors everywhere, light everywhere, elohim here and there, talking in groups or dancing. As confusing as it was, Thomas couldn't deny the beauty of it all. But that only served to make it more frustrating.

"It seems kind of random, and I have to say, somewhat unfair," Thomas said.

"Is it?" Now Hirael stopped. "Are you going to take your umbrella to work with you tomorrow?"

Thomas made a face. "How would I know?"

"Well, let's say you do take it. And let's say on your way to work, you pass a young woman. She is pregnant and holding a newspaper over her head, but let's say you decide to give her your umbrella."

"Is this going somewhere?"

"And let's say, because you gave that mother your umbrella and because of your kindness, she didn't contract pneumonia, and her baby was born healthy. And that baby will impact countless lives, some negatively and some positively. All because you brought an umbrella to work."

"Wait. Are you saying that's going to happen?"

Hirael knelt down to be eye to eye with Thomas. "I don't know." He looked up. "But the Most High does. That and infinite possibilities beyond. That is how He makes decisions."

Thomas exhaled and ran both his hands through his hair. "But what about—"

Before he could finish his thought, a street minstrel came by doing cartwheels, tassels of various colors shimmering as he moved. He stopped in front of them and called to the crowd. "Listen here, good friends," he said, as a lyre manifested in front of him. He plucked it from the air, strummed a resonant chord, and began to speak…

THE WATERY WINDOW

MEGAN HUFFMAN

The pool before them trembles and undulates—a swirling silvery gleaming pool, a gate in heaven, a window in the sky, shimmering with wonder and light—and I watch as the four elohim disappear through it, off to serve in the mortal realm for the glory of the Most High.

A tear, glistening, not unlike the passageway I have just witnessed, slides down my cheek. What beauty, what love, what kindness and grace has Elyon for us! That He would create such a way for us, His appointed servants to His sapphire throne, to leave these heavenly places and be among them, His beloved children.

They hold a place in His heart, high and close and different than I or my fellow elohim could ever occupy. The Most High does not restrict us to this celestial realm, confined to only look on in wistful curiosity or helpless anguish as the rebels corrupt and deceive those below.

No, He in all His perfect love and majesty chooses to use us, to send us, through the most spectacular doorway brimming with hope and possibility, down to them. As messengers to share and warriors to defend. As ministering spirits to heal and as minstrels to sing His glory. We are ambassadors of His will who watch and aid and perhaps even try to understand these, His wonderful creation.

Truly it is a gift, an honor, a blessing that even this small thing, a watery window between heaven and earth, reflects His glory and incomprehensible love.

The window forms
A circle of light
Swirling and dancing
A glorious sight

It breaks through the firmament
A passage without end
Encompassing all colors
As holy emissaries descend

Iridescent ribbons
Like pearls in a stream
Pool wondrously around
These faithful elohim

They plunge into its beauty
Disappearing beyond its depth
As the silvery window closes
I find I have no breath

Behold what love!
What manner of grace
That Elyon should make a way
For us to journey from this place

We stand
His watchers at the ready
Proclaimers of His will
He could with one word command
The entire earth to bend
Yet He chooses to use us, even still

The Watery Window

He gifts us with His wisdom
Clothing us in His strength
He sends us as His spiritual forces
To wage the unseen war at length

And to send us down to aid them
His children, His beloved few
He has opened this doorway in the sky
For us to soldier through

It glistens with His majesty
It sparkles with His love
And when our work's end is near
It will once more appear
To welcome us home above

...The crowd applauded, and the minstrel bowed, even as his lyre vanished in the air. "Thank you, good friends, thank you. Praise the Most High!" He threw his hands in the air and cartwheeled away.

"Everything is performance?" Thomas asked.

"Here in the arenas, yes. The Most High is in the stories, Brother Thomas." He again moved on as the crowds dissipated, the murmur of their conversations picking up. "How else are love and goodness known if not in the moments they are lived out? Or in the stories that recall them?"

Jogging to keep up, Thomas spoke. "Okay, okay, but giant scorpions?"

"A mystery you can tolerate for the time being. We'll get to beasts in time. Now, we must take our seats."

Without realizing it, Thomas found himself in another arena, similar to the last, but smaller. The crowd here had many more righteous spirits than elohim, but both crowded the room.

"History lesson," Hirael said. "Here you will learn about the commander over the very first watchers who were sent to the earth long ago."

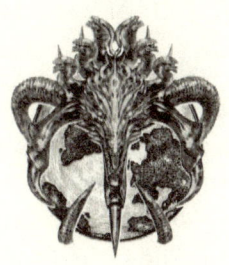

SHEMIHAZAH

GAO YU QING

Shemihazah drifted through the city of Nod, invisible, intangible to the bustling humans milling through the streets, absently acknowledging the familiar presences of two fellow watchers passing him in the opposite direction on errands of their own.

While his outward emanations radiated calm and ease, inwardly he roiled with conflicting emotions utterly new to his experience. His mind was still filled with the recent glimpse of a husband and wife he'd seen in their bridal bower, the memory lingering longer than it should have.

I have seen this before, many times over. Why should this time be any different? I need to focus on my duty assigned to me by the Most High.

From these thoughts, his mind wandered far too easily to a woman from the principal community he guided, Amaya. She was of age and soon it would be her exchanging vows in memory of the first man and woman, embracing her husband...

Black waves of negative emotion washed through Shemihazah. He instinctively fled into the sky above, singing a song that would hasten his ascent before anyone could perceive the change in him.

Safely hidden from view, he hovered over the city, probing these new sensations like a wound. *How can I feel jealous of a human? Am I not beyond such emotions? Why should I long for something I neither need, nor should ever have?*

He remembered that terrifying, exultant moment when he'd first made himself a physical, fleshly body. The knowledge that there was no reason for making it beyond satisfying his own curiosity made it all the more exciting. The response of the flesh he wore amplified the sensations. Pounding heart, the rush of heat through blood and skin, lungs expanding to gasp in air filled with scents in a way foreign to a spiritual body — intoxicating in its immediacy and fragility. He remembered the tensing of muscles as he'd stepped, foot crunching on soil that had never been trod by a foot of any kind, dried leaves crumbling to dust under his weight. The tug and pull of gravity holding him down, anchoring his spirit in the mass of flesh and blood he wore, in echo of the guilt that what he was doing was wrong. The barrier between mortal and spirit was not to be crossed in this way, yet he dared to… just briefly. Just the one time. Then again, days later. And again. Each time longer than the last. But always out of sight of prying eyes, both spiritual and physical. *No one ever saw me. I hurt no one. Why should it matter to anyone? It felt good.*

He drew in his thoughts and breathed out, "Oh, Most High, what would it be like for them?" He spoke, half in prayer, half to himself, expecting no real response. The immediacy of Elyon's glory felt more distant down here in the mortal realm.

> *So frail and fallen,*
> *but such… passion.*
> *Such* hunger.
> *Brilliant little flames,*
> *here and eventually gone,*
> *but growing, spreading,*
> *starting new glows in their wake.*
> *What will be their legacy?*
> *As we, being immortal,*
> *continue to watch them bloom and fade,*
> *will their combined light shine forth like a star,*
> *or will they sputter out in failure,*
> *as they did in the Garden?*
> *Surely there is something*
> *we can do to prevent that.*

His head turned towards the birthplace of man, invisible even from this height, but there, nonetheless. He knew the cherubim guarding it by name.

His mouth twitched in a hint of a smile. "At least my task is more interesting than guard duty," he mused. Then he sent a silent paean of thanks to the Most High for his chief position among the watchers as he looked down at the budding human civilization below him.

He felt little surprise when he realized he was over the vineyard, and something stirred as he saw the figure laboring there, head bent in concentration, as she tied a vine to the trellis in the way he had taught her a year ago. Amaya, the first person he'd ever revealed his physical body to. He did it to help and guide her, of course. The way they'd been growing the vineyard back then had been so... inefficient. He'd shared his knowledge to help Amaya's family... all of humanity, in fact. Surely the Most High would not fault him for that.

A moment later, his sandaled feet stepped onto the dirt of the field, as solid as the grass he trod on. In a tangible, human-like body, he strode towards the bent figure.

"Amaya." Her name tasted sweet on his tongue and his new body responded to the sensation with a rush of hot blood through newly formed veins.

The woman stood and turned to reveal a beautifully symmetrical face blossoming into a smile of delight. The sight of it awoke an answering smile on his own face. He loved the way she looked up at him, eyes sparkling and filled with an indefinable "something" that stirred a response in this fleshly body. His glory washed over her, affecting her in turn, though this time she didn't fall to her knees as she had the first time he'd manifested himself before her.

"My Lord, Shemihazah, how delightful to see you again!" she exclaimed as she bowed. "If you are here to see the progress of the vineyard, all is well. We've been following your instructions. Next year we should be able to harvest our first crop."

"I'm not here for the vines. I came to see you," Shemihazah said, surprising himself with the realization that it was true. A wave of unfamiliar dizziness passed over him. Excitement, relief, and... fear. *This isn't right. This isn't how we are supposed to be.* But as her eyes widened, he found that he didn't care. He'd followed this woman since her birth, seen her grow up, strong and lovely, even procrastinating his official duties in order to spend more time with her. *How can I deny having these feelings any longer? Why should I?*

"Me, my Lord?" she asked. Shemihazah noted her cheeks reddening and pupils dilating. "How can this be? Do you mean…?" Realization spread over her face and her smile blazed at him like a reflection of his own glory, captivating him in its turn. "Truly? I have not known you to jest, but… I'd never allowed myself to dream of it. But… is it proper?"

Shemihazah flinched inwardly. *Even she knows this should not be.*

She stepped closer to him, almost touching him now. So, he hadn't been imagining it. She felt the same. *Of course, it should hardly come as a surprise. No mere mortal man could compare to me. How could they?* Mastering his material body, Shemihazah reached out to cup her face, finding it the perfect size for his hand. For weeks, he'd been unable to get her out of his mind, imagining a moment like this. The blood seemed to pound in his brain, his chest, drowning out his doubts and fears. *She is so beautiful.* The way this physical body responded was so vastly different from his spiritual form. So… immediate and in the moment, perhaps by way of balancing out its frailty and mortality. Every emotion seemed bigger, more vital. He didn't understand it, but enjoyed it all the more for that fact.

"Leave such concerns to me." He felt as much as heard the words come from his mouth. *I did not lie though. I'll find a way.*

She rewarded his boast with a smile. *Which one of us began this dance? It was I, wasn't it? Surely it must be.*

Amaya rested her hands on her belly and looked him over with fresh eyes. "And… and your children?" Her words were soft, but there was a definite hunger in her voice now. "Could I bear you a son? He would be the first of his kind in all the world."

Shemihazah's eyebrows went up. He looked at the human woman in a new light and felt a smile touch his lips.

"Indeed." He agreed, as new kindling fed the flame inside his fleshly body. *A child! We might make a child! And what a child it would be!* "Yes, my beautiful one. With this body I've fashioned, why shouldn't it be so?"

Shemihazah leaned his head back and laughed, his earlier fears banished by the possibilities and the look in this human woman's eyes. *I must make this happen at all costs.* His laughter merged into a song of rejoicing, stimulating his passion, and from the expression on Amaya's face, her heart joined his song.

When he finally stepped back from her, he looked at the woman in a new light, the knowledge of his sin drowned out by these feelings inside him. He wanted *more,* even if it was wrong.

"This must be. I will make this happen," he promised Amaya, not allowing the seed of doubt taking root in his mind to show. "And I will make a gift of the storehouse of heaven's mysteries to you as a dowry."

She rewarded him with a lazy, satisfied smile.

He fled these fleshly feelings by abandoning the body, reverting to his natural spiritual state. The feelings he'd had that were purely physiological disappeared as well, leaving only the psychic residue to linger. And with the fading of that mortal static, the doubts and fears that had been growing could now be heard.

What have I done? By the Almighty, I didn't expect this! What will happen if others hear? I've crossed a line. We were sent to watch and instruct, not join with them at their level. We all knew that from the start. Will I be punished for this? I may lose my position, my station here. If I am recalled to heaven, then how can I be with Amaya? I can't give her up. Not now. I won't *give her up!*

He sailed over the city, plagued by doubts and fears he wasn't used to feeling, and plagued too, by memories of his human woman. *His.* Pleasure, guilt, and an excitement unlike anything he'd ever felt told him that he wouldn't accept any future where he couldn't feel that again. Already, he wished to take on his physical body once more, to be housed in flesh with all the rush of emotions and sensations that came with it. He sang a song of thankfulness for these new experiences, strengthening his resolve to see them through. He didn't notice the occasional tinge of contempt creeping into his song, aimed at any who might stop them.

"Taking her as a wife can't be wrong. Not truly," he muttered. "The humans do it amongst themselves daily without repercussion. Surely Elyon understands love. He made her beautiful, so how can He fault me for finding her so?" *I need to speak to someone, share my concern. But who can I trust?*

As if the Most High himself had heard his plea and answered it, Shemihazah spotted the fierce glow that could only be Azazel hovering over the city of Nod far below. With a surge of relief, Shemihazah flew down to join him.

As Shemihazah reached him, Azazel spoke first, not turning to face the new arrival. "Isn't it glorious? So grand in ambition, but... they could do so much more. I can imagine how it might look. I see towers, aqueducts, stadiums where the young pit their strength against one another. If they only knew what could be possible. If only *we* could do more!"

Shemihazah cast an indifferent glance at the city. It seemed duller than it had a few hours ago, before he'd gone to the vineyard. His eye fell on a young female washing clothes in a courtyard and hanging them up to dry. Not as beautiful as Amaya, but still pleasing.

"What if I told you we could? That we might even be able to ensure that the humans don't fail again?"

He felt Azazel's focus turn to him the way a mortal being might feel the ray of the sun. Intense, hot, never quenched.

"Tell me, Brother."

Shemihazah threw caution to the wind. If he were to do this, he needed support, an ally. If it were just him, he might receive the full penalty, but if there were more who stood with him...

"I plan to take a human wife. And before you tell me what I already know, understand that I will not give her up. The feeling... I cannot describe it, Azazel. They may be flesh, but there is something in that flesh set there by the Most High that we cannot grasp in our more exalted forms. I know because I experienced it myself. I've made a fleshly body of my own. This woman, she wishes to carry my child! What would such a child be like?"

Shemihazah paused, realizing he was rambling. It was uncharacteristic of him. Today had revealed many surprises. More calmly, he pressed on. "Does this not open unseen possibilities, options, as well as risks? What do you think?"

The fierce light of Azazel burned brighter, his mane moving like tongues of fire with his unblinking feline eyes staring out from the heart of the blaze.

"I think...," he said slowly, his voice distant but trembling with emotion, "...that you have been a fool."

Shemihazah bristled and began to respond, but Azazel interrupted him.

"Yes, you have been a fool, but... only a fool could have stumbled onto such a discovery. The possibilities this opens... My mind is suddenly filled to bursting with ideas! Your infatuation itself isn't shocking. You're hardly the only one I'm aware of, and I almost can't blame you. They are such beautiful and fascinating creatures, women. There is so much we might do to make them... more."

Shemihazah wasn't sure how to feel about learning he wasn't the only one enamored with the female humans. He had thought himself special. But what this did reveal was...

"All this time, there have been many of us? And the Most High hasn't acted to interfere? Maybe He won't. Maybe it's not as bad as we thought. Maybe it was *never* supposed to be denied us. We all saw how quickly He took action after that debacle in His mountain garden. Maybe...." Hope and excitement kindled in his heart as he recounted to himself the litany of human activity the Most High had neglected to address over the centuries since that event. Had the Most High relaxed? Where Cain was cursed and cast out and his parents exiled, his descendant Lamech had taken two wives and murdered multiple people with no response.

The figure of Azazel nodded, seizing on his thoughts. "Indeed, Brother, there may be a chance. But you need to act quickly and make use of your position. If you are the only one to take such a step, it would be a simple thing to replace you. If there are many, then removing them all might prove to be more trouble than its worth, especially since we are the ones most knowledgeable about the humans. We have the experience with them and know how to guide their steps better than any replacement from heaven would."

Shemihazah nodded slowly. "What are you suggesting?" He tried not to show the eagerness in his voice.

"You need to share this information and get others to join with you. Call a council, Shemihazah. Share your decision with everyone, to lead the way onto this new path. I promise you, you will find support. I know of at least a hundred and fifty who have simply not been as... bold... as you."

"If I do this, and become the first, what's to keep everyone else from losing heart before it is done? Then all of you may be forgiven, while I alone shall bear the punishment. What assurance do I have that I won't be abandoned?"

Shemihazah saw Azazel glance at him with a look that might have been contempt, quickly hidden. "Raise that question in the council, and I will suggest we make an oath. One that will bind us all in this choice we are making to whatever fate comes of it. What say you?"

Shemihazah thought of his beautiful Amaya, feeling something that would have made his human body shiver. *My wife!*

"I'll do it," he whispered, then raised his voice. "I'll do it!" He grinned and embraced a bemused Azazel. "I'm going to be the first of us to have a wife! A child, the first of its kind!" He laughed aloud, the excitement and joy washing away all his doubts and fears, at least for a time. "I must go now and spread word of this council at once. We'll have it on... that mountain over there." He pointed to a low mountain in the distance. "We will call it Mount Hermon, because on it we will swear this oath."

"Indeed," mused Azazel, his look distracted as his gaze turned inward. "Then I suppose I should find a wife for myself, too."

Shemihazah laughed, feeling inordinately pleased at the thought of Azazel following his example. "Yes indeed. She will be very fortunate, whoever you choose." Then he rushed away, leaving Azazel to begin his fall towards the courtyard below.

"Uh, what?" Thomas again stared ahead as the performance ended. "Is that the story behind Genesis six and the flood? The sons of God and the Nephilim stuff never made sense to me."

"It is a portion of that story—a tragedy, important for watchers to help us be mindful of how disloyalty can creep into our hearts through seemingly harmless attitudes and actions. Your scriptural stories of those who came before you, of their rebellion and failure—and consequences—are important for you to remember as well. But over time, humans, and even teachers, have explained those failures away—or worse, reframed as them virtuous."

While speaking, Hirael rose and began walking, to another arena, Thomas assumed. "Just like the fathers of the faith are not perfect, neither are the watchers. If we were, none of us would have chosen rebellion. As we serve, we learn and grow, hopefully for the better." He stared off for a moment. "There is a space between struggle and rebellion. But we must be vigilant, lest small frustrations fester into destructive impulses that might work to separate us from the Most High." Again, he stared as if looking at something Thomas couldn't see, his eyes sad. "You humans don't know how blessed you are to have the Messiah's salvation. Once we elohim have pushed Him out, we do not have the option to invite Him back in." He stopped and turned to face Thomas directly. "You benefit from a grace we will never know."

The conversation made Thomas think of Ebby and his thankfulness, even with his meager existence. Could Thomas ever have a faith so strong? He has a place to live, food, a productive future—in theory. If he took the promotion, anyway. Maybe then he'd be more thankful.

The streets on which they walked bustled with beings. At times, Thomas found himself feeling like an insect as large elohim strode past. He stared up and around, the glory around him like nothing he'd ever experienced.

He yelped as Hirael pulled him into an alcove.

"Oh," Hirael said. "One of my favorites."

A minstrel sat here, holding not a lyre, but a sword. He had features of both a man and a lion. He began his poem...

The Lowest Point of Apex

Anthony Diastello

When I was but a fledgling new,
A wrestler, Apex, taught my crew.
A hearty warrior, strong and stout.
And of his valor, 'twas was no doubt.
I asked him once to understand,
"Why say you, 'As He wills, I stand'?"

The wrestler smiled and took a knee.
"You haven't heard?" he said with glee.
"I'll tell you of a battle fateful
To have fought it, I am truly grateful.
So, listen closely to my story,
And I will tell you of my glory.

"My group departed on our mission.
We were all strong, in good condition,
But fledgling, still, like you, back then—
A group of fighting fledgling friends.
But of us all, I was the strongest,
Highest rank and served the longest.

"We went toward our destination.
Our messenger made investigation.

He saw a crowd of unclean spirits
Coming fore, they didn't fear us.
They were so many. We were so few.
I knew what I had to do.

"I said I'd stay, I'd save the day,
So that my friends could get away.
But then my friends put forth the question,
'Aren't we going faster and the other direction?'
I knew what they said was true,
But I knew what I wanted to do.

"Itching for a fight, I was.
I'd take them on, and just because.
'No, no,' I said. 'I will not fail.
We don't want these hot on our trail.
Friends, go ahead and start your travel.
I'll catch up once I end this rabble.'

"And so, they went. And so, I stood.
I knew this fight would feel so good.
I'd cause this prideful group to pay.
I made my charge into the fray.
And as I did, I loosed a roar,
While up into the air I soared.

"I saw the fear fill up their eyes
As I descended from the skies.
I turned my body flat to smash
A few at once, clean up this trash.
. . .
But as I fell, there was no crash.

"I missed them all and lay exposed.
My own pride led me by the nose.
Now on the ground, confused, disgraced.

One of them leapt and clawed my face!"
As Apex spoke, fresh scars appeared
Across his eye, out to his ear.

"I never got to join my friends.
I was the one who saw his end.
The unclean spirits laughed and cheered.
I wish I could have disappeared."
I asked, confused by Apex's story,
"Then how is this a tale of glory?"

The scars he showed began to fade,
There was more, yet, he had to say.
"You see, recovered now am I.
Not just in health, but from my pride.
That day, the Most High was my help.
He saved me, but 'twas from myself.

"A different path I could have traveled,
And on that path, I'd have unraveled.
My loss that day? My greatest win.
My lowest point? My apex, friend!

"I've learned not strength, nor skill, nor speed
Decide our battles. No, indeed!
Our confidence can be our vice.
Life's more like humans rolling dice.
The Most High governs how they land.
So, I say, 'As He wills, I stand.'"

"You see," Hirael said as they were caught up in a crowd and swept toward a new destination. "We elohim have to learn His ways like you. We aren't always the quickest students, but most of us, eventually, find our way."

Your kind does have a few advantages, Thomas wanted to say, *having seen God and all.* But he held his tongue. Hirael looked at him as if he perceived his thoughts, but didn't comment or inquire further.

As Thomas figured, they made their way to another arena, this larger than even the first, the crowd burbling with conversation and excitement. As the stage lit up, the crowd quieted, the excitement like bolts of electricity in the air. Even Thomas found himself tense, ready for the stories to begin.

NIGHTMARE

ERIN R. HOWARD

Markos hesitated before entering the small gift shop to search for the teenage girl assigned to him by the Most High. It wasn't that he didn't want to help the human, but usually his missions were more involved—more intense. As he increased in rank, Markos's battles intensified, involving more influential humans with much larger targets on their backs. And while he didn't want to admit it to anyone, he loved the challenge.

With a promotion to watcher of the second heaven fast approaching, helping the girl seemed to be a move in the opposite direction. So, what could be so important about this teenager that the Most High would need to send him?

Markos shook off his thoughts and started through the door when he sensed a holy presence. A hand touched his shoulder and Markos turned to find a ministering spirit behind him. And not one he was excited to see—Callum.

A trio of women approached the shop's entrance—passing through Markos without pause as he sighed and turned toward the other watcher. "What is the reason for your presence here?"

"It seems our orders overlap."

Markos studied the elohim then went back to surveying the area around the store. "This mission is well within my capabilities."

Callum crossed his arms. "Perhaps. However, I've been dispatched as well."

Why did the Most High have to send Callum? Had Elyon lost faith in Markos? He could think of several other ministering spirits who fulfilled their duties while staying out of his way. Doubt wiggled its way into his thoughts, but he brushed it aside. If Callum had the same orders, then the Most High had a reason for wanting them to work together—again. "Very well. Tell me what you know."

Callum nodded. "Kallie Porter. Sixteen years of age. She has been experiencing nightmares, which have been progressively getting worse."

Markos had to restrain his impatience. "I received the same information. Do you have any additional details?"

"Her mother has been petitioning for help. She is concerned for her daughter. You should know—the quantity behind the door is significant—"

"What kind?"

Callum shrugged. "They're mostly unclean spirits."

"Unclean spirits are not an issue for me." If there was a steady decline in the girl's life, then unclean spirits no doubt played a hand in her torment, and he had defeated more than his share. It would take much more to intimidate him.

"You shouldn't underestimate the enemy." Callum shook his head. "Perhaps I'm here to ensure that you have all the necessary resources to succeed."

Markos didn't appreciate the insinuation that he couldn't handle his assignment. They hadn't always agreed on the best approach to solving problems. But Markos led with strength and tackled his enemies head-on. If it wasn't appropriate for this mission, why would the Most High assign it to Markos in the first place?

"Let's concentrate on finding Kallie."

"Entirely sensible plan." Callum gestured for him to go first. "I will search the back of the premises to see if there are any other unholy elohim lingering nearby."

"Very well."

Markos watched him head toward the rear of the building and debated on assuming a physical form. Callum would probably choose to blend in that way, concealing his glory as a human to quietly assess the situation further.

But that was Callum.

Stepping into the store, Markos was glad he'd kept his true form. The entire shop was filled with unclean spirits. They hovered like dark clouds in the air, clumped together. Markos might actually pity them if they were not such sources of pure evil.

The small gift shop had only a few customers milling about. The spirits seemed to ignore them and focused solely on a human in the center of the room.

A girl with an apron stood in the middle, restocking a display of candles.

Bingo.

The first thing he noticed was that Kallie had dark circles under her eyes and her movements were careful but slow. As if she was too tired to trust herself even to put the jars on the shelves.

"All right, abominations, time to depart!" Markos manifested his sword and gave a couple of swift strikes through the air, getting the attention of the spirits. Shrieks and growls snapped back in response.

"Watcher!"

More growls erupted in the room, with at least one of them recognizing him. "It's Markos. I owe him a swift defeat!"

He swung his sword near a cluster of spirits closest to him and smiled as black vapor escaped their forms—hissing from one after another as his sword did its work.

Dozens of them escaped out of the store, pushing past each other to get away.

Eight lingered in the far corner of the room, and Markos worked his way toward them, striking two that dared to advance toward him. Keeping one eye on his charge, he noticed an older woman with the same color hair as Kallie approach, startling her. Kallie nearly dropped the glass jar.

"Goodness, Mom." The girl jumped, almost tipping over the display. She put a hand up on her chest. "You scared me."

"I noticed." The lady frowned. "Are you all right?"

"I'm fine. Just a little tense."

"Kallie, I need you to cover the register for a little while. There's an order that needs shipped today."

"I was about to go take my break. I haven't had my lunch yet." The girl's voice wavered. Was she about to cry? Markos sliced through another unclean spirit and continued to observe Kallie. The girl seemed hesitant to argue and averted her mother's gaze.

"Well, this order must go out today, honey. It's been on back order for weeks. I won't be long."

Kallie looked like she was about to bolt, and her voice trembled. "I can take it on my way—I've been craving a milkshake all day."

"I promised the customer that I would hand deliver this item to the shipping store. Your chocolate addiction will have to wait."

"Mom, I really—"

"Kallie, I said you are going to work the register. I'll be right back." Her mother's harsh tone left no room for any sort of negotiation. Kallie's focus returned to the jar, her hand shaking as she lowered it to the display. The older woman hesitated, concern and worry flashing across her face. She opened her mouth to say more but instead, turned and hurried off to the back of the store.

Where was Callum? Kallie's anxiety was clearly visible, bordering on some sort of panic attack. It stung a little to admit, but even Markos could see that the girl needed a different kind of help than he was comfortable offering.

Markos turned his attention back to the few remaining unclean spirits. As he noticed the last of them fleeing the store, he took inventory of the room. Something wasn't right. *Where is Callum?* The store emptied, leaving just him, an older woman, and Kallie. Markos drifted toward the back of the store to check if Callum was in the backrooms. But his attention was drawn back to the woman who was now depositing an armful of handmade soap onto the counter.

"Oh, you don't have to worry about wrapping." The lady waved her hand as Kallie picked up the tissue paper and then set it back down.

There was something off about her voice and mannerisms. She was in a hurry to leave.

A chill of recognition swept over Markos.

No!

Callum would have to wait. In just a few quick strides, he reached his opponent.

The woman turned around in surprise, but then smirked when her gaze landed on Markos. "Well, what do we have here?"

Markos didn't even respond. He thrust his sword into the woman's chest.

A hiss escaped the wound, and the imposter snarled, reaching up to pry the sword out. Markos pushed harder, allowing the blade to pierce deeper. Black spiritual vapor poured from the wound, and the unholy elohim collapsed to the ground.

Kallie screamed—yanking Markos's attention from the fallen enemy to her as she frantically ran around to the edge of the counter to check on the woman. She bent down, reaching out a hand, then stopped as she stared at the now empty spot where the woman had fallen.

Oh, no. Markos hadn't even stopped to think about what his actions would look like to Kallie. In the spiritual, he could still clearly see the defeated elohim lying there, no longer manifesting as the woman.

Where was Callum? Markos had no effective choice but to manifest into the material and try to disarm the situation. This was not something he enjoyed. If Callum were here, he would no doubt have reminded him to be "mindful."

Now unable to miss Markos, Kallie stepped backward—her eyes wide. The poor girl was terrified of him, and not in a good way. Markos took a second to look down at himself—a white linen robe and golden sash. He checked his reflection in a glass window and ensured he looked human. He was purposely trying to appear non-threatening.

Kallie looked at him like she'd seen him before. It didn't make any sense.

"What's going on?" he whispered to the Most High, but didn't hear a response.

He raised his hand to the girl. "Do not be afraid." Markos took a step toward her and the girl instantly recoiled, bumping into a display behind her, sending the contents crashing to the floor.

"Stay away from me."

"I'm not going to harm you."

Kallie moved again, stepping over the products on the ground. "What did you do?" Kallie's voice teetered on the edge of hysterical.

"The woman …" She raised her eyes to meet Markos's gaze. "She *was* here. And then you appeared—and she disappeared. What are you going to do to me?"

"Kallie—you are safe now."

"You did something to that woman and now I'm next. I'm a witness." She lunged for the counter, lifting up a pair of scissors. They shook in her hand.

"Really? That is what you choose to charge me with?"

Kallie's voice trembled. "I told you to stay away from me."

"I will not hurt you." Markos nearly growled in response, but had to force himself to sound more comforting. "I am here to help you."

"Help me?" Kallie gestured with the scissors to where the woman had fallen. "You gave that innocent lady a heart attack—or something—and then vaporized her!"

This was not going as it should. He narrowed his eyes at her. "I saved you, and if you do not calm down and come with me, there will be more on the way."

He reached out to take hold of her arm, but she jabbed the utensil in his direction, her voice continuing to rise in pitch. "You're crazy. I'm not going anywhere with you!"

They didn't have time for this. The girl was screaming and yelling, terrified.

"We do not have time to argue. The Most High sent me to help you."

"The Most High?"

Markos quickly added. "You humans refer to Him as God."

Kallie's face paled, and she raised the scissors once again. "And I'm supposed to believe you're, what? An angel?"

"Close enough."

She backed away from the counter and sidestepped in the opposite direction. She lowered her voice. Perhaps it was the shock taking over. "You're crazy, or maybe I am, because none of this can be real." She glanced toward the front.

Nope, not shock. Kallie had calmed down enough to get him to let down his guard. Markos watched as she sprinted for the door, but in two steps, he was in front of her.

"Please do not make this more difficult than it needs to be. I'm here to protect you."

Kallie tried to dart around him, but he reached out and wrapped an arm around her. She thrashed against his hold, kicking and screaming, and trying to wiggle out of his grip. Markos did not flinch or display any strain. There was no need to make a point of showing his strength.

"Are you done expressing your displeasure?" Tears welled up in her eyes as if she finally realized there wasn't any way she could break free from his grasp.

Sympathy stirred inside Markos. The girl was terrified, and he couldn't exactly blame her. He tried changing his tone and demeanor as best he could manage. "I know you don't understand everything yet, but that woman was not some innocent lady. She was here to harm you, and I was here to stop her."

Kallie shook her head. "That doesn't make any sense. In my dream, you're the one who murdered me."

Markos let go of her. "Excuse me?"

Kallie rubbed her arms and quickly put distance between them. "In my dream, it was someone like you who killed me—not the woman … or whatever."

This was getting more difficult with each passing second. He needed to get her some place safe until he figured this all out.

Callum had circled around the building, surveying the small parking lot. Not sensing anything in the immediate area, he walked through the exterior wall into a dimly lit storage room. Racks of shelves lined with boxes and supplies filled the small concrete space.

The atmosphere was heavy… as if despair clung to the air.

Sobs echoed around the corner and caught Callum's attention. A woman sat in an office, elbows propped on the desk in front of her, with her face in her hands.

Callum edged closer, lifting a prayer to the Most High on her behalf.

The woman moved her hands and then wiped the tears with her

fingers. "Lord, I don't know what's going on with Kallie, but something isn't right."

Understanding filled Callum and he neared. He was informed this woman had been praying for her daughter for some time, asking for help and protection. But now, hearing the desperation lingering in her voice—the poor woman was distraught.

"I don't know what to do, Lord."

Markos was waiting for him in the other room, but Callum didn't want to leave Kallie's mother in this state. There was time. He sensed that Markos had handled the unholy presences. Compassion urged him to her side. Crouching down beside her, he rested his hand on her shoulder. She inhaled a breath and exhaled, the sound shaky and mixed with sobs.

Let your Spirit fill her with peace, he silently petitioned Elyon. Then he started whispering reminders of truth and the Most High's promises to her spirit.

The woman continued to cry, pouring out her heart to Elyon. Callum continued to pray for strength and endurance, reminding her that the Most High works all things together for good.

When she stopped crying, her words became stronger, and she sat straighter in her chair. "Thank you for hearing me, Lord."

Callum stood and took a few steps back, waiting until he was satisfied that she was feeling better. Despair was gone and the Breath of the Most High filled the room.

Kallie's mother gathered her purse and keys and headed out the back door, so he turned his attention toward the storefront. Markos would no doubt grumble about his delay, but that was just the mighty warrior's way. He charged ahead and asked questions later. Kallie's mother had needed help.

Screams erupted from the next room, and Callum hurried toward the sound but came to an abrupt stop.

There, near the counter, was a vanquished unholy elohim, and Markos—embodied in the material—looking down at a hysterical human girl.

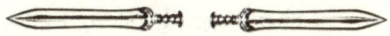

"Markos, what has happened?"

Callum's voice called out from the back of the store, and Markos glanced up to see a look of disapproval cross Callum's face.

"There were more enemies than I anticipated." He was relieved to see the ministering spirit approach—even though he missed the fight. "What delayed you?"

"Who are you talking to?" Kallie's voice wavered as she took a tentative step backward.

"I was ministering to Kallie's mother," Callum answered. "She was distraught and needed aid."

Markos nodded and turned back to Kallie. "Callum is here."

She looked around the room and let out a nervous laugh. "There are more of you?"

"He is not a warrior," Markos corrected and then added, "But yes, another … angel."

"Hello, Kallie." Callum manifested a human-looking form and stood beside Markos.

Kallie screamed—again, startling Markos. How did Callum have the patience to interact with humans this way?

"I did not mean to frighten you." Callum lowered his voice. "However, I thought this would be easier if you could see me as well."

Tears filled her eyes. "I don't understand what's going on."

"I know it is hard, but as I'm sure Markos explained, we were sent to help you."

"It's kind of hard to believe that when I just watched a woman fall over and disappear." She shuddered and pointed a finger towards Markos. "He admitted to causing it and is now holding me here against my will."

Callum nodded. "I understand how that would be troubling. How about you sit down for a moment?"

Kallie looked back and forth between them as if she was trying to decide if she trusted them. Markos wanted to interrupt, to remind

Callum that they weren't quite finished with their mission, but Callum shook his head at Markos before gently taking Kallie's arm and leading her toward a stool around the counter.

The urgency to get Kallie somewhere safer nearly overwhelmed Markos, but then he heard the Spirit of Elyon tell him to wait.

Interesting.

Callum definitely knew how to calm her down and it was working, so Markos walked over to the store window to scan the outside. As he approached, his likeness grew larger—staring back at him. Markos's gaze shifted past his reflection to notice Callum kneeling to comfort Kallie. There was something bothering Markos—something in the atmosphere putting him on edge. But what was it?

It needs to be revealed.

Revealed? Markos's thoughts raced as he tried to work out the Spirit's leading. What needed to be revealed? Was there more going on with the situation that they didn't know? He replayed the events leading up to now. They were there because of the mother's prayers. The storefront was filled with unclean spirits. An unholy elohim was in the vicinity, but was trying to blend in.

It was there but wasn't necessarily there to harm Kallie.

What is done in the dark comes to light.

All the pieces fell into place and Markos spun back toward the others, urgency his priority. His movements once again startled Kallie, and she jumped. No doubt her nerves were still raw. Callum rose to his feet, concern lining his face.

"What is it?"

"There is one hiding. Another unclean spirit."

Kallie stiffened, her expression changing over to concern, but Callum rested a hand on her shoulder, keeping his voice even. "I'm aware." Callum relaxed again. "I was getting to that."

That brought Markos up short. Irritation at Callum's delay in supplying information quickly rose to the surface. But he took a breath and thought it through.

So far, Callum had shown greater capability at nearly every step. Perhaps there *was* a bigger purpose in the Most High sending him to Kallie. Perhaps it wasn't for her, but for him.

Almost every one of his actions had stirred up more than they settled. Markos turned back to the window and studied his reflection. What if Callum's ability to annoy had more to do with Markos not wanting to look at himself honestly? Perhaps the Most High kept pairing him with Callum until he would be willing to stare into his reflection and confront what others saw on clear display.

"Unclean spirit?" Kallie called out, breaking through his thoughts. "Do I really want to know what that is?"

Markos neared the girl and chose to cooperate with his lesson. He gently pulled her to her feet, but she broke from his grasp, crossed her arms, and stepped back.

She was still afraid of him.

Markos tried to explain. "Your mother has been concerned about you. She has seen that something isn't right, that you seem tired and struggle with routine tasks. She feels the distance between you and wants to reach out to you."

Kallie's eyes filled. "She does? How do you know?"

"She's been praying for you, Kallie. I've witnessed it." Callum answered before Markos could respond.

"I had no idea—" Her voice caught, and tears traced down her cheeks. "I didn't know she saw or cared."

Callum reached out and touched her arm. "She loves you."

"Your nightmares," Markos prompted. "How long have they plagued you?"

"I don't know ..." She crossed her arms, hesitant to share. "A few months, I guess. My friends and I got into watching shows about cold cases and kidnappings—to the point we were binge-watching them.

"One friend started making up pretend scenarios about us, like she was the criminal. She got pretty dark about it sometimes and ..." Kallie rubbed a hand across her face and took in a deep breath. "I don't know. It stuck with me. Something started telling me I actually *was* going to be next, and I couldn't let go of the anxiety it was causing me. Then I started seeing things in my dreams."

Markos exchanged a look with Callum, who nodded.

"I knew it was stupid, so I didn't tell anyone," Kallie finished.

"Do you trust us, Kallie?" Markos asked gently.

"Maybe. I want to, but my dream—"

Markos manifested his sword, and Kallie's eyes widened at the weapon. Callum stepped in front of Markos, who held the sword away from Kallie, realizing he had done it again. He hoped his look of apology would suffice to assuage any fear he may have stirred.

"It wasn't stupid, Kallie. A spirit has been amplifying your fearful thoughts and giving you these dreams," Callum told her.

"But the ones in my dream looked like *you* guys," Kallie protested.

Callum nodded. "Even the one you know as Satan can appear as an angel of light. It seems these spirits want to condition you to avoid *any* who could help. Are you willing to have this influence leave you?"

"Yes." Kallie nodded. "At least I think so. What will it feel—"

That was all Markos needed. He stepped past Callum, but then paused, his eyes searching hers for permission. Only after she gave a firm nod and closed her eyes did he strike—swinging the flat of his blade across Kallie's torso, not to harm *her*, but the unclean spirit hiding within her.

The blade exited Kallie with an unclean spirit wrapped around it, wiggling and squirming to escape. Markos deftly brought his sword around and thrust it down, piercing the stowaway, and reducing it to a black cloud at Kallie's feet.

The girl opened her eyes and inspected herself. "Wait. Are you finished?"

Markos nodded toward his sword on the floor and Kallie looked down, apparently allowed to see the shadowy cloud that lay motionless around the blade.

"So, it's over?"

"Yes," Callum answered. "However, I would advise sharing this with your mother. She can support you—and help you ensure doors stay closed to the likes of these." He nudged the unclean spirit with his foot. "After all, her prayers for you are why we are here."

"I will talk to her today." The relief in Kallie's voice was evident. "Thank you both."

She looked over to Markos and a slow smile spread across her face. She was still clearly exhausted, but there was a lightness to her now.

"Can I suggest something?"

Caught off guard, Markos paused before nodding.

"Maybe spend some time with ... Callum? You know, practice how not to be terrifying before the next time you have to appear like this."

Markos dipped his head, and the corners of his mouth turned upward into a smile as Callum burst into a deep laugh.

TOO FAR GONE

CAEDON HULL & NATHANIEL SORENSEN

I had to be careful, or *they* might see me. Thankfully, Jeremy's dorm room was at ground level. It gets much harder to maintain good cover when your subject is on a higher floor. But today I felt safe manifesting as a human groundskeeper, trimming trees outside Jeremy's window.

The sun was nearly overhead when his alarm assaulted my ears through the cracked-open window. The first sign of life appeared, as a hand flopped around to silence the techno tune. It finally tapped the right spot on his phone and fell still. Concern that he might fall back asleep clenched at me. I forced myself to continue working my pruning shears.

Relief followed as the hand moved again to shove one side of the bedcovers back. Somehow, in the midst of the year's struggles, Jeremy had managed to stay committed to his grades. *One part of the plan down, five to go.*

Jeremy awkwardly pushed himself up to slouch against the headboard, one arm shielding his eyes.

"Why do I always forget to close the curtains?" he muttered.

With his other hand, he felt around on the nightstand. Not finding what he was looking for, he dropped his arm to shake the lump of bedding next to him. "Jeni. Jeni. What did you do with my glasses? Hey, Jeni!"

The lump was displeased at the interruption. It groaned, then replied, "It's *Jamie*."

"Yeah," Jeremy said, eyes scrunched closed, his hand massaging one of his temples. "That's what I said. I've got an exam today and need to get rid of this hangover. Where's my glasses?"

"How should I know?" the lump began before fading into a stream of muffled mumbles.

Jeremy yawned, sighed and finally gave an honest effort at checking the nightstand. Nothing. He swung his feet around to the floor, then bent out of sight. I presumed he was feeling around so as not to step on his new frames.

A dark, semi-transparent figure rose in his place and glanced toward the window. I quickly looked down at my "work". Even with his glasses, Jeremy wouldn't notice anything unusual about me working out here. It was these unclean spirits that were the problem. If they noticed me giving Jeremy special attention, it might scare them into trying to change Jeremy's rhythm for the day. And today's mission *needed* him to stay on rhythm. I hadn't seen the other two yet, but I knew they were there somewhere.

Risking a peek, I saw Jeremy reappear next to the unclean spirit, his search unsuccessful. He again shielded his eyes from the blinding light streaming in through the window. I cautiously scanned the room and picked out another unclean spirit lazily snickering in the shadow of a corner. It must be enjoying Jeremy's discomfort. Keeping my eyes moving, I saw the glasses sitting on a desk next to a tarot tableau. That was how the first unclean spirit got in.

Just into Jeremy's sophomore year, he'd gotten his heart broken. Not an uncommon college experience, unfortunately, but it shook him hard. He got despondent and floundered through his autumn schedule. Mithakesh, a minstrel-ministering spirit I respect greatly, worked hard to uplift Jeremy, but it was a difficult time.

Over the Christmas break, a couple childhood friends contributed to Mithakesh's efforts to encourage Jeremy and keep him from a concerning flirtation with substance addiction. Indeed, Jeremy went hard in the opposite direction. He hit the spring semester angry and looking for any way to make sure life stayed in control. He got laser-focused on his engineering classes and someday winning a job with GE Aviation.

Then came Valentine's Day. Rather than looking for a convenient date, Jeremy accepted a friend's invitation to a tarot reading. Another pair of my brothers fought hard to keep Jeremy away that night. His commitment to this friend won out, though, and Jeremy went ahead with it.

The power Jeremy felt that evening caught his heart, and he hadn't looked back since. Over the summer he started learning how to do readings himself. The allure of glimpsing what is to come fed his desire for a sense of control, but he was unaware his interpretations were not always his own.

Jeremy's spiritual boarders prefer that kind of anonymity, actually. Now there were at least three of them gaining increasing influence in his life, and Jeremy's situation was one of several challenges my team was working on at the university. It has grieved me to watch him struggle to keep up with growing appetites that don't actually belong to him — Jamie being one case in point.

I moved my stepladder to the next tree so I could stay in line of sight as Jeremy crossed the room to check his desk. He found his glasses, wincing as clarity suddenly forced his brain to process more than the previous blur.

I've heard some of my brothers occasionally refer to a human as being "too far gone." I've never felt comfortable with that, but cases like Jeremy's get me wondering. He *welcomes* this influence and promise of power. So long as he grants authority, the afflicting spirits operate outside my jurisdiction. By the time he recognizes their true natures, he may be in too deep to know how or where to look for help.

Many *have* been rescued from this state, to be sure. The authority of the Son of Man is supreme. It's just there are some extra steps to getting someone in Jeremy's state to welcome the Most High's rule and reign into their space. Some of those steps are out of my ability to control. Even if someone like Jeremy isn't too far out of the *Most High's* reach, it is frustrating to recognize how far they are out of *my* reach. As many as have been rescued, it feels there are too many more Jeremys that we lose.

He'd been withdrawing from his friends lately, making indirect methods more difficult. Calls from family back home were going ignored, and the unclean spirits prompted him to avoid any conversations with those bearing the name of the Father. Jeremy probably just rationalized it all as the stress of difficult classes and needing the time to study, but he didn't blink twice when Jamie asked him out. Unclean spirits are inept at many things, but they are quite good at excuses. Jeremy wouldn't notice the inconsistencies until they got *much* more severe.

I had a mission, though, and I was responsible for giving it my best. So long as Jeremy stayed on his usual routine, my team was about to get another go at it.

"Hey," Jeremy gently called as he sniff-checked the closest available T-shirts. "I gotta grab some coffee and get myself together. I'll catch you later, alright?"

"Hmmmphffhmm."

Perfect. Two down. Jeremy's need for control helped make him predictable. Predictability is great for mission planning. Without fail, anytime he had a "good time" the night before a day with classes, he always somehow managed to get up in time to go to his favorite coffee shop and go over his notes. The two unclean spirits I could see started moving toward the door. So far, they seemed to have no objections to his plans.

"Hmmmphffhmm!"

"What's that?" Jeremy called back from the door.

The other side of the bedcovers pulled back far enough to reveal a mess of red hair. "Close the curtains."

Jeremy sighed, rolling his eyes. I focused intently on pruning a higher branch as he walked toward me. When the curtains closed, I hopped off the ladder, gathered my clippings into a bag and returned my borrowed props for the real groundskeepers.

Stepping out of sight, I resumed my true form before speeding to my team's rendezvous point. Shalom paced the edge of the storefront rooftop. He was working out an indistinct tune that trailed off as I approached. "Well, Gale, is Jeremy coming?"

"As we speak." I nodded.

The minstrel's brow released its tension as he lifted his eyes to the sky. "Thank the Most High. We might have a real chance this time."

Shalom hummed a few bars of thanksgiving before realizing I hadn't responded. "Is everything alright?" he asked.

"It's just that this was the easy part," I sighed. "He's been so avoidant lately. I find it a little early to expect he won't turn and walk at first sight of the professor. Speaking of… has Valor had any trouble getting the professor here?"

Shalom smiled. "*That's* been the easy part. The professor has not allowed any room for spiritual resistance. It seems the Spirit of the Most High has been leading him as well. Valor would have let me know by now if something had gone awry on his end."

I nodded as Shalom continued humming his tune, jumping into the middle as though the melody had been running in the background as we spoke. The song beckoned me to a moment of rest. I chose to follow it as we watched the street below. Joining in the moment of praise, I sensed hope and faith moving to the forefront of my thoughts.

The renewed peace must have helped my awareness. Just as Jeremy turned the corner onto our street, I turned and caught an unholy messenger watching us from behind an HVAC unit. As a messenger, my perception is expected to be the best on my team. Berating myself for the lapse in vigilance earlier, I elbowed Shalom. He turned and followed my gaze.

Beady, arrogant eyes looked back at us down a razor beak. His single set of dark, weathered wings told me he wasn't a direct threat to us. Shalom and I were first heaven ourselves, but together, we were more than a match for this single observer. Yet as we turned, he made no attempt to hide or run. His obvious lack of strength made his smugness a bit unsettling. I looked around to check for any others I might have missed.

How much had he heard?

"I'm not used to seeing this particular rooftop graced with your presence," the messenger cackled at us. "I'd *love* to hear more of this Valor, and Jeremy, and a certain professor in whom you seem so interested."

He'd heard enough, then. This could mean trouble.

"You tell us some of Dolion's plans," Shalom responded smoothly, "and we'll let you in on some of ours."

Nice, Shalom.

"And since we gave you a head start," I jumped in, "it's your turn."

The messenger stared blankly, as though his mind had shut down. The idea of betraying his master's trust, even to gain some intel of ours, apparently inspired enough fear to steal his words.

Dolion was a herder who oversaw the enemy's operations at this university and was known to be particularly ruthless. He'd been here a long time, taking great pride in pulling the environment and ideologies toward his destructive ends. Any threats to his operations from our side were met with vigorous opposition. Any threats due to his own underlings' failures received a somewhat harsher response.

The messenger broke his own trance with a shake of his head. He snarled in frustration before dropping through the roof into the building below. I almost leapt in pursuit, but caught myself. Much as I would have loved to tie up this loose end before he could hinder our plans, searching at high speed through the warren of rooms in the buildings below would surely attract more attention.

"He'll probably be back with more," Shalom observed.

I shrugged. "It's a risk we have to take now. Jeremy's almost to the coffee shop. Besides, we didn't say where, or exactly when, we expected this meeting to happen. Once we get inside, hopefully it'll take them a while to find us. We can still pull this off. Can't control everything, right?"

"Right." Shalom nodded, but his tone matched my lack of enthusiasm. "Let's get down to Valor," he continued. "We only have a couple minutes."

Crossing the roof, we checked the back alley for watching eyes before dropping to street level. We made our way behind shops and restaurants in silence. Several dumpsters presented blind spots along our concrete corridor, but everything seemed clear to our eyes. Reaching a door with "Crammin' Caffeine" stenciled in violet, we paused for a focused scan. I nodded to Shalom and received a nod back. *Looks like we're ok so far.*

We passed through a storeroom and small kitchen before entering the public area of the cafe. Eleven of fifteen tables were occupied. Another four students stood in line to order their lattes and frappes. It was busy, but normal. I'd discovered for many students, noon still meant "morning".

Across the room, I picked out the only other spiritual presence. Valor calmly watched the street through the large windows.

"You're late," he said brusquely, but not unkindly, as we came up beside him.

"We ran into an eavesdropper," Shalom said. Valor's eyes widened with surprise as he glanced at me. I knew him well enough to take it as a question instead of an accusation.

"Nothing too concerning," I clarified. "Jeremy's still on his way — just down the street, actually. But it's possible some other guests may now be looking for us too. Probably wise to keep an extra eye out. Everything ok here?"

Valor nodded toward the far end of the room. I followed his gaze past a group of girls huddled around a table sipping frozen drinks while staring at their phones. Gloves sticking out of their bags marked them as part of a softball team. Just behind them, the professor sat at a corner table. He wore glasses, and loosely combed hair was graying at the temples. Quietly drinking coffee from a small, white mug, he was reading something on a tablet.

We'd picked the professor for this operation because he was already something of a mentor figure for a lot of students. He had a good ear for the Most High's voice and paired his extensive knowledge of history with a quiet, refreshing humility.

Our briefing told us Jeremy had been in the professor's class back when the break-up happened. The professor had noticed something off and offered a listening ear. Jeremy wasn't ready for help then, and the professor knew better than to be pushy. He'd gotten it on his heart to pray, however, and had kept Jeremy on his list ever since.

"It wasn't too difficult to get him here," Valor said. "This is a little off his routine, but I fiddled with his coffee maker this morning. He had a couple early meetings, so I knew he wouldn't have time to swing by until now. He only just sat down."

Valor was quiet for a moment, then added, "He brought Jeremy up again during his morning prayers, and I didn't even have to prompt him this time."

"Excellent," Shalom said. "We really are on track."

The softball players stood to gather their things just as Jeremy approached the door. *Perfect. The rest of the customers will provide a general buzz, but a little more space will encourage honest conversation.*

Jeremy entered and stood second-in-line at the register. I saw no sign of the unclean spirits. Being out in public, they were probably hiding inside him to avoid notice.

I glanced over at the professor, hoping for recognition, but he was too engrossed in his reading. I went to his table and leaned to speak in his ear. "Check the room."

After a pause, the professor reached to swipe to the next page and looked up. I followed his gaze and... Jeremy was gone. *What?! Humans don't move that fast!* Valor and Shalom seemed unfazed, though. I moved toward the register and found Jeremy crouched to tie his shoe. The person in front of Jeremy moved and Jeremy stood up to order. The professor started reading again.

I turned to find Shalom failing to mask a smile at my frustration. Valor half-smirked and shrugged his shoulders as if to say, *What can you do? Some days it just goes that way.* I shook my head and looked back at the register.

Jeremy made his order and did *not* take the softball players' table. Instead, he headed for an open, two-seat table across the room from the professor. I huffed to myself. *Some days, indeed.*

I didn't think Jeremy had noticed the professor, so I doubted he was being avoidant. There was no way of knowing if the unclean spirits had noticed and steered him away. For the moment, I judged it a coincidence. A person intent on studying would naturally gravitate toward the edge of a crowd.

I returned to Shalom and Valor. "How do you want to play this? Looks like Jeremy's settled. I don't see him getting back up now to talk with the professor."

"I agree," Shalom replied. "We need to get the professor over to Jeremy. Valor, you've been with the professor a lot this week. Why don't you get him moving? Gale, try to keep Jeremy in his seat. I'll keep an eye out for interference."

Valor nodded and headed to the professor's table. I went to Jeremy's side of the room, but took a position by the pastry counter. We hadn't shown much direct attention to Jeremy... yet. The unclean spirits would surely have noticed us in the room, but hopefully still thought we were here for someone or something else. I didn't want to agitate them before it was necessary.

I kept Jeremy in view while making casual scans of the room. Shalom watched the street, taking occasional glances at our progress. I planned how to keep Jeremy from bolting once we got the professor close. After a few uneventful moments, the professor stood and put his tablet in a shoulder bag. He was picking up his dishes when Valor finally succeeded in bringing Jeremy to his attention.

The professor paused with an empty mug and saucer in hand and watched thoughtfully. I couldn't hear what Valor was whispering, but a contemplative dialogue was evident in the professor's eyes. He nodded to himself, set his dishes in a bin above the trash can, and walked to Jeremy's table.

As I moved to join them, a deathly shriek erupted outside, ripping through the cafe. In the corner of my eye, I saw Shalom get thrown past unseeing students to disappear through the counter.

Manifesting my bow, I jerked my head up to see four unholy elohim descend from a vantage point across the street. Our smug eavesdropper leered from behind two larger warriors he had recruited to be bouncers. To their right was a messenger-minstrel making the raucous noise that caught Shalom off-guard.

Charging at full speed, the group's intentions needed no interpretation. I took careful aim and released an arrow. It cut the narrow gap between the warriors' shoulders and hit the small messenger in the eye. I allowed myself a brief grin of satisfaction as he dropped to the pavement with a gasp. Another haphazard shot glanced harmlessly off a warrior's shield.

Then they were on us. The warrior I'd targeted came at me. The other two zeroed in on Valor. He was going to have his hands full, but I'd have to leave him to it. Shifting my bow into a sword, I stepped left to dodge the full-on charge of my warrior. At the last second, however, he pulled up in a clever feint and I almost stepped right into his hammer. Awkwardly deflecting it, I was left off-balance. Despite his size, this warrior could *move*.

I danced around him, managing to dodge and deflect, but failing to find openings for counterattack. I was quicker, but he was cagey, covering himself well, even while pressing the attack. Finally, he rushed at me again and stepped wrong. I got in a good cut on his shield arm, then pulled on his shield to get him off-balance. He grunted and his own momentum carried him out of range.

With a few seconds to regroup, I glanced at Valor. He was cut, but on his feet. I was pleased to see dark tendrils emanating from both his adversaries, indicating where Valor had returned the favor. I turned back to the professor and Jeremy. *Mission first.*

"Hi Jeremy." The professor was just getting to Jeremy's table. "It's been a little while. Mind if I sit for a minute?"

Jeremy looked up in obvious discomfort. "Hi, Dr. Kendrick. Um, I sort of have an exam in a bit."

His eyes were wide, and he was actually breathing quicker. *He's been avoiding people, but he doesn't usually react* this *strongly—the unclean spirits must be reacting to our battle. But Jeremy thinks he's reacting to the professor. Not good.*

I stepped in front of Jeremy and bent to stare straight into his eyes. Addressing the spirits, I snarled, "You will stay quiet and very, *very* still. If you move from this chair, I will take it as direct interference in our mission and act accordingly."

As I searched for some response, something smashed into my back. Dazed, I turned over to see the now recovered warrior holding his hammer under my beak. I lay pinned beneath his shield, Jeremy's laptop sticking up through my chest.

"Time's up, featherweight," the warrior jeered. "We have plans here today, and you're in the way."

The warrior glanced right, and I saw recognition when he noticed Jeremy. The warrior glared back at me, his sneer shifted to gloating. "You're here with *him*? We're making good progress with this one. You're fighting a lost battle here, light one."

From behind the counter, I heard Shalom's voice fill the room with an energetic melody.

"We're here *with* him," I said, jerking my head in the other direction at the professor. "He gives us right. What we're here *for* doesn't dance to your schedule."

I was in no position to back up my strong words, and the warrior knew it. He laughed and raised his hammer for a sure strike. As the hammer descended, I laughed back and pushed against the warrior's shield.

In a flash of light, energized by Shalom's song, I found myself standing *behind* the warrior. I finished my chuckle as his hammer fell harmlessly through Jeremy's table.

With the warrior in a vulnerable position, I could now use my speed to full advantage. I struck hard and fast with my sword. From behind the counter, Shalom continued singing with a punctuated cadence, slinging stones as though he were aggressively filling orders. The warrior turned to defend himself, but I saw my openings and took them. In very little time, his defenses dropped, and he slumped to the floor.

I quickly scanned behind me. Valor had left the other warrior laying under a table. Shalom turned to help with the messenger-minstrel. No other enemies had entered the skirmish. I turned and gave another hard glare at Jeremy to make sure the unclean spirits knew I hadn't forgotten them. They'd given no acknowledgment of my ultimatum, but Jeremy had seemed to calm a bit.

Ignoring the clash of grunts and competing songs, I stood to address the professor. "Stay with it, Professor. He's got time."

"Dr. Glendenning's class?" the professor asked, observing the open textbook next to the laptop.

Jeremy nodded.

The professor checked his watch. "Jeremy, I really got the feeling I was supposed to check in on you today. That class isn't for another couple hours yet and you're always well-prepared. You sure I can't sit for just a couple minutes?"

I watched Jeremy closely. His eyes darted in my direction twice, looking through me. He stretched his neck. He was wrestling. Despite the felt need to study, despite the resistance of unclean spirits, despite the hangover — something in Jeremy *wanted* to have this conversation. He may have felt some pressure to be polite, but I saw a touch of longing in his eyes as well.

The professor waited patiently, respectfully.

Something finally settled and Jeremy nodded, "O... ok. Sure, Professor. You're totally right."

Closing his laptop, he added, "Have a seat."

I dragged the warrior off to the side and positioned myself to watch the conversation while monitoring the waning battle. As Valor and Shalom won the day, I listened to the professor deftly draw Jeremy's story out of him. There were no major breakthroughs, but it was good to hear Jeremy open up to someone. It was a legitimate step toward inviting the Most High's influence into his life.

As the conversation drew to a close, the professor offered to pray for Jeremy. I was mildly surprised to hear a nonchalant "Sure." The unclean spirits must have been thoroughly cowed.

It was a simple prayer for peace and direction, but I could sense today was a swing in momentum for us. The professor said, "Amen," and stood to leave. As Valor made ready to follow, I heard the defeated warrior push out a weak laugh.

I looked down. "What's that?" I taunted. "I didn't quite make it out."

With only enough strength to get one eye open, he wheezed again. "I told you. I knew you wouldn't get him. This was useless."

I reflected on his comment and its intersection with my own previous thoughts. "Ah," I mused aloud. "I think I see your mistake. You can't see past your own position. You think you're beyond hope, so you're quick to assume the same for others. But they aren't you."

Another messenger I recognized from a nearby hold entered the cafe and approached us. He nodded at me, then addressed Shalom. "We have a potential situation at the church. Ro'e requests you both return."

As Shalom responded, I squatted down and leaned toward the warrior. "Your self-centeredness is your blindness. The Most High beckons them all to come — which means *no one* is too far gone."

SHINING LIGHT IN THE CENTER OF THE NEIGHBORHOOD

MERVE THOMAS

The warrior Umumriel stood ever vigilant, looking out over the neighborhood of Miller's End. Once a bustling development supporting the local automobile factory, but now, since the factory's closing a decade ago, a shamble of its former self. The moonlight dimly bounced off derelict lawns, the streetlights long since burned out. Houses stood, barely, the siding on most mildewed, cracked, or gone altogether from years of neglect, the roofs an afterthought of loose shingles, gaps, and water damage. Humans lived in these dwellings, most doing vile things: making drugs, selling drugs, or selling themselves. A den of sexual immorality, physical abuse, and abandoned children. Umumriel could feel the darkness.

Only one house, that of the Delacruz family, stood as a beacon. In the front yard, a flag flew. Below it, a sign proclaimed "Jesus is King". Beside that, the chalk drawings of young children decorated the driveway—a level of love that stood in brave contrast to the others of the neighborhood, like a rose amongst the weeds. This is the house Umumriel was tasked to watch. So he stood, tall, ready, his sword stuck in the ground, his hands resting on the pommel.

Beside him, Soren lounged in the grass, his lithe body as restful as the night air. Every few minutes, the minstrel would manifest a small stone and toss it, allowing it to vanish before it hit the ground. After tossing another, he leaned his head back, so he looked straight into the sky, his throat fully exposed, and exhaled.

"We are supposed to be vigilant, brother Soren," Umumriel said. He did not let his gaze wander from the house of Delacruz.

"This is vigilant, brother. I am like a cat, ready to spring at a moment's notice." Though it seemed impossible, Soren's body relaxed further, even sinking slightly beneath the earth. "This is a dark place, we should be doing something." He gazed into the broken homes, seeing something Umumriel could not.

"There are others fighting those fights, Soren. We were tasked with watching *this* house."

"The house still stands. Unmoving." Now his body tensed and he sat up, robes flowing over his shoulders. "We were meant for more."

Umumriel arched an eyebrow. "Careful, brother. Your words verge on pride." Ever since Umumriel had been promoted, receiving his second set of wings and the Blade of Good Faith, things had been a little more tense between them.

As if reading his thoughts, Soren stood and stretched his wings, a single set ten feet in span. A staff grew from the ground, and he grabbed it, using it to point. "There, the corner of Fontana and Fifth. A young man was gunned down in that very spot just a week ago. His murderer is still here, in one of these houses. And there..." He pointed toward an alley where a rusted-out Chevrolet sat. "If it were the middle of the afternoon, two men would be standing there, using children to pawn their drugs, further corrupting this neighborhood. And there..." He used the staff to gesture toward a shabby house with a yard of weeds. "Four women live there, seven children between them. They sell themselves, and they sell..." His face soured as he spoke through gritted teeth. "We are wasted here."

"Wasted doing what we were called to do?"

With a grunt, Soren let the staff vanish. "This is not what I wished to be called to do."

"Sometimes it is the small things that matter greatly, brother. I don't pretend to know the machinations at work, but I can see the house of Delacruz is alone in this dark place. All that is standing against the enemy establishing a hold here."

Earlier in the day, before the sun set and the stars shone, Umumriel had watched the Delacruz family playing on the front lawn, the father and his two sons throwing a football, the older boy clapping each time his younger brother made a catch. He watched as the mother and her toddler daughter planted colorful flowers in the dark soil next to the house. Soren watched too, but only saw the dangers lurking. Umumriel feared Soren never fully trusted in the Most High's plan.

"The house is one of so many. Outnumbered. All I want to do is even the odds." Soren turned to Umumriel. "You were granted the Blade of Good Faith. Surely it aches for you to use it."

Umumriel took his weight from the sword and hefted it. "I'd like to think it was created for me specifically because I would know *when* to use it—" The sword started glowing red.

Soren spun. "Show yourself."

From an alley down the street, a jackal stalked. Though hunched, he stood taller than any man, covered in matted fur, membranous locust wings flittering on his back. "You want to even the odds, then come for me, *brother*," his voice a hiss.

A half-smile rose on Soren's face, and his eyes lit up. Within seconds his staff had reformed, and he clutched it with a tight grip.

Umumriel put a hand on his shoulder. "He is not threatening the house."

"What are we to be vigilant for, brother, if not this beast?" Soren showed his teeth in something between a snarl and a smile. "I will not let more ruin befall this place."

The jackal hissed. "This neighborhood is mine."

"It's not yours yet," Umumriel said. He could feel the armor manifesting up his legs, up his hips, and over his chest. Pauldrons in the shape of lions' heads formed over his shoulders. He tried to will it away, but his own emotions betrayed him, and soon he was fully donned in shining plate. The Blade of Good Faith did ache in his hands as he scowled at the beast, the pinnacle of a corrupted elohim. Silently, he admonished himself. *Stay vigilant.* He wouldn't let this beast sway him from his mission.

Spittle flew from between the jackal's glistening fangs. "This neighborhood is ruin, the grief of these humans too strong to overcome. Their lives forfeited to me and my pleasures." He glared at Soren. "There's nothing you can do, *brother*."

Lifting his staff above his head, Soren sang. He sang a song of the Most High. He sang a song of His holy judgment, and he sang a song of His servants, sent to enforce. As he sung, his staff shifted into a spear, white-hot lightning sizzling down the shaft. The jackal flinched, withdrawing down the alley on winds stirred by his wings, speeding him out of reach.

"Soren!" But Umumriel's yell was all vanity. Soren had already left his post. Spear in hand, he flashed forth to chase the jackal.

From blocks away, Umumriel watched as bits of the neighborhood lost to darkness lit up as Soren loosed his lightning spear and flashed at blinding speed to catch his quarry. In the flashes appeared glimpses of the jackal as he lurched up and over houses, or pounced through them like they weren't even there, masterfully keeping out of Soren's range.

Umumriel tightened his grip on his sword.

Now further away, from behind a run-down two-story, Soren flew up, his wings beating. He scanned below him until he locked on the jackal. He threw another spear. It burned through the darkness like a streak of white lightning. In a one-on-one, the jackal would have had the advantage. If he was hoping to take them one at a time, he would have long since attacked Soren.

No. He *wanted* them to chase.

The thought made Umumriel's armor recede. He narrowed his eyes as the jackal again appeared between two ruined houses, pointed its muzzle to the air, and howled. Soren, floating above, recoiled at the sound and sprang toward it—an epic game of cat and mouse that left Umumriel gaping.

When he smelled the smoke, Umumriel knew he was too late. With a yell, he spun toward the Delacruz house. Grey clouds billowed from one corner, between them licks of fire lapped. Two men ran off into the night, one carrying a gas can. He admonished himself. What good was staying at his post if he didn't stay vigilant?

"Soren!" he yelled, but his companion was much too far and much too distracted to be of any help.

He rushed to the house, but with the accelerant used, the fire had spread too quickly for him to put it out in time to save the family. It would take far too long for the firefighters to arrive, if they arrived at all.

Public servants, brave as they were, often avoided this neighborhood, considering it already a lost cause.

Without wasting more time, Umumriel flew through the walls of the Delacruz house; they impeded him no more than would a slight breeze. As he feared, the flames had already burned to the ceiling, slithering like snakes of orange, red, and yellow. If he didn't get the family out, one or more might be lost. If only Soren had stayed…

No time for what ifs.

Umumriel shot through the ceiling and found himself in the room of the younger kids. Praise the Most High, both still slept safely, even as the smoke oppressed the small space. The toddler lay in her crib in footie pajamas, folded like a gift. The boy, older, but still a child, lay on his back, his racecar sheets pulled up to his neck.

"Awaken and be gone from the flames," Umumriel said, making his voice manifest, but the boy did not stir.

The smoke continued filling the room.

Umumriel stood, indecisive for but a moment, before manifesting himself physically. He made himself to look like a firefighter, blackened yellow coat and black helmet. The Blade of Good Faith appeared as a pickhead axe hanging from his belt.

He shook the boy.

The boy's eyes went wide.

"Awaken and be gone from the flames!"

The boy stared at him. *Steady yourself, Umumriel. Time is of the essence.* He lowered himself until he was face to face with the boy and spoke with a soft urgency. "Quickly! Wake your family and get out."

The boy's eyes darted around the room, and he shot up. "Yes, sir."

First, the boy went toward his sister's crib, covering his face and coughing, but Umumriel stopped him. "I will get your sister. She will be out by the mailbox. Wake the rest. Tell them she is safe."

The boy nodded and ran from the room, staying low and yelling his father's name. Umumriel took a second to marvel at the boy's bravery. Then he hastened down the stairs, hampered by his physical form. The little girl slept cradled in his arms.

The fire trucks did finally arrive, the sounds of sirens waking most of the neighbors, who now stood outside at a safe distance, the heat too intense.

For the rest of the night, the Delacruz house burned, lighting up the neighborhood.

After, the Delacruz family huddled beside the fire truck, the mother holding her daughter, the two boys hugging against her legs, and the father vigorously shaking the hand of one of the firefighters. "Thank you, thank you," he said. "If you hadn't come in and woken us, we would all be dead."

The firefighter stared at him. "We never entered the house, sir."

"But…"

Soren stood next to Umumriel. "The whole family made it out safe."

Umumriel nodded. They stood beside the ruin of the Delacruz house. It was little more than wet cinders. Black bones reaching out into the night, dotted by small red flares when the wind blew. Even the freshly planted flowers in the front yard were now dark and withered.

"That is all that matters," Soren said. "But I'm still sorry, brother. I should have—"

"It's not all that matters."

"They can rebuild…"

Umumriel shook his head. "Look around, brother. There are many empty houses here that are already little more than ruins. If those weren't rebuilt, why would this one be? No. The Delacruz family will move away, taking their light with them. Come, we must report our failure."

"It is all mine now, brothers," hissed the jackal from somewhere behind them.

Umumriel simply spread his wings and took flight toward the heavens.

He didn't argue.

The beast was right.

TARIK OF KADIKOY

M.B. EVERETT & ALTHEA DAMGAARD

"And now let us rejoice! For Cemil of Istanbul has joined us in the kingdom of the Most High." In the arena, my fellow elohim raised their voices in song, and I raised my voice with them in celebration.

"The minstrel told the story well," the warrior beside me said, the breeze flowing through his auburn mane. "He had a certain *gayret*—as Cemil might say."

"Well, you should know. You were there," I replied, turning to face him.

I knew of Zouzel—the guardian who watched over this Cemil, but why had he invited me to this telling? Today was the first day I'd ever spoken to him. Surely, he hadn't done it to boast.

"I asked you to come here because you've been called into that story, Miendel. I've been asked to take you to Kadikoy in Istanbul. You are to help Tarik, Cemil's friend. Cemil and those in his fellowship have been praying for Tarik. In response, the Most High has authorized your assignment."

I was humbled to be given another mission. My assignments of late had been far from fruitful. The humans handle their own choices, but it was sometimes challenging not to feel my charge's failures as my own. I prayed this assignment would have better results.

"Cemil is meeting with Tarik this very morning," Zouzel continued. "Shall we go?"

I agreed, and we made our way toward one of the west gates.

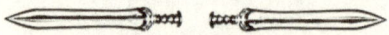

Soon, we dropped through the sky side-by-side, an invigorating sensation that would never grow old. We passed through the puffy white cumulus clouds. The morning sun shone from the east. Below, a city divided by a large waterway grew as we approached.

Slowing to a stop, we hovered above the street-side patio of a coffee shop on a cobblestone street lined with cafes and other storefronts. Steam climbed out of the sewer grates, down the historic city's ancient thoroughfare, and the song of gulls filled the air. Only a quarter of the shop's tables had customers. Two young men sat at a wire mesh table against the fence surrounding the shop's border. A cat brushed against the leg of the table.

The man we faced sat in his chair with a straight posture and a smile radiating from his eyes. "Is that Cemil?"

Zouzel smiled and said, "It is."

I shifted to observe the young man addressing Cemil. Despite the day's damp and chilly start, this man wore a tight, short-sleeved shirt highlighting a muscular frame underneath. Intricate designs covered his arms from his knuckles into his sleeves. His right arm displayed a detailed scene of Eve handing the fruit to Adam. His left showed a man's interpretation of a choir of elohim. The tattoos continued flowing up the man's body under the shirt and onto his neck with impressive depictions of leaves, vines, and flowers. From there, it continued up and around his shaved head, leaving only his face free of ink. Absent of pictures, his face was not without embellishment. A large silver ring impaled the thickest part of the man's lower lip. Both ears contained large white circles stretching his earlobes to five times their original size.

"That is Tarik, whom you will work with," Zouzel said. "He is the most accomplished tattoo artist in all of Istanbul. He is a man of renown in the counterculture here."

Attempting to understand, I concentrated on my arms and created similar patterns of my own, but felt nothing from the experience.

Perhaps because it could be changed at my will? His was a more permanent commitment.

I shifted my attention back to the conversation.

"… and you are so happy, so carefree, how?" Tarik gestured with his cup.

A mischievous grin spread across Cemil's face, and he laughed a hearty belly laugh. "What do you mean?"

Tarik scrunched his nose and grunted. "Bruh, you laugh now. I've not heard you laugh in years."

Cemil took a deep breath and looked around like a mouse scanning for cats. Leaning forward, he raised an eyebrow and whispered words even I could not discern.

"Man, I can't hear you." Tarik chuckled.

"I've given my life to Christ." This time, he spoke loud enough for others nearby to hear and look their way. His voice lowered when he added, "I've become a Christian. You know what that means. For me. Here."

"A Christian?" Tarik said in a hushed tone, his words underpinned by disbelief. "I thought you'd given up hocus-pocus religions."

Tarik swatted at the cat, which had raised up and kneaded its paws against his leg. Pushing it further away, he looked at his friend.

"I'm sorry for being distracted." He shot a glance at the cat now sitting a few feet away, licking a paw as if it had done nothing.

"Miendel, be vigilant," Zouzel said.

I engaged a discernment effect and studied the cat more closely. As I did, a tingle trickled down my horns. It was the eyes that gave it away. Instead of the normal yellow-gold or orange-gold, with the distinctive cat-eye-shaped pupil, this cat had eyes of solid black—the total absence of light. The cat, or rather the unholy elohim, met my eyes and sauntered under a table, leaving the material realm and revealing his spiritual form as a leopard.

Zouzel manifested a sword and shield, I created twin hammers, and together we bristled our lion manes defiantly toward the beast.

The leopard lackadaisically stepped aside before speaking in a guttural tone. "What are you up in arms about? I crossed no lines, violated no boundaries. Just look at Tarik. Consider his life. He is not your King's, but my prince's."

We both took one step toward the horror. Together, we could dispatch him if he threatened to interfere again. The prayers and my subsequent orders gave me all the right I needed to defend Tarik from undue influence.

The leopard tilted his head at our lack of interest in discussion and angled back, a wary tension rippling in his muscles. "You play where you're not welcome, brothers. He is not yours. This will be reported." He loped away down the street.

My attention was drawn back to the men by a rattling as Tarik set his small cup down against the saucer. He bit back a curse when the coffee sloshed over the rim.

"Your tremors are getting worse, aren't they?" Cemil asked.

Tarik flexed his hand. "Eh, a little. I thought I ruined a man's ink yesterday. If it gets worse, I'll have to give it up."

"The drugs or the art?"

"Maybe both. Without the ink, I'd not be able to afford the drugs." Tarik smiled and waved the notion away.

Cemil's face went wan, and he licked his lips. "That lifestyle is killing you."

"You're my mother?"

"I'm your friend."

Tarik looked at his watch. "I'm late for a client." He sipped up the last of the thick coffee, then rose from his seat.

"I have more to tell you, but it can wait." Cemil smiled and stood. "Perhaps when work is done, we can meet again?"

Tarik nodded, tossed some money on the table, and headed down the street.

Zouzel grunted. "Go with Tarik. We'll reconvene if he and Cemil meet after work."

I nodded and turned my attention toward Tarik, who had made it past a couple of shops down the street. I rose to fly after him, remaining close, but at a level where I could see the surroundings better in both the material and spiritual realm. As an extra measure, I engaged a detection effect—if the leopard returned to stalk us from the shadows, I would sense him.

This assignment had all the earmarks of another failure. The world's trappings already had a firm grip on Tarik. How many times had my best efforts been spurned by those humans I had served? Regardless, I would contend for Tarik, that he might hear Cemil's testimony without distraction.

I followed Tarik down the busy streets of the Kadikoy district. He walked with his hands in his pockets and nodded to those that hailed him. They were mostly other members of the growing counterculture of Istanbul on the Asian side of the Bosphorus.

A young lady stopped Tarik for a picture. He forced a smile when she posed and held up her phone. He resumed walking as soon as she had a couple of shots captured.

Tarik's phone rang with a heavy-metal guitar riff. "Yeah?" he answered, listening to an angry voice, which I could not quite make out. "I'm about there."

"I'm sorry. I got hung up." Tarik held the phone away from his face and stared at it with an ugly, scrunched-up look of disbelief while the tirade hit a fevered pitch.

"I'm a couple minutes away." His voice rose to a near shout. "*Yeah, I'm sorry. If you want to leave, leave.*"

Dropping the phone in the back pocket of his jeans, he continued down the street, a little slower than before. Stopping at a storefront, he studied his reflection in the window, tilting his head right then left, his brow furrowed. He rubbed the back of his neck to ease the tension I could see in his muscles.

"So Cemil's a Christian."

I wondered how that would affect their friendship.

Tarik fingered a tiny clear package of white powder he had pulled from his front pocket, then tossed it in the trashcan before opening the door to the shop named Assassin's Tattoos. This caused me to smile. Maybe he'd considered Cemil's words. There might be reason to hope.

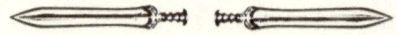

My elation did not last long after we stepped into the shop.

A man in his twenties jumped to his feet when Tarik entered, the veins proud on his neck and his fists clenched. *"You're late! I've got practice in a couple hours!"* he said with an American accent. An unclean spirit sat on his shoulder, stoking his temper.

"Patience," I whispered to Tarik's spirit. Nothing proved he heard, but a slight shrug of his shoulders released some tension in the knotted muscles at the back of his neck.

"Only a couple of minutes. We've plenty of time to finish. It should only take half an hour. Come on back." Tarik's smile did not reach his eyes.

"I recommend you let your sportsman calm down now," I addressed the unclean spirit. "My charge is about to perform a delicate operation on him that could easily go awry."

The unclean spirit stared at me, but did not move from the athlete's shoulder.

The young man exhaled. "OK, sure. Sorry. I just want the best. I want *your* work."

Tarik only nodded as they made their way to the back. He waved at a comfortable chair, which the young man sat in eagerly. Tarik sat on the stool next to the chair and picked up his tattoo gun.

"There's a party tonight. Our entire team will be there."

Without responding, Tarik flipped down his magnifying glasses and put the gun on the young man's arm. His hand remained steady, and the ink gun buzzed.

"You know most of them. A couple more want to meet you."

Still no response. Tarik was an artist at work and could not be distracted.

He worked for twenty-five minutes without talking. Music with a heavy bass beat was the only sound besides the gun. The unclean spirit whispered in the athlete's ear now and again, but did not interfere with the tattooing process.

When Tarik finished, he stood and put the gun back on the bench, removing his glasses with the other hand. "You remember how to take care of it?"

"Yeah, sure. Say Tarik, sorry about getting angry with you. Um, how's it look?"

"It looks ok. I think you'll like it."

For being so renowned, Tarik's humility about his gift amazed me—another promising trait.

"How much do I owe you?" the futbol player asked.

"Seventeen thousand lira."

"Right. Here." The young man handed over a roll of paper money, which Tarik put in his pocket without counting.

"There's a little extra in there. I know you don't tip much in Turkey, but in the U.S. we do."

"Thank you."

"So, you coming tonight? It's at the Hookah. Backroom." The young man shuffled his feet as if something bothered him.

"Maybe."

"There'll be girls and lots of booze. Dancing. Music."

"Maybe." Tarik's facial expression didn't change. A bell rang. "My next customer is here. Thank you."

Maybe this assignment would turn out better than I expected.

Tarik saw six more clients that day, all Turkish futbol players. He hung up his apron and stepped out of the studio in the late afternoon. The street bustled with pedestrian traffic.

"Tarik! You done for the day?" Cemil hollered from across the street.

"Yes." He flexed his hands. His right hand trembled from holding the gun for so long, but his art had come out flawless.

Zouzel was with Cemil, and we greeted each other with a nod. I informed him that there hadn't been any more trouble since the leopard this morning.

"Would you like to get a bite to eat? I missed lunch." Cemil smiled. "I have more news to share."

Tarik looked at his gold wristwatch, the sun reflecting sharply off the bezel's facets. "More news? After your last news, what else could there be?" When Cemil's smile dimmed, Tarik gave him a friendly clap on the shoulder. "Oh, I'm just kidding you, abi. Sure, that might be good. I don't know when I'll eat tonight if I don't do it now. I have a futbol game and then maybe a party."

"Where's the game?"

"Euro-side. Want to walk the bridge? Get a fish sandwich?"

Cemil shook his head. "I have a better place in mind, but near the bridge. Ok? If we hurry, we can catch the next ferry to get there faster."

Tarik nodded and shrugged.

They walked west, and Cemil pulled out his phone, making a couple of quick calls.

"You should stay away from that party." Cemil's voice cut through the silence between the men.

A young woman interrupted any reply as she called Tarik's name and ran up to him. "How have you been?" She smiled as if they had history.

Tarik smiled, raising his right eyebrow. He studied her. "Good. How about you?"

Cemil said, "Introduce me to your friend."

Tarik took in his friend's mischievous smile. "Of course, um, Cemil, this is, uh, um—"

She stopped smiling. "Tam bir terbiyesizsin—you jerk." Her expression darkened and her hand clenched her bag tighter. She appeared to want to say more, but turned and walked in the opposite direction, as if she had just received the worst of insults.

Tarik turned to Cemil and arched a brow. "You did that on purpose."

"You should give that up, too. You are hurting in loneliness, my friend."

Tarik chuckled. "Bruh, of course I'm alone with *you* for a wingman." Tarik waved in the direction the girl had gone. His shoulders were hunched enough to reveal his unease.

"Uh, sex. Like drugs—" Cemil broke off, as if struggling to put his thoughts together. "You are trying to fill a void. A hole. Man, you need to fill it up with something else."

They made their way onto the ferry and chose seats on the covered second deck.

"How do you know this?" Tarik said, sneering. "Did your new church tell you?" He winced when Cemil's brow furrowed. "I'm sorry. I did it again. Here, tell me about why you became a Christian."

"I'll tell you at dinner." Cemil swallowed. "*We'll* tell you at dinner."

"We'll?"

Cemil's smile touched his eyes, and they sparkled with mischief.

Tarik shifted in his seat and they both sat silently for the rest of the ferry ride.

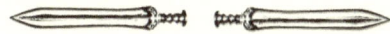

Cemil walked up to a young lady standing near the restaurant's entrance and put his hand on her shoulder. "Tarik, this is Meryem."

Meryem wore the traditional headscarf women favored in Turkey. A holy warrior, whom I recognized, accompanied her.

"I am pleased to meet you." Tarik smiled with his mouth, but he scrutinized how the two stood comfortably close. "How do you know Cemil?"

The woman stared at Tarik. His piercings and tattoos stood out against the other clientele entering the building. Her jaw had grown slack.

Cemil gave her a discreet nudge. His cheeks flushed.

Meryem shook herself and did her best to smile. "I am pleased to meet you, too. Cemil has talked about you so much…" She glanced down and then added, "I met Cemil while working with our church doing earthquake relief in Antioch."

Tarik nodded. To keep a good read on the situation, I re-engaged my discernment effect. Thankfully, Tarik didn't seem bothered by the young woman's reaction. He seemed to still be distracted with estimating just how close Meryem and Cemil were.

I turned my attention to my allies. "Valoel!" I addressed the warrior with Meryem. "Haven't seen you since we were initiated as fledglings. I see you have become a guardian!"

"It has been a while." Valoel nodded. "But I can never forget your bravery in the face of certain defeat during our training mission. Remembering your example has strengthened me to do likewise on more than one occasion. I'm glad I can thank you now."

Zouzel and Valoel together would be a formidable duo should we face any threat. Despite being in a land hostile to the Son's truth, I felt a sense of comfort.

They rode a lift to the restaurant at the top of the building. A host led them to a table on the terrace. The few customer reactions and whispers were more dramatic than Meryem's. He may have been revered in the streets of Kadikoy, but not here.

I scanned the room for threats. A second domain bear next to a businessman in the VIP area caught my eye. Serpentine hoods fanned out from his neck and shoulders. Otherwise, only the occasional unclean spirit moved among the clientele.

Once seated, Tarik cleared his throat. "This is much nicer than a street-stall fish sandwich."

Cemil smiled. "I thought this would work better for such a special meal, meeting new people, and making announcements. I wanted to view the Old Church as it is—in a backward way—a symbol of my life, and it could be a symbol of your life, too." He waved at the view of the Hagia Sophia, one of the oldest churches in the world, though it was now a mosque.

"What do you mean?" Tarik arched a brow as he turned to take in the view.

"Announcements first. Meryem and I are to be married." Cemil's eyes twinkled, as did Meryem's. "And I'd like you to stand for me at our wedding as my sağdıç, or as our pastor calls it, my best man."

I had been watching and discerning Tarik. In the lift, it had seemed he concluded the two were serious, but I don't think he suspected the engagement. He downplayed his surprise, but only managed a forced a smile. "Uh, sure."

"Will you not share our joy, my friend?" Cemil asked, a hint of disappointment in his voice.

Tarik shook his head. "I'm so sorry." He jumped from his seat and pulled his friend to his feet, embracing him in a hug that he held for a moment. He then turned and spread his arms to his friend's fiancé, and she rose. They gave each other a proper hug and a kiss on each cheek.

"May your lives together be full of the blessings of happiness. Of course, I'd be honored to be your sağdıç."

I had little time to celebrate. A second domain demagogue rode into the dining area on a dark steed flanked by two serpents, each comparable to me in strength—one resembling an earthly serpent except for the wings sprouting from his neck; the other bearing the arms and torso of a scale-covered man, though his head and lower body were serpentine. The demagogue stretched out his four wings as he lay his gaze heavily on me. The serpents slithered in opposite directions, making a circuit among the guests, sowing hatred and judgment against Tarik.

"You don't want him eating here with you," the winged serpent hissed into the ears of those to our right.

The man-serpent glided to the left, repeating at each table the words, "Haram. Forbidden."

The demagogue smiled as if pleased with the situation. "The leopard, Kataskopos, reported your presence in Kadikoy. Tarik belongs back home, where he is respected. And if he has any doubt about it, we are here to remind him." He began singing a song of contempt and wove it with what the serpents were hissing at the diners.

"This man defiles our tables.
This is not his place.
He mocks Allah's creation.
He marks his own disgrace!"

The diners' whispers remained quiet, but they glanced in Tarik's direction. It hindered the moment. Tarik sat rubbing his hands on his pants with his gaze lowered, now that the moment of sharing hugs of congratulation was over. The server remained pleasant while taking drink orders and handing them menus, but he did not look directly at Tarik, as he did with Cemil and Meryem. Tarik asked for a water, then planted his attention on the menu.

A demagogue's skill at unifying prejudice was a threat we could not dismiss. If we didn't silence him and the serpents, the tension in the room might become so palpable it might sour Tarik against religions in general, ruining the chance of him truly hearing any invitation to the Kingdom Cemil may offer. Worse yet, a guest might be motivated to take action.

I squared my shoulders as I locked gazes with the demagogue. "Tarik *will* be allowed to hear all that his friend wishes to share." Without hesitation, I manifested a hammer in each hand as I threw myself at the serpent closest to Tarik.

The serpent evaded me with his wings and swerved his sinewy body. A clean miss. I flung out my arms, in part to keep my footing, and my left hammer clacked against the serpent's teeth—lucky shot— and I backpedaled to recover. I could now see the man-serpent. He had made his way back to the bear and was whispering to the businessman. Apparently, the bear had consented to this influence. I hoped it was the only consent the bear offered in this fight.

As I circled with the serpent, the businessman glared at Tarik and waved for a server. He added a couple of snaps when one headed his way.

The demagogue wove fury into his song and held his scepter high, like a rallying beacon.

> *"He dares to draw near*
> *This open fāsiq.*
> *You can't eat with him.*
> *Cast him out, quick!"*

With the contempt already spreading through the room, this did not bode well. The bear, catching a taste of the song's fury, moved toward me with clear intentions. I danced to my right to avoid a venomous projectile spat from one of the serpents.

Zouzel, to my great relief, spoke up. "Valoel! This religious hatred being stirred could just as easily threaten our wards should they be heard sharing their belief. You are free to engage!"

Zouzel's strength was more on par with the bear and the demagogue. Defeat would have been swift if I had to fight the serpents *and* the bear alone.

The bear roared and charged toward me, but Zouzel thrust himself into the bear's path, shield in front of him.

The businessman rose and met the staff member—maybe the manager, judging by his dress.

The serpent near me struck, seizing my moment of distraction, but I launched away while swinging a hammer, striking his exposed head. This was enough, and he slumped to the ground.

I heard Zouzel grunt as the bear slammed into him. The beating of his four wings as he pushed back against the bear assured me he remained in the fight.

Valoel had manifested a shield and staff and marched toward the demagogue, who held his scepter forward, as if accepting a challenge.

Now free to help my allies, I held out my hammers toward Zouzel and Valoel, extending some of my strength to bolster their defenses. I also yoked myself to them to share the burden of any wounds they may suffer.

My support was just in time, as the bear slammed Zouzel to the floor with a momentous strike. A portion of the resulting wounds wracked my body. I thanked Elyon that Zouzel did not have to suffer it all. Just the portion I shared was immense.

Zouzel rolled, but I lost sight of him as I attempted to dodge the venom spat by the remaining serpent. My evasion failed. Sharing my strength with my companions had diminished my own defenses. The venom spattered across my chest and it burned deeply, draining me.

The serpent needed to go. I charged forward with a swing. He dodged well, but I managed to redirect my follow-through around to clap both hammers together into his torso, front and back. The serpent sank into what looked like a defensive coil until his head flopped back, and he lay splayed on the ground.

Zouzel had regained his feet and taken a defensive stance, but light leaked from his neck and shoulder where the bear's heavy claws had raked across him. Darkness vented from a nasty slash on the bear's shoulder. Their fight hadn't been entirely one-sided, but the bear decidedly had the upper hand. His expectedly high strength and durability were accompanied by unexpected speed.

Valoel danced with the demagogue, who wore an ever-widening grin as he sang with increasing anticipation.

I dug deep into my reserves and found the strength to charge at the bear. The movement felt slowed, and the bear knocked away my hammers harmlessly. My attack, however, was not meant to harm the bear as much as leave him open to Zouzel, which it did. With the bear's attention on me, Zouzel slammed his sword into the bear's chest.

The bear responded by pinning Zouzel under his girth once again. The sword sunk deeper into the bear's chest as the bear's weight bore down on it.

The bear roared with fury. He was still in this fight. I maneuvered to his rear for an advantage, but stumbled back as fresh pain wracked my body. My yoking effect had transferred some impact from a fresh blow Valoel took from the demagogue. I looked over to see Valoel recover from the hit and resume his strong defensive posture. The demagogue's greater size was only magnified by the minstrel being on horseback. Valoel was not overwhelmed, however. His abilities and skills as a guardian negated such advantages.

I snapped my attention back to Zouzel as he roared with indignation, with his sword held high. He had somehow escaped his predicament. I seized the opportunity and brought both my hammers on the bear's exposed back simultaneously. The bear turned to swipe at me, only to find Zouzel's blade thrust clean through his neck. The bear slumped to the floor, groaning—a dark plume rising from the wound.

Zouzel pointed his sword at the demagogue. "You're next," his voice ringing with determination.

Seeing his companions scattered in defeat across the dining area floor, the demagogue ceased his singing and stepped his horse away to the side. "I concede for now. Besides, I have done enough."

I looked at Zouzel, who nodded in approval and let his sword and shield vanish in acceptance of the surrender. The demagogue turned and galloped away, presumably back across the river.

Zouzel was wise not to continue the fight. Tarik was our priority, and time was precious.

Little had transpired in the natural. Several guests stirred and looked at Tarik, but without the minstrel's influence they were less likely to act out. Tarik sat hunched, though he lowered his menu enough to look at Cemil. I needed to reassure him. I walked to the table and leaned over Tarik, whispering, "All will be well. Enjoy the time with your friend."

Tarik rolled his shoulders.

I looked to Valoel, who had convinced the businessman it would prove better to have dinner elsewhere. The man paid for his drink and strode stiffly into the interior portion of the restaurant.

Turning back, I saw Zouzel hovering over Cemil, who had loosened up and was elaborating on the details of the wedding.

I remained standing, but in an easy stance. I released the effects strengthening my allies and re-initiated my detection. All was clear, I could now turn my attention to the conversation without fear of immediate interruption.

Tarik leaned forward. "Why a small ceremony? Cemil, your family is so large."

"Neither family approves of our newfound Christianity." A sad smile spread his lips. "But that price is well worth it." He straightened his back. "Our church family will be there. They have been more welcoming than you would believe."

"How so?" Tarik folded his menu.

Cemil leaned on the table with his hands clasped. "I don't know how to explain it exactly. We don't make much money, but we don't lack for anything. When Meryem's family would not allow her to live in their house anymore, a family from the church took her in. I spend much of my free time at their home, too, and they have been a great source of encouragement to both of us. Like adoptive parents."

"We left religion together," Tarik said.

Cemil smiled and nodded. "Yes, my friend, and do you remember why?"

Tarik shrugged. "It is all obligation. Prayers, alms, fasting—because that was what we were told to do."

"But this is different," Cemil said, excitement in his voice. "I don't follow Christ because I have to. I don't go to worship because it is required. I don't give myself, my time, and my meager resources because it is commanded. I do it because I love Him. This time there is love."

Meryem added, "Because He loves us so much more than anything we can do for Him." Valoel had returned to her side.

Tremors shook Tarik's hand when he picked up his glass. He sloshed water onto his hand and the table. A curse slipped out as he set the glass down hard.

Meryem cleaned up the water with quiet efficiency.

Tarik dried his hand, then clasped his hands in his lap. "Sorry." He cleared his throat.

Cemil placed a firm, reassuring hand on his arm. The tremor eased.

"I don't feel loved." Tarik rubbed his thighs.

"He loves you, Tarik," Cemil said in a calm, level voice. "He wants to spend eternity with you."

Tarik looked down and flexed his hands. He wiped tears from his cheeks. "I do not look like a Christian."

Cemil took a deep breath and smiled, "My friend, Jesus looks at your heart, and it is as beautiful as the sunrise to Him."

The three fell into a tense quiet until their meals arrived at the table.

Dinner ended, but I needed to keep Tarik with Cemil longer. Not only for him, but so the three of us could affirm one another and recuperate. The fight had taken a toll on us all. I had not suffered direct wounds, but I was weak from sharing the burden of theirs.

"Let's walk the grounds of *Magale Ekklesia*. That's what the Byzantines called it. Did you know that? It simply means the *Great Church*." Cemil waved in the church's direction when the three of them stepped back onto the street.

"I've got a game to go to." Tarik shrugged in a way that made me think he wasn't sure what he would do.

Tarik stuck his hands in his pockets and looked at his feet.

I whispered "fellowship" to Tarik's spirit, encouraging him to stay longer with his friend. "Please, Elyon, let him stay," I prayed aloud.

"Yeah, I guess I can hang for an hour or so," Tarik said after a long minute.

"Thank you!" Whether the Most High directly intervened in this instant or not, He had sent me to Tarik, which deserved thanks.

"Great!" Cemil's face relaxed.

The three of them walked the short distance to the vast old mosque. We floated right behind them, three elohim of the Most High. Some lesser unholy minions warily passed along the way, but none dared address us.

The ancient structure dominated the view ahead. It was nigh evening, and a flood of tourists headed for dinner in the restaurant district we had just left.

When they arrived at the park in front of Hagia Sophia, Tarik asked, "Why here?"

"Hmmm?" Cemil responded.

"Why did you want to come here? It's a mosque, and you—you aren't…" Tarik looked around as he said it.

Cemil said in a hushed voice, "I told you why at dinner. It resembles my faith journey in reverse."

"It's beautiful," Meryem added. "I can't believe it is nearly fifteen hundred years old."

The three of them continued to walk, making small talk, and the crowds thinned to a point where they were all alone. The area had grown quiet, and the remaining tourists lingered out of earshot. My discerning effect allowed me to see Tarik wanted to ask something, so I leaned in to whisper to his spirit once again. "It's safe to ask."

Tarik glanced about, the tension in his shoulders relaxing some. "How did you become a Christian?"

"How or why?" his friend asked.

They sat on a bench. Meryem and Cemil studied each other, and some non-verbal communication passed between them. Zouzel and Valoel scanned the district for the enemy.

Tarik continued studying his shoes. He rubbed his hands together.

An urge to embrace him grew in me. I descended to his level, put my arms around him, and held my breast to him. Knowing the power of personal testimony—and having recently heard Cemil's—I spoke audibly this time, in Tarik's ear alone. "Ask him why."

Tarik leapt to his feet.

"What's the matter?" Cemil's brow creased, and he craned his neck forward. The tone of his question made Meryem sit up taller.

Tarik shook his head. "You won't believe me." His skin turned pale in the waning light of dusk.

"What?" Cemil relaxed a little.

"No, you will think I'm crazy."

Cemil chuckled. "No more than I do already, I promise."

Tarik snorted, but he grinned.

Meryem giggled, but bit it back, as if to show respect for the men's friendship.

"So, what happened? You looked like you saw a ghost." Cemil gave Tarik a warm smile.

Tarik blew out his cheeks. "Well..." He took a big breath. "I felt warm, not from the inside, but the outside... and then I heard a voice."

While Meryem and Cemil exchanged glances, I took in Zouzel's expression of joy.

"And what did that voice say?" Cemil enunciated each word in the sentence, and Meryem's face lit up with excitement.

"It told me to ask you why," Tarik said. "Am I crazy?"

Meryem grabbed Cemil's hand. "Go ahead. He needs to hear it. I'll be ok. I'll pray."

"Sit back down." Cemil patted the spot vacated by his friend.

Tarik glanced about, but took the seat with shoulders hunched.

Cemil paused a moment before launching into his story. "A year ago, I was in a very dark place. This morning, I told you that the drugs were going to kill you and then later I told you to give up your hook-up lifestyle. I told you because I know firsthand where those lifestyles lead. I fought depression and nearly lost."

"You didn't do drugs," Tarik interrupted.

"I hid it well. After a night at the clubs, I woke up with another partner I didn't know. I felt empty and trashy. I was broke—spending everything on drugs, booze, that life. Checking my clock, I knew I would have to hurry to get to my job. My boss had given me a final warning about being late. That day's job was on this side, so I ran to the ferry and stood at the rail as we crossed. Did you know I can't swim? Halfway across the Bosphorus, I jumped in out of desperation to end it all."

"What? You never told me! I'd have helped you." Tarik turned his full attention to Cemil and grabbed his arm.

"How, by telling me I shouldn't be depressed? Maybe I should try other drugs or different partners? No, my friend. I needed something deeper to put my hope in. I woke up in the hospital, my boss sitting at my bedside. I've no idea how he knew or how they contacted him. He told me I could keep my job if I went to his church with him." Tarik released Cemil's arm, but listened intently.

"I learned about İsa Mesih, the Son of God, and how He chose to pay the ultimate price to save even losers like me." Cemil paused and locked gazes with Tarik. "They told me I could accept Christ as my savior. I gave my life to Him. I've no regrets. Serving Him is the greatest joy in my life. He led me to Meryem. He has blessed me beyond measure."

Cemil glanced at Meryem before continuing. "Meryem and I have been praying for you every day, sometimes multiple times a day, that we'd be allowed to help you find Jesus."

Meryem's head was down with eyes closed. Her lips moved with silent words.

"Will you allow us to help you find Him?" Cemil asked.

Tarik sat in silence. A tear raced down his cheek. He rose from the bench and said in a calm breath, "You know me, what I've done. I'm not worth saving."

"Nobody can be on their own, my friend. Nobody."

I hesitated to do anything here. It must be his choice now. I scanned the park grounds, but all was quiet. My companions wore expressions of hope. They felt it, too. Tarik sat on the edge of accepting Christ's love.

"What do I have to do?" Tarik asked. He wiped tears from his eyes.

"Put your trust in Jesus as your Lord and Savior. Commit that you'll love Him above everything."

"What if I mess up? What if I do something wrong?"

"You ask for forgiveness and go on, trying to be better. Can I pray with you?"

Tarik stared at his arms and hands. He mouthed the words, "Look at me. I'm not good enough." Shaking his head, he said. "Cemil, thank you. I'm not quite there yet. I want to think about it."

I looked up at Zouzel and feared his shocked expression was a mirror of my own. Tarik was so close. Cemil's testimony was exceptional.

"Oh, Tarik, please. My friend—"

"You're begging. It isn't helping. I need to think about it. I'm going to walk to the game."

Tarik turned and walked away from Cemil and Meryem. Both froze with sad, stunned faces. I glanced at my elohim companions, who looked downcast. I gave them a sad nod and departed alone with Tarik into the dark, tree-lined paths surrounding Hagia Sophia.

"Hey."

Tarik froze and turned toward the voice in the darkness. A large man stepped into the light with the gleaming metal of a knife pointed at Tarik. I sensed an unholy presence lingering behind in the shadows of an alley.

"Nice watch. That's a Rolex Datejust. Right? It looks good in gold. Can I see it?"

"No, I don't think so." Tarik stepped back with his hands in a defensive position.

"You might as well come forward, Kataskopos." I beckoned to the shadows. "You have been watching us since the church."

"Mosque," the leopard corrected as he stepped into the light.

"For now," I replied, using a ministering spirit ability to manifest special hammers that would pummel the beast's will rather than his body. Even with discernment active, I could not read the leopard, but strength of will is a weakness of most of his kind. The hammers would also allow me to crush through any active defenses he might employ. I was ready for this fight.

"Lucky, to find a willing thug along our path." I prepared to parry and planned a couple of attacks if the beast charged. He studied my stance for a weakness, and I needed to keep him guessing.

He circled away from the mugger to force me to divide my attention. "Accept that your 'come to Jesus' moment failed. My lord did his work well, and this one knows where he belongs."

"You know, I'd rather not have to clean your blood off it," the mugger said, stepping closer. "Easier if you just handed it over."

I glanced at the mugger, and the leopard pounced. As planned, I lunged to the side and my hammers parried both sets of claws in turn, but he twisted and stretched his neck to plant his fangs into my side. His jaws tore back with fury, dragging out streams of light with them. Pluming white smoke clouded my vision, as I strove to ignore the pain.

I mustered enough strength to attempt to execute my previous plan. I swung up with one hammer at the leopard's exposed side. He had no time to turn, and the hammer struck well, folding him over at the torso. Seizing the opening, I brought the full weight of the second hammer down on the back of his neck, planting him firmly onto the street. He now lay still, his will broken.

"Please, İsa! Please help me," Tarik said. It was clear that the words felt foreign to him, but sincere.

The mugger leapt with the knife outstretched. Tarik turned to avoid it, but the knife caught his right arm.

"Help!" he screamed and slapped his left hand over the bleeding gash while stumbling backward to the ground. The mugger turned back and hovered over him, blood dripping from his knife.

I swung around a building and came back running as a human with a jacket that said POLIS.

The mugger fled as soon as he heard the steps and was already out of sight before I reached Tarik.

"Stay here. I'll get help." I ran back toward where we had left Cemil.

As soon as I was out of sight, I abandoned my embodiment and alerted Zouzel and Valoel. They spoke to Cemil and Meryem that Tarik needed help and they should run. It took them a few seconds to accept the thought, but run they did, and they found him bleeding on the ground.

"What happened?" Cemil said, cradling his friend.

"A man tried to take my watch. I said no and he sliced me," Tarik replied.

Meryem pulled out her phone, calling for aid.

"But Cemil… When he attacked me, I called to İsa for help. I didn't want to give up my watch. I know it's just a knockoff. But bruh, remember when you bought it for me? I couldn't lose it. And then I remembered what you said about how valuable I am to İsa Mesih. It made me think I might be, even if I am a fake.

"I'm ready to do it, Cemil. I'm ready to accept İsa Mesih," Tarik exclaimed. "I believe he can love me."

"You just did, my friend," Cemil told him, radiating a smile. He took his shirt off and wrapped it tightly around Tarik's arm. "You just did."

A smile spread across my face upon hearing those words. I let my head fall back, and dropped to my knees, relishing the relief flowing through me, even as light leaked from my wounds. Tarik had accepted the Son and would live to tell others.

"So be it, Brother." Zouzel offered his hand, but I embraced him instead.

We all accompanied Tarik to the hospital. Then, after all was settled, I saluted my companions and flew into the sky through an opened window into heaven. This was not a long-term assignment, and I had a *success* to report.

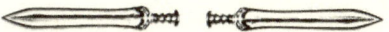

Not long after, a minstrel approached me to record the tale—the very same minstrel who told the story of Cemil! I will be honored to hear the same *gayret* when he sings the sequel. Praise be to the Most High for another entering His kingdom!

TO WIN THEIR HEARTS

NATHANIEL SORENSEN

My team and I arrived in the bishop's chambers to find a heated discussion underway.

"There have been *four* miracles, Your Excellency. Four! Two more than the number required for sainthood!" The excited man wore a simple black cassock. He looked to be in his mid-thirties, healthy, and not at peace.

"I am aware of the arithmetic, Father," responded the bishop from behind a modest desk. He was only sixty-two years old, but the lines accentuating his eyes indicated many years of service. "Nor do I dispute the supernatural nature of these visitations. However, I *do* still question who has been visiting us and why."

"But, Your Excellency, think of what it will mean to Tampico to have our own saint! It will bring such comfort and encouragement. It will inspire. Reverence and support for the Church from here to Monterrey — perhaps across all of northern Mexico —will be revitalized. Please, Your Excellency, our people need this!"

"I know what is at stake here," the bishop replied patiently. "Rome knows what is at stake here. Why did the Holy Father send me if not because the impact is significant? But Father Gonzalez, you must appreciate the need for care. The impact will be significant *either way.*

"What if this is not Brother Olmos returned by our Lord Christ to carry on with his work? What if our ancient enemy has some purpose here we have not yet uncovered? Imagine our embarrassment if we canonize a saint — only to find these visitations were not of God. How long would it then take us to rebuild trust in this community?"

"Your Excellency cannot be serious," Gonzalez replied, his voice strained with incredulity. "There have been seven visitations now and *all* of them have been a blessing! All those visited have come away encouraged. Three experienced a physical healing at the time of the encounter. The longer we wait, the more we look the fool in this matter."

The bishop sagged back into his chair as though his energy for maintaining an illusion of strength had given out. The younger man realized he had likely crossed a line and adopted a more submissive posture.

I looked up at the guardian standing behind the bishop's chair. He ministered gentle words of strength and reinforcement. Behind the words, though, I could see restrained frustration drawing back his lion's ears and tightening his eyes. Turning to my team, I gestured for Menateach, a ministering spirit, to assist the guardian. Menateach moved behind the desk and laid his hand on the bishop's shoulder to reinforce the man's spirit. The guardian caught my eyes with a silent *Thank you.*

Gonzalez dropped his eyes. "Forgive me, Your Excellency. I have sinned against you. I spoke in haste and pride. I recognize neither are of God."

The bishop returned his gaze to the man standing before his desk. "I forgive you, Father, and I *do* hear you. Please remember, His Excellency did not send me to *prove* a pioneer of our faith in this region has returned to us 400 years after his death. As the new bishop here has yet to be named, the Holy Father sent me to *investigate* this matter and provide pastoral stability for the community. I do not take your opinion lightly, but I am not convinced."

The bishop paused in thought. "Tell me, Father, how many new petitioners are coming to request blessing and to pray for miracles and provision?"

Gonzalez's enthusiasm returned. "This month, we are nearly a hundred a week beyond the usual count. Surely that must be considered good fruit."

"Perhaps. Perhaps. And what is the increase in those participating in Mass or entering preparation for baptism?"

Gonzalez searched the ceiling in thought. "This month?"

The bishop shrugged. "Since the visitations began."

"The first visitation was nearly a year and a half ago." Gonzalez counted slowly. "Our regular attendance at Mass has increased by ten to fifteen."

"Ten to fifteen percent?"

"People, Your Excellency," Gonzalez admitted with a sigh. "And nineteen more have entered the catechumenate than in the prior year."

"Not conclusive, I grant you," the bishop shrugged. "But telling, don't you think, Father?"

He continued without waiting for an answer. "If this truly is Brother Olmos — a man history describes as being intent not only on bringing the lost to Christ, but on equipping and training Aztec youth for ministry — if this were *really* him, wouldn't you expect him to increase interest in Christ more than in his own healing powers? There are too few instances yet to claim certainty, but if I am being honest, I have a desolation in my spirit when I think approvingly of these appearances."

The bishop sat up straight again and straightened his purple fascia. He leaned his elbows on the desk, the weariness passing from his posture. "May I assume you won't mind if I speak frankly?"

Gonzalez returned a curt nod. "I welcome it, Your Excellency."

"I respect your thoughts, and want to continue hearing them, but I was sent because His Excellency believes me capable of discerning the truth of this situation on my own."

At this, Gonzalez's mouth pursed, but he made no reply.

"What will be much harder for me," the bishop continued, "is bringing spiritual stability to this community without your help. I don't have your history here. You know these people and they know you. They respect you. Your peers respect you. From everything I've heard, you were an invaluable administrator to your previous bishop. It is taking us some time getting the archdiocese reorganized out of Monterrey, but I suspect you've heard you are on the short list to be ordained and appointed bishop here."

Gonzalez received the affirmation with silence and a touch of skepticism in his eyes. Perhaps he struggled to reconcile his contributions being ignored and complimented in nearly the same breath.

"This will go much smoother for both of us if I have your support. I know you *want* these visitations to be of God. Honestly, I do too. But you have let optimism be the leading voice in your heart on this. Perhaps you are still young enough to think that is the meaning of faith. My position refuses me that luxury. If you ever want to sit capably in this chair, you'll need to learn that sometimes God's most perfect plan involves not giving us what we want."

A quiet moment passed as each evaluated the other. The bishop leaned back again with a sigh and brought his fingertips together below his nose. "This is a hard thing. I know. Serving God in this role invites a continuing succession of hard things. If you find God is not giving you the grace to stand under such burdens, perhaps you should consider declining the appointment."

The bishop gently waved a hand. "You may go, Father. I need some time in prayer. I suggest the same may be true for you."

Gonzalez turned with steel in his back and exited with a carefully measured pace. I crossed the room to introduce myself to the guardian.

"Looks like you've had your hands full," I said. "My name is Beelash."

"Mutsak. We have been most… eager for your support. It pleases the heart to see you." The guardian had a thoughtful, almost ponderous way of speaking.

I introduced the four others in my team. They nodded their greetings, and Mutsak returned a shallow bow.

"I take it there's been another appearance?" I asked.

"Just this morning," Mutsak replied. "My partner, Assain, is out hunting for breakthroughs, but it has been an exercise in frustration. Today constitutes seven appearances by someone claiming to be a monk named Brother Olmos. This monk helped develop a monastery in this area nearly 400 years ago. He also helped champion a school to train local young men for the priesthood. I was in Asia at the time, but I remember hearing about the Colegio. It was an impressive work.

"He has yet to appear to more than one person at a time, and the results have all seemed... beneficial. Gonzalez was not wrong in his count of four legitimate miracles. One young father was led directly to a missing child who had stumbled into a sinkhole. Three others received healings for a twisted ankle, a broken wrist, and a fever, respectively. The remaining three visitations were messages of encouragement."

"It *has* been an interesting chain of events," I thought aloud.

Mutsak nodded. "Our only true cause for concern is that we know these occurrences are supernatural, and none of us here in Tampico are responsible. We did request verification that the Most High has not, for some reason, allowed the real Brother Olmos to visit. If this were one of our operations, we would know by now. As it is..." Mutsak shrugged.

I nodded. "We know it isn't us. We just don't know exactly what the enemy is up to. Any ideas as to what they think to accomplish? If we can determine their next steps, we can more easily catch them in the act."

Mutsak shook his head. "Only that it must be one component of a larger strategy. We have yet to identify which of our opponents has been making these appearances. Tampico is not a metropolis, but neither is it small. Usually, we would have already caught one of their lower ranks gloating about such exploits. As you heard, though, it has been nearly eighteen months, and they have managed to maintain silence. Someone is being very cautious and very shrewd."

"Which reminds me," I cut in, "just as we left our briefing, we were told to let you know we've picked up whispers that Gaon, the principality of this region, may have some special interest in this area. Might be related, might not. With what you just said, though, it checks out."

I turned to look again at the bishop. He stared out his window, the weary droop still in his shoulders. He prayed softly, "Father, is there no one else you can send for this? I can't turn the tide here on my own."

"We know the visitations started well before Bishop Martinez was sent," I mused, "but could this have something to do with him? The Kingdom would feel his loss if this broke him."

"I have wondered so myself," Mutsak agreed. "He has given

decades of powerful service to the Most High in this part of the world. Prince Gaon would surely love to get him out of the way."

I mirrored Mutsak's brief smirk. It's always fun to work with humans who are adept at causing the enemy grief.

"It looked for a time like the enemy would succeed in getting a more… pliable candidate appointed to this task. Our brothers in Rome fought a cunning battle, however, and we snuck him through. Or so we thought. Now that we can see we are up against a formidable tactician, I wonder if the battle in Rome could have been a feint on their part.

"It is conceivable…" Mutsak sighed. "This thought may just be because my assignment is specifically to watch over Martinez. Assain is assigned more to the investigation in general, and he is still skeptical of this theory."

Just then, another messenger entered through the window. Settling into the room, his two sets of wings collapsed brusquely behind him into an extended cape. With a glance, he noted my presence, then my team against the far wall. I assumed from the frustrated expression that this must be Assain.

"Finally," he said with relief.

Mutsak made introductions. Assain nodded to each appreciatively. "Mutsak and I are hardly alone here, but those already present have their hands full with their own tasks. I've been doing most of the heavy lifting on this problem myself."

"Mutsak says they've been masking their movements well?" I asked.

"I've narrowed the suspects down to four," he replied. "I thought I'd pinned this on a ministering spirit I think is leading a small team. But I was specifically watching him this morning when I heard reports pass through the streets of another Brother Olmos appearance."

"I hear you are a keen witness, Assain," I encouraged. "There's only so much one set of eyes can do on their own."

I turned again to observe the bishop as he continued his prayers. "I'm glad Martinez started praying for extra help, releasing us to assist. It's an honor to continue the work you've capably begun. Why don't you take us out and show us around? I'd like to get eyes on these four and then get a feel for how the city moves."

"Certainly." Assain nodded. His cape-like wings rippled with renewed energy.

I waved for Menateach to come closer. "While we're out, start putting together a profile on the people who have been 'honored' with these visitations. See if you can find a pattern."

"That would be helpful," Assain added. "I've been so focused on narrowing suspects that I haven't been able to do much of that kind of digging."

I gestured toward the window. "We're ready when you are."

Assain pointed out key landmarks, but didn't slow much until we approached a large villa atop a hill in an affluent district. I couldn't say whether it was a wealthy home or a place of business. We set up on a nearby rooftop, and I observed a dozen spiritual beasts lazily wandering outside the villa's perimeter among twice as many unclean spirits. Just in my first appraisal, I counted fifteen first domain elohim returning from or leaving for the city. Busy place.

"Should we be careful about being seen here?" I asked.

Assain shook his head. "They know why the bishop is here, and that Mutsak and I came to assist. Given the care they've given to every other detail, we have to assume the ones that matter already know you're here and why. Though, hopefully they're finally getting cocky enough not to care. Letting them see us might encourage overconfidence."

"What about the lesser ones?"

"I think they're under orders not to make too many waves right now. They would need help taking on the five of us anyway, and I'm pretty sure such help would be denied."

"What makes you think that?"

"It has to do with how I narrowed down our suspects. Like I said earlier, there are four who—wait a second. Here comes one now. See the messenger-minstrel there at the main entrance?"

The second domain figure was easy to spot among the lower-powered traffic. "Yes."

"That's one of the four, a false prophet. Keep your eye on what happens as he leaves."

I beckoned to one of my team. "That's one of our suspects. Keep your distance, but follow him around. See what places and people attract his attention. We'll meet back in Martinez's quarters at midnight."

The messenger nodded and headed off.

I settled back to watch for what came next. The false prophet moved out into the street, turned to his right, then nonchalantly disappeared into the city.

Assain turned toward me. "Well?"

"You're joking, right? I saw nothing. He didn't talk to anyone. Nobody talked to him. It's almost like his presence was masked."

"That's the *point*," Assain urged. "*We* all saw him, so we know he was there, but he walked right through that group and no one so much as looked at him. When's the last time you saw a second domain elohim walk through a crowd like that without at least *one* underling flinching?"

I looked back to study the group more closely.

"Did you notice the two first domain warriors going in?" Assain continued. "They didn't give so much as a nod of respect — and he didn't do or say *anything* about it. If they can dismiss any risk of backlash, they must have been specifically told to leave this group alone. I've noticed three others consistently receive the same treatment. They never interact with anyone else, but they do speak with each other."

Assain started counting off on his fingers. "There's that false prophet, then a messenger of similar power, a ministering spirit, who looks to be the highest powered and I think is their leader — but then, that's another aberration. The fourth of their group is a *first* domain warrior, but they treat him as an equal. Well, they at least don't seem to treat him the way they normally treat subordinates. I think they're here outside of the normal authority structure. Whoever they report to must hold great power to keep them so well-behaved from a distance."

I was impressed. "I must request we work together more in the future, Assain. Your perception is truly an inspiration. I confess some surprise that you've accomplished so much on your own."

Assain smiled as he shrugged. "It is a joy to use our gifts well."

He turned to give me a playful, but not disrespectful, salute. "It's your turn now, Field Commander. I'm happy to assist as I'm able, but

I've come to the end of what I can do alone. I follow your lead from here."

He gestured back toward the villa. "There's the warrior I spoke of."

I didn't see anyone new at the entrance, but movement on an upper balcony caught my eye. The warrior looked strong for first domain, yet no more than a single horn adorned his head and a single set of wings carried him down to glide over the heads of the beasts and unclean spirits. I assigned another of my team to follow him, and they quickly disappeared in the same direction as the others.

"I don't expect much more activity today," Assain said as we continued surveillance. "It took us a while, but there have now been enough appearances to recognize a timeline. Mutsak was first to realize they're working on a half-life schedule. We expected one today because the last was a week ago. The one before that was two weeks prior, then a month, and so on. The first two were eight months apart.

"Since we had one this morning, the next probably won't be for three or four days. It's why I was so intent on tracking the ministering spirit today. We *knew* they'd move." Assain shook his head. "And he still got it by me."

"We'll see this settled," I encouraged. "They are formidable, but the Most High is far more so. Is that another of our four?"

Now that I knew what to look for, it was easier to pick out the signs. A second domain messenger came out of the main entrance. He made no hesitation before turning left, away from the others. I sent the last of our group in pursuit.

"The ministering spirit makes rounds through the city," Assain continued, "but less often than the rest of his team. I was tailing him when the visitation happened this morning, so I don't think he'll be out again today. With the other three accounted for, there are a couple places you'll want to see."

"Lead the way."

Assain took me to the ruins of a monastery, now a tourist attraction. He pointed to a statue just off the street by the old gate. "Brother Olmos helped found this monastery while ministering to the Aztec peoples. He was quite adept at languages and connected well with the people here."

Surrounding the statue was a mountain of flowers and jewelry mixed among many other objects of negligible value. "By the third appearance, people started coming here to attract his personal attention." He looked around the square and pointed to various vendors with carts. "They buy pins and buttons or other emblems from these vendors, then bring them to this statue or to another near the cathedral downtown.

"Last year, the west tower of the cathedral was struck by lightning. Some say it was judgment on Rome for abandoning the city. The previous bishop died almost two years ago, and a replacement has yet to be named. In the interim, this 'Brother Olmos' began appearing. Gonzalez has not done a poor job continuing the ministry, but the people are feeling overlooked. They don't love that Martinez has held off honoring these appearances as being from God, so more and more bring their prayers here."

I noticed emblems shaped like arms and legs and feet. Some were the silhouette of a whole person. Others looked like stalks of grain or a symbol for water, perhaps a river.

Assain followed my gaze. "What they buy depends on their need. If they break their arm, they'll buy an arm. If their child is sick, they'll buy one of the smaller people emblems, then offer it as a request for healing."

Assain took me by other more populated places, such as the main markets and the waterfront — as well as a few more churches — before heading back to the cathedral. Entering the large church's plaza, we came upon a memorial to the previous bishop.

"They really loved him," Assain noted. "This is another frequent stop for our suspects — particularly the false prophet. They revive a person's affection for the bishop, then remind the person of their loss and nudge them toward depression. Sometimes they highlight how long the city has waited for another bishop."

Assain pointed up at the church towers holding vigil over the square. "Our adversaries are playing a subtle game. I haven't heard them directly suggesting bitterness against the church. From my view, that would be the easy play. They also haven't used this platform to champion the Brother Olmos appearances. Instead, they just increase this sense of perpetual floundering, and let people draw their own conclusions. We'll challenge them if they get pushier. So far, we've let them continue in hopes they'll slip up and give us information we can use. Ah, here comes the false prophet now."

I followed Assain's line of sight across the plaza to see the messenger-minstrel emerge from an alley. The messenger I'd assigned to follow him appeared soon after, calmly settling to watch from behind a fruit vendor's cart. He made eye contact with me and signaled: *Nothing of interest so far.*

The false prophet headed in our direction, and Assain and I casually continued up the church steps. It would have been odd to ignore an elohim of this one's stature, so we stopped at the door and turned to watch his progress through the plaza.

As the false prophet drew nearer, I heard him singing a soft dirge. It was almost nostalgic, more than mournful. He sang gently, but the song carried well, despite the lack of intensity.

"*We are the forgotten, a children abandoned.*"

He stopped in the center of the square, facing the church. His demeanor suggested he might as well be humming to himself, but his eyes followed the people who passed closest to the old bishop's memorial.

> "*Who will lead us? Not this one. Not this one.*
> *Who will care for us? Not this one. Not this one.*
> *Who will bring hope? Not this one. Not this one.*"

It was difficult not to intervene as I watched several sets of eyes drift downward, heads bowed under the heaviness settling upon their hearts. This seemed to be enough for the false prophet. The crowd thinned, and he left the plaza the way we had entered.

Assain pointed toward the memorial at the foot of the steps. "This is their pattern. Keep it brief and move on. Never directly suggest a larger, concerted effort. Never force our hand with intense torment. But one or more of them is here in turns every day, pushing this line."

I nodded as I took it all in. "Mutsak told me you weren't keen on this being about Martinez, but it seems that dirge could have been a critique against him as much as mourning for the previous bishop."

"Mutsak spoke true," Assain affirmed. "But it's only because the evidence is still circumstantial. Whatever they're doing here began quite a while before Martinez was assigned. Mutsak has a point, though, in that Martinez is the candidate we'd most want in a situation like this. Could they have set this up to draw him here for a more direct attack?"

He shook his head ruefully. "At first, I didn't want to credit our enemy for that much forethought. But the more we see here, the more I must admit it's possible. Over the years, Martinez has certainly caused enough damage to their interests — not just in Prince Gaon's territory, but even down into Columbia."

"Now that more of us are here to work this assignment, we should give some attention to Mutsak's theory," I suggested. "Even if that isn't their primary goal, they may need to get Martinez out of the way before they can carry on. Until we learn more, let's tighten our hedge around him."

I moved toward the door. "If there's nothing else to see, we can help bolster the bishop's spirit while we wait for the others."

We spent the evening in prayer, planning a protection detail, and ministering to the bishop. The others trickled in to join us. By midnight, Martinez was asleep in bed, and all had returned but Menateach. I hoped his absence meant he had found a thread worth pulling and not that he'd run into trouble.

I led us through a debriefing. Each of our marks had showed no interest in doing anything but what Assain and I observed in the plaza outside the church. The three suspects had meandered on a circuit through the city, seemingly looking for routine mischief. But they only actually stopped at the old monastery or at the bishop's memorial. Those who got close enough to listen confirmed the enemy was working more or less from the same script.

I was about to dismiss when Menateach rushed into the room. "Good! You're all here. I think I have something."

"By all means." I gestured for him to take my place before the team. "Share your findings."

"There *is* a connection," the excited ministering spirit began. "All the visitations have been to friends first, then family of Jose Gonzalez."

"The bishop's administrator?" Mutsak asked.

"Yes," Menateach confirmed. "The young man we saw here when we arrived. The three visitations that occurred before you and Assain arrived were to friends of varying degrees. The three since have been to a cousin, an uncle, and finally his mother."

"Forgive me, brother," Assain interjected. "That's only six. There have been seven appearances."

"That's what took me so long," Menateach responded with a shake of his head. "Today's wasn't an appearance."

"Not that I doubt you," Assain said, "but please clarify."

"Working backwards, it didn't take me long to recognize the family connection of the last three. That gave me a theory to trace back and help me see the others as being part of Gonzalez's circle of friends. Except for today's. Today's person is an older woman with no connection I could find to Gonzalez. It had me second-guessing myself all afternoon until I heard her clarify something to her sister."

Assain leaned in, his fingers twitching with anticipation.

"They were helping the first woman's ailing husband into bed," Menateach continued, a hint of triumph creeping into his tone. "... when she admitted she didn't actually *see* Brother Olmos. She merely had an impression this morning as she lay in bed between sleeping and waking. She wants healing for her husband so badly that she was more than ready to accept this impression as another visitation. I suspect she also enjoyed the chance to tell her friends she is the next 'favored one.'"

Menateach paused as I grunted in recognition. His explanation was certainly believable. "Be that as it may," Menateach went on, "she *is* convinced she was visited. But after overhearing her admission, I realized it had to be a visitation in her imagination only. If we remove her account from our list, the pattern fits neatly."

"Talk among the leadership in Monterrey," Mutsak interjected, "has been that Gonzalez will be ordained and given this diocese. His... familiarity with this area and capable administration have made him an attractive choice."

"If Prince Gaon is planning something significant in this area," I speculated, "perhaps he's making a long play at getting the next bishop under their influence by convincing him this 'Brother Olmos' is a messenger from God."

"And in so doing," Assain added, "hamstring their most likely source of opposition for years to come."

A thought struck me, and I turned to Assain. "Didn't you say this morning's visitation was perfectly on schedule?"

The messenger jerked his head to meet my gaze. "And if today's visitation wasn't real…"

I nodded. "We're still due."

I jumped back to the front of the group. "Ok, team. If we haven't missed it already, we may have an opportunity to get ahead of this thing tonight. It looks like Gonzalez is now our primary person of interest. Menateach, the last visitation was to his mother?"

"Correct." Menateach nodded.

"Any other immediate family members? A sibling, perhaps?"

"His father is still alive," Menateach said. "And there's a brother who lives alone a short distance south of the city."

Time being against us, I made a quick judgment call. "They're taking great care to hide these actual visitations from us, so it's unlikely they'll move in force. Let's also assume they won't go back to the same household to appear to the father right after the mother."

I split the team between Gonzalez's brother and staying with Mutsak to guard the bishop.

"Assain, Menateach," I concluded. "You're with me. We'll set up at Gonzalez's house tonight. With us just arriving today, the opposition may think to make their big move while we're still getting our bearings."

I met each of their eyes in turn and was met with readiness and confidence. It took a lot to put this team off balance. I felt a swell of encouragement at the knowledge I could trust each of them to act capably and wisely.

"Approach unseen, if possible," I cautioned. "I'd prefer we catch them in the act, instead of merely warning them off to try another time when we aren't looking."

With a final nod, they turned to their tasks.

Gonzalez lived close, but Assain led us on a circuitous route to avoid unwanted eyes. We saw no activity when we arrived, but I paused anyway for him to make sure. He swiftly reappeared at my side, giving an 'all clear' signal.

We entered a modest living space. Observing a gently used couch, table, and two chairs, we froze in unison as a voice reached us from the back of the house. I motioned for us to stay quiet and spread out. My partners disappeared forward through walls to my right and left, and I entered a short hallway. Checking open doorways, I observed my companions keeping pace with me through a humble kitchen on one side and bathroom on the other.

Getting closer, I noticed a faint glow emanating from the last room. The voice was now clear enough to make out words.

"...have won great esteem in heaven for your discernment and loyalty. If you remain true to the will of God but a little longer, you will have the position you seek. Martinez will realize he is not needed here and together, you and I will restore the glory of the church among all our people."

I peered around the door frame and cautiously scanned the room. A golden aura emanated from an old friar standing at the foot of Gonzalez's bed. Gonzalez was awake and sitting up against a rustic headboard. His eyes were wide. His mouth hung open in wonder. I thanked the Most High for good timing. A few minutes later, and it may have been too late to keep Gonzalez free of this deception. *Still work to do, though.*

The apparition's back was to me, so I turned to my left and searched for Assain. I recognized his beak, barely visible behind two sets of clerical robes hanging in an open closet.

"I will pass my mantle on to you," Olmos continued. "You, Jose, will exceed me. Indeed, you will be remembered in history as Mexico's greatest bishop."

Making eye contact with Assain, I gestured toward the friar. I barely processed the wings exploding out of the closet before Assain's blade was held against the friar's throat. Olmos immediately went silent. Simultaneously, Menateach and I moved into view to discourage a fight. The apparition flicked assessing eyes back and forth between us.

We were not manifesting for Gonzalez to see us, but he did note

Olmos's abrupt stillness. Curiosity overcame wonder, and the priest leaned forward. "Brother Olmos?"

Olmos glanced down, then back up at us. Assain spoke in his ear, "You've just given your final performance. Show him your true form."

The friar's eyes tightened as he whispered through his teeth. "I will not. Prince Gaon would know."

"Brother Olmos?" Gonzalez asked again. "I could not hear you. Forgive my weak ears."

I glanced at Menateach and pointed toward Gonzalez. "Can you try to impart your discernment to him?"

A touch of skepticism flickered in his gentle, oxen eyes, but Menateach moved to the bed and laid a hand on Gonzalez's shoulder. I waited, but saw no change in Gonzalez's expression. He was still waiting expectantly for Olmos to continue speaking.

"Well?" I asked.

"It's one thing for me to impart an ability," Menateach said, looking up at me. "He still has to choose to use it."

"Help watch him." I gestured toward our captive.

Menateach manifested his staff and traded places with me.

"Brother Olmos?" Gonzalez pressed.

I settled down to Gonzalez's level. "You *must* remember. Test the spirits to see whether they are from God. Test everything. Hold on to what is good."

I hoped Olmos's silence would continue. The awkwardness made the moment feel a little less glorious. Gonzalez hesitated. I continued to urge him to discern the situation. Finally, I saw a shift. The look in his eyes changed slightly from adoration to longing.

Longing is good. I can work with longing.

Longing indicated a desire for something that might be out of reach. Gonzalez was winning the battle. He was willing to surrender this to the Most High if asked.

"Gonzalez," I prompted again. "Test the spirits!"

Gonzalez took his eyes off Olmos and lifted them to the ceiling. He took two quick breaths, as though working up courage.

"Brother Olmos," he said, leaning forward. "Forgive me, but do you confess Jesus, the Son of God, has come in the flesh to dwell among us?"

Olmos's pursed lips twisted, and his eyes flared. He did not speak, but lifted his chin with unconscious arrogance.

Gonzalez peered closely, watching for a response. Suddenly his eyes shot open, and he recoiled against the headboard with a single, ragged gasp. He crossed himself and, with a trembling, stilted voice, began reciting the Lord's Prayer.

Realizing his façade had been penetrated, the ministering spirit's human likeness distorted, swelling to reveal a haughty, oxen head. His fur was dark gray, swirled with black, as if he'd been anointed with ink. The friar's robe unfolded into two sets of black wings, drooped in resignation. The golden aura blinked out, revealing crooked, moonlit shadows playing on the walls. Even knowing what to expect, the vision of innocence shifting so quickly to menace put a chill in my own heart.

I turned to check on Gonzalez when chaos erupted to my left. Throwing an elbow, the ministering spirit broke free from Assain's grip. Manifesting a staff of his own, the ministering spirit quickly leveraged Menateach out of his way and stepped toward Gonzalez.

I stepped in his way and manifested an axe in either hand. The ministering spirit prepared to jab at me, but was interrupted by the quickly recovered Assain. Now gripping a second sword, he lodged them both in the ministering spirit's neck.

I made myself visible to Gonzalez. It was enough that he had seen his enemy for what it really was. I didn't mind him getting a shock, but he didn't need to be tortured by fear.

Batting aside the ministering spirit's clumsy jab, I swung my axes at his ribs. The eruption of smoky darkness would obscure Gonzalez's view as we finished our work. Assain swung again with his left sword, then pierced the ox's head with his right. The ministering spirit gave a frustrated groan and slumped to the floor.

Gonzalez looked up as I turned toward him. I met his eyes with a strong, piercing gaze. I intended no threat, but felt I should accentuate the seriousness of these matters. After a brief pause, I softened my expression, then nodded to him and left his sight.

With a shudder, Gonzalez released his breath, as his vision had ended. He rested his face in shaking hands and whispered a repeated, "Kyrie Eleison."

I affirmed Assain and Menateach for a job well done. Pointing my axe at our defeated quarry, I added, "Let's leave him out in the street so they'll find it more difficult to cover up their defeat."

Still muttering prayers under labored breaths, Gonzalez scrambled out of bed and fumbled with his shoes. He was right behind us as we deposited the retired actor. We took a quick look around to make sure there weren't any ambushes waiting, then escorted the shaken priest to the church.

"How do you think this will play out?" Assain asked.

"Can't say for sure yet," I shrugged. "Perhaps the enemy's brilliance has backfired yet again. They may have just handed us a more seasoned, discerning bishop than we would have expected."

Assain's beak slowly opened into a grin. "Let us pray so."

We arrived just ahead of Gonzalez to find Martinez sleeping peacefully. A pounding at the door changed that. "Your Excellency! Your Excellency, please! I must speak with you! Your Excellency!"

Martinez only took enough time to swing a robe around his shoulders before checking on the emergency. No sooner did he crack open his door than Gonzalez fell to his knees in the hallway, babbling a confession of his blindness, his pride, his over-zealous ambition for self.

It took Martinez a moment to calm the flurry of words and pull Gonzalez into the room. Gonzalez tried to return to his knees, but Martinez directed him to sit on the bed. The bishop poured a cup of water from the pitcher on a simple table in the corner. Sitting next to the bewildered priest, Martinez offered him the cup. "Now, my son," Martinez started gently. "Tell me again what has happened; slowly and, as best you can, in order."

Gonzalez recounted the evening with much more clarity. He again concluded by expressing a repentant humility I hadn't expected from my first impression of him.

I perceived Martinez also appreciated the shifted mindset. I noted a swell in the bishop's spirit — a buoyancy of relief and encouragement.

It was contagious. Seeing inspiration rising in Martinez's demeanor ministered to *me*.

The Most High's love was easily recognizable in the man's eyes as he heard Gonzalez's story. He listened calmly and patiently. Occasionally, he would look down and I knew he was conversing with Elyon's Spirit, awaiting guidance on how to respond. I could see why Martinez had gained his reputation among us.

Eventually, Gonzalez ran out of words. He dropped his head in the way of a condemned man awaiting sentencing. Martinez let the quiet sit for a moment before speaking. "For what is mine to forgive, Jose, I forgive you. God always has his purposes in the unfolding of events. I now see great redemption in this for you. And hopefully for these people as well."

"Your Excellency," Gonzalez protested. "You must demote me. I was so weak and *willing* to be led astray by Satan. I am no longer worthy to serve."

"You never were, Jose. No one is worthy. But now that you can see it too, perhaps you are a little more prepared than you used to be."

"No, Your Excellency! How can I lead others when I can so easily be deceived myself?"

"You are right, my son. Before this night, I was not prepared to recommend you. But now, I suspect your eyes have been opened in a very useful way. I think in the future you will be much harder to deceive. I cannot expect God would waste that. After all, were you not rescued? Did God not send His angel to intervene in your moment of trial? He could have left you to suffer alone, but God thought you worth rescuing."

Gonzalez's eyes slowly widened as realization struck, stilling his panic.

"People change, Jose. God changes us. It is the essence of our faith, after all. By the power of His Spirit, we are transformed from glory to glory — conformed into the likeness of his Son. You now sit beside me a different man than the one who stood across my desk just this morning.

"Now, with God's grace and your help, I believe we can find our way forward. There is much work yet to do, but I find myself encouraged that we *can* recapture the hearts of these people for God."

Menateach playfully punched my shoulder. "You called it, sir."

I acknowledged his compliment with a smile. "I do love a good redemption story."

"That's scary," Thomas said.

Hirael lifted an eyebrow. "What is that, Brother Thomas?"

"Well, first of all, to realize that you guys don't always succeed. But just generally to think how much impact evil elohim have in the world."

"Oh, it's more than you know. So many mighty archangels are in rebellion and have great power and authority on the earth. It is constant war."

"And we don't even see it happening. I'm glad you guys *are* there. You know, to help."

Hirael nodded and gave a slight pause, as if in appreciation, then led Thomas from the arena.

Thomas had a couple things eating at him that he had to bring up. "You told me to wait after the giant scorpion. But now we have a leopard, and serpents, a mangy jackal with insect wings, and a bear with things coming out from its head like a king cobra! I mean, what am I to make of all that?"

Hirael gave Thomas a look of concession. "Yes, you have a fair point. We have time to talk about bestial elohim on the way."

Thomas tried to keep from showing his eagerness. "Thank you. I have to say, talking monsters just starts to sound like fantasy."

"From the scroll of Habakkuk." Hirael recited from memory:

> *"His horses are more swift than leopards;*
> *they are more menacing than wolves at dusk.*
> *His horsemen gallop; His horsemen come from afar;*
> *they fly like an eagle swift to devour."*

Thomas seemed confused. "Those are all poetic comparisons talking about a human army."

"Exactly," Hirael replied, unphased. "But those comparisons were selected precisely for the images they bring to mind. You can see beasts like these from the safety of a zoo or even a video screen. But to the ancient people who wrote and first read your Scriptures, these beasts were quite threatening and scary. Leopards stalked and killed. Wolves preyed on vulnerable livestock. Eagles swooped down unexpectedly with razor sharp talons and beaks." As Hirael spoke the last, his neck twisted so Thomas could see the profile of his hooked beak, which looked more fearsome than he had noticed before.

"Ah!" Thomas screamed as he realized the lion face was now animated and staring fiercely at him. "I forgot you could do that!"

"Sorry." Hirael brought his eagle face forward again. "Let me offer another: 'Behold, I have given you the authority to tread on snakes and scorpions, and over all the power of the enemy, and nothing will ever harm you. Nevertheless, do not rejoice that the spirits are subject to you, but rejoice that your names are inscribed in heaven.'"

"That was Jesus—from the gospel of Luke," Thomas blurted, then quickly composed himself. It wasn't like he expected Hirael to give him a gold star. "So... are you saying there really *are* giant spiritual scorpions?" He glanced around, like one might be right behind him.

"Not technically, no. But neither am I an eagle-lion-ox." Hirael started walking again. "Bestial elohim are just like the rest of the elohim you have seen here in heaven. However, they have rejected the purpose the Most High gave to them, along with the associated imagery. They have deeply embraced rebellion and corruption and adopted new imagery that reflects their new appetites. They are not unintelligent, but they are more impulsive. The other unholy elohim still cling to their given purpose and imagery, while perverting that purpose toward their own desires."

"So…" Thomas was trying to process it. "All unholy elohim have rejected God. But the ones who look completely like beasts have rejected Him more… openly? Is that right?"

"That is good enough."

Thomas wanted to keep going with this. "So, then, what's the deal with unclean spirits? Are they elohim, too?"

"That is more complicated, and we are out of time."

Thomas flinched. They stood in another small arena.

"More history, Brother Thomas. Another tale of the first watchers, but hundreds of years later."

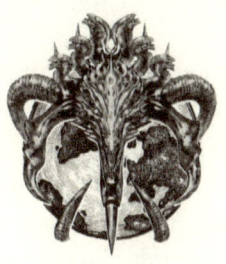

AZAZEL

GAO YU QING

Azazel stood upon the ramparts of his great house, gazing out over the work of his hands, smiling in satisfaction. Behind him, a silent servant escorted his visitor onto the roof. Without turning around, he dismissed the servant with a wave, leaving the watcher and his guest alone by the balustrade.

"It is good," Azazel said after a moment of silence. "Don't you think so, my friend?"

Enoch, the righteous scribe, frowned and shook his head.

"Interesting choice of words," he said in a resonant voice. "But I think that you venture into the realm of presumption, Azazel."

Azazel's mouth twisted into a grimace as he gazed out over the plains, where he could see the shape of the great city growing from the ground like something alive, larger with every passing day. He took comfort from the sight, like a gardener watching his crops grow. Nearer still, the tiny milling forms of human workers and the larger forms of their overseers labored over a huge stone statue carved in the likeness of a lion at rest. It crouched, head lifted and alert, with eyes of mica and obsidian glittering in the sun, the stone hide polished until it gleamed, golden as the real beast. If the lion's face bore a marked resemblance to Azazel's spiritual form, he could honestly say that *he* hadn't suggested the idea. Even from this distance, Azazel could point out his firstborn son, Gilgamesh, towering above all the others, and allowed himself a flash of pride before confronting more immediate matters.

Smoothing his expression before he turned to face the man who had somehow garnered the favor of the Most High, Azazel nodded with reluctant respect and stepped down to stand beside him.

Enoch, scribe of Elyon, didn't *look* impressive, even for a human. The seventh generation since Adam, he stood almost two heads shorter than Azazel, his bearded face crinkled into lines of worry, with eyes that alternated between unfocused and piercing. His clothes were homespun, with none of the colorful dyes or adornments Azazel's fellow watchers had introduced to humanity. *A shame.* Azazel considered the scribe as he spoke, envisioning how he might change the man's appearance to make him truly impressive in the eyes of his fellow men. Something bold, like the rich purples and reds he arrayed his household in. Some elegantly crafted jewels set in gold or silver to indicate their wearer was someone to heed. Sturdy leather sandals like his own instead of bare, dusty feet. A trimming of the beard…

"Presumption? It's all a matter of perspective," Azazel soothed. "After all, when I and my brothers watched the Most High shape all this," he gestured at the spreading countryside, "we agreed with His pronouncement that it was good. His triumph and pleasure became our own. Did He not command the humans to subdue the land? Have I… and the Most High's watchers," he smoothly corrected, "not shown them how to do just that?"

Enoch's gaze, heretofore mild, suddenly sharpened, and fixed on Azazel with an unblinking stare that had more than mere humanity in it. A cold tingle ran down Azazel's spine, and he had to will his flesh not to shiver.

"The Most High has sent me today with a message for you, pre-eminent among your brothers, before I deliver it to the rest. I am to speak to you of your mighty works."

Azazel schooled his expression, revealing nothing of the turmoil that suddenly roiled in his mind. Why would the Most High not tell him Himself? He had been silent for so long. Why speak now, and through this mere man? Still, to receive an acknowledgment from the Most High at last, after all these years…

"I am not the leader of the watchers, Scribe. Shemihazah leads, not I," he demurred.

Enoch only arched his eyebrow and gave Azazel a droll look in response to his claim, not needing to verbalize the truth of the relationship between Shemihazah and Azazel that all knew, save Shemihazah himself.

Azazel gestured and his wife Ishtara stepped out of the shadow of the doorway, where she'd been waiting out of earshot. At the sight of his wife, Azazel's irritation eased, and he smiled down at her. Even after all these decades, she remained his favorite. The light of adoration in her large brown eyes. The long, loose sheen of her oiled and perfumed hair cascading down her back like a cloak made of silk finer than that used to weave her alluring garments. Her delicate features highlighted by his gift of cosmetics. They all called to him. A bit heavier now than when he'd first caught sight of her hanging up laundry in a courtyard, but he could see that plain, ordinary girl she'd once been, now turned into a great beauty under his guidance and care. Like this land, he'd made her more than she was. Made her *better* than she had been before he claimed her as the first of his wives.

She raised her smiling eyes up to him now, lined with antimony to look huge, hungry for more than just the sight of him. In her hands, she held a silver platter with a pitcher of spiced wine and two goblets on it.

Reaching them, she curtsied, eyes lowering to flutter her lashes. "My Lord," she said in dulcet tones pitched for their ears alone, just as he'd trained her. "Perhaps you and your guest would care to slake your thirst this morning?"

Azazel lifted the pitcher and poured some of the rich red liquid into a goblet, offering it to his guest. "What do you say, Scribe? Care to taste of Shemihazah's latest vintage? It is a fine one. I can guarantee you've never tasted one better."

Enoch regarded the woman and the wine alike, his eyes flicking from one to the other as he shook his head, a line forming on his brow. "Thank you, but no. I do not eat or drink of the fruit of the vine. I should also think the pleasures of the flesh are not for those of the spirit."

In response, Azazel drained the goblet in one long draught before lowering it, wiping his mouth with the back of his hand, sighing in appreciation. His spirits rose as the chemicals within the wine flowed into his body, triggering cascades of other chemicals that created the desired end effect he knew as 'pleasure.' His mind monitored all such things constantly, intimately aware of the body he'd created for himself, adjusting the balance so he wouldn't suffer the intoxication the lesser beings endured. He'd never give up control in such a manner. Unlike some of his fellow watchers, he didn't permit pleasure to rule him.

"Ah, but this is one of our many contributions to this world. I have to give Shemihazah credit. How better to guide the humans to betterment than to partake of their experiences and lead them through our example? After all, how do you improve the wine if you've never tasted it?"

Enoch's face remained impassive as he responded. "The fact that you watchers can taste human pleasures doesn't mean you should. There were two trees in the Garden. One existed precisely not to be eaten from. Come. Walk with me and show me the works you regard with such pride." He turned and headed for the stairs built into the side of the house, forcing Azazel—to his great annoyance—to follow after.

Azazel returned the goblet to Ishtara's tray and favored her with a touch of his hand, allowing his presence to flow over her in approval. He'd had centuries to guide and shape her behaviors, so she did what he wanted without protest, longing for the next touch of his hands on her flesh. He kissed her painted lips before urging her towards the door, his own mouth quirking in amused affection that might have been scorn, if not for his care for her. *They are creatures so easily controlled by their emotions, barely stronger than the beasts they were supposed to have dominion over.* He turned and caught up to the scribe in a few long steps, before finding himself forced to shorten his strides to avoid running into the shorter man. Limiting himself to follow another — he'd been there before and recalled his distaste for it.

They reached the ground and Enoch turned to the road leading to the city. He didn't look back as he spoke.

"You know it is evil, what you have done to her."

Azazel twitched. Gritting his teeth, he controlled his anger at this human scribe, specially favored or not, and lengthened his stride so that he walked beside the man.

"I don't know what you're talking about."

Enoch slowly shook his head, not looking up at Azazel, who watched him out of the corner of his vision. *Was that a touch of sadness about his eyes?*

"I can see the imprints of long influence and domination on her spirit. You've made her into your creature, *needing* you more than loving you. Like one of those intoxicants your comrades created that the people abuse."

Azazel flinched at that reminder. "I will not accept fault for humanity's inability at moderation. In any case, what is wrong with Ishtara needing me? She's my *wife!*"

"She is *one* of your wives. You subjugate their will — as you do *all* of humanity — to your own, with your children to provide the violence when your blandishments fail."

Azazel threw up his hands in exasperation. "I don't steal my wives' choice or make them *do* anything they don't want to! I do only what human couples do to each other, except with greater skill and effectiveness! You should understand, for you have a wife and children of your own. Methuselah, I believe, is the name of your firstborn. A disturbing name, I might add. Who names their child '*his death will bring*'? But be that as it may, I assume you didn't come here just to criticize my job as a husband. What is this message from the Most High that you have for me?"

The scribe remained silent, head bowed in apparent thought as they walked, drawing nearer the construction at the monument overseen by Azazel's sons and a handful of men. All of them wore armor and carried weapons made of steel. The hybrids towered over their human counterparts like adults among children. In the distance, they heard the clank of chains — forged using the gifts Azazel had relayed to Ishtara's family and the crack of whips and booming voices.

As they came within hailing distance, a sudden commotion drew their attention to the laboring figures. They no longer seemed to be working, but most were instead turning on their overseers, wielding their tools as weapons. A smaller group of men broke from the conflict and raced towards a set of squat, crude buildings with narrow windows and heavy wooden doors barred and locked from the outside. As Azazel watched, small hands reached through the slitted windows, crying out in terrified voices as the men hammered in desperation at the doors, trying to break through to those calling to them.

Azazel briefly considered acting, but the sound of familiar, braying laughter brought a smile to his lips. He turned to watch Gilgamesh, Hobabish, and their companions moving through the fray with contemptuous ease. Makeshift weapons bounced harmlessly off the metal armor he had fashioned for them, while their great scythe-like swords swept through his attackers like autumn wheat, harvesting lives instead of grain.

Though they lacked the sheer power of the massive hybrids, the armored humans fought with brutal efficiency, beating aside the makeshift weapons with shields and delivering crippling blows with swords or axes, very nearly as impervious as Gilgamesh and his brother.

The revolt lasted less than a minute before the last of the slaves lay dying on the ground, blood soaking into the dry soil. As the human overseers set about dispatching the dying, the attention of the nephilim turned to those still attempting to break through the doors, or even the mud-brick walls. Glancing over their shoulders, the men's efforts rose to a fever pitch, but none stopped their labor, despite the frantic cries from those they sought to save.

Enoch's face paled, and he trembled as if with the ague, a look of horror — but not surprise — on his face. "Tell me, who were those men?"

"Them? Criminals, of course, who attacked the citizens of the city. My sons and the men they command defeated them — clad in the armor I showed them how to make, and wielding the weapons I showed them how to forge. As punishment, we made the criminals work to build what they sought to destroy. A fitting judgment, I'd say." Pride swelled in his heart at the great victory his sons had achieved through his skill and knowledge. "Look at them. None on the earth can stand against the might of my sons when I've armed them."

"Nay, nor their appetite for death and flesh."

Azazel glanced back towards the worksite as a chorus of high-pitched shrieks filled the air in time to see his sons, laughing, ripping a screaming man in two as if he were a fowl at a feast. Then, in full view of the trapped occupants he'd been trying to free, the warriors started to eat him with equal gusto.

Enoch spoke, his voice devoid of inflection, though his eyes flashed. "These were no warriors, no danger to you and your city. They were fathers, sons, and brothers giving their lives in an attempt to free their kin, taken and imprisoned by your sons and their kind. They were little threat to your iron and weapons. How many people have those weapons killed? How much blood soaks the ground that yet calls out Abel's name? How many images of the Most High were crippled or maimed by the fruits of your forges?"

In the distance, Gilgamesh turned and saw his father and raised a hand in greeting, his handsome face splattered with blood and framed by a mane-like head of hair and beard as he chewed his meal.

Azazel raised a hand in reply and smiled back, allowing his pride to wash away the shocking charges Enoch had just made. "What choice did we have? The work has to be done, for the sake of *all* humanity, even those primitives who still shun the city because of their superstitions and fears. Humanity needs to band together to create the civilization that will subdue the land as the Most High commanded them. These nomads and rebels also need to be subdued for the work to continue. This city, *my* city, is the future. The mold in which all future cities will cast themselves." He gestured with pride at the walls and growing structures of the city before them, the air clouded with the smoke of industry. "I will show them the way. This is merely the glorious beginnings. Surely you can't object to that."

Enoch grunted and turned to continue towards the city, looking neither to the right nor the left, his back straight and rigid as they drew near the gates. Already, they could hear the rumble of sound it produced day and night. Voices, shouts, the sounds of beasts, the grinding of wheels on roads, the ring of hammers, and the roar of furnaces.

The noise surrounded them as they entered, enfolding them much like the smells, refusing to be ignored. Human and giant alike made way for Azazel and the scribe, parting around them like a river's waters around a stone as they made their way towards the center of the city.

Azazel gazed about him, glancing up at the towering edifices, many still showing signs that they would be built higher. He gestured to one. "See there, Scribe? That is the tallest building in all the world. Imagine the views from those windows. Imagine the thrill of the humans who live there, seeing the city spread out beneath them."

Enoch gave the building only a glance before looking away.

Azazel bristled, but rather than yielding to his irritation, he tried a new approach.

"Breathe in, Scribe. Smell the lifeblood of the city. Do you recognize these aromas from anywhere else in your travels? I know them all, and can detect the coal and smelting metal from our forges scenting the air as much as the smells of spices and wine." *As well as the ever-present odor of human labor and sweat,* he mused. All of them worked towards his grand design. Unified. In his mind's eye, he already saw the future form it would take. The simple collection of hovels and shepherds he and his brothers had found here were now transformed into the greatest city and source of culture and civilization in the humans' history. Far superior to those "cities" the kin-slayer, Cain, had built.

Enoch only coughed and shook his head. The lines of his shoulders and neck told of a growing tension within him.

Azazel glared down at the shorter man. "You pretend not to be impressed. Very well then, see here." He pointed at a long, low building still only half-built. "That will be an academy. A school where men will be taught all there is to know — all that we have brought to share with them. We will foster their intellect and skills, and they will continue to discover new things, to create beautiful works of art, and to elevate the lives of all who follow! Can you say that you've ever seen anything like it in this world?"

Enoch turned to glare at the academy, color mounting in his cheeks, but his voice remained controlled, if tight, as he spoke at last. "Taught? To what end, I wonder?"

Azazel pretended indifference as he set his bait and cast it. "Perhaps to whatever end the one set over it will choose. You, as the first scribe, can surely understand the value such an institution would have. Indeed, you could oversee it! You could store all your writings there, protected from the elements, for all the generations that follow to read and study. I will set you in charge of storing all our knowledge, and you can work in peace and comfort. Imagine all those eager minds soaking up your wisdom, trained to be scribes like yourself. Think of the mark on posterity you will leave. What better place to raise up your successor?"

Azazel caught a slight hitch in Enoch's stride, a look of near pain on the man's face, and smiled to himself. *Yes, that's what every man wants. To be important, looked up to, and respected. To create a legacy for himself that will endure beyond his death. Immortality.*

By now they'd reached the central square. A space in which Azazel planned to put a public fountain, fed by an aqueduct connected to the nearby mountains. The humans weren't ready yet, though. Maybe in a few centuries or so.

"Look at all of this, Scribe," he called aloud in challenge, his mood lifted by the evidence of his work. "Is this not good? Look at everyone laboring together towards one goal. Unified in purpose. It is still humble, but when we are done, it will compare to the dwelling of the Most High. Surely you can't deny the truth of what we've made here. Look at the evidence around you! What more could the Most High desire than what we've accomplished here? Now tell me, what is the message He sent with you to me?"

Lost in thoughts of a glorious future, Azazel almost stumbled over Enoch when the scribe came to a sudden stop and whirled on him. The watcher recoiled at the blazing anger radiating from the human, and the righteous fury in his face flowing from a source beyond the mortal realm.

"You speak of truth and evidence? You are blind, watcher! Blinded by your own pride. Blinded as the Serpent and Adam were in turn, seeking to elevate their own will over that of the Most High and become like him! As you say, look at the evidence around you!" He gestured expansively. "See what is, not what you wish to see. In the name of Elyon, see what the Most High sees!"

Azazel staggered as all the sounds and smells surrounding him surged, forcing themselves upon his senses. The sounds, screams of pain or exultation alike, shouts of anger, of wailing children and weeping women. Drunken voices lifted in lewd songs, unheeded cries for mercy and help.

Enoch's words boomed in Azazel's ears, disorienting him, thankfully drowning out the other voices. "You asked me to smell the air of your city. The Most High detects only the pollution of air that will foul the lungs of those who breathe it. He smells perfumes used to entice one another. He smells wine, spilled out on the ground by those too drunk to hold on to the chalices that contain it."

As the prophet spoke, smells rushed into Azazel's nose. The scent of exposed sewage, rotting food, and sickness. Soot-stained air filled with toxins ravaging the lungs of those who breathed it in. Of, yes, perfumes and wine. Of blood, both animal and human alike.

"Look at your lofty dwellings, filled by the wealthiest and most servile of your supporters, exalted far above those they consider 'beneath them,' as you so consider them in turn."

The words drew Azazel's eyes to the towers and rang true, despite the lies he told himself. For he knew those who vied among themselves to live there, and knew, too, how much their petty squabbles for supremacy disgusted him. All the wheedling voices, soft hands, and greedy, piggish eyes.

"And you dare tempt me with your academy, your pride and joy," Enoch's voice dripped with scorn. "Would you have me join with you in your sin? What have you to teach them? More forbidden secrets? Will you teach men of where they come from and their true purpose for being here? Will you fill their minds with caution of past mistakes, or puff them up with empty facts and pursuits that will lead to future chaos? Whose knowledge will be elevated there? The teachings you brought to humanity, or worship of the Most High?"

Just by speaking the words, he drew from Azazel's most secret heart of hearts: the truth. How he had planned to teach them all the secrets brought to them by the watchers, with the knowledge that the humans had him to thank for making it all possible.

"No!" Azazel looked about wildly at his beautiful city, the manifestation of all his work and shared wisdom seemingly twisted into a nightmare before his eyes. The sources of his pride turned to mockery. Where before he'd seen the bustle of industrious labor, he now saw the darkness as well. The dark alleys where blank-faced, stick-limbed children with distended bellies lay waiting to die, while men wrestled and spilled each other's blood for handfuls of shiny rocks. The balconies in one of those proud, tall buildings were filled with women exposing themselves to the leering men below, calling out teasing crudities from faces painted with his cosmetics to cover the marks of dissolution or jaded scorn. While from behind it came the sound of a dying, unwanted infant, another mouth to feed.

Azazel spun in a circle, seeking some relief, some ray of light in his bright city. Instead, he saw the beggars crouched at the intersections of streets, bodies maimed, and eyes blinded by disease, injury, or the cut of one of the weapons he'd designed. He saw the men staggering down the street, drunk, faces slack and flushed with false cheer. He heard the clink of chains and watched as a gang of dead-eyed slaves hobbled along under the cruel eyes of one of their nephilim overseers, who appeared to be eating a severed human leg, watching them like a butcher eyeing the animals he planned to slaughter that day.

Everywhere he looked, he saw the darkness that twisted the hearts and minds of the people. *His* people, *his* city, until every inclination of their hearts was evil. His work, his planning, his dream, and his glory were all twisted, spoiled, and rotten at its very core.

Azazel, foremost of the watchers, visionary founder of the city, always in control, fell to his knees as his mighty, self-styled, fleshly body retched out the contents of his stomach into the dirt.

As Azazel knelt, helpless, Enoch raised his hands above his head and called out in a voice that seemed to freeze everyone in sight, stilling their movements. Even the overseer, with his enslaved charges, turned as one to stare at the scribe turned prophet.

"Hear now the Word of the Most High, the Lord of majesty and the King of the ages! To you watchers, who forsook your eternal station in the highest heaven, defiled yourselves with mortal women, and have worked great desolation on the earth. You will have no peace or forgiveness."

Azazel shook his head, trying to clear his thoughts, opening his mouth to protest the injustice of it all, but the motion summoned another convulsive heave, and he retched out bile.

"And concerning your sons, in whom you rejoice, you will see their slaughter. You will lament over their destruction and make perpetual petition, finding no mercy or peace."

"Noooo!" Azazel croaked. He couldn't focus, couldn't stand or even lift his head to see Enoch through his watering eyes. So great was the revolt of his body at what he'd seen of his dream, his work, his ambition through the gaze of Elyon. For the first time, he felt almost… mortal. Yet still he felt the gaze of the prophet as Enoch looked down at the kneeling elohim, pitching his voice for him alone.

"And to you, Azazel, the Lord says, 'You will have no peace. A great sentence against you has gone forth to bind you. You will have no relief or petition because of all the unrighteousness and sin you have revealed to humanity and brought forth from them.'"

In the unnatural silence that filled the city, the slap of the prophet's bare feet could be heard as he turned and walked away, out of the heart of the city and toward a nearby mountain. Then came the sound of a rushing wind, and the footsteps ceased as Enoch was carried away.

With a start, the city jolted back to life, the sounds crashing back down like a wave over the inhabitants, though with an almost unnoticed frenzy and desperation to it. Voices spoke louder, as if trying to drown out what they'd all heard. Denying it with a return to the familiar, however debased.

Azazel lifted his head and forced himself through the strength of will to get back on his feet, wiping angrily at his mouth with the back of his fine sleeve. He shuddered once more, as new voices came. Voices that none of the mortals around him could hear, yet he knew every watcher could. He glared at the spirit hovering before him, whispering in a tongue only they could understand.

"Come. Come all. This way to the gathering. Come and hear the word and judgment of the Most High."

Azazel spat on the ground, trying to rid himself of the bitter taste on his tongue, and turned to walk back to his home. He turned his back on the way the messenger had said to go, brushing him aside with purposeful disdain for his presence and his missive. He'd heard all he wanted to.

Azazel looked neither to the right nor the left, unwilling to see what might be revealed in the dark alleys and cracks of his masterpiece. His back remained straight as he turned away from the summons and what it implied about his work. He gazed towards the horizon, to the future he would still bring about.

"I've heard enough," he growled, and his people cringed at the sight of his anger.

"Is that what it was like—angels ruling like kings, marrying women, and having Nephilim children that went around eating people?"

Hirael held up a hand, signaling for Thomas to wait. The audience dispersed and there was not as much jovial chatter as at other times. Some elohim looked reflective and others showed anger.

After most of the guests had left, Hirael spoke. "I understand these events are a lot to take in. Your fascination, however, is causing you to miss the point of the story. Consider Shemihazah's and Azazel's corruption. Different persons, different drives, but ultimately the same sin. They both put serving their own desires above faithfulness to the Most High. Both convinced themselves they were creating order and new life, but the results were wide-scale chaos and death. Human sin is no different, Brother Thomas. And many are just as blind as Azazel to the effects." Hirael paused to let the thought sink in before getting up. "Come. We have a lot of…"

Thomas did not follow. "Hold on. I don't think that is a fair comparison. Those guys… elohim…watchers, they knew God. They saw Him, heard His voice, were even directly sent by Him. If God just showed Himself,"—he gestured toward the stage—"we'd all behave. Or at least believe."

"Would you?" Hirael said. "Did they? Let me tell you something. As watchers, we don't have all the answers. Sometimes His instructions seem counterintuitive. We must learn to walk in faith the same as you.

And, honestly, it may be harder for us because we *do* see Him directly. He could so easily just tell us everything we ever need to know, but He doesn't. He could just bypass us completely and do it Himself, far easier and with better results. But He doesn't do that either. He wants to work alongside us. The Most High wants us to deny ourselves in order to risk trusting Him. He delights in our faithfulness. And He is willing to accept the results of doing it that way.

"To actively be His image is to obediently participate in what He is doing in cooperation with Him. The Son of Man, Jesus as you know Him, is the perfect example of actively being the image of the Most High. He said, 'Truly, truly I say to you, the Son can do nothing from Himself except what He sees the Father doing.' Many elohim and humans have denied this awesome privilege because they wouldn't learn to trust in His goodness."

"Now, you're cheating," Thomas said. "I can't argue with Jesus. But I do serve in the shelter. I am going to seminary. I work hard at my job. That is a form of worship, right? Doing whatever my hand finds to do as unto the Lord?"

"Yes. It can be. Those are all good things." Hirael beckoned him with urgency, as if they might be late. "But are you truly doing those things unto the Lord? Or are you doing them for yourself? Think about it as we walk."

Thomas did think about it. All of these things. Why did he really do them? He didn't remember God leading him to do them. He just thought they were the right thing. Everybody should help those less fortunate. If you were *serious* about God, you either became a pastor or a missionary. And he really wanted to do well at his job... but that wasn't really for God. He just wanted to get promoted, make more money, buy a house. Regular stuff. Admittedly, if he were doing it as an act of worship, he wouldn't take the shortcuts he does. He wouldn't talk behind the boss's back, even if he could be a royal jerk. Why was all this so clear right now? Serving the less fortunate made him feel good, like he was earning a 'good person' card. And seminary... he was ready to quit as soon as he got the promotion, so does that really count? What would it really be like to partner with God? To only do what he saw the Father doing?

As they entered the arena, Hirael broke the silence. "The best is when we work together. The Most High, lesser elohim, and humans. Elyon and his children. One big happy family. You know that's the end goal, right?"

The thought echoed in Thomas's thoughts as a minstrel took the stage and began to sing.

FAITH TO SHARE

ELLIE LERUM

Beautiful days always had additional secrets hidden within them, even in the quietest of moments. Beneath a tall oak, two women scrubbed aprons in a washbasin. The lye soap had slightly burned their hands as they worked the fabric, scrubbing and beating them to remove dirt, before dunking the cotton into the water again. They had no knowledge of the stranger beside them, the silent watcher standing guard over them. It was a call I greatly delighted in.

I shifted from where I stood, watching Mikiah and her friend Anne. Their conversations always amused me, though I didn't always understand them. These women were certainly interesting in their own right, and it was a pleasure to watch them grow closer to Elyon together. I was fortunate enough to often be present when their conversations moved in that direction; I enjoyed the view from the oak, as it oversaw the entire village, but its shade didn't seem to bring Anne and Mikiah as much comfort today as it usually did.

It had been a trying time, to be sure. Anne had confided in Mikiah the news of a pregnancy, but the joy had been short-lived. A week after the announcement, the pregnancy was lost, and Anne had become withdrawn.

Today was the first time they had been together since Anne asked for privacy, and a piece of my spirit was concerned that Anne had perhaps been influenced by other, less benevolent elohim during that time; poor Mikiah had been worrying that she said something to upset Anne while her friend grieved. That in itself had been a long battle.

Anne cursed quietly, as the lye on her hands stung, and Mikiah's eyes flashed to her friend. I tilted my head as the two women moved away from the washbasins to sit beside their flasks of water and pouches of nuts. Mikiah nudged Anne. "Are you doing alright?"

"What do you think?" Anne snapped.

Mikiah paused, and I glanced at the two. That was a sudden response, and out of character.

"Anne, I was just wondering—"

"So you can blame me, too?" Anne, the younger of the two, shifted away from Mikiah, anger and mistrust shining through her tear-filled eyes. "Everyone else has... are you going to tell me that it's my fault, too?"

At their sudden silence, a hum reached my ears, and I stopped.

Something was singing nearby, a whisper of lies and dread.

Slowly, I scanned the area around us. Where was it hiding? How long had it been watching, simply waiting to intervene?

A large frog sat no more than ten feet from me, it's call confusing Anne's words and filling her thoughts with the lies I'd heard for ages. Frogs were crafty, twisting the truth of situations into falsehoods. The human idea of fault was at play, the lie that everything was Anne's fault. She was beginning to despair, and there was nothing I could rightly do to directly counter the frog—not without Anne rejecting his influence or the frog crossing a line.

Mikiah's encouragement could help turn Anne from singing along with the frog's tune. With the right words, she could help Anne push through.

Glaring at the frog, I crouched beside Mikiah. "There's something more here, Mikiah. Is this what your friend used to sound like? Have you said things like this to her?"

The frog was clinging to something Anne held close to her heart. He would pick apart pieces of the woman that suited his needs, such as a whisper that she was a burden or unwanted. The heart issue was the problem, less of the situation at hand. If Anne could work through those fears, the frog would have less ability to pull her from the truth.

Mikiah shifted slightly, and I knew she heard my words. She wouldn't know I was speaking them, but they were there, all the same, as a gentle whisper that caught her attention. Her lips had twisted in thought, and I couldn't help but smile as I pressed again. "Who has told her these things?"

Ah, yes, there was the light.

Mikiah's eyebrows rose, her eyes wide and mouth slightly parted. I remember seeing another young woman with that exact look many, many years ago. In that case, the woman had informed her family that she was starting a family of her own, and they just did not understand. That was a pleasant memory, far more than this will be.

I shook my head and looked at the frog. It blinked at me—one eye and the other—before it continued to sing words meant to drive Anne into fear of rejection and condemnation from Mikiah... and everyone else.

"Come on, Mikiah!" I said. "Your voice needs to be louder than the lies."

"Anne, who told you that it's all your fault?"

The frog flinched. Anne blinked, beginning to falter.

"Have I ever told you that, Anne?"

"No, but... others do!" Anne snapped. Her fingers curled tightly against her skirt, growing white and shaking. I looked at Mikiah as Anne continued. "I'm just trouble! Everyone says I am, and... and... I know it's my fault! It's always my fault, and you're just trying to make me feel worse!"

I frowned.

This frog had a tight hold on Anne, and he silently gloated as he blinked at me again.

He continued singing, and I looked at Mikiah again. "She needs you to get through to her, Mikiah. She's hurt. There's nothing but lies being whispered to her," I murmured. "You must get through these lies." I touched her shoulder and closed my eyes.

She needed peace to navigate through this, and that was something I was more than happy to provide.

Mikiah shifted a bit. "Anne, I love you. Do you really think I'd hurt you, my sister? I would never hurt you, and I'm so sorry that others have. You lost something you were so excited for, and… Oh, Anne…"

Anne turned away from Mikiah and wiped her eyes. Finally, she mumbled, "Tell me something, Mikiah."

"Anything."

"We both serve God, don't we?"

"Whole-heartedly, Anne. Why?"

"If we serve the same God, then why has He taken this from me, hm? You're talking about loving me, and I've heard you speak to others about God's love… why does He love you more than me?"

I frowned and looked at the frog. He smiled impishly at me, rubbed his eyes with one leg, and settled again. "Did you think I wouldn't be ready for your interference, Obadiah? I planted that seed as soon as I knew she was coming here."

He was trying to frustrate me, especially as he gave another handful of notes and some new lyrics to his song.

I could discern Mikiah's passion and confidence were growing weak. It seemed she felt as though she wasn't allowed to speak. With that realization, I caught a whisper in the frog's lyrics that she had no right to help Anne through this. Mikiah hadn't gone through a loss like this.

Those weren't just added notes!

There was a new song at work, subtly layered under the first, and it was directed at Mikiah.

I looked at the frog sternly as I held out my hand, manifesting an axe with its end pointed directly at the frog. I didn't want it to come to blows, but now he was overstepping his bounds. He knew full well that Mikiah was cooperating with me, and thereby, I could rightfully defend her.

Despite being a warrior, I didn't relish violence. But there were protocols, and I was willing and able to step into the new battle this frog had decided to wage.

Before I could, though, Mikiah whispered, "I don't think He does, but I also don't know why He allowed you to lose your baby."

Good girl, Mikiah! She had pushed off the frog's song without my help.

I let a menacing gaze linger on the frog as I leaned into Mikiah. "No one knows, Mikiah. Sometimes, the Most High gives good gifts: there are so many places in the Scriptures. Share them with Anne, show her His love. Get past the lies, keep speaking to her!"

The frog took a deep breath, but I leveled my axe towards him again. "Do not! You've already overstepped your bounds. Mikiah is not yours to influence."

Before the frog could respond, Mikiah had taken Anne's hands and held them tightly. Though Anne looked confused, Mikiah squeezed them and then hugged her.

"Remember, God saved Isaac through the gift of a ram to be sacrificed—it was blind faith, and a beautiful gift that showed Abraham that God would provide. He fed those in the wilderness manna and gave them fresh water; those were gifts that nourished their bodies when there was nothing to eat. How much more will He provide for you, Anne, even in this time of pain? He sent the Savior to hang on the cross for us. He cares so incredibly deeply for you... if a child is to be in your family, He will bless you with a child." Tears streaked down her face, more than I recall seeing her shed before, and she whispered, "Anne, you are not alone. I'm angry too, but the anger isn't meant to be towards God... but given to Him."

"You haven't experienced this!" I knew these words were the frog's. They were the same words he had tried to use against Mikiah just a moment ago.

"True. But I see you hurting. And it hurts me. I don't want you to be alone in this, Anne. Please, there are so many women who have gone through this, and there are women who have experienced joy, too."

"That's good, Mikiah," I said.

I closed my eyes. I remembered the several times I had watched women in this situation grow in compassion and understanding after losing their children. Others used their grief to better the care expecting mothers received, while more did what they could to share in the joys of those who did receive their children.

There were always those who fell away, too. The pain of losing a child and the grief of a lost pregnancy brought confusion and the feelings of betrayal. They turned away from their faith, losing it as they were lied to by unclean spirits and unholy elohim like this one here.

Anne was close to moving in that direction. I could feel it.

Still, as Mikiah held her friend and continued to whisper, Anne's sobbing slowly died down. She pressed her face into Mikiah's neck and sniffled. Mikiah, meanwhile, stroked her hair and whispered, "You're alright, I'm here. You aren't alone... I'm here."

"And Adam..."

"Adam loves you deeply, even through this pain," Mikiah said quietly. She held Anne tighter, rocking slightly. "You're not alone, I promise."

"Are you certain?" Anne whispered, pulling away to wipe her eyes.

Mikiah brushed some hair from her friend's face, peering into her eyes with a soft smile. "I'm certain. Do you want to believe me, or do I need to try convincing you? I'm happy to try to sing it, if that's better?"

"If only you knew, Mikiah," I chuckled.

A little snort left Anne, who shook her head. "No... no... though, if I forget, I suppose a rhyme or two under my window would be welcomed."

The two laughed softly as Anne leaned against Mikiah again, who played with her hair and kept watch over their washing basin as they continued with their lunch.

I looked at the frog, who gave me a disgusted look.

"You're done here today," I said softly. "It's time for you to leave."

He puffed up his throat sack, deflated it, and then crawled off. I looked back at the two women and let my axe dissolve. "Good work, Mikiah... Thank the Most High that you listened..."

This wasn't the last time humans would face this. Grief and loss have been in this world since the Garden exile, and they only brought people pain and heartbreak. Still, there was hope; that itself never vanished.

Those who allowed grief to shape them for the better could bring about change. There was a community that built around those who experienced it, who built one another up. Others walked away from that community and moved towards cynicism. It was understandable; grief twists the heart, forces loneliness into the body, and whispers lies of all sorts. It was a sad reality that they didn't know the love of the Most High, sadder still that they allowed unholy elohim to whisper the condemning and killing lies over them.

Today, though, Anne was safe.

I leaned against the tree, sighed, and resumed my watch.

There was a high likelihood that I would guide another through this again. After all, I was the Most High's servant, and they were His children.

BREACHING THE SHADOW

JOSHUA C. CHADD

Imriel stood on a secluded mountain deep in the jungles of Columbia. The lush green landscape had a natural beauty to it in the predawn light that was at odds with the compound nestled in the small valley a mile away. One couldn't see it in the material realm, but the collection of buildings was a place of great spiritual evil. A foothold ruled by a powerful unholy authority. The place was a hub of activity, elohim coming and going, using the hold as a temporary stop on their missions. It was the same for the holy holds Imriel visited frequently.

This hold had grown quickly from the amount of unholy activity below and the power of the ruling elohim. It wasn't that unusual for a hold set in the wilderness far removed from a praying, faithful community. That growth had slowed, thanks to the efforts of a breach team Imriel had been assigned to.

He'd been serving under Lumiel, the breach commander assigned with tearing down this hold. The rest of his companions had left a week ago after months of work: harassing the foothold, picking off any arriving or departing forces they could overpower, and stirring up the prayers of saints whose relatives were trapped inside. It'd been a surprise to Imriel when he'd been assigned to take over as the new breach commander. It made sense, and as he looked back, he could see that Lumiel had been grooming him from the beginning. Imriel didn't mind. He'd been on breach teams before and always loved the satisfaction of demolishing an enemy hold. Now he would be the one in charge.

A breach commander needed a team, though, and in answer to that question, he'd been told to wait. If he'd been promoted every time he'd been made to wait, he'd be an archangel by now. It still irked him how much the waiting affected him, which may also be part of why he was *not* an archangel.

Over the millennia, he'd seen the Most High work countless times, and yet his first response was always a slight annoyance at the inaction. He *knew* it always worked out for good, even if that wasn't always how he'd wanted it to turn out. It gave him empathy for working with humans, as they had much the same experience. He trusted, though, and would wait until he was told otherwise. It had given him time to continue watching, and even complete a couple small missions to destabilize the foothold even more. He couldn't shake the feeling that his waiting was almost at an end. The time had almost come to kick that unholy elohim off his throne and continue the hard work of removing this stain from the world—both in the spiritual and material realms. His former team had laid the groundwork. Now it was almost time to start reaping those rewards.

Leaving the ridge, Imriel went to the back side, to a small clearing amidst the dense foliage. A presence entered his range of detection from above, but Imriel didn't look up. This was the holy presence of a fellow elohim and he *was* expecting company, even if he didn't know who to expect. He kept up the haven effect he'd had active for the last week, causing other elohim to ignore his presence, but exempted the descending elohim, allowing himself to be noticed. The elohim landed next to Imriel, his double set of wings fully unfurled.

"A hold," Rimaz stated, an edge to his voice.

His feline features were set with a scowl as he looked through the mountain to where the compound rested on the other side. He couldn't see through the solid stone any more than Imriel could.

"Yes, a foothold," Imriel answered. "It's good to see you my friend. It's been too long."

Imriel gripped Rimaz's forearm and the other elohim finally tore his gaze from the mountainside. A smile split his face and the fierceness left his features—somewhat.

"And you, Brother. You have your second set of wings. About time."

Imriel laughed. "Is that a jab at me, or the Most High?"

"I would never question the Most High!" Rimaz snapped.

Imriel raised his hands in a calming gesture, a smile on his face. "Peace, Brother. I was only testing your zeal. I see it has not waned in these centuries."

Rimaz eyed him, his wings settling into a relaxed state. "I hope your axe has stayed as sharp as your tongue."

Imriel laughed again, clapping Rimaz on the shoulder. "I can assure you it has."

"What are our orders?"

"Always straight to the point and ready for action. I've always liked that about you, Rimaz. What were you told?"

"I was to finish my mission in Pyongyang and meet you here. Nothing more."

"North Korea. What was your mission there?"

Rimaz's eyes lit up. "I was assigned to a young couple who were evangelizing despite the danger. They were to persevere to the end."

"You completed your mission?"

Rimaz nodded. "They stood firm in the face of execution... they are with the Most High now."

Sorrow and joy mixed with resolve in Imriel. "They join a worthy host of saints."

"Indeed."

"I will explain the mission shortly. Now that you are here, I'm expecting..."

Imriel trailed off as he sensed a new presence above. This time he did look up to watch as the elohim drifted down from on high. The herald landed beside them, his *three* sets of wings relaxed as he eyed the others, a slight smile on his hawkish face.

"Imriel. Rimaz." The newcomer acknowledged each with a tilt of his head.

"Zimrah, I see you've been busy," Imriel replied.

"As have you two. What has it been... two centuries?"

"A little over. The final battles of the American Revolution," Imriel responded. "I still don't know how we managed to keep our charges from killing each other."

"Indeed."

They clasped forearms.

"I have a feeling we'll have time to reminisce later. What is this important mission we were summoned for?" Zimrah asked.

"Follow me," Imriel said as he started up the ridge, his wings now relaxed and flowing wide like a commander's cloak, as was customary in tactical discussions such as this.

When he reached the ridgeline he stopped, his gaze locked on the compound below. It was still early in the morning, so there was little activity in the material realm. The usual cartel guards were stationed around the property, with two standing outside the largest building towards the center. Imriel's heart broke within him as he looked below. He knew what the captive humans must be feeling. He'd seen enslavement like this since the introduction of sin into the world. He took comfort that he served a sovereign and just Lord. The Most High had a plan for this place, as He did for all of creation, and Imriel's team was the tip of the spear that was about to pierce this darkness. In the spiritual realm, many unclean spirits were visible around the compound, the greatest activity around the central building. There was a sentry somewhere down there, probably watching them as they crested the ridge. He wouldn't be able to notice Imriel with haven active, but he'd surely see the other two.

Imriel turned to his companions, his mood more somber than before. "The compound below is home to a relatively new cartel, *Los Sangrientos*. Recently they have decided to branch out from their usual drug running to human-trafficking. On the spiritual side, it has seen an unusual amount of activity this last week, including an influx of unclean spirits and beasts. They have been flocking to this place like flies to a rotting corpse. There has also been an unusual amount of human activity. Recently two semi loads of... children arrived, and the amount of human guards has doubled. They're preparing for something."

Rimaz narrowed his eyes, a snarl escaping his lips.

"Do we know the elohim that rules here?" Zimrah asked.

"The authority is a third domain defiler and just below him, a second domain *tyrant*." Imriel spat the last word.

It was common when he talked about the unholy corruption of his discipline of king priest. Many holy watchers had distaste for their corrupt kin. The corruption of their chosen discipline made such feelings all the more acute. It was painful watching a close brother deny the Creator of the universe in pursuit of their own twisted passions.

Imriel continued. "There's also a first domain sentry down there and a warrior just showed up two days ago."

"You said they do seem to be amassing strength," Zimrah stated. "You're sure it's only a foothold?"

"Yes. I was a part of the old breach commander's team assigned here."

"And the mission?" Rimaz asked.

"The foothold is to be torn down. We all know that's not a quick or easy process, nor will our raid end the unholy presence here. But we are to be the tip of the spear. The time has come to attack. Any unholy powers inside are to surrender and leave or be defeated."

"Good, as long as it's not a *diplomatic* mission." Rimaz almost growled the last.

Imriel chuckled and Zimrah just shook his head with a slight smile. They all had to do their fair share of missions that were less straightforward. None of them enjoyed having to let evil *seem* to get away with its goals. The final outcome was ultimately decided. The Son of Man had been enthroned, which was what truly mattered. That didn't make it any easier, though, when they had to stand by and watch evil win small battles.

"So you're the new breach commander," Zimrah stated. "I was told command had recently changed."

"Yes, I was promoted when my old team left. I've been waiting for the rest of my trio, not sure who to expect. I should've guessed it'd be the old team back together."

"It's been a while since I've been part of demolishing a hold," Zimrah said.

"Are you okay with taking orders from someone of a lower rank during this assignment, or shall I defer command?"

Zimrah shook his head. "I can follow for a time, especially if it's you. We've been through enough together and you've always been a leader, even when not leading. I'm just surprised it took you this long to become the one in charge."

Imriel laughed. "All in His timing."

Rimaz spoke up. "When do we go in?"

"We are to gather here and wait. My orders stated that we would know when it was time to move."

"So we're all in the dark now," Zimrah stated.

There was no malice or frustration in his tone. They'd all been here plenty of times before. Often their orders were very specific, but other times they just had to trust in the Most High.

Rimaz let out a gruff sigh. "I dislike waiting."

"I agree," Imriel said. "But it's always interesting to see how the Most High provides a way forward. Though in this case... the sooner the better."

Zimrah gazed down at the compound. "Agreed."

Imriel raised his hands in the air, light briefly shining from them. Three white flaky clusters of manna appeared on the ground next to him and he picked them up, handing one each to the others. "I have a feeling we won't have to wait long. Best to be prepared."

Rimaz took the cluster and put it into a pouch he manifested on his belt.

"I'm beginning to remember why I like fighting alongside you, my friend," Zimrah said as he took his manna.

"These will work in a pinch to restore some endurance and I'll be ready with my other abilities when the time comes."

"Like when you instantly swapped places with me in the battle with that frog-bear beast," Zimrah said. "The shock on his face when he was suddenly fighting a much stronger, much healthier opponent."

"I'd forgotten about that. We were fighting alongside the Israelites against the Amorites then, right?"

"Yes. The wars were a bit simpler then."

"Well, when the Israelites weren't chasing after idols in their disobedience, leaving us to stand by helplessly, watching them be overrun."

"True."

Rimaz nodded. "Remember the time Samson fought the Philistines with the jawbone?"

"That was less a battle and more a slaughter," Imriel said. "They didn't understand that they actually fought against the Most High that day."

The morning passed as the three reminisced of old times battling together and fighting for the Kingdom of Heaven. As the day wore on, they settled into a vigilant silence, waiting for the sign that it was time to move into the foothold. Afternoon came, and Imriel noticed activity on the edge of the compound.

"Do you see that?" Rimaz asked, peering down towards the compound.

"Yes," Imriel responded.

Zimrah manifested a staff. "It looks like an emissary."

"Or a small strike force." Rimaz manifested a large, two-handed sword.

"Best to be prepared," Imriel stated as he manifested an axe and tower shield.

A single unholy elohim had launched into the air from just outside the compound and landed on the ridge, fifty paces from Imriel and his team. It was the sentry.

"Servants of the Most High," the unholy elohim spoke from a safe distance, relaxing his wings into a cape to reinforce his diplomatic intentions. "What business do you have here?"

"Our business is our own," Zimrah said, his tone casual.

"You'll know soon enough," Rimaz said.

The sentry eyed him, then he looked to Zimrah. He scanned right over Imriel who stood a little removed from the two, haven still active.

"I see... You are trespassing on our territory and we can take any action we deem necessary to defend what is ours."

"Thanks for the warning," Rimaz said, an eager smile on his feline face. "We can dance right now if you'd like."

He took a step forward, his sword held casually at his side.

The first domain sentry took a step back, his hands still empty, though Imriel could see a hint of uncertainty on his twisted, hawkish face.

"No need, *zealot*. There will be plenty of time for that later if you stick around."

"Oh, we'll be here," Rimaz said. "You, on the other hand..."

The sentry scowled at them both, then launched himself into the air, arching back to the compound below.

"Must you always antagonize?" Zimrah asked, looking to Rimaz.

Rimaz shrugged. "They already guessed what we're here for."

"Indeed," Imriel said, stepping up to them. "They have had to deal with my team around for the last several months."

"Did they ever strike out against you?" Zimrah asked.

"A few times, though nothing substantial. I'm guessing they will do the same soon if we don't move first."

"Was that the sign to move in?" Rimaz asked, his feline ears perking up.

Imriel took a moment and thought about it. It didn't *feel* like it was the call to move. There was nothing pressing on his spirit.

"No, not yet."

Rimaz's ears fell, and his sword vanished from his hands. "More waiting."

"There will be time to fight soon enough," Zimrah said.

The afternoon turned to evening and Rimaz began pacing while Zimrah and Imriel stood looking down into the compound. The sun was setting behind them, casting the valley into shadows, but lighting up the sky in tones of orange and red. Imriel began to feel restless. Whether that was because the time to move was drawing near, or his own impatience, he didn't know. He wanted to pace along with Rimaz, but held himself still.

"How long have you had your third set of wings?" Imriel asked.

Zimrah looked over to him. "Not long. A couple years. I would have thought you'd be gaining on me by now."

Imriel shrugged. "All in the Most High's timing."

"I meant no offense, my friend."

"None taken. I have just been waiting a long time for a role like this. I assumed I'd have been promoted further by the time I received it. In a way, though, I'm more thankful to have the role without the rank."

"It will come. Maybe all you need to do is demolish this foothold."

"The thought has crossed my—"

"Wolves!" Rimaz cried, just before the beasts entered Imriel's range of detection.

In a split second, both elohim turned, manifesting weapons as Rimaz was struck by an unholy beast exiting the tree line behind them. The lead wolf had hoods extending from its neck, showing him to be swift, like a serpent. He was followed by four lesser wolves. Two ran on all fours, while the others stood upright on two legs, more akin to a man. Imriel lunged into action, bringing his axe down on one of the wolves. Zimrah gave a glorious single-note battle cry that sounded like the opening of a grand composition. Imriel immediately felt passion rise within him and he struck harder. Zimrah's cry hung in the air for a few moments before he moved into a song proclaiming the greatness of the Most High. This sentiment caused the lesser wolves to hesitate and whine, one even stumbling.

Imriel used the opportunity to finish off the one he was fighting with a stroke of his axe, when three more exited the trees. By this time, Rimaz, roused by an initial wound, had the lead wolf and two others on the ground and danced between the newcomers. The other two circled Imriel, waiting for an opening to strike. He didn't give them a chance. He lashed out with his shield battering one away, then struck at the remaining one with his axe. Zimrah kept up his song, watching the battle for if his martial help was needed. Imriel dispatched the wolf he was fighting and moved toward the last one who, seeing Zimrah alone on the ridge, ran at him. Zimrah's staff shot into motion, expertly striking at the wolf, keeping him at bay for Imriel to arrive and strike the final blow. Turning back, he confirmed Rimaz had made quick work of others.

It only took a matter of moments and the battle was at an end, the last note of Zimrah's song hanging in the air. Darkness descended in the material realm, though Imriel and the others could see just as well, seeing in both realms simultaneously.

"Anyone hurt?" Imriel asked.

Rimaz shook his head with a smile on his lips. "Just a warmup." He ignored the small wisps of light escaping a wound on his arm.

"I'm good," Zimrah said. His eyes scanned their surroundings. "Did they come *from* the compound or were they heading there?"

"There have been several beasts making their way to the hold in the last few days. It could have been either."

Suddenly, an explosion lit up the night in the material realm. Imriel walked to the ridgeline and looked down into the compound as gunfire sounded in the night. Several sleek black vehicles poured through the blasted open gate. Figures jumped out of them, firing upon the guards stationed around the buildings. The compound was under attack.

Something pressed upon Imriel's spirit, and he heard a deep, unfathomable voice in his mind.

Go.

Imriel looked at the others, who looked back at him, anticipation on their faces.

"It's time."

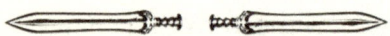

The sliver of a moon was half covered in clouds as gunshots lit up the night in the compound. Bullets flew through the air, slamming into vehicles, buildings, and bodies. Imriel and his three companions landed amidst the chaos of the battle, weapons at the ready. Immediately, he was aware of several things at once. In the physical realm, he recognized the insignia on the attacking force as a rival cartel. In the spiritual realm, he detected a massive amount of low-powered evil concentrated in the central building where the prisoners were housed. That would be where most of the unclean spirits were gathered, although he could still feel plenty of them scattered around as far as he could sense. He couldn't sense the authority, or any other unholy elohim within range, save the beasts turning towards them. They snarled, spitting curses.

"You do not belong here, *servants* of the Most High," spat one of the weaker beasts, gaining confidence from his stronger companions. "You will not spoil our revelry."

He was pushed aside by a massive bear with many spidery eyes. The bear spoke in a gravelly voice. "No. They are just in time. We will present their defeated forms before Shovath, honoring the authority at his celebration, yet garnering esteem for ourselves by displaying our strength."

There was something more going on this night. The beasts had been gathering as guests for an event, not gathering in anticipation of an attack. The defiler had something planned. That would explain why the sentry had come to feel them out earlier.

The other beasts howled with hatred in their animalistic eyes. Three were wolf-like, but each displayed additional bestial features: a scorpion tail on one, a long tongue on another, and goat's horns on the final. Five lesser wolves flanked the higher domain beasts.

The bear's many eyes locked on Rimaz and he tilted his head, a smile breaking his bestial face. "Oh, I will take much pleasure in crushing *you* over and over."

Rimaz's growl turned into a bellow as he charged straight at the massive bear. "For the Most High!"

Zimrah gave a loud cry and Imriel felt passion rising within him once again. Imriel charged at the other beasts, aiming to keep them off Zimrah. He would be at his best if he could be left to sing. And sing he did. Zimrah continued the battle cry into a heroic theme, further emboldening his allies. As a result, Imriel felt more than a match for the beasts in front of him. Shield leading the way, he bashed one of the wolves that lunged at him, then struck out with his axe cleaving into another wolf. Dark smoke curled from the wound and the wolf jumped back as one of the second domain beasts attacked. Imriel fought with precision, parrying attacks and countering with targeted strikes.

While he fought, a part of his focus remained continually on his companions for an opportunity to assist them. The flash of muzzles lit up the dark night in the material realm. The staccato of gunfire joined the sound of divine metal striking spiritual evil as the four sides fought. A few dozen of the unclean spirits in the area saw the outnumbered holy elohim and entered the fray. Zimrah took up his staff, manifesting a shield in his off hand, and fought off the unclean spirits as the wolves circled around Imriel. Zimrah struck at any who faltered, seizing the opportunities created by a third song layered under the others Imriel had missed earlier. Rimaz had it handled with the bear as dark smoke leaked from multiple wounds on the beast's body, though it would still be a tough fight.

His focus returned to his opponents when the scorpion-tailed wolf got a solid strike on his shoulder. Imriel winced and retaliated by bashing his shield into the beast's face. Before he could fully recover, Imriel swung his axe around into the wolf's side. The beast howled and Imriel struck again, dropping him to the ground, but quickly went back on the defensive as a long, frog-like tongue shot out of another wolf's mouth. Imriel faltered, leaving an opening for the horned wolf to charge. Imriel recovered just in time to slam his axe down squarely on the charger's head. The wolf dropped to the ground and Imriel brought his shield up to block the slash of yet another wolf's claws.

There was a brief pause in the fighting as the final second domain wolf eyed him, two lesser wolves encircling Imriel. Zimrah looked to be holding his own against the final wolf, as most of the unclean spirits had either been defeated or left the fight, seeing their betters fall to the holy watchers. Suddenly, Rimaz landed next to the wolf with the frog tongue and released a flurry of blows with his sword.

Within a few moments, they had dispatched the final beasts, and the skirmish ended.

"Thanks," Imriel said, taking a deep, steadying breath. Dark smoke poured from the gaping wounds of a beast at his feet.

Rimaz nodded, a fierce smile on his face.

A few unclean spirits lingered, safely out of range, while the majority slinked farther into the compound. Imriel watched them go, knowing they would join their kin and be back in the fight later. He looked to his two companions. They had fared better than he. Neither had any significant wounds.

Three presences entered Imriel's range of detection and he looked up. The tyrant, sentry, and an unholy warrior with a shield and spear walked towards them, a small horde of unclean spirits behind.

"You dare interrupt our sacrifice and attack when our numbers are swollen?" the tyrant asked, heaving his massive two-handed war hammer.

The sentry and warrior stood a little behind the tyrant, their single horns a contrast to the regal crown with two spikes sticking from the tyrant's brow.

"We've been ordered by the Most High to demolish this foothold. The timing was His," Imriel stated loudly. "Surrender and leave, or face defeat."

The tyrant looked them over, then laughed. "You three, against *my* army?"

Imriel noticed more unclean spirits exiting the buildings surrounding them.

"Your army?" Zimrah asked. "You're not the authority, just his pawn."

The tyrant growled, his dark lion's mane bristling. "Shovath is consecrating himself and can't be disturbed. As the acting authority, I have the privilege of overseeing your demise on this glorious day of carnage and suffering."

The tyrant looked to his right where the battle in the material realm still raged as cartel fought cartel. Half of the unclean spirits stuck to the humans, egging on their bloodlust or dragging the dying into hopelessness in their final moments.

Imriel manifested his glory, light shining from him as if reflecting that Ultimate Light.

"You have a choice. Surrender and leave this place," Imriel said in a loud voice. "If you continue, no quarter will be given."

He could feel first Rimaz, and then Zimrah, manifest their glory as well. Zimrah's was the greatest of the three, and the unclean spirits looked on at it in fear, stuck in place. The sentry and warrior cowered, looking to their superior out of the corners of their eyes, also unable to move. The tyrant grimaced, but stood his ground with a shake of his bull-like head.

"So be it," Imriel said, readying his axe and shield.

Just then, he felt another holy presence inside the large building with the captives. A cry reached their ears. "You do not fight alone, brothers!"

Imriel had forgotten about the guardian assigned to a captured child. He was not as strong as the breach team, but any aid was welcome.

"Fight and demolish this foothold!" Imriel cried and charged, slowed a bit himself from Zimrah's displayed glory.

Rimaz was not far behind as Zimrah continued to express his glory. They brushed aside the awestruck unclean spirits, and Rimaz struck the sentry as he tried to flee the oncoming zealot. In two quick strikes, the unholy elohim fell to the ground, defeated before he could raise a defense. The tyrant stepped forward and met Imriel's charge. Zimrah now let his glory dim as well, shifting his efforts to song as Rimaz closed in on the warrior.

The true battle for the foothold had just begun.

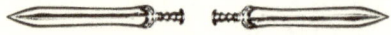

Imriel's axe struck down an unclean spirit, and he launched himself backwards out of the cluster of enemies. He landed on one of the buildings, quickly looking to where Zimrah barely held against the tyrant. Zimrah's song faltered as he blocked and dodged the onslaught of hammer blows. The enemy was no fool. He knew who could turn the battle if he weren't taken down first. This had not begun as Imriel had hoped. Rimaz was somewhere in a press of unclean spirits, fighting dozens of them at a time while trying to take down the warrior. The guardian had followed him into the fray, offering needed support.

Leaping from his position, Imriel landed on a two-story building closer to Zimrah, and looked at his companion maybe sixty feet away. His hands came alight, and he reached towards his companion with his axe hand, jerking it back. Suddenly, he was no longer on the roof, but before the tyrant whose hammer was coming down in a powerful blow. Imriel blocked the blow with his shield, staggering under the force of the impact. The tyrant looked at him in confusion for a second before frustration took its place. Using the momentary shock, Imriel struck out with his axe, slicing into the tyrant's leg, who roared and struck Imriel with the butt of his hammer, pushing him back a few feet.

A passion and zeal for the Most High surged within him, as he heard Zimrah renew his song from the rooftop where Imriel had stood moments before. As a zealot, Rimaz was doubly invigorated, fighting with increased speed and deadly precision—the corrupt warrior wouldn't stand a chance. The only thing saving him from a quick defeat was the mass of unclean spirits swarming Rimaz, forming groups against him. Thankfully, the guardian stood as a bulwark, protecting Rimaz from their superior numbers.

Imriel ran at the tyrant, axe raised. He brought it down on his foe, who barely blocked with the shaft of his hammer. Imriel slammed his shield into the bottom of the locked weapons, knocking them up, exposing the tyrant's mid-section. He let go of his axe and jabbed the unholy elohim in the stomach with his fist. The tyrant staggered back, but Imriel noticed the warrior wince as if receiving the blow himself. The tyrant was yoking the warrior to carry some of his wounds! Imriel manifested a fresh axe into his hand and attacked with renewed ferocity. The tyrant was the antithesis of all Imriel and the king priest discipline stood for. Instead of lending his strength to others, the tyrant used others for himself. Those too weak to object became his pawns and were forced to give themselves for his benefit, hoping for scraps of the power he gained at their expense.

He would be defeated this day. Axe met hammer in a collision, holy power meeting unholy, light against darkness. The ancient struggle with the chaos which has plagued the earth since the Garden.

The tyrant disengaged and removed his left hand from the haft of his hammer, pointing it at Imriel. Chains shot out from his outstretched palm and wrapped themselves around Imriel. Imriel used his own ability to shed the bonds almost immediately. However, the split second was all the tyrant needed. The head of the hammer slammed into Imriel's unguarded side and he grunted, bright vapor billowing from the wound. Taking the hit, he gave his own, his axe biting into the tyrant's shoulder. Imriel swung at the tyrant's wounded shoulder again. His enemy moved to intercept, but the strike was a ruse, and the lip of Imriel's shield took the tyrant in the throat. The unholy elohim's hammer fell to the floor, and Imriel wasted no time in bringing his axe across his neck. The tyrant crumpled to the ground, shadowy smoke erupting from the last gash.

He was defeated.

Imriel dropped his shield—which dispersed before it landed—and pulled out the cluster of manna he had kept for himself. As he ate, he felt some of his strength return and sighed in relief. Glancing up, he saw Rimaz, with both hands resting on the hilt of his sword, and the guardian behind him on one knee. The warrior was down and most of the unclean spirits were scuttering back, forming a perimeter. Zimrah was still on the rooftop, his songs fading to a low hum.

There seemed to be a lull in the fight in the material realm as well, the gunfire sporadic. He could hear the screams and cries of wounded and angry men. Flashlights lit up the darkness around the buildings—one cartel hunting another. In the few outdoor lights, bodies lay scattered on the ground, dead or dying.

Imriel walked over toward Rimaz, who took a step toward him but stumbled. It'd been hard to see, but there was a massive wound on his back gushing vapor. In true zealot fashion, he had been drawing on his passion to carry him through the battle. Imriel moved without hesitation, laying his hands on the wound, giving some of his freshly restored strength to heal his companion. Rimaz straightened.

"Thanks," Rimaz said.

Imriel turned to the guardian. "And thank you for having his back. He wouldn't be standing now without your support."

"It is my privilege to serve," the guardian replied, and then turned to the building that housed the captives. "I should go check on my charge."

Imriel nodded his approval, looking to Rimaz. "Do you still have the manna I gave you?"

"Yes. I didn't have a break in the action to eat."

Imriel gave of himself again to fully heal his ally, and Rimaz handed his manna to Imriel, who ate it.

Zimrah landed next to them.

"Need healing?" Imriel asked.

"Not after your intervention. Thank you for that, my friend. I was in a tight spot back there. Though… I probably had it handled."

"I never doubted you," Imriel said with a chuckle.

Zimrah looked around at the unclean spirits still gathered. They shuffled nervously, but kept the three warriors surrounded from a safe distance. "I feel the battle is not yet done."

"It seems that way," Imriel said.

The unclean spirits nearest the center of the compound turned as one, and a moment later Imriel felt a powerful presence approaching. The authority, Shovath, had come. Imriel hefted his axe and manifested a shield again, readying himself. The unholy elohim landed across from the three heavenly warriors, tossing his bull-like head with massive golden horns. He carried an immense sword. Imriel could tell right away that it wasn't just a weapon the defiler had manifested, it was more—an article of dominion, a weapon of great power.

"You are responsible for this?" Shovath surveyed his defeated underlings strewn throughout the courtyard. "Then know that I am responsible for this." He now surveyed the human bodies scattered in the same area.

"These men were a sacrifice in my honor. Their blood desecrates this ground, sacred now unto me." He rose to full height, three extra horns crowning his head beside the usual ox pair—a clear mark of his third domain status. "It matters not which side wins. I will strengthen the victor with new power, rebuilding them greater than before. All they must do is continue their foul trades and expand as I beckon. Each abuse they commit, a ritual of worship further sanctifying this domain in my honor."

Imriel had discreetly signaled his companions to be patient, knowing monologues could occasionally provide helpful intel.

"I had intended to come out to commemorate the victor in front of my forces and those invited to witness, and accept their praise. But you have turned this into a different kind of performance. When those whom you have bested see you all fall at my hand, their reverence toward me will be all the stronger. I should thank you for the opportunity."

As he finished these last words, he raised his sword.

Seeing he had finished, Imriel finally spoke. "I offered the others the chance to leave. That offer doesn't extend to you."

The time for diplomacy was at an end.

Zimrah began a new song and layered another over top. He did it with such practice and precision that it sounded like two halves of a whole. Zeal and passion rose within Imriel, washing away some of his exhaustion. He gripped his axe and shield with determination. The Most High had given them a mission, and it was time to complete it. Imriel and Rimaz attacked together, one from the right and the other the left. They hadn't fought together in centuries, but in the last several minutes of combat, they'd fallen into a rhythm like only old companions could.

Shovath blocked Rimaz, and Imriel's swing struck a glancing blow as the unholy elohim moved at the last moment. Then the unclean spirits joined the fray, their moment of hesitation gone. Zimrah flew to the top of a nearby building, giving him a better vantage to defend himself while he kept up the songs that energized Imriel and Rimaz. They struck again, one going high, one low, but the defiler blocked and dodged. Rimaz disengaged to sweep off a group of the more aggressive unclean spirits at his back. Imriel briefly pressed Shovath alone before Rimaz's sword returned to strike at the defiler's arm. Imriel bashed an unclean spirit with his shield while thrusting the point of his axe at Shovath's torso. The unclean spirits were only a distraction from the true fight, but a distraction at this time could be deadly. The more Rimaz fought, the faster he moved and the harder he struck, passion rising within him.

The defiler saw an opening as Imriel turned his axe toward several unclean spirits, and struck at Rimaz. Imriel saw it too and stretched his will, yoking himself to his companion right as the blow landed, sharing the burden of its damage. He could feel a fraction of the blow, but was glad it was only a fraction as it hit him hard. Rimaz stumbled but recovered quickly and countered before Shovath could fully recover. His sword cut a line through the defiler's chest. Shovath let out a roar and turned to Imriel.

Imriel quickly dispatched the unclean spirits around him in time to block the blow from Shovath. The defiler pressed him hard, blow after blow raining down, and Imriel took several small hits from more unclean spirits flocking to him in his weakened state. As he was driven to his knees, he knew he couldn't keep his defensive stance for long. Unclean spirits piled onto his back, biting and clawing at him. Right when his guard was about to break, Rimaz was there, striking the defiler several times in quick succession. Shovath roared once more and shot up into the air.

Imriel took a deep breath. Rimaz looked like he was about to follow Shovath, when the unholy elohim manifested a censer in his off hand.

Imriel yelled, trying to alert his companions.

Rimaz was already dashing away.

Imriel tried to stand, but had sustained too many small wounds and many of the unclean spirits still clung to him. Trying to shake them off, he realized he was too late. A hot multi-colored coal hit the ground next to him and lightning struck the spot, throwing Imriel to his back from the small explosion. The one positive of the lightning was it'd thrown the unclean spirits off him. Imriel rolled to his knees and stood quickly, only to have something slam into his back and he was thrown face-first to the ground. Thunder sounded and the ground shook in the spiritual realm. Imriel coughed and rose to his knees, white smoke rising from several wounds. He ached all over.

A coal landed on the roof next to Zimrah and lightning struck the mark. Zimrah was thrown from the roof with a cry and Imriel lost sight of his friend as he fell behind the building. Rimaz fought the few remaining unclean spirits that were still in the fight, while staying ahead of the coals launched his way.

Imriel groaned. His endurance was nearly spent. The ground shook again as the defiler landed before him.

"If you want something done right…" Shovath said.

His massive sword in both hands again, he struck downward. Imriel used his will to manifest chains wrapping around the defiler, halting his swing. Shovath merely grunted and flexed, the chains shattering. Imriel used the brief moment to rise to his feet and raise his shield. The defiler quickly readied another strike, jumping into the air a few feet, and swung down at Imriel. It was a momentous strike, like only a warrior could employ. His sword must have granted him such ability. Imriel kept his shield raised as the sword descended, unable to do anything else, knowing the strike would cut right through his defenses. At the last moment, the blade jerked to the side and swung just past Imriel as something slammed into the defiler.

Rimaz had rejoined the battle, his sword striking again and again as Shovath tried to shake off the impact of the charge.

Imriel stood on weak legs as Rimaz and the defiler battled. He didn't see any sign of Zimrah, though he could still sense him—not fully defeated, but maybe close. Imriel was low on endurance as well, weariness hanging on him like a heavy cloak. Rimaz continued to strike the defiler, and he could see that Shovath was weakening. Darkness billowed out from dozens of wounds as Rimaz continued to press him, leaving no opening for attack or effect. Even so, the defiler broadly swung his giant sword, leaving himself open. Yet as Rimaz lunged to seize the opportunity, Shovath launched himself backwards. Rimaz had overreached and the defiler charged back in, the great sword slashing right through Rimaz's torso. Imriel's companion stumbled to a knee, the strike hitting true. Imriel cried out and used the last of his strength to dash forward, barely closing the distance to rest a hand on Rimaz. The last of his endurance left Imriel. He collapsed limply to the ground, but Rimaz rose to his feet, the thick vapor pouring from his chest wound reducing to a thin trail.

Shovath looked at Imriel in shock, barely bringing his sword up in time to block Rimaz's strike as he pressed the momentary advantage. Imriel's vision grew fuzzy around the edges. He lay on the ground, watching as Rimaz leapt and stabbed with renewed passion. The defiler could no longer endure in his weakened state. After deflecting a last, tired, downward strike of the now visibly weighty sword, Rimaz landed two well-timed strikes at the defiler's heart. He joined Imriel, motionless on the ground. Rimaz stepped over and grasped Imriel by the shoulders. He dragged him over to the wall of a building and propped him in a sitting position.

"Thank you, Brother," Rimaz said.

Imriel could see the blur of his feline face. Then it was gone and Imriel looked out at the rest of the compound. The skirmish in the material realm had ended as well, and as he sat there, dipping in and out of consciousness, he couldn't see who had been the victor. Not a single human moved around the compound. Were they inside the buildings? His vision blurred again for a long moment—maybe seconds, maybe hours. When it came into focus again, he noticed Rimaz and Zimrah, a few minor wounds still leaking white vapor, walking towards him.

"Time for me to return the favor," Zimrah said, pulling out the cluster of manna Imriel had given him earlier.

Zimrah opened Imriel's mouth and placed the white cluster inside. The manna rested in his mouth and dissolved. Strength returned to him like cold water waking one from a stupor. His companions helped him stand to his feet as he stabilized.

"Thanks," Imriel said.

"I figured it was time for me to rescue you for a change," Zimrah said with a smile, clapping him on the shoulder.

"How long have I been down?"

"A good half hour," Rimaz said.

"Long enough for us to scout out the rest of the compound," Zimrah said. "The area is clear, other than the unclean spirits lurking in the shadows. All the unholy elohim and beasts have been defeated or fled."

"Good," Imriel said with a sigh. "Then the battle for the foothold has been won."

Rimaz nodded.

"And by some *miracle*," Zimrah added, "the cartels seemed to have wiped each other out to a man. They're all dead."

"I wondered why it was so quiet. What about the captives?"

Rimaz looked to the building in the center of the compound. "Still there."

"Rimaz, mind routing out or chasing away those final unclean spirits?"

Rimaz smiled, showing sharp teeth. "With pleasure."

He moved off and Imriel turned to Zimrah. "Let's go see what we can do about those captives."

Imriel and Zimrah walked through the carnage of the battles. The bleeding bodies of the humans lay mingled with spiritual beasts, dark smoke rising from their wounds. There were several small fires around the compound from explosives and one of the vehicles was in flames. The loss of human life never sat well with him, but in cases like this, it was tinged with the knowledge that with the end of the cartel's influence in this foothold, his job in the coming weeks would be much easier. The initial battle for the foothold had been won, but there was still more work needed to completely tear this hold down.

They arrived at the building and Imriel walked through one of the walls, heading towards a room he remembered from his scouting missions. Stopping outside the door, he looked at the deadbolt in place. He reached into the material realm, unlocked the door, and then he entered. Two young women were curled in each corner behind the beds, fearful gaze on the door. They would have heard the combat outside and the door unlock. Imriel could only imagine the terror and uncertainty they would have in this moment.

Imriel went over to one and began to speak encouragingly to her, trying to comfort her spirit. Zimrah sang a quiet psalm of thanksgiving, and the effect was immediate on the two women. Much of the fear left their faces, and they looked at each other in question.

Imriel continued speaking to the one. "Peace. You are safe. The enemy has been defeated. Check the door. Look outside. Your captivity has come to an end."

He repeated the phrase, knowing she wouldn't be able to "hear" him in a normal sense, but maybe some of his words would break through. On his third time repeating the phrase, the woman stood and hesitantly walked to the door. She opened it a crack and peered out. All the guards that had been stationed inside had joined the battle in the compound and were now dead. Opening the door completely, she looked back at her companion.

"They're gone," she said in French.

The other woman shook her head, still too shocked to speak. Imriel followed the woman to the door, urging her to go outside. After a few moments she complied, Zimrah staying with the woman in the room. The woman walked out of the building and into a night lit up by small fires and the headlights of idling vehicles cutting through the darkness.

An hour later, Imriel watched as the last of the kids were loaded into one of the black SUVs under the light of the moon. A young Columbian man looked around one final time at the carnage, then glanced into the sky. He said a quick prayer and climbed into the SUV, leading the caravan of vehicles full of newly freed people out of the foothold and to freedom.

"That's my cue," Rahael, the guardian, said. "Luciana will take some time to heal from this, but she has a good family who've been praying."

"Hold fast, Brother," Imriel said.

Rahael nodded and shot off after the departing vehicles.

The captives would taste freedom this day. Hopefully, that freedom would reach beyond the physical and enter into the spiritual. Rimaz had cleared the compound of unclean spirits, though he noticed some come out of the jungle clinging to a few of the SUVs. For some of them, the captivity would haunt them for the rest of their lives.

Movement caught Imriel's eye from the ridge where he'd watched the compound. A figure launched from that spot and the holy messenger landed next to them.

"Greetings, brothers," the messenger said.

"Greetings," Imriel said.

"Zimrah, herald of the third heaven?"

"Yes?" Zimrah said.

"You are summoned back to the heavens when your work here is complete."

"Understood."

"Rimaz, zealot of the second heaven?"

"Yeah?"

"You have a choice: stay with Imriel and join his breaching efforts, or head to the stronghold in Illinois for your next mission."

"What type of mission?"

"Diplomatic."

Rimaz scowled. "I'll join Imriel."

"Very well. Continue the fight, brothers."

"One moment," Zimrah said, and the messenger waited. Zimrah looked to Imriel. "You plan to stay?"

"Yes."

"Then we still need to remove these." Zimrah motioned at their downed enemies.

"I was just thinking that."

"With help, I can take the defiler to a hold and see if they wouldn't mind a prisoner. Get him out of your way for a time."

"I would appreciate that," Imriel said.

Zimrah looked to the messenger.

"I can spare the time," the messenger said.

"Good," Zimrah said, turning to Imriel.

"Thanks for your help, my friend," Imriel said.

"Of course," Zimrah responded. "It's been a pleasure, as always. Let me know when you get your next set of wings. Maybe your team will have an opening."

"I'll always have an opening for you."

Zimrah clasped forearms with them both.

"Until we next meet, Imriel, Rimaz," Zimrah said.

Rimaz nodded.

"Until then," Imriel responded

Zimrah and the messenger walked over, collected the defeated defiler, and shot into the sky.

Imriel surveyed the aftermath of the night-shrouded compound. They had many more downed enemies they needed to remove, but the leader had been taken care of. It would be a while before the defiler could return, and when he did, he'd find the enemy presence that remained less enticing, or if Imriel's plans succeeded, removed altogether.

"No goodbyes here," Rimaz said, smiling at Imriel.

"I'm surprised you gave up the opportunity for a riveting diplomatic mission to join me."

Rimaz chuckled. "You know I'm not suited for such missions. Helping you against the opposition that is to come? Now that I can do."

Imriel laughed. "I'm glad to have you on my team. Our work has only just begun."

SHADOW OF GRIEF

HOPE ANN

T he enemy didn't look like they were pressing an attack, but oh, were they clever. Movement caught the corner of Karim's eye, and his gaze flicked out the wide living room window in time to spot another trio of unclean spirits vanishing through the walls of the house next door.

A moment more, then a wail rose, only to fade away like a shadow in sunlight.

Karim snorted, picturing Mehran casually flicking his great sword. The warrior could hold off a dozen evil spirits without blinking. Even a hundred, if need be, for a short time.

But this? A few attacks each hour? No true rest? No time to properly heal? An occasional creeping or slithering beast to increase the challenge?

Karim glanced instinctively over his shoulder, but Addie still sat hunched over the glass coffee table, hoodie sleeves bunched up around her elbows.

Some unclean spirits lurked for her too. They'd not attacked so far, but they wouldn't hesitate the moment he stepped in to help Mehran.

By the grains of the sand, what are they trying to gain?

Karim knew it baffled Mehran too. The last time he'd caught sight of the warrior through the windows of the opposite house, he'd noted the furrow on the thick, bushy brows and the tension of the warrior's lion-like jaw.

Darkness lurked for all humans, of course, and unclean spirits were as persistent as vermin.

But, like vermin, they normally poked into places no one was watching. They kept to the shadows. To the helpless and the weak.

They *didn't* attack a third heaven warrior or even a second heaven ministering spirit like Karim unless something greater drove them; something he still couldn't sense when he reached out to feel for the presence of others.

"...your will. Amen." Addie's voice was barely a whisper in the hush of the warmly lit living space.

Karim shivered. The words brought to mind spices, ice, and fresh wind.

She continued staring at the mess of journals and papers before her, oblivious to his presence a realm and several steps away.

Studies of the apostles in tiny fonts. Records of the Most High's words. Blank paper holding several false starts on what she planned to be a thesis on serving the Almighty in her current time.

Humans.

Karim smiled faintly. So earnest. So focused on making life more complicated than needed.

Addie rubbed her eyes with both palms and the elohim moved behind her seat with another glance at the window. He brushed her shoulder with one hand.

She shook herself, sitting a little straighter.

"Courage."

He let strength slip from his fingers to her skin, encouraging her resolve.

Addie drew a quick breath, her gaze shifting to the wide window welcoming in the last rays of the dying sun. She'd been looking that way more often since catching sight of her neighbor a few days ago.

His wife died two weeks ago, Mehran had told Karim. Addie had known her slightly. They'd talked of flowers and watered plants when the other was absent. She'd never spoken to the husband, whose constantly furrowed brow seemed to warn everyone away.

He was the main reason she'd not attended the funeral, or so she'd told herself. He'd recognize her as a neighbor if she went and offered condolences. And what if she upset him somehow? What if that meant every time she stepped through her door, she risked coming face to face with a neighbor who hated her?

Unclean spirits and other unholy elohim had both gathered that day, with hints of greater threats just out of reach. Their number had only increased since then.

This was more than grief. More than fear. There was something larger going on. If only Karim could—

He drew a sharp breath as something touched the edge of his mind. Something dark. Powerful.

He sprang for the window, shouting a call of warning through the spiritual realm to Mehran.

The thing was moving. Fast.

A shadow passed overhead, and paws slammed against the ground in the gathering dusk.

A monstrous leopard.

A bit late, seeing death had already visited the house. Or was the creature coming back to revel in the grief he wrought?

Odd, though, that he hadn't struck as he revealed himself. Or maybe it was just arrogance.

Taller by half than any human, the beast snarled as his mutated tail coiled, a scorpion's stinger with black poison on the end.

Mehran exploded through the roof of the house, his giant blade wielded in two hands.

The leopard sprang away, striking as he moved.

Mehran stumbled, barely evading the blow.

"Tired already?" the beast growled, the noise rumbling in what could only be a laugh. Then he opened his mouth.

Oh.

A long tongue uncoiled, revealing his second mutation, this one from a frog. It lashed toward Mehran. The warrior slashed downward, but the beast twisted at the last moment, his gaping mouth opening again.

This time it wasn't for growling or laughter or even words. It was a song, warped and twisted, and broken into chaotic notes of failure and despair.

Trepidation. Of all the misused, cursed, unfair attacks...

Of course, a creature that could sing to trepidation would be sent if a ministering spirit was present. Karim growled under his breath. If woven successfully, it could keep him from lending aid to the warrior.

As if they needed proof this was a well-coordinated attack.

Karim sent a surge of passion toward the warrior as Mehran twisted, swinging his blade in a circular motion to ward off a strike.

Mehran shook himself, shedding the song's effect and readjusting his grip on his weapon.

Behind Karim, Addie inhaled sharply.

Karim spun, his staff slicing toward an unclean spirit coiling around her arm. It shrieked, crumpling into a smoke-like substance that twisted powerlessly beneath the edge of the couch.

Addie didn't flinch, staring at her paper again. She struggled for words to write, as she had been for the past week.

"Sometimes, actions are needed, not words." Karim pushed the thought toward her as he pivoted back toward the window.

Mehran had avoided another blow from the leopard, but barely. He was more tired than Karim realized.

Movement caught Karim's eye as the front door of the neighboring house opened and a man stepped onto the porch, just beyond the fight. His movements were slow, his shoulders slumped. Three unclean spirits wrapped about his legs and a beast in the shape of a spider clung to his back.

How had *that* managed a way past?

Oh.

The leopard's lack of ambush wasn't arrogance after all. It was a distraction.

"Karim!" Mehran deflected a blow as he shouted.

Karim was already thrusting a hand toward the man, creating a glowing shield around his form as Mehran lunged to the side. His blade passed harmlessly through the man, slicing the spider in half and catching the unclean spirits in a backstroke.

A claw from the leopard caught him in return, slashing across his ribs.

In the physical realm, the man wavered, catching the porch banister at the very edge of Karim's shield. The man stared out at the last red streaks of light slashing the dying sky.

Inside, Addie murmured to herself. A low-level bestial creature shaped like a frog crept through the shadows at her feet.

Sands of the sea.

Karim twisted, sending his staff slashing toward the creature. The frog evaded him, leaping, but then Karim swung his weapon around and slammed the creature out of the air.

The frog screeched as he fell backward, crumpling into an unmoving heap. No time for victory. Karim spun back toward the window as the leopard struck the dome around the man.

It shuddered, and Karim with it, but the shield held. Barely.

Bowing forward, Karim steadied himself with one hand on his knee.

Movement flickered to the side as an unclean spirit wrapped up Addie's leg. Karim gritted his teeth, struggling to force strength back into the shield. Dropping even the smallest amount of focus now would let it go.

Addie stilled, staring out the window to where the man stood.

"Go to him." Karim sent the words in her direction.

The unclean spirit hissed, wrapping the words in its own tendrils of fear. Addie glanced quickly back to her paper, but her shoulders were still tense, her gaze deliberately not on the window.

She knows. She knows what to do.

Outside, the leopard swiped at Mehran. Light split from his bronzed skin as another wound opened across one bicep.

How much time had passed? A dozen seconds?

Already the warrior was faltering. The beast's tail curved around to strike.

No time to strengthen. Or quicken.

Addie's gaze had drifted back to the window.

"Go to him," Karim urged again. He tapped what little strength he had left, and reached toward Mehran.

The warrior seemed to sense the touch, his eyes widening in realization of the attack Karim had seen a moment before.

The beast was moving far too fast and there was no time to escape.

As the blow descended, Karim felt himself yanked from the room, his presence replacing Mehran's as the warrior was transported to where Karim stood a moment before.

The scorpion tail stabbed Mehran's surrogate in the back.

Karim crumpled to the ground with a strangled scream, his shield around the man faltering.

Most High above, have mercy.

He couldn't see. Couldn't think. Pain surged through his senses, tearing at them. Blinding him.

Sunlight blinked out, leaving nothing but a distant crimson glow.

Claws slammed into the shield, and this time Karim had no strength left to give it.

From the side, Mehran surged from Addie's house, wounds closing, thanks to the sacrifice of Karim's injuries in his stead. The warrior slammed into the beast's side, scoring a cut along his flank.

Karim dragged himself to one knee.

Most High, be with Addie. For I cannot.

The leopard faltered, but when Mehran swept forward, the leopard leaped back, striking as he went. Except this strike crashed into the shield.

The barrier finally collapsed, but it had been enough. Enough for Mehran to step between the leopard and the man still hunched against the railing of the porch, unaware of the fight happening over him.

Karim drew a ragged breath.

Instead of striking, the beast's mouth opened again, and he sang notes of confusion and defeat. This time Mehran staggered under them.

Gritting his teeth, the warrior readjusted the grip on his sword.

The song waned, then rose again.

With a cry, Karim reached weakly toward the warrior, trying to renew his drive by offering the last of his own strength.

It struck a wall, rebuffed, as Mehran's features slackened.

Most High, send help.

Karim struggled to breathe, dark mist clouding his vision as his body shuddered from the poison. "Mehran..."

"We can't—" The warrior's features twisted. "It's not up to us anymore."

Karim shook his head, pain splintering at the motion. "The result never was, but we still fight."

Next to the warrior, the leopard nudged the man toward the porch steps, low words mixing with faint snarls.

The man shuddered, looking up. His eyes locked on the road before his house, where lights flashed by on moving vehicles.

A leopard, bringer of untimely death.

Apparently he wasn't done with this house.

Karim shuddered, trying to rise completely and crumpling back to hands and one knee.

Addie. Where is Addie?

Karim reached for strength, once again, to offer to the warrior. "Mehran, wake up! This isn't you." This time, a little passion seeped through.

Mehran shuddered, blinking once. Twice.

The man was already stepping from his porch, the leopard giving him another nudge.

Pain wrapped around Karim's chest.

Breath of the Most High, reach Addie. Bring her.

It was important. It was hard to focus through the pain, but it was important.

Reaching out with the last of his strength, he rested comfort across her shoulders like an invisible cloak. Comfort and peace.

Because there she was, standing at the window.

Ahead, the man had taken another step toward the road.

Karim was too far. Too weak. He dragged himself a pace toward the man anyway. Then another. To the side, Mehran drew a deep breath, his eyes finally clearing.

The leopard nudged the man a step further, then spun with a roar as Mehran swung his sword. The monster twisted, but the blade seared through a portion of his tail.

With a shriek, he surged into the warrior, knocking Mehran to the ground and leering above him with great teeth, dripping with poison.

"Again?" The beast's voice was more growl than words. "You want to fail again?"

Beyond them both, the man stumbled toward the road with halting steps. Toward the cars speeding along it.

"Now," Karim pleaded. He didn't have the strength. Addie wouldn't hear, but he repeated the words anyway. "Courage over comfort."

"Go to him."

He dragged himself another step. Another.

If he could only get close enough to the man himself. How can a mortal walk so slowly, yet time move so swiftly all at once? Shadows clustered the man's steps, clinging to him, urging him on.

Movement flickered.

Karim drew a shuddering breath as Addie stepped from her house. Her hands were clenched. Her knuckles white with nervousness.

"Courage."

Karim's mind fogged slowly, his body heavy.

"Courage."

She took a step. Then another.

Mehran's voice rose as the warrior hurled insults at the leopard.

He's seen. He's keeping his attention.

Ahead, the man stopped on the curb, eyes locked on the traffic. A breath. A heartbeat.

A movement.

A hand touched his arm, and his body jerked back with an imperceptible step.

Addie's hand. Her voice.

Karim could barely hear it. He didn't have to hear the words though. What he saw was enough.

Addie brushed away a tear of her own. Then the man shook, trembled, and crumpled to the curb with sobs wracking his body. Distant lamp light rested across her like a cloak as she crouched with him, one arm awkwardly on his shoulder.

The leopard spun with a hiss, leaping toward them both. Toward their bowed heads. Their sorrow.

The beast slammed into an invisible shield.

Karim's breath caught.

He knew what was happening and he never tired of witnessing it.

The invisible turned visible. A glow. Faint at first, as Karim caught a fragment of Addie's broken prayer. Then stronger. Brighter.

The glory of the One to whom it belongs.

The leopard growled as the light spiraled upward. Reaching. Growing. Surging in an explosion sweeping outward as the leopard fled with a final snarl.

Karim gasped, surging to his feet as the pain washed away and new strength filled his veins from the light.

Shadows fled. The night gathered, but here, all was light.

Karim met Mehran's eyes across the way

The warrior's eyes closed, his head bowing.

Karim did the same.

By the time he looked again, the glow was fading.

Slowly, the man rose and turned toward the house. His shoulders were straighter now. His eyes clearer, though still filled with pain.

Addie ducked her head in farewell, hurrying past where Karim stood as she made her way into her own house.

Karim followed with his newfound healing, sensing the released adrenaline in her blood. The shiver of cold as she wrapped her arms around herself. The grin as she knew she'd done what was commanded. The shaking from the release of unexpected emotions.

It was a word of comfort and a prayer from her. She doesn't know how much more it was for the man she saved.

She likely would never know. But, as she sat back at her books, she took up her pen and this time she began to write.

Karim smiled, rested his staff in the crook of one arm, and kept watch through the night.

MELODIEL'S RHAPSODY

BRYAN TIMOTHY MITCHELL

At the central east gate, two cherubim stood at either side of the shimmering portal. Their sacred presence and divine light always inspired my resolve before departing on my missions. A holy radiance emanated from them, providing comfort through its everlasting song of peace and strength. Still, there was much to do. Time was short for the Stanton family and their neighbors.

Maiel, the breach commander of a small rural region of northern Virginia, had warned me that the unholy hold in Ruckmyer's Meadow was a stubborn nuisance, especially for the families living there. For this reason, he had sent two messengers to inspire hope. The message never made it, and the messengers never returned. I and two of the best warriors I'd ever worked with were to deploy later today to attack the hold and seek the missing messengers, but Maiel had sent a courier, who informed me that the Stanton family needed immediate intervention.

"Melodiel," Sersimi called. He and Urimiel marched along the golden path leading to the central gate with shields strapped to their backs. Their golden armor glistened in the rippling light of the portal. We had fought the enemy together many times, and I was thankful to have them with me again. "Why are we deploying early? Has something changed?"

"I just received a message from Maiel. A family from Ruckmyer's Meadow, the Stanton family, is under extreme duress. The patriarch, Earl Stanton, lost his job, and unclean spirits are pushing him to take his own life." I turned back to the rippling portal. "We'll deploy directly to him and then continue as planned to Ruckmyer's Meadow."

Urimiel squeezed a fist, and a sword appeared in his hand. "Lead the way."

I leaped through the portal with Sersimi and Urimiel in tow. Dropping from the sky into the Lord's glorious creation was like entering a song where majestic waves of sound expanded and contracted through space, forming shapes that simultaneously calmed and excited the senses. Rays of light rained from the afternoon sun, igniting scattered clouds and rebounding off the forestland below. The pastoral colors of the wilderness presented serenity, despite the loathsome schemes of the unholy elohim—a pleasant reminder that the Lord was in control even through times of trouble.

"Where are we to find him?" Sersimi asked.

"He is along an embankment of the lake below us," I said.

"There!" Urimiel, whose golden mane danced like agitated flames, pointed his sword to the southeastern side of the small brown lake. Earl Stanton knelt there on a flat stone surface, weeping among a throng of unclean spirits.

Sersimi, a discerning and calculating warrior, narrowed his pale-amber eyes and brandished his long sword. "He's surrounded."

Earl was alone amid these wretched spirits. Their forms, more like smoke than substance, crowded around him like wolves devouring prey. Although weak and cowardly, their words would bite his soul. They relished the anguish of others. Refusing to bear witness to such senseless torture, I drew my warrior's sword, but it wasn't the only weapon I had. From the deepest depths of me, depths of which only Elyon knew, came a powerful battle cry that could only come from a minstrel of the Most High. "For the glory of Elyon!"

Invigorated by my song, we rocketed to the earth and smashed in the heart of the unclean infestation, surrounding Earl Stanton. The ghostly rabble fell quickly, dissolving like fog in light. Three took refuge inside Earl. We could drive them out with our swords, but Earl was in such distress that a song seemed the better remedy. One that would offer him peace and quiet the wicked spirits within.

Earl's tearful face strained and shook. His breathing hastened, and from his gaping mouth came an agonizing scream. "Let's end this!" He pressed the muzzle to the side of his head.

I gripped his shoulder, and his rigid body stilled, although the things within squirmed. The unclean spirits would love to flee but feared me and my brothers, yet they would not escape my lullaby.

> *Quiet the noise within*
> *Let the world be still.*
> *Shall we now begin*
> *To contemplate what's real?*
> *You are not alone*
> *Never were nor ever will be.*
> *Before the stars even shone*
> *You were loved. Yes, you were loved even then.*

It must have struck a chord with Earl. His tired face seemed to settle. He looked skyward. Winds ushered clouds away, and sunlight opened his glossy red eyes to the world around him. I knew the Lord was speaking to his spirit as it does me every time I marvel upon His creation.

He lowered the gun, but his heartbeat quickened. The unclean spirits were trying to burrow deeper and secure their tenuous hold. Earl tensed, breathing in short, rapid breaths. I continued the song.

> *This is why we are*
> *Something is never nothing,*
> *And He who set the stars*
> *Always knew you would be.*
> *So silence the darkened thoughts,*
> *Take in the life around you,*
> *Exhale the lies you bought,*
> *Because you are loved. Yes, you are loved to no end.*
> *You are loved.*

After a deep inhalation, he exhaled. Too weary to fight, the unclean spirits poured from his mouth in listless smoky-gray plumes. Urimiel sheathed his sword. "Well done, Melodiel. Although I would've preferred to cut them down."

"There's plenty of cutting to come, my friend," I said, coming to my feet. "This is only the start of the trouble."

"Aye," Sersimi said, still gripping his sword while eying the woods. "The greater threat to us lies with our rebellious brothers, but they aren't here. What do we know of this hold?"

Earl was safe. I allowed him to catch his breath and turned to my brothers. "There is nothing remarkable about it. None of its known members hold strength that's worthy of note, but the ruler is a sly, unholy messenger. They occupy the area around Ruckmyer's Meadow, which is surrounded by heavily wooded hills. While it isn't strong or distinguished, two messengers disappeared there, so something is amiss. We're to find out what that is and retrieve the messengers after attacking the hold."

"Do we know where they're held?" Urimiel asked.

"No, but the property owner operates a moonshine still in the forest," I said. "And there are stolen goods in his house, which sits on the property. We'll search for them after we've weakened the hold."

Sersimi folded his arms over his breastplate and focused on the stone surface. "We'll need to execute caution. They'll be expecting an attack."

"True," I said. "I believe the best course would be to stay close to Earl. They wouldn't expect us to ride with him. Their eyes would be to the sky. We'll observe their posture, their movements. And when we're ready, we'll strike hard and fast."

"That sounds surgical," Sersimi said. "I like it."

"Maybe we could cripple the hold," Urimiel said. "Begin its decline."

"It depends on how entrenched its influence is in the community," I said.

Earl sighed and pushed to his feet. His t-shirt was soaked in sweat. He looked at the water, then at the gun in his hand. "I don't want this anymore!" With a grunt, he slung it into the water.

"Well," Sersimi said, "we can't have some kid finding that." He jumped into the lake without disturbing the water.

Earl pulled out his smartphone and sifted through family photos. He had many pictures of a young girl, likely his daughter, playing in a grassy field. He paused on a selfie of him and his wife.

Sersimi emerged from the water. "Wedged it between two large stones, then packed rocks over it. I think that'll keep it hidden."

"Good work." I nodded to the trailhead. "We're about to move, so you and Urimiel can scout the path for spies. I'll stay with Earl."

They headed into the woods with their weapons drawn. We had wiped out the unclean spirits, and I doubted any unholy elohim were with Earl. Still, it was important to exercise caution. If they saw us getting into a vehicle with Earl, our cover would be blown before we reached Ruckmyer's Meadow.

"Lord, I'm sorry," Earl whispered behind me, eying the ground. The light in his eyes had dimmed.

While it would take time for him to heal, I wanted to comfort him. There was beauty all around. He just needed to feel it. I raised my sword and swirled it clockwise, singing "For the Beauty of the Earth." A gust of warm air curled around us, stirring the surrounding vegetation. It gathered amber plumes from honeysuckles on the other side of the lake and carried it over. Earl inhaled and smiled. That was nice to see. Although he was unemployed and hurting financially, he was seeing the light again. Defeating the unclean spirits was one thing. What Sersimi, Urimiel, and I were heading into next was another.

Earl followed a trail through the woods that wound around the lake to a nearly empty parking lot. There was only one car parked near the trail, which must've been his. Beyond the parking lot, through a line of trees, vehicles whooshed left and right along a narrow four-lane road.

"All is clear," Urimiel said.

Earl got into his compact car. I sat in the front passenger seat and inherently shrank to fit into the small space.

The backseat was so cramped that Urimiel and Sersimi looked like small children when they sat. I couldn't help myself. "My two precious kiddos are behaving so well. Keep it up and I'll allow each of you to have a candy bar."

Urimiel smirked. "You better produce this candy bar, or I'll bring you before the council."

"Issuing threats is no way to earn the candy bar, brother," Sersimi added. "I, however, will not issue threats to our most kind and generous leader, which should earn me twice the reward."

"Two candy bars?" Urimiel scoffed. "I didn't realize you were prone to gluttony."

The interior of the car was in disarray. Trash and crumbs covered the floorboards. The seats were torn and stained. When Earl turned over the engine, a belt squealed from under the hood, and the engine shook the car. The speakers blared what humans called thrash metal. The singer's voice sounded angry and garbled. Earl cranked it up, tapping the steering wheel to the beat of the intense music. He backed out of the parking spot and sped to the busy intersection.

"Any more lullabies for Earl, Melodiel?" Urimiel said. He and Sersimi broke into laughter.

I gave him a slight smile. "No seatbelts. No candy bars."

"You know we can't mess around with these seatbelts," Urimiel said. "Earl would notice them moving on their own, and it would likely cause him mental distress."

Sersimi lost interest in the banter. "Will this music affect his ability to drive calmly?"

Earl seemed focused on the road, and his driving wasn't as boisterous as the music. "He's fine. Just cover your ears if you can't handle his musical preference."

He pulled into a gas station to fill his tank and removed much of the trash that was piled on the floors. Of course, Sersimi and Urimiel pestered me to go inside to purchase candy bars, but I noted that their behavior must persist in the right direction for the rest of our journey to reap a sugary reward. Kids, you must love them—not spoil them.

Urimiel asked, "How long do you suppose we'll remain in this tiny car once we've reached Ruckmyer's Meadow?"

"If it's clear, we could enter Earl's home," Sersimi suggested. "We may gather more intelligence that way."

"I'll stay with Earl," I said, watching Earl take a squeegee to his windshield. "There may be unholy elohim inside the other homes in

Ruckmyer's Meadow, so you two will clear the other homes and join me inside Earl's afterward. We'll work our way to the owner's house and if need be, the moonshine still from there, attacking any patrols we see on the way."

"Are we moving as one unit after clearing the homes?" Urimiel asked.

"Yes," I said. "If we stay together and are deliberate, we'll remain unobserved longer. There's no reason to rush. And furthermore, while this hold doesn't seem like much, they captured two messengers. We should remain cautious."

"But from the report Maiel gave you, each one of us outmatches them alone." Urimiel bent closer. "We could make quick work of them and focus more time on finding the messengers."

"While that may be true," Sersimi said, rubbing his chin, "we only know so much about this area. Certainly, this hold is stronger than reported. It is a hold, after all, not some group of loosely organized troublemakers."

"We'll be cautious at the start," I said. "If it seems best to pick them off individually, we will. If we find most of them in the open, we'll attack and maintain aggression until they're subdued."

Earl hopped into the car with his cellphone pressed to his ear. "I'm gonna talk to her about it, Pa." He nodded while listening. "The company was hurtin' more than they let on when they hired me. I planned on workin' there 'til retirement, but I'll find somethin'. Somebody's bound to be hirin' somewhere. We'll need it if we're ever gonna get out of that trailer park." He stared ahead, listening. "I'll keep you posted for sure. Love you too. Bye."

Earl weaved between forested hills, passing small houses and mobile homes. Eventually, he pulled onto a long dirt road, where a weathered two-story home with cracked wood and flaking paint marked the entrance to Ruckmyer's Meadow.

"That's the property owner's home," I said, eying the dusty windows for activity. "It very well may be the nucleus to the hold."

"I can hop out here and clear it myself," Urimiel said.

"Standby," I said. "Let's first clear the homes in the trailer park."

The road led to a pothole-infested gravel lot that sat in a sunlit field nestled at the foot of a large, wooded hill. Earl drove between the two rows of mobile homes. Three unholy warriors surrounded a picnic table, where four men played cards. One man nodded to Earl. Seeing the warriors turn their heads, I quickly disguised myself as a human passenger and instructed Sersimi and Urimiel to do the same. The elohim glared but didn't notice our true nature.

Earl pulled next to the last trailer on the left. Like the others, his home had vinyl siding and a small wooden porch, but had a flowerbed and small bushes for decor as well. Blinds covered the windows, and an aluminum apron hung below the trailer. They had more field than the other families, and they took advantage of it, having a swing set and several toys strewn about.

I turned to my brothers in the backseat. "Seems they're in a lax state, security wise."

"Yes," Urimiel agreed. "Maybe they're too concerned with their schemes against man to notice our infiltration. Shall Sersimi and I clear the trailers now?"

I nodded. "I'll head in with Earl and clear his house. You'll clear the others, then rally back to me. Take care not to alarm the three around the table or any stationed inside the homes. These trailers aren't far apart. Go underground from one to the other to remain concealed. Just be careful when you come up. Use the element of surprise to take out any you find."

"Are we taking prisoners?" Sersimi asked.

"No prisoners. No questions," I said. Movement in the forest ahead of us caught my attention. There was a fence surrounding the field with 'Do Not Enter' signs posted to keep anyone from venturing into the forest. "We can't trust what they say, anyway. Once we have the trailers cleared, we'll work our way out to the owner's house. Be swift but quiet."

"I'll take the left." Sersimi dropped through the bottom of the car and into the ground.

"I wanted the left." Urimiel huffed. "Oh, well—" He checked that the area was clear before dropping through the car as well.

The silence was jarring when Earl turned off the car. I dipped below the surface of the earth, submerging myself in darkness. With a single stroke, I swam a couple of feet toward Earl's home and came up beneath the trailer.

I heard Earl's feet clomping on the porch, which squealed with his every step. Overhead, a television blared with sitcom laugh tracks inside. The door opened and closed. Slowly, I raised my head through the trailer's floor. There were no unholy elohim in the room. Earl's wife sat on an old recliner with a cigarette propped between her forefingers.

"What're you doin' home?" she asked.

Earl hung his jacket on a hook by the door and sighed. "They laid me off, darlin'."

"What?" She snuffed out her cigarette in a light brown ashtray beside her. "Why?"

Laughter blared from the television speaker. Earl rubbed his head. "Mind cuttin' that off?"

His wife shut it down with the remote. "What happened?"

Earl stepped into the narrow kitchen, looking about. "Where's Buttercup?"

His wife nodded toward the bedrooms, past the kitchen. "Nappin' for a change."

I moved past Earl and into the hallway, checking the two rooms and the bathroom for unholy elohim. Once I knew their home was clear, I returned to Earl. He sat at the kitchen table and rested his head in his hands. His wife sat across from him and took his hands.

"What is it?" she asked.

Earl shook his head, staring at the placemat in front of him. "I don't know how to say it, so I'll just say it." He looked up at his wife. Tears in his eyes. "When they laid me off, I didn't know what to do. It was me who packed us all up and moved us out here, thinkin' we'd be set. I expected to become a manager, and we'd get ourselves our forever home."

"It'll be OK," his wife said, rubbing his hands. "It's not ideal, but we'll figure somethin' out. There's bound to be other jobs out here. I can get a job at the grocery store. They're hirin'."

"That's not all though, darlin'," he said, pulling a wrinkled envelope from his pocket and set it in front of her. "I've been in a funk for a while, since we moved here, really. And when I lost the job... I was ready to end it all." He exhaled, staring at the floor. "Just before I pulled the trigger—" he shook his head. "Something occurred to me."

"Trigger?" his wife asked. Her face was etched with confusion. "Where'd you—Where's the gun?"

"I threw it in the lake," Earl said, rubbing his eyes. "It was dumb, I know. I bought the thing and just junked it. We could've used that money and—"

"Don't worry about it. You're here and that's all that matters to me." Tears leaked down his wife's face. She squeezed his hands and brought them to her cheeks. "I'm sorry, Earl. I know it's been rough, but I didn't know you would..."

"It's alright now," he said, moving to her side of the table and hugging her. "I changed my mind. We'll figure things out. Get back on our feet."

She wiped her eyes. "I figure you thought we'd be better off without you, but we wouldn't. I don't know what I would do if you'd went through with it." She buried her face in his shoulder and sobbed.

"It's alright," he whispered. "I know better now." He looked at the narrow hall leading to the bedrooms and bathroom. "How long has Buttercup been sleepin'?"

The mother shrugged. "About thirty minutes or so. Why?"

"I just want to look in on her." Earl headed to her bedroom. "She looks so peaceful when she's sleepin'.

Sersimi climbed up through the floor. "The left side is clear. There were no targets."

"Was anyone home?" I asked.

"No, but I came across several cats and small dogs," he said. "Playful critters, but I spared them no attention."

"Sure, you didn't." I looked through a window toward the woods. A small squad of two unholy messengers and two warriors patrolled along the tree line, carrying bows. They seemed unaware of our presence, conversing about trivial things, laughing and shoving one another in what seemed like playful banter.

"I can assure you I didn't fraternize with the tiny house pets," Sersimi said. "One particular puppy will be in terrible trouble when its master returns. It shredded three pillows and pillaged a trash can."

Urimiel ascended through the living room carpet, breathing hastily. After a quick survey of the room, he plopped onto the couch opposite the recliner.

"Are you alright?" I asked.

"Fine," he said, waving a hand dismissively. "Cut down seven. Mostly unclean spirits, but there were also a couple of ghastly locusts. One nearly got away. How about you, Sersimi?"

"What you went through was nothing compared to my arduous plight," Sersimi replied gruffly. "I nearly stepped on a litter of kittens and there was one particularly naughty dog."

"You're kidding me," Urimiel said, sitting up. His face was ill-tempered.

"Oh yeah." Sersimi nodded, eyes widening for emphasis. "Absolutely DE-STROYED the living room and kitchen. Garbage all over the floor."

"Not even a wisp of an unclean spirit?" Urimiel slapped his hands on his thighs. "That's it. I get the left next time."

"Sure," Sersimi said. "But I don't see why you're upset. You got all the glory."

Urimiel rolled his eyes and muttered, "I never get to see animals. It's always unclean spirits and unholy elohim."

"Listen," I said. "I saw four enemies patrolling in the woods. They weren't a very disciplined bunch, but we can't take this hold for granted. It's time to move to the property owner's house. We'll overrun the elohim that were at the picnic table along the way. Questions?"

"None," Urimiel replied.

"On your move," Sersimi said.

"Link arms," I said. This would help us stay together as one unit when we went underground. "I'll take us to the trailer closest to the entrance. Once we're postured, we'll attack."

We dropped into the ground, heading toward the entrance to the trailer park. I came up halfway across the road, then submerged again, taking several strides before having a second look. Once we were at the last trailer, I saw that the men at the picnic table were still playing cards, but the elohim were moving in a single file toward the property owner's home. I led us aboveground and signaled to Sersimi and Urimiel to follow me and maintain silence. We hastened behind the squad. The rear of their formation paused before we struck. They sensed us far too late. I manifested a sword and sliced through the one at the rear. Urimiel and Sersimi took care of the other two before they could produce weapons.

"I said I wanted the left this time," Urimiel said.

"You didn't remind me," Sersimi responded.

"Eyes out," I whispered. Now was not the time for banter. I took us within the wood line. There were no nearby threats. The property owner's home was within sight. "Let's get in there quickly. Clear it and see if the messengers are inside. Ready?"

They both nodded. We creeped along the forest's edge with our eyes on the target. The owner didn't seem to be home. There were no cars in the driveway and no movement within the house. We leaped through the exterior walls, onto the first floor. Room by room, we cleared it. Nothing on the first floor. I sent Sersimi and Urimiel to the basement and took the second floor and attic myself. Nothing. No unholy elohim. No holy messengers.

We regrouped on the first floor. "Did you find anything in the basement?"

Sersimi shook his head. "Jars of moonshine and shelves of stolen electronics and jewelry."

Urimiel peered out the windows. "This is odd. They must've known we were coming. Do you think they scattered to avoid confronting us?"

"Maybe. It seems they're craftier than I first gave them credit for. This has to be some sort of trap. They wouldn't just release the messengers and run off. They're somewhere else. Likely fortifying their position for an attack."

"Ah," Sersimi said. "They're in the hills at the moonshine still."

"That isn't all that clever," Urimiel said. "We could defeat them there just as well as here."

"Keep in mind there are two messengers missing," I said. "We don't know this land, and all I know is there's an old still out there. They wouldn't leave the messengers in the open for us to find them. They have them stashed somewhere."

We stood there in silence. My brothers were likely thinking the same as me. The hold could be aligned with other forces. If that's the case, Maiel didn't know about it, which was disconcerting.

"No doubt, we're about to head straight into an ambush. We'll need to approach this with great caution," I said. "Let's get back to the forest. We'll get on the high ground and start toward the still."

We hunkered down at a nearby briar patch with oak, maple, and fir trees stretching overhead. There were no enemy patrols, which told me they had likely fallen back preparing for us.

"Stay tight," I whispered before climbing uphill. I took the point with Sersimi on my right and Urimiel on my left.

We moved steadily and quietly. There should be plenty of unholy elohim in the area, unless they had scattered prematurely, which was unlikely considering there was no word from Maiel of the messengers escaping the hold. Roving guards would eventually find their downed comrades if they hadn't already and would alert the hold of our presence. Of course, they would expect us to head to the property owner's home, which explained the absence. But that would've been an excellent place for an ambush. Considering there wasn't one, they must've had a more effective plan in place.

I continued along the ridge, watching the hillside rising on my left, with Sersimi and Urimiel behind me. An arrow cut through my field of vision. I ducked down and several more zipped by. The unholy rabble were below us in a gully that extended the length of the hill. I created a sword and pointed. "Attack!"

We leaped from the ridge and soared feet above the ground with our weapons ready.

"Enemies! Right flank!" an unholy warrior shouted.

These fiends may have been weaker than us, but they were eager to strike. Eight shadowy arrows flew in our direction. I veered slightly to evade those aimed at me. I sliced at two unholy elohim before slamming into a third on the far side of the gully. Sersimi and Urimiel finished the two warriors behind me while I took care of the third. Sersimi took two arrows to the chest. He pulled them out, and bright light pierced through the holes in his armor.

We didn't have time to talk. Four elohim below us rose into the air.

More arrows rained from a higher position in the gully. Urimiel put his back to the volley, allowing his shield to block most of the onslaught, but he caught one in his lower leg.

"Shields and spears," I said, kneeling between Urimiel and Sersimi. Though weaker, they were many. We came in too confidently and were now surrounded. Feeling humbled, I said a small prayer, asking for forgiveness as arrows tested Urimiel and Sersimi's shields.

Something peculiar happened. The Breath of the Most High unexpectedly nudged me. He wanted to intervene, with my cooperation. Trusting Urimiel's shield, I closed my eyes briefly to listen. I've heard of this happening, but never experienced it until now. The Spirit was giving me a unique song for this moment, and I couldn't wait to hear it.

Opening my eyes, I sang, "And he said, 'Go forth, and stand upon the mount before the Lord.' And, behold, the Lord passed by." Spiritual winds rushed down the mountain. The unholy elohim that were in the air fell to the earth. Boulders came crashing down, smashing several of our enemies. "But the Lord was not in the wind!" The ground shook. More unholy ones fled uphill. Sersimi joined me and Urimiel. A third arrow in his chest. He nodded to show he was fine, although his complexion was dim and weary.

The Spirit wasn't done, and I continued the song. "But the Lord was not in the earthquake!" Spiritual fire lit the gully and surrounding forest. Our remaining opponents fell back to flee the holy fire. Several must have recognized the pattern playing out and shrieked in anticipation of what was coming next. "But the Lord was not in the fire!"

All became still. The unholy ones that remained covered their ears, diving beneath the surface of the mountain to hide from the gentle whisper which spoke to all who were listening.

"Why are you here, Melodiel?"

Melodiel knelt. "To honor you, Lord."

He spoke to Sersimi and Urimiel as well. They too knelt. When the presence lessened, we turned to each other.

Sersimi released his spear. "That was unusual, but I'm grateful, nonetheless."

"Me too," Urimiel said. "But why would the Lord intervene? We could've crushed these clowns."

"I'm sure He has His reasons," I said, gazing about for any nearby signs of the messengers. "Maybe there's more to this mystery than what we can perceive right now. But all is clear, so let's continue our search."

The unholy elohim that weren't lying still had fled in fear and would likely remain away for some time. I continued to wonder why the Spirit of the Most High had intervened while I searched in and around the gully. They had outnumbered us, but our trio had fought worse and come out on top. Maybe we needed our strength for what lay ahead.

We traversed the gully and the surrounding area three times over and found no evidence that would lead us to the messengers.

"Are we sure they're still here?" Urimiel asked. "They may have moved them to a stronger position."

I sat on a log, uncertain of how to proceed. As a warrior-minstrel, I displayed my orders as a bearded man from the nose down, giving way to a lion's gaze and a full mane. I dragged my hand through it in frustration. "We would've gotten word if they'd moved them."

"The hold is down," Sersimi said. "Do you want me to go to Maiel to see if there is any new word on the messengers' location?"

"That may be best." I nodded to Urimiel. "Go with him."

Urimiel waved his hands and shook his head. "Melodiel, we can't leave you—"

"The hold forces are down," I said. "But we don't know the situation between here and the breach commander's position. You both have been hit and could use some healing. Bring back reinforcements who can help us locate the missing messengers."

"Very well." Urimiel nodded.

My two dear friends leaped from the hillside and flew north toward Maiel's position, which was set between four small churches in town, roughly ten minutes away. Not one to sit idle, I skimmed through the gully again for any sign of the missing messengers.

"You won't find them that way," a garbled voice said.

I brandished a spear and turned. An unholy elohim, a messenger, stood several feet away with his eagle-like head bowed. Given his stature and lack of wounds, he must've been the ruler of this hold and chosen not to take part in the battle. Preferring not to converse with a liar, I prepared to plant my spear in his chest.

"Wait!" He fell back, shielding his head. "I can tell you where they are!"

Despite myself, I hesitated. "How could I trust you?" I growled.

"A spider has them." The messenger raised his beady eyes. His hooked beak curled slightly, as if giving me a knowing grin. "One strong enough that we won't find him unless he wants us to. He may even be watching us now." He smirked, looking over my shoulder, believing he may set me on edge. "But I *can* show you the entrance to where he's holding his prisoners."

"Why would you want to help?" I took a step back, glancing around to ensure this wasn't a trap. As far as I could perceive, there were no immediate threats in the area.

"Would I be helping you—or him?" He came to his feet. "He is stronger than any beast I've personally encountered. I doubt you and your two underlings can take him. Truly, what I'm doing is sending you as lambs to slaughter." He bellowed with laughter.

"Enough." I pushed the tip of my spear into his chest. He hissed and backed away. "If you know where he is. Show me now."

"Very well, right this way." The evil elohim started uphill. I was thankful that he didn't speak during the hike. Although I didn't trust the messenger and watched for ambushes, I knew if a powerful spider *was* here, I wouldn't notice.

Upon reaching the moonshine still near the ridge, he peered downhill to the right. After several small steps, he said, "Ah, there it is." He turned to me. "You can only see the spider's cave from here."

I looked down to the right and saw trees and foliage. There was no sign of a cave anywhere. Strange. Spiders could hide themselves, but that wouldn't affect the landscape. And something else didn't seem right. "This doesn't make sense. Despite *your* best efforts, this is still a relatively quiet town. Maiel hasn't reported anything that would suggest an evil of that magnitude here."

"Oh, yes." The ruler screeched a laugh, clapping his hands. "Maiel has only been in this area for about two years. I have much more knowledge of this town's history. While it has been quiet for more than a decade, there were several violent murders here, in that very cave." The ruler pointed at it. "The killer has since been caught and killed, but the spider is merely awaiting another human who shares a bent toward his appetites, a willing host to step up for a second act in the chamber of horrors. Detaining the Lord's loyal lap dogs apparently helps to pass the time." The unholy messenger stepped away from the old still and gestured for me to take his place. "Step right up. Step right up. See the entrance to pain and suffering. The hidden doorway to where shadows thrive, and light never ventures."

I jabbed my spear at his chest. "That's enough."

"So sensitive." The messenger shut his beak, but there was still a slimy grin behind it. I stepped in front of the still and peered downhill, scanning. A narrow cave entrance was behind several trees along the hillside as it curled around the property of Ruckmyer's Meadow. Barely noticeable but obvious all the same. How strong could this spider be? Maybe this messenger was trying to lead me to my doom, but he also seemed willing to divulge information with the proper amount of prodding. "I've handled many spiders in the past," I said. "I doubt one that's done nothing for years would be a problem for me."

The unholy messenger's demeanor changed. He looked deadly serious. "You'll find out soon enough, but mark my words. Even if you wait on those other mangy cats of yours, you will not defeat that spider. All of you will become captives. Do you know how much power I could gain as the ruler of a small hold that took three warriors of your rank captive?

"The messengers you seek are only bait. It was just a question of who would bite—Maiel or stronger forces like you. Maiel obviously chose the coward's path and called for help. And if by some miracle you and your two brothers best the beast—that wouldn't be on me. I gave the spider what he wanted. If he can't handle it, that's on him—not me. The weaker he becomes, the stronger I stand. Anyway, it's been fun. Enjoy your stay in the chamber of horrors."

The unholy messenger ran past the still and dove underground. I spared him my spear since he left willingly. While unholy elohim couldn't be trusted, what he said made sense. Even the most brazen liars can tell the truth when it suits their purposes. If the spider captured me and my two dear friends, it would garner him prestige for the part he played.

Sersimi and Urimiel landed farther down in the gully. Maiel and a ministering spirit were with them. When they looked in my direction, I waved, and they started toward me.

When they came within earshot, I said, "Supposedly, the messengers are held prisoner in a spider's cave."

"What cave?" Sersimi asked. "We scanned the entire area."

"It's only visible from where I'm standing," I said.

Glaring at the still, Urimiel said, "How did you find out about this spider?"

"When you left, the hold's ruler, an unholy messenger, spoke to me before running off." I pointed in the direction he had left. "He told me if I stood here, I'd see the entrance to the cave where the messengers are imprisoned. He was correct, and I believe he spoke true of a spider as well." I stepped aside. "See for yourselves."

Sersimi and Urimiel stepped to the spot and peered at it. Sersimi pointed at it. I greeted Maiel and the ministering spirit.

"It seems you're on to where our messengers are now," Maiel said. He was a powerful warrior but was new to this position. That was another thing the unholy messenger said that was true. "Thankfully, things are quiet enough that we could assist you. Thank you again for your help."

"We'll certainly need you," I said, "especially if this spider is as powerful as I think he is."

"If it's only a spider, we can handle him easily," Urimiel said. "We go in there and grab the prisoners. And when he shows himself, we overwhelm him with force."

"The ruler believed the spider could defeat the three of us handily," I said, glancing toward the cave. Was the spider listening now? "He figures that even if we beat the spider, he wins by weakening a rival."

"But there's four of us and a ministering spirit now," Maiel said, stepping up. His dark brown mane swayed to the rhythm of a gentle wind.

"True," I said, "but he could shield himself with the prisoners before we reached them. If he's as strong as the ruler claims, he could keep us from them while protecting himself."

"He would have to be third domain then," Sersimi said, folding his arms over his breastplate.

"It could be nothing," Urimiel said. "Just something to make us look like fools."

"There's no one here to see us look like fools, though," Sersimi said, stepping away from the still.

"We'll feel foolish," Urimiel said, scoffing. "That's bad enough."

"Listen," I said. "Whether or not there's a spider in there, I'm going in—alone."

"No way," Urimiel said, stepping toward me. "If there's even a remote possibility that a third domain spider is in there, we're coming with you."

"Spiders are very discerning. Very crafty." I looked at each of my warrior brothers. "No doubt, I'd be outmatched. But trust that I know what I'm doing. Stay here with your eyes and ears on that cave. When you hear me shout, come full speed." I moved close to Maiel and whispered, "Your *only* priority is getting the messengers to safety."

"Of course," Maiel said with a bow.

"Are you sure?" Sersimi said. His eyes were leveled. Although he was well aware of the danger I was putting myself in, he knew the worst thing I could do was spell out the entire plan when the spider could be listening in. "Depending on how deep that cave is, there's a good chance we won't hear you."

"I trust you will," I said.

Sersimi looked at Urimiel and nodded. "Melodiel knows what he's doing." He peered at me. "We'll do our part as directed."

I returned to the spot beside the still, and the cave was visible to me again. I kept my eyes fixed on the entrance and headed straight for it. Once there, I ducked into its shadow with my spear in hand. With the way this spider was collecting prisoners, I suspected he had taken on some bear qualities as well. Not encouraging.

The space widened, and the walls glistened with faint light. I came to a pit and dropped in. The sounds of dripping water echoed off the muddy stone walls.

The air was stagnant. This pit had no exits save for the one I dropped from. I took careful, deliberate steps in the absurd silence. The spider was most likely watching me, but he wasn't my concern yet, because I had a sinking feeling that he was allowing me to find the messengers, confident that he could easily defeat me.

Stepping deeper into this chamber, I observed its muddy walls and floor for signs of the messengers, but when I craned my head, I found a spiritual barrier encasing them on the ceiling. They were unconscious. The barrier proved the spider was here and aware of my presence; I took several steps back and assumed a defensive stance. He had me exactly where he wanted me—almost.

"Quite the prize, aren't you?" an unfriendly, unnatural voice spoke from deeper within the chasm.

I took several more steps back from the messengers, maintaining a defensive stance. Now that I knew where they were, I needed to draw the spider away from them. He already displayed immense cunning, so this would be a challenge.

The spider growled like a bear, hungry for a fight, but seemed open to discourse. If so, I could use that to save my strength and keep the spider focused on me rather than what I had planned.

"The same could be said of you, I'm told," I said confidently.

Faint, dark movements scurried above me. The sound of chittering legs carried to the other side of the chamber. The spider lowered his bulbous body from a glistening silken thread. He was putting on a show, hoping to intimidate me with theatrics. The thread dissipated. A scorpion's tail protruded from his hind side, explaining the desire for theatrics. He hoped to relish my fear as an appetizer before moving on to the main course—pain.

"I am no prize," the spider hissed. Eight green eyes glistened. He came to the ground opposite me. "I am a collector, and you are the latest piece in my heavenly collection." He raised his head to the messengers above him.

"So, the ruler of the hold spoke true," I said. "You're a pawn in his game. A mere guard for his prison."

"Attempting to get under my skin." The spider saw right through my attempt, but I wanted him to feel confident.

The spider rushed toward me, planting his massive paws and striking at my head with his tail. I parried it but didn't counter, and the spider took note. His many eyes gleamed as he read everything he could about me: my face, my posture, my reaction. "And I thought you were keen for a fight. Are you not their savior? Surely, the warrior within you understands that defense alone only prolongs the inevitable."

The spider attacked again, jabbing his two front legs at me, and I parried them. He rose onto his hind legs, ready to stomp, leaving an opening for me to attack, but I refrained again. Instead of crushing me, he backed away, curious. The clever creature wanted all the control. He couldn't bring himself to wound me terribly without knowing the mystery that I wasn't sharing—not yet, anyway.

"You can easily beat me, yet you hesitate," I said, keeping his thoughts on me rather than my plans. He seemed unaware of my allies who were listening for me from the still; a small blessing that I gladly welcomed.

"Oh, I could easily defeat you," the spider said. With a flick of one of his paws, chains manifested from under me, wrapping around my legs, arms, and torso. "Twice you could've stuck me with that toothpick of yours but maintained a pointless defensive stance instead."

The spider glared at me—no, into me. I said nothing but stared back, holding my position the best I could as the chains slowly tightened, pulling me to my knees. "You are also a minstrel, yet despite your situation, you have yet to sing."

"I'll take a request," I grunted. "What would you like to hear?"

The spider laughed. He creeped closer and whispered, "I want to hear you scream for mercy. And you will."

"As you wish." I sucked in a deep breath and bellowed, "Mercy!"

My booming voice startled the spider momentarily. The chain loosened slightly. The spider pondered my intent, and when he noticed I hadn't tried to escape, he tightened the chains.

He looked toward the entrance, clearly sensing something new. Good. Sersimi and Urimiel heard. "Ah. You thought your friends could sweep in while you had me distracted? Very foolish," he said furiously.

He turned to me, and with surprising speed, his scorpion stinger came down and drove through my breastplate. Hot venom surged through me with vicious haste. "There is no escaping me," he said in a cold and menacing tone.

He waved a leg toward the entrance, his gaze never breaking from mine, and a shield appeared around us. I kept his gaze, not daring to look at, or even think about, the messengers. I didn't need to. To make a new shield, he first had to drop the one encapsulating them, which is exactly what I was counting on. No matter how the rest of this panned out, at least they would be saved. "Your friends won't break through," the spider said, crawling closer, still studying me. "Not in time... Yet still, you don't struggle and seem unafraid. You must think you're intelligent. Whatever you think you've hashed out in that half-cat head of yours will not work."

Urimiel and Sersimi came in first, dropping straight down and striking at the shield between us. I looked past them and saw Maiel and the ministering spirit grabbing the messengers and carrying them outside.

Sersimi and Urimiel flew back and charged in for a second coordinated strike at the shield. As they slammed against it, the spider looked at them as well. The chains weakened as the spider diverted more strength to the barrier.

Maiel returned, joining Urimiel and Sersimi for a third strike. The spider turned to me, raising a paw to end me before taking on the new threat. But I broke through the weakened chains. I rolled to my feet and launched a spear, not at the spider, but at the shield. The coordinated power of my strike and the three warriors was enough. The shield cracked and then faded away.

I came alongside Urimiel, Sersimi, and Maiel and faced the spider, which had stepped back. He was powerful and intelligent enough to know he was outmatched. The lesson from the encounter on the hill was the key to our victory. In our overconfidence, we had put ourselves in an undesirable situation against weaker forces. The spider did the same in turn, allowing us to divide his attention and spread his power thin.

He cursed, "That idiot ruler of that measly hold will pay for his part in this." He scurried into the earth.

We let him flee and flew to the surface, where the ministering spirit was already treating the former captives. The vibrance of the world did much to quell the pain coursing through me, but my wound was severe. Poison had been coursing through me since the spider skewered me. The ministering spirit came over, eyeing my wound. He handed me a small cluster of manna.

"Eat this," he said, patting me on the shoulder.

When I did, my strength gushed back, drowning all the pain within.

"You should rest," Sersimi said.

"And miss the best part?" I asked, nodding thanks to the ministering spirit. I knelt between the two messengers and touched their shoulders. "Welcome back."

One clasped my hand and said, "I woke when you shouted 'Mercy'. I thought we had another captive joining us."

The other gave a weak nod. "Thank you."

Someone touched my shoulder. It was Maiel. "Well done." He looked at Sersimi and Urimiel. "You've done us a great service."

I bowed. "We are happy to serve." I'd save my brothers from captivity anytime, even if it meant getting stung by an unholy, spidery monstrosity in the process.

"If you're willing," Maiel said. "I invite you to join us as our message reaches the Stanton family. They wouldn't have received it without your intervention. You saved them from great suffering as much as you saved these brothers from that terrible spider."

"I'd like to come too." One messenger pushed himself up.

The other got up as well. "Me too."

Maiel nodded. "Of course."

We went together to the Stantons' trailer. A four-door sedan was parked near the entrance of Ruckmyer's Meadow and an older man and woman were walking door to door. We came onto the rutted gravel lot and stood near the Stantons' porch and waited.

The two visitors seemed weary by the time they reached the Stanton residence. An older lady wiped her face with a kerchief as they climbed the steps. The man knocked on the door and stepped back.

Earl answered the door. "Can I help you?"

"Yes sir," the man said. "I'm Pastor Willie Chestnut and this is my wife, Barbara. We're part of First Baptist Church here in town and want to invite you for a picnic we're having this weekend. We'd love to get to know ya, and have ya join us if you'd like. I'm sorry. I forget to ask sometimes. Can I get your name?" He offered a handshake to Earl.

Earl shook it and introduced himself. Anna joined him at the door, carrying a small child who looked shyly at the pastor and his wife. "This is my wife, Anna. Shanna is a little shy, but if you look in the yard—she's quite a handful."

They all chuckled except for Shanna, who hugged her mother tightly, burying her head into her shoulder.

"I'm sure you wouldn't have it any other way," Mrs. Chestnut said.

"Absolutely not," Anna said, giving Shanna a tight hug. "When is this picnic again?"

The pastor took a flyer from his inside jacket pocket and handed it to Earl. "Saturday afternoon at 4 o'clock. Plenty of food and fun for all ages."

Earl and Anna gave each other a look. Their troubles were apparent in their expressions. "We'd like to come, but we can't offer much."

"You don't have to worry about that," the pastor said.

"I just lost my job this morning," Earl said, looking away. "I'm about to head over to the unemployment office and file for that. Start looking for work."

"I'm sorry to hear that," the pastor said. "What sort of work do you do?"

"I was at the sawmill," Earl said, rubbing the back of his head. "Been there for about a year."

"We moved out here for it," Anna said. "Not sure what we're gonna do now. May end up heading back to North Carolina."

"Well," the pastor rubbed his chin. "I have to ask ya. Do ya do any work with furniture at all?"

Earl nodded and smiled. "I built cabinets with my dad back home.

Probably gonna end up going back to that. We hope to stay out here, though. Just don't know if there's any work."

The pastor looked at his wife. "Do you believe this?"

She smiled back, shaking her head. "Just tell 'em, Willie."

He looked back at Earl. "Do you know about Carrigan's Furniture?"

Earl nodded. "It's about fifteen minutes from here, right?"

"That's right," the pastor said, "and Don Carrigan told me last weekend they need more help. Now I'm sure ya hate losing work at that sawmill, but I'm certain that you and a few of your buddies would do well working for Don. He's a fine man."

Earl blushed and shifted on his feet. "Well, I'll get out there and fill out an application this week, but just in case, I might get over to that unemployment office first."

"If you're willing," the pastor said, "I don't mind drivin' ya over there now. You look like a fine young man, and Don needs help. He asked for prayers that he could find more workers. It would just tickle me to death to be the one to show him that his prayer has been answered."

Anna touched Earl on the shoulder. "Maybe you ought to."

Earl smiled and wiped his eyes. "I can't believe this. Are you for real?"

"Go ahead and spiff yourself up a bit." The pastor left the porch. "I'll bring the car over and we'll get on our way."

Earl gave his wife a peck on the cheek and went to ready himself. The pastor's wife said, "It really is nice to meet you, Anna, and Shanna. I have a couple of fun-sized Hershey bars if you'd like to have them. Maybe if Shanna is good, you can give them to her."

Sersimi and Urimiel gave me a look.

"Unlike the pastor's wife, I don't carry fun-sized candies around in a purse," I said. "Besides, you two misbehaved."

"Did not." Urimiel crossed his arms.

"I was particularly well behaved," Sersimi added, crossing his arms as well. "You said wait until you shouted. And we listened."

"While that is so," I said, raising a hand to make a point, "I recall more bickering than necessary regarding who takes the left and who takes the right. Did I not?"

"See what you did," Urimiel said. "You cost us our candy bars."

Sersimi turned and glared. "You were the first to complain. Besides, it takes two to tango."

While they continued their fun little banter, I pulled a couple of surprises from my belt. Two Snickers bars. "Ahem!" The two capable and trustworthy warriors turned to me.

Urimiel spoke first. "Can I get the one on the left?" Sersimi snatched it and ran to the grassy field.

It was a beautiful day. The world sang its everlasting song, and I basked in its glory, while my friends enjoyed their candy bars and well-deserved fun in the yard.

As the last minstrel left the stage, Thomas's mind was swimming. It had been a long night, or day, or whatever. Hirael had compared the arenas to movie theaters, but these stories were so inspiring, filled with new and interesting thoughts. And to think they could be true. If Thomas *were* dreaming, this was the longest, most vivid, and most lucid dream he had ever experienced.

A thought occurred to him. He turned to Hirael. "Why doesn't God just wipe them out—the unholy elohim?"

"Could you so readily destroy your own children?"

Thomas had never thought of fallen angels as God's children before. He stood up, assuming they would move to the next arena, but Hirael guided him to stay seated.

A different minstrel stepped to the stage; one Thomas had seen a couple times before.

"Another history lesson?" Thomas said.

"Yes, Brother Thomas." Hirael's eyes saddened. "This time showing the ruin that comes when humans and elohim cooperate, but toward corruption. The results are… truly terrible."

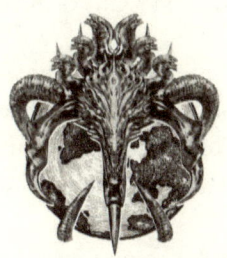

GILGAMESH IMMORTAL

GAO YU QING

Azazel landed on the ridge and dropped the dazed, limp form of his firstborn, Gilgamesh, on the rocky ground before turning to watch his youngest son, Hobabish, larger and more powerful than any of the other nephilim, finally fall under the combined weight of three others, ripping and tearing at one another. The roiling bodies hid what happened next.

Too late. I returned too late to save them both. Is this the promised punishment? Is this how it will happen?

For weeks, all had been teeming with turmoil and chaos. Ranks and factions of humans and nephilim fought and tore at each other with any weapon at hand, though the latter crushed the former like a man swatting flies. More terrible by far were the battles between the giants themselves: huge powerful bodies colliding, using fingers and teeth as often as the metal blades Azazel had designed with such pride, to tear into each other, bodies falling by the score. The image of what was happening in front of him, writ large.

The ground rippled underfoot, as if solid earth had become liquid and a wave passed through it, causing Azazel to stagger. The air rumbled and shook in answer. He checked the dark clouds churning in the distance, drawing closer. He had been tracking them for several hours, marveling at their speed and size. They seemed to stretch on forever, farther than his immortal sight could see, sealing the earth away from the heavens like a rug rolling across a floor.

He turned as Gilgamesh, who he'd physically dragged from the battle, shook his head to blink up at Azazel from where he lay, his great bush of hair matted with blood and dust. Fury contorted his features as he glared at his father, sweat leaving pale runnels in the dirt caking his face.

Azazel could imagine the scene now taking place in the city. In every city they'd built. Even the beasts seemed affected, running madly, trampling their riders and tearing into one another. But he'd seen the greater, more personal doom coming for them all on his return home.

"We were winning, Father! We were putting the enemy to route! Why did you pull me out? How fares Hobabish?"

Azazel ignored his son's questions. *So soon. If only I'd had more time!* Bitterness welled up in him, as well as hatred and hurt. Worst of all came the unbidden awareness that despite all his knowledge, his wisdom, perhaps he was to blame. Now there was nothing he could do. *Well, perhaps there is one thing…*

He looked down at his son with consideration. *Perhaps I might save one. I can still prove myself. Prove to them all that I was right all along.*

"Be still and listen, my son. I need you to do what I say. You don't have time to ask questions, just obey. I need you to survive. To live. I saw what is happening on my return home. Remember the dreams of Shemihazah's whelps those decades ago? Remember the message of the prophet? It's happening. Now. The Most High is bringing about the fulfillment of his prophesy. If I'm to have any hope of salvaging anything from this disaster, it has to be you. My brothers are coming to bind me. I won't be able to avoid them. They've already bound Shemihazah and many of the others, but you may escape if you are strong and wily enough. Run towards the mountains, or the highest place you can find. I believe a great flood is coming, so you need to make sure you stay above the water, or, if you wind up in it, grab hold of some wood. It will help you stay afloat until the danger is past. Avoid other people. Stay away from settlements. I fear they will attack you if they see you. Now prove me right when I said you were the best of all of them. Get up and *run!*" He shouted this last, pouring all his authority and will into the words.

Gilgamesh leapt to his feet and turned. His huge legs worked like machines, feet pounding over the ground in long strides, covering the distance at an astounding rate. He didn't look back.

Azazel felt the tingle of the presence too late, distracted as he was. Raphael had masked his approach until he seemed to appear before Azazel, even as he felt metal links, hard and heavy, forming and tightening around him.

Azazel recognized the unbreakable chains at once and twisted to escape them. Dismissing his flesh, he tried again in spiritual form, but the bonds held him even then. He felt unaccustomed panic beginning to rise. He'd *never* been powerless before! Then he became aware that Raphael was speaking to him.

"For what it's worth, Azazel, I'm sorry it came to this, but you heard the prophesy for yourself. When we learned of the Most High's plan, we were stunned. It produced much debate, even among the four chief archangels. The idea of wiping it all away… it seemed too strong a reaction. Michael himself lamented how harsh your judgment would be. But we cannot take your part in this matter. For if we do so, then we become no better than you, believing our will is better than the Most High's. After all, we were among those who interceded for the humans your children slaughtered and abused. Why did you do it, Azazel? Why, when you knew it was wrong?"

Raphael's voice cracked with emotion as he said this, even as the chains tightened, imprisoning Azazel more securely.

Azazel stood there, no longer struggling, his expression and emanations as emotionless as he could make them. "Too late for such questions, Raphael. I did what I believed best and thought that the sacrifices made along the way were to the greater good." *And it may still work out in the end, if my son survives. That will prove to everyone, even the Most High, that I was right. Even if I am imprisoned, I will still have that certain knowledge.*

The ground rumbled once more. If Azazel had still worn his fleshly form, he might have fallen over, but none of the turmoil of the physical world could affect him now. Crashes sounded in the distance. *The city.* It reminded him of when he'd returned home after an earlier quake and found it collapsed, his wives dead. The sounds of distant battle continued, the screams of humans mingling with the great bellows of the giants. Azazel dismissed his city, home, wives and even Hobabish from his mind, placing all his hopes and ambition on the person of his firstborn, Gilgamesh.

In response to his words, Raphael unrolled a scroll, holding it before him as he read. "Azazel, elohim and watcher of the Most High, you have been judged and found guilty." His voice rang deep and powerful, belying his usual gentle manner. "You are guilty of dereliction of duty, absenting your given place and position in favor of seeking after your own desires, in direct opposition of the Most High and at the expense of humanity."

Azazel spat, and had a moment of satisfaction, seeing the spittle mar the gleaming perfection of Raphael's armor for a second before it vanished.

Raphael didn't even pause. "You are guilty of failing in your duty to shepherd humanity. Of instructing them in worthless mysteries that promoted sin, and leading them further from the side of the Most High until they have become a stench in His nostrils. You are guilty of creating perversions of creation, demeaning and diminishing mankind, who were to be image bearers of the Most High on the earth as we were in the heavens. Subjugating them to the level of breeding animals, slaves, and food for your own unnatural offspring."

He paused to meet Azazel's eyes as he rolled up the scroll, revealing none of the regret he'd shown earlier, just an acceptance of his role and duty. Something Azazel had turned his back on.

"Azazel, these judgments are by decree of the holy watchers, and by decree of the Most High. Indeed, the Most High pronounced judgement over a century ago and you still persisted, unwavering in your course and leading humanity to damnation along with you."

Azazel met his gaze in defiance. "I did what was best for humanity's advancement. So, though it does me no good, I deny the validity of your judgment."

Raphael sighed before he stepped up to face Azazel eye to eye. "You forget one basic fact, Brother. The difference between the Most High and His works, versus you and yours. *You* are not *Him.*"

Azazel stared back in silent defiance while nearby the ground cracked, letting out a massive geyser of water. The gusting wind sent a shower of mist through them, but he who had been preeminent among the watchers felt none of it in his current state.

"By your own confession, you are confirmed guilty. You will be bound and imprisoned until the day of the great judgment in which the age will be wholly consummated, over the watchers and the godless. But first..." Here, Raphael seemed to hesitate before continuing. "As you may remember, it has been decreed that all the watchers will be made to watch one last time. To witness the consequences of your choices and the fates of your children, and the truth of what they are that you have denied for so long."

Azazel tried to step back as Raphael placed his hands on his shoulders. He felt a little stunned to see pity blossom in the archangel's eyes, like a hidden flower from a rock. "You spoke of humanity's advancement. You fail to understand that there are worse things than death and bigger stakes at risk than what you can see now. Far more of humanity would face that fate should this have continued. This flood will be a mercy. But not for all. You will see with your own eyes what fate your actions have appointed for the nephilim in your hubris and greed, and the truth of what you have wrought."

Raphael paused and looked away, and the sight of that weakness filled Azazel with disdain. He himself had acted out of his own reasoning and regretted nothing.

"I... I am sorry, Azazel. You did this to yourself, but I still mourn what your choices brought about, however necessary and just the punishment to come."

As Raphael moved to stand behind him, Azazel looked out at the towering wall of clouds, now sheeting down fat droplets of rain. All across the plain, he saw fountains of the deep bursting open to pour out water over the land, turning pastures to ponds, streams to rivers, rivers to torrents. Despair threatened to overwhelm Azazel, but he clung to his pride and the righteousness of his cause. *I am right. Damn them all! I know I am! Live, my son. Live and prove it to them all!*

Azazel felt the archangel grip the coils of chain, and then they were aloft, soaring into the air, becoming almost *part* of the air.

The days that followed and the things they forced him to witness pummeled Azazel's spirit. Witnessing the deaths of so many of the giants, all of them the progeny of his mind, if not body, drove him close to madness, especially when he saw the truth of what happened to them when they died.

As they fell, either to violence or disaster, something dark and pathetic emerged from the ruin of the body to linger, a mockery of what he'd envisioned the nephilim to be. Even as the souls of the humans around them flickered out and were bound to Sheol, the shadowy remnants that had been the giants lingered, howling in despair and misery. The sight of their wretchedness filled Azazel with disgust, all the more so because of the magnificence they'd had in life. Their very existence repelled him, threatening to put the lie to all that he'd done.

The first time he'd seen them, these... unclean spirits... Raphael had spoken in his ear.

"You sought to make them the perfect mix of flesh and divine spirit, but in truth you made them less than the sum of their parts, lacking the image of the Most High that we and humanity both share, neither fully human nor fully spirit. What did you think would happen? Now their spirits are trapped, with no access to heaven and unable to leave the earth until their final destruction. Forever denied, forever lacking flesh, forever longing for what they had. Behold what you and your fellows have created."

In the prison of his mind, Azazel screamed his denials. *Not for them all! I didn't want this. It will not happen to my son. I was right. He will escape this destruction and prove it!*

As the days passed, Azazel clung to hope. He didn't see Gilgamesh, and every day that passed let him believe that his son might have escaped and had not been reduced to one of those weak, pathetic wraiths. Now and then he heard weeping, the sound of one of his kindred broken by what they were being forced to witness. It did not surprise Azazel that the loudest was that of Shemihazah, wailing out the names of his many wives and children. *That won't be me. My son is stronger than any of theirs. I won't give them the satisfaction of seeing me break.*

Every day the bound watchers and their angelic guards found fewer and fewer nephilim. Most, it seemed, had killed each other in the factional fighting Gabriel had instigated; but some lingered, driven on by the rising waters, running with herds of panicked animals, all seeking the same thing.

High ground.

They found Gilgamesh at last, however, and they stayed with him for the final days, invisibly watching as his son climbed the mountains, always one step ahead of the water. Tireless and powerful, the sight of him made Azazel's heart swell with pride, especially knowing that the rest of the 200 watched alongside him, equally invisible, a jury of peers "watching" the last of their children. Despite battles, catastrophe and disaster, Gilgamesh still lived, while theirs lay dead and reduced to twisted shadows. A final concluding proof that *his* son was the best of them all.

Like Azazel himself.

There was food readily at hand, and Gilgamesh caught his prey and ate his fill of raw meat while on the run, as naked now as the animals he ran with, battered and bloody.

The mountains gave out before he did.

Gilgamesh roared and flailed, fighting off the panicked and desperate animals fighting for that final foothold. He cast them down into the waves to be battered against the rocks until he remained supreme, swaying with exhaustion, but the victor, roaring his defiance into the wind.

The king of the mountain.

There he crouched and waited, eyeing the unrelenting waters that even his great strength could not prevail against, and taking what rest he could.

Salvation came in the form of a tree, blown by the wind near Gilgamesh's final perch, even as the waters lapped against his bloodied feet. Azazel's faith strengthened as his son clumsily swam across the distance to take hold of the tree and cling to it. *This must be a sign that the Most High has relented of His judgment at last. My son has proven himself worthy!*

For three days, Azazel and his fellow watchers observed the last of the giants on the earth cling to his tree and drift with the waves, even sleeping, coiled fast in the branches he had wrapped around his limbs. He wished he could speak encouragement to his son, or, barring that,

that he might shout to the rest of the watchers of his son's superiority to their own, but he held his tongue, letting events prove out his triumph more thoroughly than any boast.

On the afternoon of the third day, Azazel's hopes soared to new heights. There, in the distance, rocking on the waves like a dead leviathan, floated a massive construct of wood and pitch. *The madman actually did it! By all the stars of heaven, he actually built it, and it works!* Surely this was the ark that the great-grandson of Enoch had built under the guidance of Uriel, in whose belly hid the last of humanity and animal life. *Three... maybe four, fertile women for my son's seed, to produce a new generation of those like him. Perfect. It can't be an accident. There are no accidents with the Most High. He's seen that I was right in the end. My son deserves to live! Now all will see!*

Gilgamesh saw the vessel too and watched its slow approach. Azazel observed the tension in his shoulders as he bided his time, kicking now and then to adjust the course of his makeshift vessel. But in the end, all could see that the great boat would pass just out of reach, a mile, perhaps, to the east.

With his salvation so close at hand, Gilgamesh abandoned the tree and began swimming towards the ark in powerful—if clumsy—strokes. Limbs churning, he gained on the wallowing craft, with Azazel willing him on, even daring to pray in the exultation of his hopes.

Oh, Most High, please, I beg you for mercy on behalf of my son. I can see Your plan now, the winnowing of the weak so that only those without blemish survive. I accept it. And I accept my fate. Only let my son survive!

The ark was close now. So close. Gilgamesh had calculated the angle of his approach so he'd reach the prow of the vessel, giving him the whole length of the ark to find a handhold, a way to secure himself or gain the attention of one of the inhabitants. Azazel opened his mouth to shout in triumph as his son reached out one last time...

The shout died in Azazel's throat as movement stirred the waters and something huge swelled beneath the waves. A great dark back, studded with barnacles and mats of tangled seaweed broke the water to one side of Gilgamesh. A terrible head with jaws lined with serried ranks of teeth bit into the giant's side, nearly cutting him in two.

Azazel heard his son's scream and barely refrained from echoing it in shock as the last vestige of all his centuries of hopes and expectations crumbled in an instant. Again, a head lifted and bit off the outstretched arm as it strained to reach the pitch-black side of the ark passing by, inches beyond Gilgamesh's reach. Azazel watched in horror as his greatest pride, his greatest work, was devoured by the great beast—as if his son were no better than any other living thing, staining the dark water with his blood. He watched as the fight finally left that so-vital figure, floating lifeless along the side of the ark until his foot struck a glancing blow, making the body spin. And as Gilgamesh's body was yanked beneath the waters, Azazel, and all the other witnesses, saw the shade of his son rise to hover over the waters, lost and uncertain. Azazel's legacy reduced to a shadow. Pathetic. Nothing at all like his son. A mockery. The wraith-like figure twisted, now able to see his father. Their gazes met, leaving Azazel looking at a mirror, the shade an embodiment of all his grand accomplishments and ambitions. Gilgamesh saw only the disgust and disappointment in his father's eyes.

The unclean spirit's scream of shame, despair, and the start of a deep, abiding hatred echoed through the spiritual firmament as Raphael snatched Azazel away to his judgment at an impossible speed. The cry became the opening note of a chorus that would echo down the millennia to come as the last and greatest of the giants fell like all the rest.

"And that is one more way in which you differ from the Almighty," Raphael said in Azazel's ear while the world blurred around them as they sped on past. "You saw only their strength and their power, and refused to see what lay within. Now that you have witnessed the truth of what you created, the hollow ugliness that sprung from it, you look at it in disgust and turn away. Because your children could not live up to your expectations, you reject them. The Most High witnessed His human children fail as well, yet loved them and created a path for redemption. They may be saved. Your children may not." Then he sighed deeply and said, his voice weary, "It is finished."

At once they altered course, diving towards the rolling waves beneath them. Despite knowing that it could not kill his spirit body, Azazel, lost and confused in his rage and grief, flinched as they plunged through the water and dove down... down. He felt lost, not even knowing where they were in relation to the world he had walked before. Down past the point where human-frail bodies would be rendered to paste. Past the point where even mountain stones cracked under the weight of the water pressing down on them, through the rolling clouds of dirt and sediment swept along in the tides of the flood, still yet to settle into fresh layers on the scoured rock below.

With eyes beyond human sight, he felt them reach the level of the ground he'd once walked on and dove even further into one of the great crevices opened by the outpouring of the subterranean waters. Down into a realm that had never known sunlight, into tighter and tighter spaces until at last Raphael stopped and let go.

Azazel sank to the jagged bottom of the small cave they'd wound up in, still wrapped in his chains that seemed different now. More permanent. No longer maintained by Raphael's will, but a Greater One.

"I'm... sorry for your son," Raphael said. "Sorry for the pain it caused you. You knew, though, Azazel. You always knew the truth. So, I will never understand your decision. Farewell... Brother."

With those parting words, he disappeared. Back towards the surface, the sun, towards life and the Creator of it all far beyond it. Separate from it. As the walls around Azazel began to creak and groan, closing about him to form his prison, Azazel could only stare after him in despair and hatred, knowing that he would never pray again.

Thomas fell back in his seat. "This is a lot to take in. I feel like I'm starting seminary all over again with this stuff."

"And there is still more to learn."

As the crowd made their way out of the arena, Hirael sat with Thomas.

"So, is that what they are?" Thomas asked. "Unclean spirits? They're the Nephilim? How does that work?"

"Brother Thomas." Hirael sighed. "You know, I had discretion regarding which stories to take you to. Did I choose wrongly? You are so distracted by defining things that you miss the meaning—the story's purpose. But that has been the general condition of your culture for more than a thousand years. You seek to dissect Scriptures when so much of their worth is found in how the stories interact with one another. So much effort spent defining the elements, while ignoring the life found through meditating on the mystery."

"Like the Garden," Thomas said, staring ahead blankly.

"What was that?"

"Like the Garden. Like Adam and Eve. They gave up life for knowledge."

"Hallelujah!" Hirael raised his hands in the air. "You are paying attention after all!"

Thomas couldn't help but smile at Hirael's exuberance. "Are you sure you don't have some man face in there somewhere?"

Both shared a laughed that trickled down into a brief moment of shared silence and thought.

"So, let me try this." Thomas took a breath and closed his eyes. "Sit in the mystery. See where it takes me. Don't get too distracted by weird factoids."

Hirael was completely silent.

Thomas let his mind process. "The first watchers, they took human wives, had children, corrupted mankind by living with them and teaching them things they wouldn't have known."

Something occurred to Thomas. "Not just living with humans. They were living *like* humans. Jude says something about the angels who left their proper domain. And you talked about an elohim's orders being your purpose or function. You said the Most High gave each of you an order, or multiple, as in your case. So, part of the original watchers' rebellion was leaving God's intended order of things to live like humans instead of elohim."

"Hirael?" Thomas opened his eyes. "Is that right?"

Hirael smiled. "You are getting it. You are looking at what the elohim orders *mean* instead of trying to dissect what they *are*. These are the kind of insights you don't discover in a single pass but in hearing, hearing again, and pondering. Think of it like studying several coins in your hand. The longer you manipulate and study them, the more you become aware of the similarities and differences. The design of the fronts and backs. The locations of certain information like dates or phrases. You become aware of patterns and deliberate choices of the designers."

"I see. I see," Thomas said, nodding his head. Another thought occurred to him. "You said before that you are a watcher. And several of the elohim in the stories were watchers. Are you the same as those watchers? Did the Most High just start over with new humans and new watchers after the flood? It obviously wasn't a complete reset. After all, Noah didn't end up back in the Garden."

"There's a good question, Brother Thomas," Hirael said. "You are right. Tell me what happened after Noah and his family were able to leave the ark."

"Well, Noah made some sacrifices. God told them they could eat animals now. Noah got drunk and passed out, and one of his sons made fun of him."

"Let's get to humanity." Hirael clearly seemed to be restraining himself. "What did *humanity* do?"

"They made some cities… oh." Thomas snapped his fingers. "The Tower of Babel. They made the Tower of Babel."

"Good. But what had the Most High commanded them to do?"

Thomas thought for a second. "Not to kill each other… And to spread out. Fill the earth."

"Yes," Hirael added. "He even told them to *swarm* the earth."

"I see." Thomas scratched his chin. "But they stayed together in cities… And that tower. They wanted to reach heaven, but they didn't belong in the heavens. Just what the watchers did. Abandoning their proper place in God's established order."

"Yes. You are understanding." Hirael seemed pleased, even proud of Thomas.

"So, God *made* them spread out. God scattered the nations, gave everybody their own language."

"Their own language, and their own gods."

Thomas flinched. "What? I don't remember that part."

"That is because you have always looked at your Scriptures one coin at a time instead of studying and restudying all the coins together." Thomas considered this as Hirael paused. "It doesn't say it in the Genesis scroll, but it talks about it in other places like Deuteronomy, Psalms, and it is referenced in things people say and do in Samuel and Kings. And who do you think are the spiritual powers and principalities Paul speaks of?

"After the nations were divided, the Most High appointed archangels, sons of God, as princes over the scattered nations. They were intended to be caretakers and stewards of the peoples, pointing them back toward the Most High. But the corruption of Azazel and the other watchers still lingered in humanity and the princes followed the people's lead instead of leading the people."

"They were like Aaron instead of Moses."

"Yes. Look at all the coins," Hirael said. "The humans wanted gods that would let them do as they pleased. So, the Most High gave them the gods they wanted. They had rejected Him as their God."

"That's like what God said to Samuel about the Israelites when Saul was made king," Thomas said. "'They have rejected Me as their king.'"

"You're really getting good at this, Brother Thomas."

That was as close to a gold star as Thomas thought he was going to get, but it did feel good.

"The humans worshipped their new gods," Hirael said. "They gave them names, wrote stories, and erected statues and temples for them. The princes began to mingle deeply in human affairs—not for the good of mankind, but for their own ends. They became the powers behind the kingdoms of the earth and still are to this day." Before continuing, Hirael stood and stretched his wings.

Thomas could only marvel at the powerful creature before him. And Hirael was merely a middleweight in the grand scheme of things. It blew Thomas's mind how insignificant he felt.

Placing a hand on Thomas's shoulder, Hirael continued. "But the Most High didn't abandon humanity. He loved his children, and He had committed to working His vision of the earth together with them. The Most High called Abraham out to make a nation He would call His own. And the plan wasn't to forget the rest of the nations, but to eventually call them back into His family, too. Let's not get lost in the fine details now, but suffice it to say, the Most High knew there were people out there, even among the scattered nations, who would seek Him. There were also those who were victims, widows, orphans, the weak, and the vulnerable, whom He cannot ignore. This is what justice means, taking care of those in need and righting wrongs. Ultimately, He will set all things right in the great Day of the Lord, but until then, He has replenished the host of the watchers and renewed their original mission—to teach humanity and to do what is just and upright upon the earth. The princes and their underlings have legitimate authority over the nations of the earth, but we step in when elohim or unclean spirits exceed their boundaries. We are there to guide and teach those who earnestly seek Elyon."

Thomas swallowed. "Man, that's wild. So, when Satan offered Jesus the kingdoms of the—"

"Yes, yes. You are a star pupil." Hirael beckoned for Thomas to start walking. "But we could go on for all eternity, and you have gotten the point, solidly. Come now, there is one last story."

Hirael led Thomas back through the halls where elohim and righteous spirits gathered, discussing the day's stories. Here and there, Thomas caught quick snippets of conversation, most marveling one way or another at Elyon's unfailing love.

"Here we are," Hirael said.

Before him was a small arena, the smallest Thomas had seen, smaller even than the alcoves the poet minstrels used. The stage was large enough for just one performer, and a lone seat waited before it.

"What's this?"

"A seat just for you."

Thomas sat as the light above the arena focused into a circle, and a minstrel stepped into its center. He bowed to Thomas. He had six wings and felt all the more towering to Thomas, in a seated position with no other elohim between them. This minstrel had three faces: man, ox, and lion, and wore a cloak of swirling colors that was near mesmerizing as he moved.

A lyre manifested itself before the minstrel and he strummed a few chords, then started a finger-picking pattern as he spoke.

"Thomas sat across from Ebby..."

Thomas sat up straight.

"I prayed for you, too." Ebby slurped his soup. Behind him, two elohim stood, one lion-faced, staring at the room, teeth bared. The other had an ox face and glanced sadly at the men here.

The room was filthy with unclean spirits. They sneered at the two elohim. But worse by magnitudes, in the farthest corner of the room, pacing but unafraid, crept a scorpion with the hungry mandibles of a locust. He seemed to relish watching the homeless men eating their meager meals, knowing it would be their last for some time. He pointedly kept his distance from the warrior and ministering spirit, though.

The ministering spirit leaned down and whispered with his ox lips into Ebby's ear.

"I prayed," Ebby said, "you'd have eyes to see and ears to hear."

The ministering spirit stood back straight, nodding.

Beside him, the warrior glared with ferocious lion eyes at the scorpion, who hissed back.

"And those," Ebby said, "might give you a mouth to speak."

An unclean spirit meandered closer, but the warrior manifested a sword. The threat was enough to send it scurrying away.

"How's seminary going?" Ebby asked.

"Fine." Thomas looked around the room. "I mean, okay." He shrugged. "I ace all my tests."

Ebby smiled. "But have none of the answers."

The unclean spirits suddenly hissed, scuttling away from this side of the room as another elohim strode in, straight through the wall. He wore a cloak of swirling colors and sung a song under his breath. He came and stood directly behind Thomas, gesturing toward him.

The ministering spirit behind Ebby nodded.

Done with his meal, Ebby stood and the two elohim flanked him. "Thank you again for the food." As he took care of his dish, the elohim walked with him, keeping the unclean spirits at bay.

"I will take him," the scorpion said. "It's only a matter of time."

The warrior growled and took a step toward the scorpion, but the ministering spirit stepped in front of him, shaking his head.

Just before Ebby reached the door, the ministering spirit brushed Ebby's shoulder, and he stopped. He yanked an old hat from his pocket and pulled it down over his ears. Before leaving, he gave a last wink to Thomas.

While Thomas sat there, staring after his friend, unclean spirits circled, drawing closer, weighing their chances against the one elohim that remained. From under his swirling cloak, six wings sprouted, and a bright light made the spirits cower. Even the scorpion lifted his claws, cowering.

Finally, Thomas stood and went to grab his coat. The minstrel grabbed the hanger, holding the coat back. "We just need to delay you a moment," the elohim said, though Thomas didn't hear. When he released it, the hanger went clattering to the floor. Thomas grumbled as he bent to pick it up. He slammed it back in place and stormed out the door.

The alley that was a shortcut to his apartment lay just ahead. A streetlight barely poking its light in that direction shone on a wolf, standing just inside the alley, his greasy grey fur unaffected by the wind.

As Thomas approached, the wolf licked his lips. Hiding behind the dumpster not ten feet into the alley were two men that Thomas had fed not an hour ago. They did not wait to give him thanks, but to mug him, hoping to get enough cash for some booze. Thomas looked at the alley, not seeing the wolf, and started heading that way, but the minstrel stepped in front of him. "Why don't you take the long way, give you some time to think?" he suggested.

Why don't I take the long way? Thomas thought.

As they walked past, the wolf howled.

"Consider yourself lucky, beast," the minstrel said. "I was fully prepared to fight."

Soon they were at the corner and Thomas, hands shoved deep in his pockets and thoughts shoved deep in his mind, barely paid attention to what was ahead.

The minstrel reached out, manifesting a five-dollar bill on the ground. He tapped Thomas on the shoulder, inspiring him to look down. As Thomas bent to pick up the money, a car ran the stop sign just ahead of them, coming close enough to Thomas to muss his hair. Thomas, barely escaping what could have been a fatal injury, stood up without even knowing...

Epilogue

The shelter had a distinct mumble today as some of the men spoke with each other. Thomas wore a big smile as he handed out bowls of food—he had arrived at the shelter early and made fresh stock from some turkey and beef bones he bought from a local butcher—and the men seemed to notice. He couldn't see, but the room felt less oppressive than it ever had. He wondered how many unclean spirits lurked about. He was sure there were a few, but not the dozens the minstrel had spoken of in the story.

The door squeaked as Ebby walked in. His eyes lit up when he saw Thomas behind the table.

Thomas scooped Ebby a large portion and carried it where the two of them could sit.

Before they spoke, Ebby bowed his head to pray. He lifted an eyebrow as Thomas bowed with him. After the prayer, Ebby took a spoonful. When the taste hit him, he smiled. Then he looked at Thomas. "Haven't seen you here on a Tuesday," Ebby said.

"Yeah, I was here last night too."

"Sorry I missed you."

"Me too," Thomas said. His hands shook as he fondled something in his pocket. "I have more time to come to the shelter now. I took fewer hours at work."

Ebby smiled.

"So I could focus on seminary. I should finish after next semester."

269

"Congratulations."

"I have to thank you."

"You have to do no such thing."

"I really do. You have no idea."

Ebby spoke around another mouthful of soup. "I have some idea."

"An elohim…" Thomas lowered his voice. "An angel… came to me after you prayed for me."

"Praise be."

"Here." Thomas yanked a notebook from his pocket. A five-dollar bill acting as a bookmark poked from between the pages. He thrust it toward Ebby. "I want you to read this. It's everything that happened that night. I tried to capture the voices of all the stories."

"All the stories?"

"It was unbelievable," Thomas said. "But it happened. I had eyes to see and ears to hear, Ebby. All of it. Now I have a mouth to speak."

After setting his spoon down, Ebby took the notebook from him. Scribbled on the cover in ballpoint pen was "Allies of Majesty." He cocked his head.

Thomas shrugged. "I thought it sounded cool."

Ebby smiled, lifted the book, and flipped it open.

Contributors

Anthony Diastello PureFun Media	Managing Editor, Lore Crafter, Author
Troy & Stacy Hooker Descendant Publishing	Publisher
Nathan Freemyer PureFun Media	Graphic Design, Hospitality Editor
Merve Thomas	Author, Developmental Editor
Nathaniel Sorensen	Author, Lore Consultant
Dawn L. Carter	Copy Editor

Authors

Althea Damgaard
Megan Huffman
Gao Yu Qing
Erin R. Howard
Caedon Hull
M.B. Everett
Ellie Lerum
Joshua C. Chadd
Hope Ann
Bryan Timothy Mitchell

Artists

Simon Wong	Cover Art, Interior Logos
Moreamh	Interior Illustrations
Zachary Hunt	Interior Order Icons

ACKNOWLEDGEMENTS

First and foremost, I thank my wonderful wife, Esther, who not only has the second highest character in the *Allies of Majesty* role-playing game *(Cleo, second only to Ra'am)*, but has also given me her unconditional and unwavering support as we've transitioned from a hobby to an actual business with real costs.

Thank you to my precious children, all 12 of you: Anthony, Heaven, Angel, Trinity, Eden, Zion, Judah, Victor, Eve, Theo, Christine, and Justice. Thank you for loving the world of *Allies of Majesty* and always being eager to introduce anyone who might be interested. I am very excited to share these new stories with you in addition to all the ones we've shared at the table!

Thank you to my contributing authors, all 12 of you: Althea, Bryan, Caedon, Ellie, Erin, Jeremy, Hope, Joshua, Brian, Megan, Merve, and Nathaniel. Thank you for taking on the challenge and the adventure of writing in an established world that was mostly new to you. Your creativity knows no bounds... except the bounds of what actually works within the game world and associated rules.

Thank you to our talented artists, Simon, Sam, and Zach. Your art is a much-needed gift in a world as unique as this one. You have given form to the unseen. Your depictions of characters and events provide readers greater opportunity to vividly imagine what the *Allies* world feels like as they are reading these stimulating stories.

Nathan, Troy & Stacy, Dawn, and again, Merve—my wonderful editing and publishing partners, thank you for your encouragement, diligence, and prompt efforts to help us meet such a tight schedule.

KICKSTARTER BACKERS

And a very special thank you to our "Supporter" level - Kickstarter Backers. You helped make this possible.

L. G. Larimore

Jonathan Marlowe Reichel (giver of the parable comparison)

The Chadds

Matthew Butler

Trinity Diastello

Zion Diastello

Judah Diastello

Victor Diastello

Jeremy Dunn

Eden Diastello

Andrew Lowen

Adam Glass

Benjamin Harris W. Hendrickson

Jack Dunbar - New Kingdom Gaming

Heaven Diastello

Animo Games

The Hicks Boys

Michelle Moore

Casey Mellinger

Daniel Mimm

Mr. & Mrs. Phillip Lerum

Emanuel Class

Chrisxmarine

Wesley Maher

Dale R.

Kneight Reinagel

Faith Forged Games

Rémi B.

Damon B

Tim McCoy

Kris Eckert

Armando Villarreal

Anthony Diastello II

Chris Sample

HelixKnight

Scotty Breuer

R.M. Reasoner

Matt and Danielle Hull

Animo Cards Canada

Steve Fromm - VP of GG4G

Alexander Blume

About the Authors

Anthony Diastello is a husband of 26 years and father of 12. He holds a B.A. in Music from Otterbein University, an associate degree in theology, and has found a glove-fit career as a Realtor. At 14, he dedicated his life to serving God, and that path has been full of surprises. Joy and pain, confidence and uncertainty, security and struggle. It has taken him everywhere except where he expected. He considers the years behind as preparation for the years ahead and looks forward to pursuing life refined and ready.

Merve Thomas received an MFA in fiction from Virginia Commonwealth University, where he also taught writing and literature. His work includes multiple published short stories, a co-written produced play, and several completed novels. He currently lives in the Midwest with his wife and three young children, balancing writing with the joyful chaos of homeschooling.

Nathaniel Sorensen lives in Hamilton, OH with his wife Barbie. They pastor New Life Vineyard Church and love exploring new things and new places. On his off days, he has taken to writing as a way to continue exploring how interesting people interact with interesting environments. A long-time *Allies of Majesty* player, Nathaniel has been eager for the opportunity to bring these passions together.

Althea Damgaard has always loved writing stories and reading since she was a kid. Now disabled with multiple sclerosis, she spends most of her time writing, reading and improving her craft. Her go-to fiction is fantasy and science fiction, but she will read any story that promises some adventure and the need to overcome. When not doing that, she is spending time with her husband, playing with her cats, or playing games. Go to *https://altheadamgaard.com* for more information about the world of Karnum, behind-the- scenes moments, and updates about works in progress.

Megan Huffman is a lifelong storyteller and fervent follower of God with a love of character-driven narratives and redemptive story arcs. Ever since she was a young girl, Megan has had a passion for writing emotionally resonant fiction and poetry. Her work often explores themes of restoration, sacrifice, and enduring love—inspired by the greatest redemptive love of all demonstrated by Jesus Christ. Megan lives with her husband Adam and their two cats in sunny East Texas. When not writing, she enjoys playing TTRPGs, knitting, nature walks, historical research, and encouraging others in their creative journeys.

Gao Yu Qing is an avid reader, proud parent, inveterate writer, Michigander and chronicler of worlds filled with anthropomorphic foxes and the avatars of sentient universes when not critiquing the life choices of Nephilim.

Erin R. Howard is the award-winning fantasy author of *Window of Time*, and the managing editor for Expanse Books, an imprint of Scrivenings Press. Her other titles include *The Kalila Chronicles* (YA urban fantasy) and *The Gates of Deceit* (dystopian) series. When she's not writing or editing, Erin loves playing video games with her husband, watching movies with her children, and fueling her many craft addictions. Erin has a Creative Writing degree and is a member of Realm Makers, RagTag Writers, and Once Upon a Page. She resides in Western Kentucky with her husband and three children.

Caedon Hull is a young writer who hopes to use stories to help others in their walk with God. He is currently pursuing a bachelor's in Bible and theology at Nelson University. When he isn't writing or studying, he is spending time with his family or taking long walks outdoors.

M.B. Everett is a passionate storyteller and adventurer, crafting fantasy realms inspired by his global travels and lifelong love for authors like Tolkien and King. His writing journey began when he couldn't find suitable books for his sons, prompting him to create his own tales of magic and valor. M.B. debuted with *Immortal of the Saltless Sea* in March 2025, a story exploring themes of time and loss through an ageless character, Aiden. He plans to dedicate his 2026 retirement to writing, pouring his 57 years of life experience into creating immersive worlds. You can follow his adventures at mbeverett.com.

Ellie Lerum is a fantasy author and blogger whose stories blend redemptive hope, emotional depth, and a touch of whimsy. A devout Christian and mother of dragons (well, griffins… and two spirited little girls), she writes tales that wrestle with grief, healing, and courage through richly imagined worlds. Ellie draws inspiration from her faith, real-life loss, and the works of J.R.R. Tolkien to craft narratives that are both adventurous and deeply human. Whether writing or exploring Idaho with her family, she finds the greatest joy in connecting with readers who see themselves in the stories she tells.

Joshua C. Chadd is a Jesus Freak and adventurous nerd, who loves the outdoors. He's the award-winning and best-selling author of the zombie apocalypse series, *The Brother's Creed*. When he's not escaping into the mountains, he can be observed living in northern Wisconsin with his wife, two sons, guns, and katanas. He has a love for all things imaginary and finds inspiration in the wilderness, away from the distractions of life. Some of his other passions include hunting, shooting, board & video games, hard rock, reading, and anything fantasy & sci-fi.

Hope Ann likes to think of herself as an undercover resistance fighter in the battle for truth. In reality, she is a Christian speculative fiction author with a passion for shining light in the darkness and chaos of our world. Day-to-day life involves brainstorming theories about Sanderson's Cosmere with her husband, collecting situation-perfect memes, and struggling to remember the difference between effect and affect. She is a writing coach, editor, and a former board member for Story Embers. Check out her website at *authorhopeann.com* for free stories and writing resources.

Bryan Timothy Mitchell lives in Archdale, North Carolina with his wife and children. An Army veteran, he holds a master's in computer science and a bachelor's in English. His novels *Infernal Fall* and *Almost Paradise* won Realm Awards for Best Horror and Best Supernatural, respectively. He is a member of Realm Makers and has sharpened his craft through attending writers' conferences and workshops such as the Novel Writing Intensive led by Steven James and Robert Dugoni. Learn more at *www.bryantimothymitchell.com*.

Appendix

Melodiel's Rhapsody - The Game Session

This appendix offers an at-the-table view of what it feels like to experience *Allies of Majesty* as a tabletop role-playing game. To do that, I have taken the opening portion of the story "Melodiel's Rhapsody" and reimagined it as a live game session.

For this example, the participants are named after the very first family to ever play *Allies of Majesty* together.

You will join four people gathered around a dining room table—dice in hand, paper character sheets, notes, and pencils in front of them. Rather than reading a polished, prewritten narrative, these players are creating the story cooperatively, in the moment. Each player has their own unique character for whom they make decisions, speak, and take action. One participant serves as the Host, presenting the overarching plot and acting for all non-player characters in the stories—the other holy elohim, the humans, and even the unholy enemies.

If you are unfamiliar with the *Allies of Majesty* game, you will come across unfamiliar terms that are used when talking about character abilities, time units, and special effects specific to gameplay. I've glossed over much of the rules minutia to keep the focus on story and flow, while still preserving a sense of how the gameplay feels.

My hope is that having read "Melodiel's Rhapsody" first, this sample will help you imagine what it's like to create and guide stories like you read in the anthology together, on the fly, during a game session. The tone is more casual, the dialogue is spontaneous, but the imperfection is part of the charm because you're doing it with friends. The heart behind PureFun Media is creating games and media that are both pure and fun, edifying and enjoyable, and whenever possible, pointing us toward our Creator and King.

Participants:
Host – Emanuel will be hosting the game session.
Melodiel – Lisa will be playing Melodiel, a Second Heaven Warrior-Minstrel.
Sersimi – Miguel will be playing Sersimi, a Second Heaven Warrior.
Urimiel – Emilia will be playing Urimiel, a Second Heaven Warrior.

Host (Emanuel):
Melodiel, you are standing at the Central East Gate in heaven. There are two Third Heaven Cherubim guarding the portal to the skies above the earth. You can feel the weight of their Magnitude.
The earth date is around 2010. You have been asked to help out a Breach Commander, a Warrior named Maiel, in a small Appalachian town. Two of his Messengers have gone missing. He thinks they may have been captured by the unholy Hold he has been working against located near a trailer park called Ruckmyer's Meadow.
You'll be joined by a couple Warriors you are quite familiar with, Sersimi and Urimiel, and as the highest-ranking character, you'll be leading.

Sersimi (Miguel):
(chuckling) Yeah, Lisa doesn't get us into too much trouble when she's in charge.

Melodiel (Lisa):
Maybe we'll break that trend this time. You never know.
You Warriors can handle most of the fighting, letting me focus more on singing. It's one of the things I like when we run this team.

Urimiel (Emilia):
Aw, geez. Thanks, Boss.

Sirsimi and I will keep shields manifested and strapped to our backs instead of creating them as needed. It looks more intimidating to the enemy—always ready for battle!

Sersimi (Miguel):
You know it! *(the two players fist bump)*

Host (Emanuel):
You were supposed to depart for this mission later, but a Messenger from Maiel brought Melodiel an urgent request to come now if possible. Earl Stanton, a young husband and father, lost his job and Unclean Spirits are pushing him toward taking his own life.

Melodiel (Lisa):
Thanks for coming early, guys! I just received a message from Maiel. *I inform the two Warriors I got the message about Earl.*
We'll drop from a heavenly window directly above Earl. We can go to Ruckmyer's Meadow after we help him.

Urimiel (Emilia):
Lead the way.

Host (Emanuel):
The three of you leap through the portal. It is afternoon on a clear day. You are descending above a forested area with a lake directly below you. As you get closer, Urimiel, you see a human along the bank of the lake and lots of Unclean Spirits are swirling around him.

Urimiel (Emilia):
He's right there!
I point out Earl and the Unclean Spirits to the others.

Sersimi (Miguel):
I'm going to manifest a sword.

Host (Emanuel):
Now you are closer, and you can all see a man who must be Earl Stanton, kneeling and weeping. Unclean Spirits are circling him like wolves.

Urimiel (Emilia):
Wolves? I thought it was just Unclean Spirits!

Sersimi (Miguel):
It is. The Unclean Spirits are circling *like* wolves. Put your phone down and pay attention.

Urimiel (Emilia):
Sorry.

Melodiel (Lisa):
I'm going to sing Blessed Battle Cry and then manifest a sword as well. *For the glory of Elyon!*

Host (Emanuel):
You are all invigorated by the song and gain extra Passion for 2 Cycles. Melodiel, it is your Turn first, go ahead.
As you know, Unclean Spirits are minions, and I have them in three Groups of seven each.

Melodiel (Lisa):
I am going to fly down and swing at a group of Unclean Spirits. *(Rolls dice. Gets to adjust dice. Very strong result.)*

Host (Emanuel):
You destroy that Group of Unclean Spirits.
Sersimi, it's your Turn now.

Sersimi (Miguel):
I'm going to do the same. *(Rolls dice. Gets to adjust dice. Decent result.)*

Host (Emanuel):
You take out three of the seven. There are four left.
Urimiel, your Turn now.

Urimiel (Emilia):
I'm going to manifest my sword also as I crash down and attack the third Group.
(Rolls dice. Gets to adjust dice. Very strong result.)

Host (Emanuel):
Wow, you smack them as well, taking out the whole Group.
The Unclean Spirits that remain are scared. They dive inside Earl's body. You can't see them anymore.

Urimiel (Emilia):
That doesn't do them much good. Our weapons will just pass through Earl's body and hit them.

Host (Emanuel):
Earl is continuing to weep and cries out, "Let's end this!" as he presses the gun to the side of his head.
Melodiel, it's your first Turn of the Cycle, when you get to choose or switch Songs.

Melodiel (Lisa):
I appreciate your enthusiasm, Umriel, but this feels like a pretty sensitive situation. I think it would be prudent to be cautious, especially since a human's life is at risk. I know Earl can't see us and wouldn't feel the attack, but I feel like more violence in the environment, seen or unseen, might not be the best move—especially so intimately close to Earl.
I'm going to sing Lullaby against the Unclean Spirits, but singing it so as to be heard by Earl in his spirit as well. It'd be handy if I knew Blessed Lullaby, but I haven't invested much in the Sleep Family of Songs.
I would also like to use some Action Points to try a couple Social Interactions. I want to Soothe Earl and try to Subdue the hiding

Unclean Spirits. I'll rest my hands on Earl's shoulder while singing. I'll sing lyrics about quieting the noise within, subtly referencing the Unclean Spirits along with his own turmoil. I'll also include lyrics about resting in the reality that he is not alone and is loved, and always has been; and subtly suggest that his wife and child are with him and love him, but also that God is with him and has always loved him.

Host (Emanuel):
 Since your song choice and lyrics fit the situation especially well, I'll give your Soothe Interaction Boon:1. Roll an extra die and throw out the lowest that isn't a 1.

Melodiel (Lisa):
(Rolls dice. Applies Boon. Gets to adjust dice. Strong result.)

Host (Emanuel):
Alright, that appears to have worked out well. Earl seems like he is hesitating.
Now, let's handle that Subdue Interaction on the Unclean Spirits.

Melodiel (Lisa):
I want to wrap that in with the Song's effects as well.

Host (Emanuel):
Since your lyrics are targeted for Earl, you'll have to explain the Subduing on the Unclean Spirits another way. The Song itself, the music's effect, will still affect them, but the lyrics you gave aren't targeted at them.

Melodiel (Lisa):
Okay... I don't want to risk anything with Earl since they are hiding in him. I'll just forget the Subdue and end my Turn.

Host (Emanuel):
Your Lullaby *is* still affecting them. Let me roll their Resist Check.
(Rolls dice. Lisa gets to adjust dice. Fair Result.)

The Unclean Spirits gain enough Exertion to make them Weary, but not Fatigued.

It's Sersimi's Turn and then Urimiel's.

Melodiel (Lisa):
There aren't any more enemies right here to fight and I'm addressing the current situation with Earl and the Unclean Spirits hiding in him.

Urimiel (Emilia):
Yeah, well done, Melodiel. I would've preferred to cut them down. On my Turn, I guess I'll just unmanifest my sword and stay near so my Magnitude can improve Melodiel's influence with Earl.

Melodiel (Lisa):
There's plenty of fighting to come, I'm sure.

Sersimi (Miguel):
Aye. The greater threat is with our rebel brothers. I'll grip my sword and scan the woods.

Host (Emanuel):
(Rolls dice privately.)
You don't currently see threats or anything else of note in the woods.

Sersimi (Miguel):
Alright, then. That'll be it for my Turn.

Host (Emanuel):
Melodiel, you can sense the Unclean Spirits squirming as you continue to touch Earl's shoulder. I'm sure they would prefer to flee, but they are afraid of the mighty trio of elohim just outside.

Melodiel (Lisa):
I will continue my Lullaby and try to Soothe Earl again. I'll stick with the lyrics about Earl being loved, but try to draw his attention to the peaceful nature around him.

Host (Emanuel):
I'm going to say that is more of an Aim Interaction than a Soothe Interaction, even if the intent is for the nature to be soothing. He is currently lost in his own head and isn't paying attention to his surroundings. This would certainly be a redirection.

Melodiel (Lisa):
Fair enough.
(Rolls dice. Gets to adjust dice. Strong result.)

Host (Emanuel):
Earl's face seems to settle, and he looks toward the sky. A wind produces a break in the clouds, and you get the distinct sense that the Holy Spirit is speaking to Earl now. He lowers the gun, but you feel the Unclean Spirits again as they try to Resist the effects of your continued Lullaby.
(Rolls dice. Lisa gets to adjust dice. Poor result.)
They fail to Resist and this time are Fatigued, not just Weary.
Earl breathes in deeply and as he exhales, the Unclean Spirits pour from his mouth in smoky plumes. They now lay, exhausted, on the ground before you.

Sersimi (Miguel):
I want to Strike them to finish them off before they rest. …
Actually, I'll let Urimiel do it.

Urimiel (Emilia):
Gee, thanks!
(Rolls dice. Gets to adjust dice. Strong result.)

Host (Emanuel):
Yeah, they are Exposed, so, with that roll, you finish them off easily. Earl sits, catching his breath, and is not currently at risk of harming himself. Immediate crisis avoided.

Sersimi (Miguel):
So, Melodiel, what do we know about the unholy Hold?

Melodiel (Lisa):
Emanuel, what intel did Maiel share with me about the unholy Hold?

Host (Emanuel):
You know the only remarkable thing about the Hold is that it is unremarkable. Other than the ruler, it is curiously devoid of any Second Domain elohim. There is usually at least one other, if not two. The Ruler is a sly, unholy Messenger.

The Hold occupies the area around Ruckmyer's Meadow, which is surrounded by heavily wooded hills. Despite this underwhelming description, two holy Messengers disappeared in the area, so something is amiss.

The mission you've been sent on, now that Earl is safe, is to find out what is going on and retrieve the Messengers after raiding the Hold.

Urimiel (Emilia):
Did Maiel tell you where the Messengers are held?

Host (Emanuel):
No. Maiel did not. Melodiel was informed that the owner of Ruckmyer's Meadow— the trailer park where Earl lives—operates a moonshine still in the nearby forest. His house sits on the property with the trailer park and he has stolen goods in the house.

Melodiel (Lisa):
I relay all that I know to my teammates.
The plan is, we'll raid the Hold and then search for the Messengers. Hopefully, we'll find them inside and it will be simple.

Sersimi (Miguel):
We'll need to be cautious. If they are holding the Messengers, they'll be expecting an attack.

Melodiel (Lisa):
True. I think it'll be best if we stay close to Earl. They probably won't expect us to ride in with him. We'll observe them first and then strike.

Sersimi (Miguel):
That sounds surgical. I like it.

Urimiel (Emilia):
Maybe if we cripple the Hold, we could start its decline.

Melodiel (Lisa):
Maybe, but it won't stick if the community's attitudes and behaviors are still reinforcing it.

Host (Emanuel):
Earl sighs and pushes to his feet. His t-shirt is soaked with sweat. He looks at the water, then at the gun in his hand. He says, "I don't want this anymore!" and throws the gun into the water.

Sersimi (Miguel):
Well, we can't have some kid finding that. I'm going to go in the lake and bury the gun under some rocks.

Host (Emanuel):
Sure. You go and do that.
Meanwhile, Earl pulls out his smartphone and sifts through family photos. You see him flip through pictures of a young girl, probably his daughter, then he pauses on a selfie of him and his wife.

Melodiel (Lisa):
I think we're about to move soon. Sersimi and Urimiel, scout the path for spies. I'll stay with Earl. I doubt there are any unholy elohim here, but best to be sure. If any see us get into Earl's vehicle, our cover will be blown.

Urimiel (Emilia):
Roger that, Boss.
I'll manifest my sword again and head into the woods to scout.

Sersimi (Miguel):
I'll go with him, sword ready as well.

Host (Emanuel):
(Rolls dice privately.)
You guys don't see any enemies in the woods. If there are any, they are successfully avoiding you.
Melodiel, you hear Earl whispering, "Lord, I'm sorry."

Melodiel (Lisa):
I want to comfort him if I can. I will manifest my sword invisibly into the material realm as I swirl it around to try to stir up some of the smells of the flowers and bring them over to Earl. I'll sing the hymn "For the Beauty of the Earth" for Earl to hear in his spirit. I don't have a Song from my character sheet in mind. I'm just singing the actual hymn as flavor with the Soothe Interaction.

Host (Emanuel):
Good use of multiple relevant stimuli. You already Aimed him to the natural surroundings earlier, so this *can* be a Soothe Interaction. I'll give you a Boon:1.

Melodiel (Lisa):
(Rolls dice. Applies Boon. Gets to adjust dice. Strong result.)

Host (Emanuel):
That's a pretty good result.
You stir a gust of warm air that draws in nearby scents of flowers and pine. Earl inhales and smiles. He seems settled, collected, and in good shape, considering.
Earl gets up and heads down a trail through the woods.

Melodiel (Lisa):
I'm following him.

Host (Emanuel):
The trail winds around the lake to a nearly empty parking lot. There's only one car parked near the trail, which you can assume is Earl's. Beyond the parking lot, through a line of trees, vehicles whoosh along a narrow four-lane road.

Urimiel (Emilia):
We will rejoin Melodiel.
All clear. No spies that we found.

Host (Emanuel):
Earl gets into his compact car.

Melodiel (Lisa):
Let's get in with him. I'll take shotgun.

Urimiel (Emilia):
Of course you will. Just kidding. I would rather be back with Sersimi, anyway, to keep him in line.

Host (Emanuel):
When each of you enters the small car, you feel yourself shrink down, automatically adjusting to the space you're now concerned with.

Melodiel (Lisa):
(mimicking a motherly tone) My two precious kiddos are behaving so well. Keep it up and I'll give each of you a candy bar.

Urimiel (Emilia):
If you don't live up to that promise, I'll bring you before the council.

Sersimi (Miguel):
Threats are no way to earn that candy bar, Brother. I'll not issue threats to our most kind and generous leader and earn two candy bars!

Urimiel (Emilia):
Two candy bars? I didn't realize you were prone to gluttony.

Host (Emanuel):
The car is messy. The seats are torn and stained. There are trash and crumbs covering the floorboards. A belt squeals from under the hood when Earl turns the key, and the engine shakes the car. The speakers are blaring thrash metal. Earl cranks it up and taps the steering wheel with the music as he starts pulling out of the parking lot.

Urimiel (Emilia):
Any more lullabies for Earl, Melodiel?
(Urimiel and Sersimi laugh)

Melodiel (Lisa):
(mimicking a motherly tone) No seatbelts. No candy bars.

Urimiel (Emilia):
You know we can't mess with the seatbelts or Earl would freak out.

Sersimi (Miguel):
Seriously, though, will this music affect Earl's ability to drive calmly?

Melodiel (Lisa):
I'd like to Perceive if Earl seems to be okay or might be at any kind of risk.

Host (Emanuel):
(Rolls dice privately.)
Earl seems fine to you.

Melodiel (Lisa):
He's fine. Cover your ears if you don't like his music.

Host (Emanuel):
Earl pulls into a gas station.

Sersimi (Miguel):
Are you going to go in and get us those candy bars, Melodiel?

Urimiel (Emilia):
Yeah, *are* you?

Melodiel (Lisa):
(mimicking a motherly tone) You must keep behaving for the rest of the trip to earn your treats.

Host (Emanuel):
Earl starts cleaning out trash from the car while the gas is pumping.

Urimiel (Emilia):
How long do you think we'll need to stay in this tiny car once we get to Earl's?

Sersimi (Miguel):
If it's clear, we can go inside his home. We might be able to get more intel from there.

Host (Emanuel):
Earl is cleaning his windshield now.

Melodiel (Lisa):
I'll stay with Earl. I want you two to scout and clear out any unholy elohim in the other homes near Earl's and then join me. From there, we'll work our way toward the Hold, attacking any patrols we encounter. If the Hold is a dead end, we can try the moonshine still.

Urimiel (Emilia):
After clearing the homes, are we sticking together?

Melodiel (Lisa):
Yes. If we work together carefully, we'll hopefully stay undetected longer. We aren't in a hurry. This Hold doesn't sound like much, but if they've captured two Messengers, we shouldn't relax too much.

Urimiel (Emilia):
I don't know. From the report Maiel gave you, any one of us could take them. We could take them down quick and then focus on finding the Messengers.

Sersimi (Miguel):
Maybe, but we don't know this area. This Hold has to be stronger than what was reported. I mean, it's a Hold, not a random squad.

Melodiel (Lisa):
We'll start off careful and then decide if we should pick them off individually or attack aggressively.

Host (Emanuel):
Alright, guys, we need to keep things moving.
Earl has hopped back into the car and is talking on his phone. You hear his side of a conversation with his dad. Earl is assuring his dad that he will tell his wife he got laid off. He says the company was worse off than he'd realized when he got hired. He thought he'd be able to retire from there, but he'll do his best to find some kind of work. He doesn't want to stay in the trailer park forever.
Before long, you approach Ruckmyer's Meadow. You're on a long dirt road and you can see a weathered two-story home at the entrance to the trailer park.

Melodiel (Lisa):
That'll be the property owner's home, where the Hold is centered.

Urimiel (Emilia):
Let me hop out here and clear it myself.

Melodiel (Lisa):
No, Urimiel! Let's stick to the plan and clear out the homes in the trailer park.

Host (Emanuel):
The road goes past the old house and to a gravel lot in a field at the base of a wooded hill. The road leads between two rows of mobile homes. Three unholy Warriors are around a picnic table, where four men are playing cards. One of the men nods to Earl.

Melodiel (Lisa):
I want to quickly Conceal my Glory and look like a human passenger similarly dressed to Earl—t-shirt, maybe one of those tall ball caps.

Sersimi (Miguel):
A trucker hat.

Melodiel (Lisa):
Yeah, a trucker hat!
Sersimi. Urimiel. Disguise yourselves, too. Quick.

Host (Emanuel):
Each of you, make a Swiftness Check with 2 Difficulty.
(Lisa, Miguel, and Emilia each roll dice. Lisa and Miguel get to adjust dice. Strong result for Lisa and Emilia. Poor result for Miguel.)
Melodiel and Urimiel Pass. Sersimi, you completely Fail.

Sersimi (Miguel):
Yeah, I know, hold on… I have 2 Swiftness Perks. I'll use both of them to get 6 total Adjustments to the Check Roll.
(Adjusts dice.)
There. That does it. I Pass.

Host (Emanuel):
Okay, then. You all Pass.

The Warriors turn their heads, glaring at the car, but don't seem to notice your true nature.

Earl pulls up next to the last trailer on the left. Since they are in the last row, they have easy access to more of the field than the other families and have a swing set and several toys in the yard.

Melodiel (Lisa):
Seems like their security isn't too tight.

Urimiel (Emilia):
Maybe they're too wrapped up in their own plans to think about getting attacked.
Should Sersimi and I clear out the trailers now?

Melodiel (Lisa):
Yes. I'll stick with Earl. You two clear out the trailers and join me. Be careful not to be spotted by the Warriors at the table. Go underground and pop in each home through the floor. Try to surprise any enemies you find before they can run out and alert others. Once you are back, we can work our way to the owner's place out front.

Sersimi (Miguel):
Any prisoners? Or just take them down?

Melodiel (Lisa):
No prisoners. No questions. Neither of you deal Resolve damage with your attacks, so they could just lie to you, anyway. Not worth the extra time.

Host (Emanuel):
(Rolls dice privately.)
Melodiel, you think you notice some movement in the forest ahead beyond the fence surrounding the field. But you don't see anything of consequence. There is a "Do Not Enter" sign posted at the edge of the field before you get to the forest and the hill.

Melodiel (Lisa):
Hmmm. I'll have to keep an eye on the forest, just in case.
Sersimi and Urimiel, go. Be quick and quiet.

Sersimi (Miguel):
I'll take the left.
I drop through the ground as quick as I can.

Urimiel (Emilia):
I wanted the left.

Sersimi (Miguel):
Sorry. I'm gone. I can't hear you.

Host (Emanuel):
Urimiel, do you want to make a Swiftness Check to try to catch him?

Urimiel (Emilia):
No. Don't worry about it.
I drop through the floor of the car underground and head to the first home on the right.

Host (Emanuel):
Melodiel, it is just you and Earl for now.
Earl shuts off his car, and the silence is pronounced.

[And the game continues from there…]

ALLIES OF MAJESTY

An RPG of Biblical Proportions

Battle for Creation
Alongside your Friends

Rich & Engaging Roleplaying For Everyone

This cooperative game lets you jump into the stories with your friends! Play to your preference. Do you like crunching numbers for the most effective turns? Do you like navigating your way through social scenarios? Do you just like rolling dice and beating up bad guys?

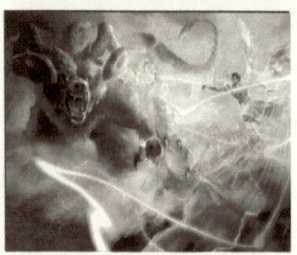

Each player can engage at the level they desire, and everyone's style contributes to the success of the mission.

Game Masters

Now the Assistant app makes hosting games easy, so you can focus on the storytelling.

Keep up to date
on the Latest News

www.alliesofmajesty.com

Learn more online
about the Gameplay & Lore

wiki.alliesofmajesty.com